THE CEORAN CHRONICLES VOL. ONE

THE REAPER'S DESCENT

VIOLETA M. BAGIA

PRESS

Published by Vulpine Press in the United Kingdom in 2021

Cover by Claire Wood

ISBN: 978-1-83919-375-0

www.vulpine-press.com

To all the big kids who love to go on adventures

Acknowledgements

Where do I even begin with the acknowledgements for this book? Of course there are the usual suspects, my husband, my sister and my parents, my best friend, my fans and the wonderful writing community I find myself surrounded by.

But it wasn't always a smooth ride. Years ago when I first started penning this idea, it was a small flicker of inspiration that quickly turned into a flame that was all consuming. Years later, I had finished the book, found it a new home and then began the exciting process of getting it ready for the world.

Unfortunately, as with life, unforeseen circumstances thwarted the progress of the book and I found myself once again, back at the start. Editing, rewriting, pitching.

Then, the amazing people at Vulpine Press saw something magical in this story, the same thing that kept me going through the motions when sometimes, the only thing I realistically wanted to do was wave the white flag—it was all too much. The story and the book had become bittersweet, sometimes a bit too harsh for me to digest.

Thankfully, Sarah and the team were so supportive and encouraging and gave me the space and time I needed to breathe life into this story and bring it back from the brink.

So, after all these years and after all the tears and sometimes childish outbursts, here it is, *The Reaper's Descent.* My first foray into the world of YA, which began as a story I wanted to write for my sister who was a teenager at the time.

Now as I hold this book in my hands and expect my first child later this year, I know there'll be many more fun adventures that my kids and their kids can someday go on. And a lot of that is thanks to Vulpine Press who saw something in this book and saw something in me.

Thank you for reading and as always, onwards and upwards!

PROLOGUE
THE DESCENT

They count, and they wait. Anticipating the end of what they'll come to remember as the last year their lives mattered.

Tonight, everything will change. Tonight, we will take this world and they will bow to us.

Moving into position, I nod at my soldiers; they're preparing, eagerly awaiting my order.

The mortals watch on, laughing, eating, sharing stories; completely ignorant as the ball prepares to drop in some sort of bizarre commemoration of a new year, a tradition I've never seen other races engage in.

They fascinate me, they intrigue me with their curious ways. The order in which they live, the class division they implement, the way they kill and torture each other for belongings, for things their earth harbors.

They have no idea such a powerful, dormant race lives just under their noses and they have no idea their downfall will be because of them.

Millions of them spill into the streets, filling the crevices of their dying city, a concrete jungle heaving and struggling through its last days. Yet, they're here to celebrate.

1

A city they call New York, a city that never sleeps. My lips quirk up. After tonight, this city will be plunged into an endless slumber, one which no magic will touch.

Five, four, three, two, one.

An explosion, louder than anything the mortals have ever heard, rocks their celebration and throws them into unprecedented chaos. But there is no room to move, nowhere to run. They've crowded themselves into the maze and like a sickness, it quickly spreads.

Celebration quickly turns to panic, laughter quickly turns to screams, and I grip the railing in the cool January air and breath it all in.

Yes. This is what we've been waiting for.

I smile, watching from afar. They have no idea what's coming, no idea how quickly their world and everything they know is about to come to an end.

"Commander Silus."

I turn my head slightly, acknowledging the soldier. He is still young, still too eager to please, to harbor any form of control. But soon, soon he will be invaluable like the others I have raised.

"We're ready," he says, standing tall.

"Then we shall proceed," I agree and return my attention to the quivering veins of the city. "You know your orders?"

"Yes, sir," he replies, standing to attention. "Draw out the Ceoran, find the Map."

"Precisely," I say. "And the Halfling. It must be brought to me."

"You really believe it's here?"

"Yes. I know it is."

"And the Map?"

"The Halfling is priority."

"Understood."

With that, he leaps from the building and disappears into the sea of humans.

What hope did they ever have?

This is beautiful, this is poetry, this is how we were meant to live, not hiding and dying in the shadows of the Ceoran.

But out in the open, embraced by the anomalous lightning and cracking sky.

CHAPTER ONE
THE BEGINNING

Alex

The city of burning embers smelled like death and charcoal.

Each rushed step I took, stumbling over charred bodies and remains, sent a spluttering of ashy air into my lungs.

I couldn't tell whether I was running or being dragged. I couldn't see through the tears in my eyes or through the ash falling down around us. Mom and Dad gripped both of my hands and pushed through the forming crowds; all around us, families were doing the same.

Somewhere over all the noise of people screaming and mumbled cries of confusion, I still heard the music blaring through speakers scattered all around Times Square. The distorted sound carried through the city as everyone ran, wherever they could, going and going until exhaustion took over.

Mom gripped my hand tighter as we navigated our way through the crowd, with people running in every which direction.

Couples were being separated from each other, kids were left behind and the elderly trampled.

My chest heaved with an ache I couldn't shift, and as I spotted a girl close to my age sprawled dead and bloodied on a park bench, I was certain I never would. Her pink beanie was soaked red and half her perfectly made-up face was gaunt, like the blood and muscle had been sucked from it. Bile rapidly filled the back of my throat as Mom yanked me toward her.

My eyes darted between the descending creatures and the green Christmas pines lining the brightly decorated city streets.

Baubles fell, shattering beneath stampeding feet as their branches rapidly decayed before my eyes when they neared.

Whatever they got close to began to break down or fail. Lights, cars, planes. Everything stalled, everything died.

In the distance, a plane carrying hundreds of people to their New Year's destination fell. I watched as it took a nosedive, no sound, no smoke. Just silent destruction lost in the noise of the chaos below.

"Keep moving!" my dad shouted as Mom and I fell behind.

"There's nowhere to go!" she screamed back.

She was right.

The city was falling down around us.

Plumes of orange and black reached far into the sky, rain of ash and fire sprinkled down around us. There was nowhere to go. Nowhere safe.

"Up there." Dad pointed toward the Chrysler Building.

On any normal day, it would have taken us about twenty minutes to get there. Today, with all the bodies and chaos, I was questioning whether we'd make it at all.

My heart thundered with each step that was hindered by a blockade of panicking people and charred remains dropping from the sky.

I held in a scream as the creatures dropped another body in front of us. Mom yanked me off to the left but my eyes remained fixed on the unmoving gaze of the man in a suit whose face looked like

5

the girl in the beanie. He had been someone's dad, someone's friend, son...someone who was also probably dead among the sea of unrecognizable bodies.

"There!" Mom dragged my attention to the steps coming into view.

Other people seemed to have the same idea. Hundreds of us tried to cram in through the art deco revolving doors which had since stopped revolving. Instead, the panes of glass separating the cold and snowy world outside from the toasty warmth of the Chrysler's lobby were shattered into makeshift doorways.

We ran through, pushing past whoever tried to get in before us. Dad gripped Mom's hand, who in turn pulled me in after her. We managed to get through the majority of people and follow a smaller crowd up into the service stairwell.

"Get inside and stay hidden," Dad ordered as we reached a floor that was unoccupied.

My eyes darted around. Every so often, a flash of orange would tear through the sky and filter through the large windows, then it would go dark again until a loud explosion sent ripples of light outward. I'd never seen a weapon do that. I had no idea what was happening outside, but I knew that this was coming, I knew that we weren't going to see the end of them, whoever they were. They had come with one goal in mind and they were just getting started.

***

We were holed up in the boardroom on the seventeenth floor of the Chrysler Building for three days. We would go out, find food, and then come back. It was safe to say that we were all getting edgy, and waiting for them to find us was horrific.

I clutched my glittery purse like a lifeline. It was a birthday present for my sixteenth birthday; I'd eyed it for months and months and then Dad surprised me with it. Honestly, it was probably a bit childish, but it was sentimental as hell.

"How much longer can we honestly stay here, Richard?" Mom strode across the boardroom, shoved a wheelie chair out of the way, and stopped directly in front of Dad.

He scrubbed his beard and looked across at me, giving me a tight smile before looking back at Mom. He squeezed her shoulder and then spoke to both of us.

"Whatever those creatures are, they're here to kill us. That's the plain and simple of it. We stay here as long as we possibly can. Logic dictates that they'll clear out of the city when there's nothing left for them here."

"And how long will that be?" I asked.

"I don't know, angel, but we're going to stay as long as it takes."

I sighed, peeled open a trail bar from the latest haul, and nodded.

Mom wasn't satisfied though. "Richard, we have to get her out of here, it's getting dangerous."

Getting? I raised my brows while opening another trail bar. Maybe she missed the end of the world, death, and destruction scenario out there.

"We're better off staying here for a few more days," Dad insisted.

"If they find her—"

"They won't," he said, giving me another tight smile. "Alex, angel, will you see if the vending machine has any water?"

"Sure." I jumped to my feet and gave them both a pointed look.

7

They continued arguing in hushed voices while I snuck out of the boardroom, checked twice before running across to the machine, and lo and behold, there was water.

Thankfully someone else had done the smashing and took only what they could. These bottles were stuck inside the coils which is probably why they were left behind.

I carefully pulled them out and shoved them under my arms.

When I came back, they were done arguing but Mom had resumed her pacing.

I plopped myself down in the corner and opened one of the bottles. Mom paced up to the windows, hovered for a moment and then came back to me, gently pressing her hand to my cheek, over and over until my dad called her to the far corner of the room.

I couldn't make out what they were saying but they were huddled by the window, occasionally looking out over the skyline.

The gunfire below had since stopped, and the sky only lit up a few times throughout the night now. Maybe our army was done, maybe they'd won, but I knew better. If our army had won, there'd be choppers in the sky searching for survivors, there'd be rescue teams scouring the buildings and calling out for us, there'd be something other than the painful silence sending waves of terror through the bricks and mortar of the building.

"It's going to be okay, Alex," Dad said, startling me.

"I know, I trust you."

He smiled.

"We're not going to let them hurt you, sweetheart," Mom said. "We're going to do everything we can to make sure you're safe."

If anyone was going to keep their word, it was them. Dad knew how to evade terror threats, he knew how to keep soldiers safe, he knew what he was doing. But it was still terrifying. There was no knowing what would happen if they found us. Maybe Dad's military knowledge wouldn't be enough against them. I shuddered and huddled closer to the wall.

I pulled my knees to my chest and wrapped my arms around them tightly.

A few bumps and thumps somewhere beyond these walls caused me to jerk and look up at the door. Oh crap. I'd forgotten to lock it.

My eyes rapidly welled with tears and my heart sped up. I messed up and we were going to die because of it. I didn't want to die, I didn't want to look like that girl, I didn't want my mom to see my face like that.

The fear totally caught me off guard.

The bumps got louder and closer.

They'd be coming through that door and when they did, they'd kill us, they'd suck my face off and I would be dead, just like all the bodies out there.

I jumped up, leaving my sparkly purse on the floor.

"Mom," I whispered.

Dad rushed over to me and gently pulled me back pressing his finger to his lips.

"I'm scared."

"I know, angel, it's going to be alright," he said softly.

The bumps and thumps grew in frequency, there was a scream which caused me to jump and then there was achy silence once again.

He turned me toward him. "We have to keep moving, they're coming."

"Can't we just lock the door?"

"That won't do anything to stop them, angel," Dad explained. "Now, we have to get moving."

"Where?" I whispered.

They gave each other knowing looks which did little to comfort me.

Before I could ask, he jerked his head toward the door.

Outside.

He wanted to go outside to where the creatures were waiting.

Dear God no.

"When I say, we move. Okay?" he said.

"I don't think I can run."

He glanced down at my heeled boots and frowned. Like I could have foreseen the end of the world on New Year's Eve to prepare a better outfit. I was just grateful that I wasn't wearing one of my Alex specials—sequined skirt and blazer combo. At least I was wearing jeans and a coat, for once thankful that New York turned up the snow show for the holidays.

"No more running, just fast walking," he said.

"Dad, no, that's not funny, and I can't. I'm pretty sure my toes are bleeding inside these bad boys."

"Then I'll carry you."

"And that's a definite no." I frowned. "I'll slow you down."

"Then keep up," he offered with a small smile.

Ever the positive, silver lining kind of guy. I couldn't help but smile back even though I was sure it looked like a really awkward grin. I was so far from smiling it was actually funny, ironically.

He pressed a gentle hand to my shoulder and squeezed it, kind of like when you're trying to prepare someone for some shitty news. And the shitty news story here was that we had to run, out there, where the creatures were.

10

Pepping myself up, I nodded. "Okay, I can do this."

"I know you can. Now, we'll have to move quickly. They'll be searching for us." He looked over my shoulder locking eyes with Mom again.

When I caught her gaze, she looked away which immediately made me think that he wasn't talking about us as in the general human populous, but *us* us. Before I could say another word, a loud crash sounded just outside the door and Dad immediately pulled me back, pressing his body in front of mine, Mom taking shelter behind a column off to my left.

He held up his hand as we all listened out to what was going on just behind the thin sheet of wood keeping us hidden from them.

"The Halfling has to be here somewhere," I heard one of them say, its voice sharp and thin, like it was lacking more than one range of notes.

Dad's gaze locked onto mine, his jaw set into a tight line that sent shivers all over me. Had it been any more silent I was certain that they'd be able to hear how loudly my heart was cracking against my ribs.

"The Halfling has guards and watchers everywhere, what makes you certain it's here?" another said.

"Silus tracked it here, it won't be far from the Map."

"The Map is second priority. Don't forget that."

"But Commander Silus said—"

"He said to keep searching for both, now move."

My eyes snapped up to Mom's. What was a *Halfling* and what map were they looking for?

As they kept talking my mind kept snapping back to the name Silus. It was unusual, yet I could have sworn that I'd heard it somewhere before.

11

Every thought stopped in my mind as the door handle to the boardroom moved. In that moment, my emotions spiraled, my heart slowed and every hair on my body stood on end.

If they found us, we'd be dead, if they came through that door, my mom and dad would die, and I couldn't let that happen.

Panic consumed every logical thought and then, suddenly, there was a warm feeling, something that completely caught me off guard yet felt so incredibly natural.

It started in my core and then spread out, weaving and spinning through my blood and bones, and then it coated my mind like a warm blanket.

I staggered backwards, my eyes darting from corner to corner feeling Mom and Dad's eyes on me. They were saying something, moving slowly like they had been slowed down. My chest rose and fell in sharp bursts but no matter what I did to push the feeling out, I couldn't. It consumed me, pouring through every vein and every crevice making a flush of fear rise to the surface chilling my skin.

No. There was no time to panic. The sounds outside had grown quiet and they were right there. I didn't know how I knew, but I felt it through my entire being.

The feeling coursing through me intensified, hammering through my skull, the pressure rising making my ears pop and then, there was quiet. I didn't have to be afraid. *It* kind of told me that and like a switch had been flicked, I knew what I had to do.

I had to save them.

I closed my eyes and as each shallow breath came out in tiny puffs, I felt the blood slowing inside me and my dad's hold around my hand tightening.

He was saying something to me, but I couldn't make it out over the deafening roar of my own words in my head.

They can't come in here. They have to leave. You have to save your family; you have to do this, Alex. You're the only one who can. Save them. Over and over I repeated it.

"It's empty, go to the next floor," I heard the first voice order.

And just like that they were gone.

My eyes snapped open and darted to the door. It was still closed, and we were still here.

I collapsed back against the wall and let out a low breath.

"Alex." Mom's face appeared in front of mine. "Are you alright?"

"What happened?"

"They were called away," Dad said, his gaze stopping on my face and hardening.

"How?"

"It doesn't matter," he said. "We've got to keep moving."

"Wait, what?" I got up and stumbled after him. "They were coming in, why did they go?"

"Lucky break," he said.

"What is going on?"

"Keep moving, Alex," Mom said. "We can talk about this later."

Knowing that the stern look she gave me meant business, I clamped my mouth shut and followed her.

Dad ran up ahead and Mom stayed behind me.

I kept moving, ignoring the blisters on my feet and the aches and pains from the grinding of those blisters on my shoes. Something told me that complaining about that would go unnoticed, especially considering what just happened.

Surely it was just like Dad said: *lucky break.*

Though a niggling feeling in the pit of my stomach said otherwise, it said that I had somehow done it.

13

And that same something told me Mom and Dad knew exactly what was going on, not just with me and not with what I'd done, but with the creatures and what they were looking for.

***

Cold, calculating eyes looked down at me. I was frozen, on my knees in the dirt, wherever I looked, they stood, wherever I tried to run, they blocked.

His mouth spread into a grin, the kind that said I was screwed. I balled my fists in the dirt and looked up through strands of hair.

Blood pooled in the back of my throat and the burn, stinging through my singed shirt was merely an afterthought.

I grinned through the blood, despite the horror pulsing through me.

Whatever I managed to do was shot down as soon as I looked up at him.

"You gave yourself up, for him," he said.

"No, not just for him. For all of us. For everyone you would have killed if I hadn't come here tonight."

He laughed. "I hope they know how brave their hero was."

Holding my hand out, I felt the pull of power inside me. He stepped back, mouth slightly agape as I raised my palm ready to release a kill shot.

"Oh, they will."

His electric blue eyes widened, and I released the blast.

***

My hand jerked up hitting the wall making me force back a choked cry. Damn. I inspected the damage, opening and closing my fist to

14

make sure everything worked. When I was sure that nothing was broken in my hand, I released a sigh and then jerked back as my eyes coasted across the wall beside my head. There was a very deep crater that webbed out like something with serious force had hit it.

I traced my fingers over the fractures and tenderly withdrew my hand.

This wasn't possible. It was nearly inch-deep drywall with a beam of wood directly behind it. The impact should have broken my fingers and mashed up the bones inside my hand.

"Alex, are you up?" Dad asked.

"Yeah." I peeled my eyes away from the wall. "I'm up."

"Can I come in?"

"Yeah." I pulled on a sweater and started packing up my things.

We'd taken whatever we could from abandoned stores. I'd found myself flat boots, a warmer coat, and this sweater. Funny what sorts of things brought you comfort when everything else had been taken from you.

Outside, the city was slowly getting quieter and quieter; the crying and screaming was dying down with each passing day, and people scarcer. A week ago, we'd been sharing makeshift sleeping quarters with complete strangers huddled throughout department stores. Today, we'd be lucky if we saw another soul.

"I have something for you," he said, kneeling beside my makeshift bed.

I watched as he presented me with a gun.

"Whoa, Dad, I don't think that's a good idea."

He placed it into my hand. "This is the safety, and this is how you load the bullets." He cupped his hands over mine and made my fingers do the work.

My heart kicked up.

"Daddy, I can't do this."

"Yes, you can, angel. This is the world we live in now; I need you to be prepared and be ready. You've done this before; you've shot loads of guns and you know how to do this."

"That was just the shooting range."

"Same concept, aim and fire."

I expelled a long breath and looked at the Glock.

"I engraved your name into the handle. So you'll never forget who you are and where you come from."

"Where did you get this?"

"I actually had this ready for you months ago, but it never seemed like the right time to give it to you. I carried it with me instead."

"This is crazy," I found myself whispering.

How did this happen? *Why* did it happen?

He pressed a kiss to my forehead and then cupped my cheek.

"Take only what you need, we're leaving in ten minutes."

"Where?"

"Into the woods, we're going to have to find other survivors and stick together."

"Okay."

"Okay." He smiled and left.

I carefully tucked the gun into a bag I'd pulled off the sporting department shelf, and kicked off my ridiculous boots and swapped them for the pair of flat ones. I paused when my eyes landed on a torn newspaper that had made its way inside. The picture on the front page was taken at Times Square.

A cold rush swept over me as I read the article. There were silhouettes of people against the burned backdrop of the ball, people who had leaped from the building, people who had been killed by the creatures.

My eyes burned as I kept reading.

The journalist explained that it wasn't just America that was affected, it had happened all over the world. The UN were doing their best to scramble enough troops to make our stand, but no one knew what we were making our stand against. They were stronger, more equipped than us, and our weapons were about as effective as a knife against a grenade launcher.

They spoke about mysterious balls of light which seemed to fight on our side against the creatures but even they didn't have the capacity to fight them all.

As it stood at the time this article was written, we were on the losing side of a very serious battle.

Two weeks. Two weeks since the end of the world started, and we finally understood how hopelessly unprepared we were for this war.

Mom appeared at the door. "Ready?"

I dropped my gaze to the image that would forever be burned in my head and gently folded it up and placed it inside the bag I'd claimed as my own.

There was no glitter, no sequins, there were no heels and no dresses.

There was only surviving.

"Ready."

Chapter Two
The Aftermath

"Please, Alex, please don't make me do this."

His piercing green eyes floored me.

I closed my eyes for a moment and tried to remind myself that I'd made this choice and I was responsible for everyone here. I leaned back in the cot and opened my eyes, meeting his.

He couldn't understand why he wasn't fighting me on this.

And I couldn't tell him because he would never understand, he would never forgive me or himself. He would rather die than do this to me.

But I knew what I had to do.

Tears brimmed as he stepped closer and I cupped his hands, pressing them flat to his chest.

"It has to be you; it can't be anyone else," I said.

"There has to be another way."

"There isn't, you know that."

He closed his eyes and I let my power course over him and lock onto his mind.

"It's okay. I trust you." I pulled his face down to mine and kissed him. "I could never forget you, not completely, even after everything."
When I pulled back, his vibrant green eyes were rapidly replaced by icy, blue glowing eyes that seared into my mind.

My body jerked up, my face coming within inches of the fabric of the tent. I groaned and sat up, following the small sliver of light seeping through the zipper.

The chatter outside grounded me and reminded me where I was. I ran a hand through my hair and shook away the residual guilt.

We were lucky to have found the others when we did.

Several of them had been battling alone and without weapons, and we weren't faring much better without food, but together we were able to combine forces and before long we had a small group.

Several had the foresight to bring tents, and others, cooking utensils, pots, pants, the lot. We had brought blankets, comfortable clothing, and toys for young kids. That was Mom's idea. It worked a treat. At least they had something to hold onto, to keep their minds off the rest of the world.

Had it not been obvious by the continuous plumes of smoke visible above the tree line, you never would have known that a catastrophic disaster had taken place.

Here, in the forests, we were secluded enough to allow the younger children to sleep easy, pretend we were all just camping while the rest of the world burned.

"Did you have another one of you dreams?" Mom's voice and the sound of the zipper drew my eyes up to the entry.

"Yeah." I looked away. "Something like that."

"What was it?"

She asked me every morning, and every morning I'd tell her all about the weird dialogue between me and the creatures and she'd always tell me how it was just my mind trying to make sense of the world and what was happening, psych 101 she'd remind me. But this dream was different. It wasn't about the creatures, and I wasn't scared, I was just sad.

"Saw the guy again."

"Your dream boyfriend?"

My cheeks immediately heated up. "Mom, he's not my dream boyfriend."

She smirked. "We all have to have something that makes us smile, and besides, who wouldn't find a man with green eyes and dark hair sexy, he sounds mysterious." She winked.

"You're not wrong," I mused. "But no, he's not my dream boyfriend and this wasn't a happy dream."

She frowned and then placed herself at the end of my inflatable mattress. "Tell me."

"I really don't think it's important."

"Maybe not, but I'm your mom and I'm here. You can talk to me."

I sighed. "I don't know what to tell you, I was asking him to do something he didn't want to."

"What?"

"No idea, but I told him that despite what he was doing, I could never forget him, not completely. I don't know."

Her eyes shot up to mine, immediately setting me on edge.

"What, Mom?"

"Nothing, sweetheart, that sounds terrible."

I frowned. "It's just a dream, no big deal, right?"

"Right." She forced a tight smile and got up.

"Why do I get the feeling you're hiding something?"

"I'm not hiding anything from you, Alex. We're all under a lot of pressure, and I'm sorry if I've been hard on you these past few weeks."

"It's fine, don't worry about it."

Satisfied with my response, she curtly nodded and then left.

20

Through the opening in the tent I could make out the brightness of the day and, despite the winter chill, it was nice.

I rubbed the back of my neck and stretched out the muscles.

There was work to do—it had been more than four weeks since we watched the world as we knew it fall to its knees.

Missiles, bombs, and grenades; I couldn't tell which brought New York City down first. Some of the papers I found said we did it, some say the military reacted too slowly, some say it was just terrorists but those of us who'd seen *them,* and what they could do, knew better.

I was there, up close and personal watching them carry people off, kill them and then discard them. I was there when they scoured floor by floor of every building picking off whoever they could get to. This wasn't a terror attack, at least not by a human threat.

It didn't take long for everything to go quiet; after about two weeks all broadcasting ceased, power went down, and communication went silent.

A few weeks after that, the groups of people who were left got smaller and the injured started to die. There was no medicine, no hospitals. Mom did whatever she could to help, but some people were beyond what she could do. They needed surgery, antibiotics. All we could offer were words of comfort and some Advil for the pain.

Eventually, they went to sleep and never woke up.

Their beds were cleared and given to the next in line.

It was all so clinical, so *inhuman*.

My heart tightened with familiarity each time I saw them clearing out another bed.

It was the same feeling that had consumed me the night it happened when I watched as the snow and the creatures fell from the sky. Their flaming bodies melted everything around them and turned the snow into endless rivers of glowing light.

Something deep at my core felt drawn to it, like I'd seen it before, though I'd never confess that to another soul, not even now.

But that wasn't the only thing we had to contend with, there were bad people out here too. The kind that killed for food or supplies, stole what they couldn't find and other awful things I didn't want to think about. One night I swore I heard a woman get dragged off. I never heard from her again. I shuddered.

The cries that echoed through the forest at night weren't just of wounded and dying people, they were of people who were being tortured…attacked…

Collecting what I needed for the day's jobs, I slipped out of the tent and crept past the others. Most people here tried to make daily life as normal as possible, which meant small talk, but I just wanted to be alone.

Over the past four weeks, something had started to change inside me. Things I couldn't explain, things that resembled superpowers of the characters I'd read about in books.

At first it was small; I could predict what someone was about to say or do, then, stuff started to move just by me thinking about it, and the more these things developed, the more I kept to myself, never daring to stay around someone long enough in case they saw.

I laughed to myself. I'd loved parties, going out and being around people. Now, all I could think while I kneeled in the overgrown shrubs surrounding the riverbank near our camp was how much of a stranger that girl was.

Today, I had more in common with the girl in the beanie on the park bench on Broadway than I did with the girl whose reflection was staring at me in the water. I could hardly remember what it felt like to go to school and do homework, and I had no idea what the dreams meant, or why I could suddenly move things with my mind.

"Alex?"

My eyes shot up and I stopped scrubbing the bottom of the pan and looked across at Mom.

Her long blonde hair fell neatly over her shoulders in perfect waves. How she managed to keep it so nice out here was beyond me.

"Are you done with the pan?"

A quick glance down confirmed it. The pan was done for, another one, in less than a few days. Frowning, I held it up and shook my head.

"I don't think these are meant to be used on open flames."

"Another one, already?"

"Sadly, yes."

"We have to think of something else." She looked down at the pot in her hands. "They're just not lasting."

"I don't know. Maybe we should try to find some camping stores…they can't all be cleared out. They'll have the cast iron stuff. That's good, right? For flames?"

She placed the pot down beside me and smiled, squeezing my shoulder.

"We'll tell the others."

She smoothed her hand over my left arm and sighed. My eyes traveled down to the small, distinctive pink scars that served as a reminder of a burn I couldn't remember. It happened when I was a child, apparently, I left a toy on the heater and set my cot on fire.

Smiling up at her, I cupped my hand over hers.

She had the same light blue eyes as me, but her blonde hair was much lighter; mine was sort of mousy, like Dad's. I seemed to have caught the short genes as well as the slightly darker features.

"Your father wants us to move out before nightfall."

"What?" I knotted my brows. "Why?"

"He said we have to get moving."

"I don't understand, there are people here, good people. We're safer in numbers, aren't we?"

"He thinks we're better off alone."

"What if we're overrun by Scavengers?"

"I wish you wouldn't call them that." She frowned.

"Well, that's what they are. They scavenge from people."

"They're people too, Alex. Just not good people."

"Exactly. *Scavengers.*"

She sighed but dropped it.

"We can handle the *Scavengers*, if they come."

Refusing to accept her roundabout answer, I shook my head and opened my mouth to protest when she stepped closer to me and snapped back.

"I need you to trust me and I need you to listen, okay?"

The sudden change in her tone kind of stunned me.

"Alex?"

"Yeah. Got it."

Satisfied with my response, she forced a tight smile and gave me a quick hug.

"Get your things, we'll talk more after we eat."

Leaving me no choice, I returned my attention to the busted pot with a sigh. *Okay, guess we'll talk then.* I held my hand out and with little more than a simple thought, it flew up into my palm and I continued scrubbing it.

24

After suffering from a broken nail, scraped knuckles, and way too much effort, I gave up. There was no saving it. I dropped it beside the river and collected the few things I'd brought with me. Most of my days were spent doing chores which were divvied up between whoever was able. Today was no different. Today I was helping an elderly couple with their towels. I scrubbed each one in the river using barely a drop of liquid soap because you know, I was still conscious about looking after the environment. I scoffed, taking in the charred, scattered mess of trash and other things that had gathered around the edges of the riverbank. Still, I couldn't bring myself to stop caring. If I stopped, it meant accepting that the world was changed for good. Maybe the kid in me was still holding onto hope, the eighteen-year-old in me wanted to slap some sense into myself. Once the towels were more or less, clean, I squeezed out the excess liquid and slung them over some lower hanging branches I could reach.

Then I continued with the next set of chores on the list.

Mom had asked me to walk the four younger kids around the camp while the adults held a meeting. It was scheduled for the remainder of the afternoon.

"Alex!"

"Yes?" I turned and smiled at the little red-head girl running toward me with a stick.

"Can we go down there?" She pointed to the riverbank.

"Sure, but you all have to stay together. Got it? I'm not a good swimmer so I can't save your butts if you fall in." They all giggled but accepted my terms.

Once we were all down by the water again, I sat against an old Oak and watched them play. In their little minds I'm sure the world was no different. Maybe being out here *camping* with total strangers was a bit strange but nothing too wild for them to conceive. How I wished I could feel the same. The distant chatter of the adults in the camp made a dull ache settle into the pit of my stomach. I could handle whatever they were talking about, why wouldn't they let me? Instead, I was here playing babysitter and washing pans that should have been tossed out weeks ago.

"Alex, I think it's time to go back," the little girl said startling me. "I'm hungry and Tommy's cold."

Was it? Already? I looked up as the sun began to dip below the dark clouds and the moon crept across the sky. Wow. The days really were flying by. I gathered the kids, picked Tommy up before he started freaking out about 'catching frostbite' and we walked through the woods back to the campsite. Moments like these, when the world was silent save for my own feet crunching across the dried terrain, were the moments when I felt it stir inside me.

It was a feeling I couldn't explain to anyone. But I knew it better than I knew the normal things in my life. It was a feeling that consumed every fiber of my being, like it was a part of me, whatever it was, and it was strong, running through my veins, filling up every pore and every cell. It almost hummed in tune to the steady pulse of my heart, ever since I watched them fall from the sky.

As I made my way through a clearing, a shiver ran up my spine making me straighten and then stop walking. It was impossible to describe, almost like the familiar sensation of butterflies whenever you saw someone you really liked. My eyes swept the dark trees, there were voices up ahead carrying though the canopy of still leaves above—nothing out of the ordinary. But something was out of place and when I couldn't find the source, I hurried my pace and made it back to the campsite, kids in tow.

"What's wrong?" Tommy asked, his little face turning in every direction.

"Nothing, kid, go back to your mom and we'll hang out again tomorrow."

"Bye Alex!" they said in unison and disappeared back to their parents.

Elly, a girl who was a few years younger than me, was talking loudly to her sister about that night. They were sitting around a small campfire. As I approached, I noticed that two of the others my age were eagerly listening. She believed, with her hand on her heart, that they were demons sent from hell like in *Supernatural*, while Alice, her older sister, shook her head and rolled her eyes. *Why were they never stuck with babysitting?*

Both girls were petite brunettes, though Alice looked like she could kick your butt without a second thought. We didn't go to school together, but I recognized the hockey training top she practically lived in now. My school had played against them a few times. My parents had wanted to send me there before I ended up at Mission Lodge.

"I'm right, come on, Alex, tell me you're on my side. They're demons."

"I'll agree to anything as long as you promise that Sam and Dean will show up to kick some ass." I shrugged, pulling my hair up into a bun.

"See!" She threw up her hands when the guy sitting closest to her laughed.

As soon as his eyes locked onto mine, I felt my cheeks flush and suddenly my Sam and Dean comment seemed super lame. Last week when he and Alice got into a fight, I discovered that his name

27

was Evan after she screamed at him from across the campground and that they were a thing, past tense.

"What do *you* think about them?" He smirked, patting the spot beside him.

In the flickering glow, he had an almost celestial look about him, he was a gorgeous guy, chocolate brown eyes with perfectly tousled dark hair accentuating the jock build he had going for him.

But the more I focused on his eyes, the more I started thinking about how green would suit him…a deep, rich emerald…

"Alex?"

"What?" I snapped my attention back to Alice.

"You zoned out."

"Oh." I rubbed my hands together, trying to play it down. "Sorry."

"So. What do you think of them?" Evan asked again.

What did I think about the demons? That they fascinated me? That they seemed familiar?

"I don't know. They're creepy."

He didn't take his eyes from the flames, but he nodded. When he did finally bring his attention back to us, his eyes landed on me and he smiled. Instantly, my heart warmed, and Alice's eyes snapped to me. I reactively looked away. I didn't want to start any trouble and quite frankly, she scared me. But his smile was the kind of smile that broke down whatever barriers you thought you'd built and smashed them all over the ground. So, I smiled back.

"What did you do at school before the Takeover?" he asked.

It still felt weird talking about the event that way. A Takeover. Something so simple to explain away a life-altering, universe-changing event. But someone called it that and it stuck.

"I played tennis."

28

"Alice was a cheerleader, before she realized she likes to slam people into walls." Elly nudged her sister in the ribs earning a smack to the back of the head.

"I don't always slam people into walls." She grinned, breaking the tension. "Only if we're behind."

"Did you ever try out for the cheer squad?" Alice asked, rubbing her hands together in front of the flames.

Shaking my head, I did the same. Wow it was getting cold.

"You have the build for it," Alice said, sizing me up.

Maybe she was trying to figure out whether she needed to slam me into the wall. Deciding that I definitely didn't want to become one of her outlets for aggression, I inched away from Evan.

Before my mind registered what he was doing, Evan wrapped a blanket around my shoulders and I quickly noticed that everyone had one.

"What did you want to do when you finished school?" he asked, making me laugh nervously.

Alice and Elly looked at me, waiting for my answer.

"I guess I hadn't really thought about it."

Alice shrugged. "My parents wanted me to study psychology, join the family business and all that, but I didn't want to. I guess now that we can't do any of that, it doesn't seem so bad."

Evan smiled. "I know what you mean. My dad wanted me to go to college, study anything. No one in our family finished school."

"Guess the record stays, then," I said lightheartedly.

Evan chuckled. "At least I can say I was almost there, that's got to count, right?"

I laughed. "Absolutely."

"So, you've really never thought of a career?" Elly asked.

I brought my knees to my chest, anchoring them on the edge of the log and shook my head.

"Doesn't matter now, does it?" Evan threw his head back in a dramatic gesture as though he was searching the stars for answers. "We're free to be whoever and whatever the hell we want."

"Amen to that!" Alice laughed. "And on that note, get your skinny butt up, we have to get to bed." She nudged her sister.

"Okay," Elly muttered, "I'm going."

I laughed as they walked off leaving me and Evan alone.

He stirred beside me. "Where do you think they came from?"

"Who?"

"The Reapers."

"Reapers?" I tilted my head.

He shrugged. "I've heard some of the others call them that."

Huh. I guess it made sense, they were kind of like the bringers of death, though I'd been calling them creatures, because like creatures of literature, they were evil, they were monstrous and inhuman.

"Alice and I spoke about it a few weeks ago, when the first group of campers left. She thinks they're from space," he said.

"What, like aliens?"

"Why not?"

The whole thing made my skin crawl. "What if they're from another time?"

He turned his whole body toward me, shooting me a look. "What?"

"Nothing, I'm just making things up. I don't know why I said that."

"Are you talking about time travel?"

"Nah." I shrugged, desperately trying to downplay what I'd just said. "Different dimensions. Things like that."

He chuckled. "Are you a Trekkie?"

I stuck my finger up at him.

"You could be right, you know?" he said, suddenly serious.

"Hardly." I laughed and turned my eyes back to the stars. "That's just crazy."

"And what's happening in the world now isn't?"

"That's a different kind of crazy."

"You're not wrong." He shivered, turning his head back to the stars. "I wonder if there's anyone out there, trying to help us, or figure all this out."

"There has to be. I don't believe that this is it."

For a moment he kept his eyes on the stars and when I moved on the log beside him, he turned his head toward me, a slight glimmer flickering through his eyes, and my heart did the thing.

It sped up, raced like I'd drank way too many Red Bulls and then, as he leaned toward me, the worst case of bad timing stopped him from kissing me.

"Alex?" Mom called, stopping a few feet away. "Time to come to bed now."

"Seriously?" My cheeks reddened. "I'm not ten."

"And that response makes you sound like an adult." Mom's brows quirked.

Immediately I shut my mouth, ignoring the smirk on Evan's face. I groaned and gave Evan the most natural smile I could muster before collecting myself and whatever was left of my crushed ego.

If Dad really was going to make us leave tonight, this would be the last time I'd see him. As I stood there in the stillness of the camp, looking at him, my heart kind of stilled and for a moment I contemplated whether I should say anything.

But there were no words that seemed to suffice. I didn't know what to say, I didn't know what I wanted to tell him.

Because as stupid as it was, my mind kept returning to the painful feeling of watching the boy in my dreams with the emerald eyes cry and plead with me.

So, instead, I gave Evan a quick hug.

"Good night, Alex."

"Good night."

Mom was serious about the move. She'd packed everything. Even my stuff. I used to hate when she went into my bedroom—it's not like I had anything to hide, but it was annoying. Now I owned like ten things, and she didn't need to pack them for me. I balked when she pushed aside my bag and handed me an empty one.

"You know life is different out here now, same rules don't apply."

"What are you talking about?" I asked, glancing over at all the bags strewn across the floor.

"I know you wanted to spend more time with that boy, but we don't have the luxury of that sort of thing anymore. I'm sorry, sweetheart."

My cheeks flushed and I immediately changed the direction of the conversation. "What is all this?"

"You're taking those two bags."

My eyes swung down to my packed bag and then back to the empty one in my hands.

"Why?"

"Can we save the questions for later?"

"Later, when?" I stood my ground. Something about this was so off. She'd never been so short with me.

"Alex. Pack."

Throwing my hands up, I scoffed but did as she said.

I stuffed the remainder of the ten things into the empty bag and when nothing else would fit, I shoved my knees on either side, pushing it closed. The zipper barely made it all the way up, but I managed.

"Where's Dad?"

"He's getting some more supplies."

That set off alarm bells. Supplies. Supplies which were guarded by the leaders of this group and proportionately handed out to each person and family. Before I opened my mouth to argue, shouting outside forced it shut. My mom pressed her hand to my mouth and pulled us both down to the ground.

My face came within inches of the zipper closest to the ground, which was open just enough for me to see outside. The tiny, glistening blades of wet grass rapidly began to decay. From the vibrant green they were moments ago, full of life, they became brown, turning black until they wilted away.

They were here.

When she released me, my eyes widened as the yelling continued and we lay in silence, waiting. It felt like eternity and with each passing minute, my heart thundered louder and faster.

A voice I recognized shouted for them to stop and then my heart stalled when the voice was cut short. Evan…oh my God.

Several shrill screams sounded following the next round of shots. Alice and Elly.

Tears rapidly filled my eyes and before a choked cry could escape, Mom pulled me down further into the rough ground of the tent.

Another loud crack echoed through the still night. Followed by another and another. My heart lurched into my throat, but it was too late.

The people we'd been living with, traveling with, were screaming. Hurried footsteps crunched the dry leaves lining the floor and through the sheer fabric of the cheap tent, the surrounding darkness was lit up by blinding flames. Orange and red sparked to life as the trees began to burn.

"Where is it?" I heard a voice yell.

"You can go to hell!" my dad replied.

Oh God, no.

"We know you have the location of the Map."

"And that location will die with me," I heard Dad say.

My eyes widened. What? No, what was he talking about?

"So be it." A shot sounded and no more replies came from Dad.

No! Struggling to keep up and make sense of what was happening, I shook against my mom's arms and all I wanted to do was scream but she pressed her hand to my mouth again silencing me.

My heart slowed and then sped up, bile filled the back of my throat and a rapidly building scream was stopped by a choked sob.

And as more screams filled my ears, gunshots broke out. This time, there were no pauses, there was no stopping.

The leaders had begun to fight back. How many were left, I had no idea, but my heart was hurting, and my eyes burned. I could barely see through the hot tears as they streamed furiously down my cheeks. My body was frozen like it refused to work, but then

Mom grabbed me, her wide eyes locked onto mine, and shook me from my trance.

"Sweetheart, I need you take your bag and run."

My head shook on its own.

"Alex, please, you have to."

"No!"

"Alex, now!"

Panic rolled through me, wave after wave of horror mounted as the voices outside grew louder and the heat forced beads of sweat to start dotting my face.

"I, I can't, I can't leave you, and Dad…oh God."

She pressed her hands to my cheeks and smiled, her wet eyes glistened in the glow of the orange aura.

"Take your bag and run. You can do it, sweetheart."

Before I could argue again, the fire roared and caught the fabric of our tent. Mom pushed me back toward the rear exit and with a final shove, she forced me out and threw my bag to me.

"Remember what you promised him in your dream?"

"What?" My eyes darted between her and the fire outside.

"You'll trust him, even after everything. Remember. Now go, run!"

There was no time to process what she said, because in the second it took for me to understand the words that came out of her mouth and for the roaring outside to get closer, the cheap fabric went up in flames and for the first time since it all began, I saw the reality of the situation.

Flames, angry and raw, billowing around the makeshift camp, snuffing out screams and silencing cries, charring trees and tearing down tents. I was frozen.

Mom was fighting off an army of them, there were so many, so many and no one would be coming to help.

Anger quickly replaced the horror inside me and I dropped the bag, rushing back into the fire. Three Reapers up ahead stopped and turned abruptly, their gazes landing on me. One of them had distinctively larger eyes than the others which made it look even creepier.

Crap.

Fear was not an option; like I said, the world changed people, it had changed me.

They wasted no time leaping over the burning tents like it was no effort at all and within a heartbeat, they were coming right at me.

I should have run or hid or done what every other normal person would have done. The old me would have bolted, but I wasn't that girl anymore.

These creatures had taken everything from me, and I'd be damned if I let them take anything else. I stood with my feet apart, my eyes narrowing in on the one closest to me and deep inside, I felt the familiar spark. My hands reached out instinctively, as if my body knew what it was doing.

My eyes coasted across the expanse of the burning surrounds. One of the Reapers had broken off and was coming right at me. At first glance, I recognized its overly large eyes as the one who'd broken formation first. Its reaction quickly earned the attention of the other two, while I stood, hoping that my self-acting hands knew what they were doing.

They ran at me. I braced myself for the impact, and probably my imminent death, but as the first Reaper closed in, breaking the last foot between us, my hands rose and a force field type gust of wind hit the Reaper square in the chest. A feral sound resembling a hiss left its mouth and my own startled cry left my lips.

Its pale eyes widened in momentary shock and as soon as it wore off, it regained its composure and stood tall.

Its lanky body moved in a fluid motion. They tried to dress like humans, but the sickly pallor of their off-white skin was hard to miss. No matter how much they tried to assimilate, they were so unmistakably alien. Some of them, though, looked less like this pasty creature and more flesh toned. It made me wonder whether they morphed into this over time or if this is just what they looked like from the onset. From what I'd worked out so far, the pastier ones were more unpredictable—maybe they were new or something, but it was as if they didn't want to follow orders or maybe they were incapable of critical thinking.

The two others quickly took its place and came at me. This time, I threw my hands up, ready to do whatever that was, again.

But nothing happened.

Nothing at all.

My stomach dropped through the floor and that higher reasoning I was missing before found me.

Spinning on the spot, I grabbed my bag and I ran.

Up ahead, my eyes landed on the carnage: bodies were strewn across the charred landscape, burning tents and trees filled the forest.

My eyes burned as the embers filled the night and the reality of my world struck me. I wasn't just a teenager running through the forest. I wasn't just on a camping trip. I wasn't about to go back to school and see my friends. Everything I did now was about survival. Keeping my head in the game was getting harder as each step became more difficult. The Reapers were gaining on me and the terrain was getting rougher. I was alone and I was outnumbered. I didn't know how to fight. Dad never showed me more than a basic choke hold and those few sessions down at the firing range were more fun than educational. And God help me if I needed medical assistance. Mom tried to teach me the basics, but now, should an issue arise, I dared to think I knew more than to staunch the flow of blood. I should have listened. I should have been more present.

Useless tears quickly filled my eyes.

As I turned, making it through a smaller clearing my eyes landed on my mom. She'd made it out past the fighting. Her wide, terrified gaze held mine for a moment, and then a long silver blade was thrust into her, all the way to the hilt, forcing a choked scream from my lips. I didn't even see the Reaper or where it came from.

Everything slowed, my heartbeat thundered loudly in my head and my body refused to move. The Reapers who'd been chasing me were closing in, but I didn't have it in me to care.

My whole world was ripped apart and the last remaining part of it was just taken out in front of me.

Mom didn't say a word, she didn't blink or even cry, she just dropped as the Reaper pulled the blade out and discarded her like trash.

The only thought that registered was the long, shiny knife in its hands covered in her blood.

It stepped toward me, the blood glistening in the amber hue of the night. A sickening grin adorned its pasty face, and the two behind me stepped around to the front, the third joining it.

"You've got quite a bit of power in you," one of them said.

"I think you might be who we're looking for," the other cooed.

My eyes darted between them.

The third stepped closer wordlessly.

My mouth dried up. The spark inside me started to grow again and the confidence that last burst gave me was back.

They'd killed my parents.

Tears welled.

They'd taken everything from me.

Anger grew.

I'd kill them all, or I'd die trying.

The Reaper closest to me took a small step back.

Anger fueled me, and adrenalin and probably irrational fear, but I wasn't going down.

With a scream and burning anger, I ran forward and threw my hand out, a bolt of power rushing out of me and hitting the Reaper. It went down.

For a moment the other beside it looked just as stunned as me. But that moment rapidly passed as it lunged again.

I kept going, one after the other, bolt after bolt. The energy was consuming, the rush flowed through me. My heart raced with ecstasy and then, as I readied myself for the next attack, a large burst of energy hit me in the chest throwing me down.

I tried to scramble to my knees but failed miserably, dropping back into the blood-stained earth.

A shrill laugh filled my ears, somehow managing to sound through the blood rushing in my head.

That was the moment I realized there were at least a dozen now, a dozen Reapers and me, all alone. My heart cracked as the thought that I might not make it out of these woods dawned on me.

The one holding the blade stepped closer and whatever the crazy power was that I had inside me before was a no show now. There was nothing, not even a drop to squeeze out.

Panic set in hard and fast. My eyes darted around, assessing and trying to work out what I could do, what I could use. There was nothing.

Doing the only thing I knew I could, I pushed up to my feet, throwing my weight into the closest Reaper and ran.

There was a small window of opportunity and I took it. I sprinted through a small clearing, pushed through another Reaper and broke free.

I ran and ran. I lost count of the hours and of the days, I didn't know how long I'd been going but all that mattered was never stopping.

I was on my own now and this was how it was going to be.

I would regroup, find my strength and then, well I had no idea what would happen next.

CHAPTER THREE
THE GIRL

A shout echoed somewhere off in the distance sending my body jolting upright and out of a broken sleep. Before I could stop the response, my head smacked into a low-hanging branch and sent a rush of reactive tears to the back of my eyes.

I wanted to tell myself that it wasn't because I was so, so sad and alone. I wanted to tell myself that it was because my head hurt and not because I'd lost everything in one night.

But that was a lie.

Pain ate away at me, ripping apart every small fragment of strength. My head did hurt, but my heart hurt more.

All I saw were my mom's eyes, her smile and her singing, her soft voice and Dad's strong hands, cradling me when I was hurt, telling me he'd beat up any boy who broke my heart.

They were both gone.

My family…my whole camp…my entire reality.

No. There was no time for that. I swallowed the tightness in my throat and looked around. Rubbing the rapidly forming lump, I strained my eyes in the dark and focused.

Shuffling footsteps off in the distance alerted me, jarring me from my thoughts. They were much too loud and much too clumsy to belong to Reapers which meant that they were most likely Scavengers, and that put me on edge.

I reached across the nearby cover of grass and let out a breath of relief when my fingers ran across the cool, smooth metal of my Glock.

As silently as possible, I kept my eyes sweeping the surrounding woods with my hand firmly clasped around the grip of the gun.

A quiet echo of chatter filled the deathly still space.

"It's been four weeks since we burned that camp down and everyone in it. You really think she's still out there?" A voice broke through the clearing.

It sounded human.

"Of course she's still out there. You think they'd let her die, they need her."

"I'm just saying, they killed her guardians and she's out here alone. She's just a girl."

"She isn't *just* a girl. Keep looking and keep your thinking to a minimum."

My mind raced. *Who are they talking about?*

"Remind me again why she's so important," one of them muttered.

"She's supposed to be some mythical being, half them half those other guys."

Other guys? There were more?

"So, are we looking for the Map or the Halfling?"

There it was again, that word. *Halfling.*

"Look, mate, I have no idea. Silus's orders are to search for both."

These guys weren't Reapers...but they were working for them. Why? And there was that name again, he, or *it*, must have been a leader or something.

A quick glimpse of a shadow off to my right drew my attention and forced my heart into my throat.

Crouching, I stayed in the shadows and repositioned myself among the shrubs, and the rustling footsteps drew my attention back to them. They neared me but stopped several feet away; they were too close for comfort.

Just as they swept their weapons over my area getting dangerously close, a rustle of leaves high in the tree line a few yards away drew them in the opposite direction.

I exhaled slowly and stayed low. Perfect timing, wind.

"There's no one out here," one of the voices shouted.

"Clear here too," another one yelled.

"Keep moving east," the first voice said.

But the guy closest to me stayed rooted to the spot making my heart lurch into my throat.

"You heard the boss. Keep moving."

When he remained unmoving, the first guy barked his orders again.

Finally, he left.

When the footsteps moved again, I took the opportunity and ran.

I didn't stop to hear whether they found my tent or whether they were coming after me. I'd been out here long enough to know when to run and when to fight—right now wasn't the time for heroics.

I tightened my hold on the strap of my bag and moved through the wooded area, glad that I had enough foresight to keep my bag with me at all times.

Taking a right, I continued through the darkening tree line, keeping my eyes on the horizon and my mind on alert. I hadn't stayed alive this long without being good at staying out of sight. Though I had my family then and the others at the camp. Now I was alone. That was sobering and quite frankly terrifying. But more than that, my brain refused to catch up—deep down, where my weird power came from, there was an answer I think I knew all along but denied. And it came in the form of the beings that fell from the sky and the *other guys* the Scavengers were talking about.

As a clearing up ahead caught my eyes, a gut-wrenching jolt of dread rushed through me. Throwing my hands out I stumbled and barely caught myself against a trunk. I hid behind the cover of the low hanging branches and pressed my back against it, letting my eyes scan the nearby trees.

My hand instinctively went to my heart. I'd never felt that before. Dread swallowed me completely and coated my insides with icy fear.

The temperature rapidly dropped, and an eerie, unnatural silence descended. My eyes coasted along the nearing tree line. If I were susceptible to persuasion, I could have honestly thought this forest was haunted, coming to life with the spirits of the deceased. The way the mist descended and ghosted around me forced a chill to settle over my bones. Ghosts weren't real. The paranormal wasn't real. I was just overreacting. I evened out my breathing and looked around. Nothing but the hypnotic cover of mist hovering above the forest floor moved, yet there was something else here with me. Something I couldn't see or hear but something I could *sense*, deep in the pit of my stomach, where that weird feeling I knew all too well coiled around my heart, coursing through my veins. Something which didn't want to be found. I took a deep breath and drew my gun. So much for the paranormal not being real.

The painful silence deepened, and my eyes darted from corner to corner taking in the blackness surrounding me, and a few feet away, looming closer and closer, two glowing, deathly pale eyes stared right at me. And then, like a vacuum sucking the life out of this world, the air became stale and everything near the Reaper started to decay.

My breath stopped short and my body froze as my eyes took in what was happening.

No, this couldn't be it. They couldn't have found me. I'd been so careful, I'd done everything I'd been told, everything Mom and Dad had said... and then, like a slap to the face, a sense of dread replaced the shock.

"We've been looking for you, Alexia."

How does it know my name?

A sheen of tears coated my eyes. I wasn't going to go out like this.

The eyes came closer and in the dim light of the moon, the creature's sickly face was illuminated. It was one from the camp. The one that killed my mom.

The tears burned my eyes.

With each step it took, the glistening blades of vibrant grass decayed beneath its feet. My eyes shot back up to it. Dark shadows surrounded its glowing eyes, cuts and scratches covered the grey skin.

A sickening stench permeated the air, stinging my nostrils, and the back of my throat tightened as the bile began to rise.

Dead, dried leaves from up above floated down around us and disintegrated as soon as they reached the immediate area surrounding it.

The Reaper circled me, sweeping its rough hand along the hem of my collar, its sharp, black nails scratching along the skin on my neck making my body jerk in response.

This one was less pale than the others I'd seen, one of the mature ones I assumed. Its clothes seemed to fit over a more filled-out body and it seemed to be more *human.*

"You've been very hard to track." It spoke in a very deep, raspy voice.

Track? My head instinctively shook.

A sour taste filled the back of my throat and coated my insides with terror.

"Your guardians did a good job."

My body tensed. As it moved around me, taking the time to *smell* me, a feeling I recognized filled my veins.

It was the same feeling that had made me stop in the woods before my last night at the camp; a shiver ran up my spine and the butterflies were back. And again, I knew I didn't need to be afraid of whatever it was because *it* felt like the giddy joy when I dreamt about the boy with the green eyes. I looked around, there was nothing but the darkness, nothing but the stillness around me, but the feeling was growing, it was getting stronger, it was fueling me, giving me courage, urging me to move, to react, to do anything other than just stand here and wait to die.

The Reaper stilled beside me; it'd sensed the shift too.

Without hesitation, I clamped my jaw shut and turned sharply. I didn't think, I just reacted. I clenched my hand at my side and launched my fist into its face, bracing for the impact when it connected. I yelled out as my knuckles screamed in protest. The Reaper jolted backward. It wouldn't keep it down for long, but it would be enough to make my move. I ran. I didn't stop, I didn't look back. I pushed myself harder than I ever had in my life.

And as I placed more and more distance between us, I couldn't help but think…how did I just execute a perfectly placed right hook? I'd never trained in any form of combat, let alone hit anyone. Sure, I'd watched *Supernatural* enough to know what it looked like. But watching and doing were two very different things, and something deep down told me I knew the answer.

Maybe I wasn't ready to accept it yet. Maybe it wasn't time.

CHAPTER FOUR
THE FAMILIAR STRANGER

My feet ached with every rocky step I took, and my legs screamed in protest. The terrain was rough, trees lay strewn across the forest floor like they'd lost a battle with a category five storm, and remains of campsites lay scattered among the debris.

I'd been walking, running, sleeping, whatever I could do to survive, wherever I could. I'd almost lost count of the days. I carefully stepped over a large branch and my eyes settled on a broken doll. It was half buried in the soil and missing an arm. Its long black hair was matted and dirtied from months of rain and mud washing through this area, but I could still make out the pale pink dress it had on. It looked like it had been loved and cared for dearly at some point.

Did the little girl this belonged to miss her doll? Was she even alive? Thoughts like that quickly crept up on me and it shocked me that that was pretty much the way I lived now, always on the move, always alert, always *realistic*.

It didn't elude me that the weather had gone crazy too. Everything was strange; the sun shone in an unnatural hue, the rain came and went in completely erratic patterns and the temperature dropped and rose like someone was playing with the thermostat.

It wasn't the only unnatural thing. I was one of them. I didn't waste time pretending that I'd imagined the things I could do, so now I spent my time working on perfecting whatever it was. A lot had changed in that time. It had been over a month since my family was killed and since I'd seen another soul that wasn't out to kill me.

Stopping the quivering in my lip, I pulled my eyes away from the doll and moved on.

There was a motel somewhere down here, I remembered it from a trip I took years back with Mom and Dad. We'd stopped there on the way to Greenwood Lake because Dad said there was a great spot by the water to have lunch—he was so excited to show us the rock formations. I looked through the tree line spotting the glimmer of the Sterling Forest Lake on the horizon. I swallowed hard and walked. He was right, the spot was beautiful just like the last time I'd seen it—some things never changed while others became painfully unrecognizable.

Using the water as a marker, I walked along the bank in the nearby trees, conscious to stay hidden. Although it was dark, the light cast by the moon was enough to draw attention to me and that was something I desperately worked to avoid. The motel would only be a few miles from here if my calculations were correct.

Hours passed as another familiar path came into view. I stepped around an exposed root and continued. A chill settled in my veins as I moved through the dark night. I shivered. It wasn't just cold, it was abnormally freezing. My breath escaped in short gasps into little white clouds and while I did my best to conserve energy and keep my body warm, I was turning into a popsicle. I hurried my stride along and tightened my arms around my chest hoping that somehow it would help.

As the mind-numbing silence consumed me, I found myself straying toward those green eyes I dreamed about whenever I fell asleep. They carried me away with soft whispers of words I knew I'd never heard. How could I have? A love like that wasn't something you could forget. But God, it felt real.

Up ahead, a clearing came into view and brought my focus back to my walk. A quick glance at the road confirmed that it was empty. I stepped over another upturned tree and rushed across the paved section and into the woods on the other side.

A subtle gust of wind threw loose leaves up into the air and twisted them around me in a gentle breeze. I scanned the area and stilled. It was too quiet. I'd been so used to hearing screams, echoes of gunfire, anything. I tightened my grip on my bag and as a shift off to my right caught my attention, I sidestepped out of the tree line and pressed my back against the trunk of a large pine and hid.

Further down the path, my eyes fell on a small crowd gathered around a fire. One of them kicked a can and laughed loudly taking a swig of whatever he was drinking.

Hoping that the cover of trees and the low brush would hide me, I kept low and quiet.

But, just behind the group of loud men, a very distinctive set of glowing eyes, followed by several more, shone through the trees a few feet from them. Oh no. They were all about to get slaughtered.

Frozen in place, I watched on in horror as the group of Reapers stepped out of the trees and made a line for the men.

They weren't good people but they didn't deserve to die like that. I should have done something. Useless anger tightened my muscles. I couldn't do a thing. I was outnumbered just like they were. I moved closer and focused on them with morbid fascination, waiting for the attack.

As the Reapers came into view, I held my breath and waited, but they didn't slaughter them. They didn't even attack. Instead, they joined the humans around the fire. They were talking but I couldn't make out anything they were saying. And when one of them stopped, and turned toward me, I could have sworn its eyes focused on me through the woods. Without warning that same feeling from earlier filled my heart, distracting me. As I jerked back, I knocked a branch and made a very loud, very obvious noise. God. Could this have been any more of a cliché? I gritted my teeth and tried to move out of the way, mentally slapping myself. How did I make such an amateur mistake? It was too late.

Without a second to react, panic set in and I jumped to my feet, rushing to get away. My legs moved like jelly and the unnerving feeling of eyes on me filled every void inside my veins. I threw everything into the motion and ran.

A loud crash sounded through the woods and I didn't dare look back.

The loud crash sounded again and this time a roaring sound like fire flaring through a contained space penetrated the tree line. I stumbled over an upturned root and despite my desperate and feeble attempt to reach out for a trunk, I fell.

When I looked up, my heart came to a screeching halt and all the will power and fight inside me seized up.

They were right there and there was nowhere to go.

My brain tried to kick my butt into gear, and it did, but a few seconds too late. As I raised my hands, calling on the shallow burst of power inside me, a small gust hit them, but nothing compared to the retaliating attack.

A strong force smacked straight into me, throwing me back several feet until I landed in a painful heap.

Curling to the side, I forced my hand down to the dirt, praying that I'd have more in me to force another shot. I did. It was nothing compared to the force it threw back at me, though, and this time, I was flung into the air and suspended.

When the Reaper neared me, it released its hold and I crumpled at its feet.

In one fluid motion its hand shot out and tightened around my throat. Excruciating pain radiated through me as the edges around my vision grew darker.

My hands desperately clawed at its cold, clammy wrist and as the suffocating pit of terror reached around my heart and consumed every logical thought I felt consciousness slip away from me.

As I spiraled into the unknown, the same deafening explosion filled my ears and the Reaper released me.

It didn't take too long to regain my bearings. I scrambled to my feet and bolted. I sucked in greedy breaths of air, ignoring the burning in my muscles and lungs as I leaped over an upturned root. I didn't even make it a yard before a powerful burst of wind knocked me straight down, and when I chanced a look back, my heart stalled—the Reaper was closing in with slow, purposeful steps. It looked amused, its brows were arched, and its thin lips quirked into a smile.

Ten feet from me, a man stepped directly into the Reaper's path. His back was turned but the unmistakable sensation of familiarity winded me.

Subtle waves of energy—what I'd mistaken as the nervous feeling of butterflies—were now pronounced. I realized as I sat on my butt behind him that it wasn't nervousness, or unease, but whatever this was, it was strong, and good, full of positive and energetic vibes.

And the origin of that feeling stood between me and the Reaper, towering menacingly, broad shoulders pulled back and squared, dark strands of hair falling around his face under a black baseball cap. I scrambled to my feet and pulled out my gun.

Hesitating for a moment, I looked back and forth...*who am I meant to be fighting here?*

Deciding that I'd take my chances with the stranger, since there was only one of him, I turned my gun to the Reaper. Through strands of sweat-soaked hair, I forced my attention between the two and let out a ragged breath trying to compose myself.

The stranger turned his gaze to me, and my breath stopped short. *It's your dream boyfriend,* a small voice whispered inside my head. No. Hell to the no. This was insane, I'd clearly hit my head too hard. And besides, this guy didn't look exactly like my *dream boyfriend.*

This guy had a large, deep scar that ran from his right eye down over his cheek and disappeared into his collar where I noticed an angry splattering of red and pink scars—he'd been burned.

His eyes found mine and then traveled over my left arm, like he was looking for my scars. I instinctively turned my shoulder away. There was no way anyone would have seen them. I always wore long sleeves to cover them. But this stranger's eyes seemed to know exactly what lay beneath the surface of my thin sweatshirt.

But more than that, it was what I'd remembered from my dream, the feelings, the emotion, right here in front of me in high definition and unmistakable clarity.

Slowly, he brought his eyes back up to mine and when he swept his gaze over my face, something quickly flashed across his features, making us both flinch.

53

But before I could register what I'd just seen, he moved. The whole exchange took literally seconds. He stepped forward placing his body between me and the Reaper who had been joined by the rest of the group I'd seen earlier.

There were eight of them and two of us…if he was on my side.

"Back up," he ordered. A dangerous edge laced his words. "I won't say it again."

Okay, he was American. That much I gathered and he didn't sound like the Scavengers, he sounded refined. His accent was sharp like someone who grew up on the East Coast.

Immediately, I bit my lower lip and remained silent. Not only did he look like he could kick all their asses, he'd probably look amazing doing it.

Stop it, Alex. I chastised myself.

"Eric Raine," the Reaper muttered with a hefty laugh. "Guardian extraordinaire."

Eric smirked, casting his eyes over each of the Reapers.

Do they know each other?

"You know I hate repeating myself," he said tightly.

"And you know that you can't save them all," the Reaper spoke, casting a quick look over me.

Eric gave it a tight-lipped smile, the kind where one corner quirks up and the other tells you it's all business. How I knew that was beyond me.

My stomach did summersaults. He was confident, unshaken, and despite what hellish past I imagined he'd faced, he was strong, someone you didn't want to mess with.

"Though I think it's heroic of you," the Reaper added.

My mind went into overdrive. But Eric stood silently, listening to every word the Reaper was throwing at him.

"You won't be around all the time."

Casually, Eric swept his hand across his jaw and let out a low laugh.

My brows shot up.

The Reaper, now holding the attention of the others in its group, smirked and stepped closer. Eric didn't flinch.

He was completely nuts, or he was one of those weirdos who loved to live life on the edge. He was squaring off against eight *Reapers* with a serious arsenal which resembled something our own army would utilize; guns, rifles, and other weapons I didn't recognize, not to mention serious supernatural abilities, more serious than mine. I tightened my grip on the gun, glad that at least my butt was protected.

When the Reaper smirked, Eric stuffed his hands into the pockets of his dark army pants. As he moved, I noticed that his black sweater, which was hidden under a tactical vest, had a logo attached to the sleeve—one I'd never seen before. Having Dad and all his friends around pretty much clued me in to all the insignia the US government used, and some of the international ones too. This wasn't anything I recognized. It was made up of a large V with a smaller one inside it surrounded by seven stars forming a U shape.

As he spoke again, my eyes swung back to his face. His sharp jawline was covered with a dusting of dark facial hair and where the scars cut along his skin, the hair was a little thinner. His biceps tensed with the pressure he was exerting as he stood his ground against the small army, and with each deep and calculated breath his muscles flexed slightly, drawing me in.

He wasn't just attractive he was intoxicating. Something about him was dangerously addictive.

"I don't need to save them all," he responded, turning his face slightly toward me, letting his gaze linger before turning his attention back to the Reaper. "I'm just looking for one."

"And what will this one cost you, aside from the obvious?"

"Not as much as it will cost you if you don't walk away now."

What the hell?

The Reaper laughed.

Well, I was glad someone was finding this whole exchange funny. I, on the other hand, was seriously contemplating making a run for it. Yet for some reason, I stayed, eyes fixated on Eric. That lack of common sense I seemed to sport these days was really irksome right about now. Why wasn't I running already?

"Fine," the Reaper agreed, "go."

No way. My eyes shot back and forth between Eric and the Reapers. They were sizing each other up. Tension was growing but the Reaper did as he said and stepped back.

Angry protesting erupted behind it, but it held up a hand sternly, silencing the others before returning its attention to us.

"Silus will hear about this."

"I have no doubt," Eric muttered. "Tell him we will speak when I'm ready. For now, Silus stays away."

The Reapers remained still. Were they in shock? I knew I was.

"Leave, before I change my mind," the Reaper said.

My eyes shot up to the Reaper. Eric gave a quick and curt nod and before my brain could tell my feet to move, I was struck with something I couldn't place. A warmth began to spread inside me originating from my heart and spreading out into my arms and into my fingers.

Looking back at the Reapers, I watched as they dispersed.

What just happened?

As I opened my mouth to demand an explanation, darkness edged around my vision, and when I looked across at Eric, his eyes narrowed and focused on me, my legs gave way and I began to fall.

As the darkness swept me up, and the last glimpse of his striking eyes burned into my mind, I could have sworn I heard him whisper, "You said you'd never forget, even after everything."

CHAPTER FIVE
THE SIBLINGS

Strong, warm arms circled me and the intoxicating aroma I loved so much filled the air. It was a mix of the cologne he wore and the ever-present scent of trees and grass. We'd all spent so much time out there now; it was a wonder we didn't all smell like a garden.

When I chuckled to myself, he drew his thumb along my lip, silencing me.

"You're perfect."

I snorted. "So perfect."

"You are."

Reaching up, I closed my hand over his cheek. "Tell me the story again."

"What story?"

"The one where we leave this life and live our own. The one where it doesn't matter who you are and who I am."

"Oh." He chuckled. "Come here then."

I scooted over, nuzzling my face against his chest.

"It's the greatest story of all, the one where you understand the meaning of true love, of crossing worlds and time, to protect the only thing that matters," he whispered, tightening his hold on me.

A choked laugh escaped before I could stop it.

"What?" He laughed. "Too much?"

"A little. But I like it."

"I like it too." He flipped me on my back, and carefully lowered himself over me.

His vibrant green eyes closed for a moment, his dark lashes fanning his smooth, tanned cheeks before he opened them, and his gaze hardened.

"What is it?" I asked.

"I'm going to miss this."

Before I could ask what he was talking about, the green orbs that had looked at me with such love and care were gone, in their place, terrifying, blue eyes I couldn't tear my gaze from. I screamed.

The sound of a horrifying cry penetrated through my ears, jolting me awake. *Was someone in trouble?*

I fanned myself desperately trying to catch my breath, and as my eyes darted around trying to figure out where I was, another presence in the room forced me to stop. The scream had been my own.

It dawned on me then, I was lying in someone else's bed, in different clothes dressed by a stranger. My ripped jeans were replaced with yoga pants and the tattered sweater I'd worn to death was replaced with a black hoodie.

I shot up and scrambled back, and unfortunately for me, coordination was not a gift of mine, nor were quick reflexes. I was still groggy and recovering from whatever he did to me and as I rushed to get off the bed, I tripped over the blanket and found myself careering toward the ground, hard and fast.

Before my face smashed into the light brown floorboards, two strong arms wrapped around my waist and steadied me, pulling me up to my feet. Those haunting, green eyes shattered my composure.

Once my brain forced some sense into me, I pushed him away and moved against the wall, quickly glancing around for anything that I could use as a weapon.

My bag was gone which meant my gun was gone. Not good—I'd never been without it, not since all this started.

My eyes swung up and fell on his, and my breath stopped just short, butterflies rippling through my insides.

"You screamed, you were having a bad dream."

"It wasn't bad…" I began to say then stopped and corrected myself. "It wasn't all bad."

"Well, that's good…" He looked at me suspiciously and when I remained transfixed to my spot, he changed his approach. "I didn't undress you. If that's what you're worrying about."

When my eyes flicked away from his and traveled across the line marring his features, I couldn't help but frown which caused him to look away. Crap. He probably thought I was…God that was insensitive.

"My sister dressed you. They're her clothes," he added, shaking me from my thoughts. "She's just outside and I was bringing you food."

My mouth refused to work.

He nodded to the small tray beside the bed. There was a trail bar, some water and an apple. I didn't know why, but the gesture made me incredibly sad and I felt totally stupid.

I wrapped my arms around my body and looked back at him.

He stuffed his hands into his pockets and raised both brows. He wasn't dressed in the combat gear I'd seen him in yesterday, he was more casual now. Dark jeans and a light grey T-shirt.

60

Now in the less obstructive outfit, I noticed that the burns went further. They reached over his right shoulder and crept down to his forearm to where mine just stopped above my elbow.

When I remained awkwardly still, obviously staring, he shifted and scratched the back of his neck, repositioning the cap he had on.

Oh crap. I looked away. I hated when someone made it obvious they were staring, so why I did it was beyond me. God I was such an idiot.

"Say something." He raised his brows again, creasing his skin slightly. "You do speak more than a few phrases, don't you?"

I wanted to say I was sorry, for whatever he went through, for staring, for making him feel awkward. But when higher reasoning returned, I released the breath I'd been holding and nodded, letting my eyes drift over him.

"I do," I said.

He raised a brow in question.

"Speak, I mean," I shot back, clarifying my less than eloquent response. "I do speak."

God. I was such a freak.

I cleared my throat. "Where are we?"

A smile broke out across his face and it was breathtaking. I reminded myself to stop staring this time.

"We're at my grandparents' farm in Mansfield."

"As in Pennsylvania?"

"Definitely not Australia."

I shot him a look.

"Anyway, you took a pretty hard hit, had to make sure you didn't have a concussion."

"I didn't hit my head," I countered. "I, there were Reapers and you were there…"

"Yes. You tried to run from them. You tripped over a branch."

"There was no branch…" My voice trailed off. "You were talking to them. They let us go…"

"Like I said. You took a hit; I'm not surprised that your memory is scattered."

"My memory isn't scattered."

He chuckled. "It's okay, I'm sure the memory loss isn't long term."

A scowl crossed my face before I could stop it and that only earned me a grin from him.

Why does this all seem so normal?

"Come on, Alex, you should meet my sister."

"How do you know my name?"

"It was engraved on your gun," he explained without a second thought, "unless you stole it from someone named Alex?"

"Uh, no, I did not steal it…" I snapped my attention back to him. "Where is my gun?" I demanded. "Where's my stuff?"

He stood silently, until he cleared his throat and jerked his head toward the door. "It's safe, my sister put it all downstairs."

This didn't sit well with me.

"I'm not going to bite." He laughed. "Unless you're into that sort of thing."

"Definitely not."

"Coming?"

"I'm not going anywhere with you."

"Okay, that's fair." He held his hands out. "I'll be downstairs. Come out when you're ready."

He disappeared out into the hallway and I quickly shut the door, jamming a chair under the handle. I looked around. The room was bare save for the bed and the table with the tray. As if on cue, my stomach grumbled. I rushed over to food and snatched up the apple, taking two quick bites and chowing it down without taking a breath. Once I was done with that, I walked over to the window and looked out over the landing below. Good, it was only one floor and the roof below would be a good buffer if I jumped—

I paused when I spotted him crossing the yard.

He came to a stop on the porch below and leaned against the wooden banister which overlooked at least ten acres of land.

Across the field my eyes fell on a girl as she galloped along the perimeter on a white horse. The picture was stunning. As she came closer, I noticed how her eyes were as vibrant as Eric's and her long brown locks fell around her shoulders in silky waves, over a dark navy blazer buttoned up around a silky white blouse with tan pants.

I forced my eyes back to Eric. He shook his head, but the unmistakable pull of a smile creased his brow. I relaxed and watched the exchange.

The girl on the horse did an over-the-top bow and then laughed when Eric stuck his finger up at her.

The apprehension that had forced me to stay up here suddenly melted away. I immediately felt stupid for jamming the chair under the handle and before I could regret what I was doing, I pulled it away and made my way downstairs.

I traced my fingers across the white panes of wood on the walls and across the patterned wallpaper above. It was everything you'd imagine a picturesque farmhouse would look like. Antique, aged furniture, white and pink picture frames, quaint décor.

Stopping just short of the porch, I stood back beside the door.

"She's a show-off," he said without turning.

"She's pretty good."

He chuckled, leaning back against the porch with his arms across his chest.

"You never actually told me your name," I said, keeping my eye on the girl and the horse.

"You know my name," he said simply, his voice suddenly a lot more serious than I'd heard before.

I looked up at him and wet my lips. His shoulders were rigid, his body poised defensively on the steps.

"My name is Eric Raine," he said keeping his eyes on the horizon.

"Eric Raine," I repeated softly.

A very small, almost silent breath came from him.

I tore my eyes from the back of his head and looked over at the girl as she approached.

"And that's Emelia, my sister," he said, taking the steps down the porch and across to where she'd just tied up her horse.

She looked across at me with a wide smile and an enthusiastic wave. I found myself awkwardly smiling back and taking the steps down and walking toward them. As she made her way over, I noticed how Eric's eyes were focused on me, like he was searching for something, almost expecting it. I didn't know what he was waiting for…maybe recognition? Maybe something else.

I cast my eyes away from him and smiled, genuinely this time as Emelia approached. I felt a pull to her warmth, like a friend I'd known a long time ago, one I might have even shared boy secrets with.

"Alex!" she squealed, pulling me into a bear hug.

Jerking back, I pulled free. *Whoa. Personal space?*

Eric shot his sister a quick look, but she shrugged and smiled. "Sorry. I'm a hugger."

Her eyes narrowed, searching mine and then, just like Eric, she kind of sulked back, looked dejected before turning to her brother. A knowing look crossed his features before he turned to the horse.

"How are you feeling?" she asked, bringing her smile back to me full force.

Something weird was going on.

"I'm fine." I smiled, smoothing my hand over the black hoodie. "Thanks for the clothes."

"Sorry, I had to change you. When you went down you ripped your jeans."

I shot a look across at Eric and he instantly returned his attention to the horse.

"It's fine." I nodded. "Hope my spotted bra didn't scar you for life."

She laughed and led me inside.

"I've seen worse, believe me. Cleaning up after that animal makes you develop a strong tolerance." She pointed her finger at Eric and shuddered, making a face.

Somehow, I couldn't believe anything could be gross when it came to him, but I laughed at the face she pulled.

"Gosh, I'm so rude. I'm Emelia."

"I know," I admitted, "Eric told me."

A small, sad smile crossed her features before she cleared her throat and pushed the door open. "Are you hungry?"

Am I really doing this? Really engaging with a pair of strangers I don't know from a pair of serial killers. But a calm voice in the back of my mind told me they were neither strangers, nor serial killers.

The voice came in the form of my mother and I couldn't argue with that. It was a compelling argument.

"My parents had backup generators running for a few weeks after the world shit itself, but that's since stopped working too. I cook on open flames now," she explained, shoving the door shut, with a little more force than I thought necessary. She turned to me and smiled sheepishly. "The wood is kind of old and splintered. Doesn't close the way it used to."

"Oh," I said, looking at it, not sure what I was looking for.

She smiled again. "Come on. The kitchen's this way."

Everything about Emelia seemed so *normal* but when it came to Eric, well, that all got strange.

As we walked through the beautiful house, my eyes swept across the walls and shelves. *Didn't they say this was their grandparents' farm?* I hadn't noticed anything that would belong to *an elderly couple,* nothing cute and kitschy that I remembered my grandparents hoarding, there was just a bunch of stuff covered by white sheets and a broken-down truck out the front with half its insides missing. Unless of course, they were minimalists and total clean freaks. I pushed that thought away when we rounded the corner and my eyes fell on framed photographs of a very happy family.

When Emelia caught me looking over the immortalized memories, she came to stand beside me.

"Mom passed away when all of this started." She pointed to a beautiful woman dressed in a bright yellow sun dress perched on a rock by the sea. She was caught mid laugh and she was so charming. "She got sick, toxins I think. She used to love to sing and dance, she was so much fun, but in the end, she wasn't herself anymore."

My cheeks reddened, and I dropped my gaze. I was an idiot. Discretion was definitely something I had to work on.

"What about your dad?"

She paused for a moment, briefly looking away before giving me a tight smile. "He's out there somewhere."

"I'm sorry," I whispered, bringing my eyes back to hers. "There was a swarm of Reapers back at my camp, and we were overrun."

"When did it happen?" Her soft voice drew my eyes to her.

"More than a month ago now, I think," I said, following her through another door which opened up into a very beautifully styled kitchen.

I sat down and watched her. She was lost in thought for a moment as her eyes scanned the framed photos which continued into this room too.

"If you'd stayed, you would have died too." Emelia sighed and then pushed a plate toward me.

"When did you make all of this?"

"While you were sleeping." She shrugged.

The conversation died at the point, mostly because I didn't really know what else to say and Emelia was starting to look uncomfortable.

"Aren't you hungry?" she asked, changing the subject. "I can make you something else, I'll just get more firewood."

"It's fine. This is good. Thank you," I shot, before she could get to her feet.

"Maybe you just need to regain your bearings."

"Right," I began, "after tripping on the branch."

Searching her eyes for any sign of deception, I slumped back in my seat when I came up empty. Instead, she smiled back and nodded, keeping her expression completely neutral while she picked at her food delicately.

I didn't get that dangerous vibe, but I felt that same confusion and again, that distant memory just out of reach.

"Eric said we're in Mansfield?"

She nodded, cutting a strip of bacon in two and popping a piece into her mouth. "We're just on the outskirts of Hammond Lake."

"How long was I out?"

She cut a slice of bread from the loaf and thought for a few moments. "About seven hours after Eric brought you here. He said he found you near the Sterling Forest Lake."

"Yeah." I toyed with a piece of bacon on my plate and remained quiet for a moment crunching the numbers.

That was at least a four-hour drive from here. Sure, it would have made sense had there been a car or even a bus or a horse and carriage. But all I'd seen on the expanse of the property was a beat-up truck with no engine…unless they were stashing it under a tree or something.

She finished the rest of her food and folded her hands neatly on the table in front of her. The vibrant green of her irises found me and again I felt that familiarity start to pulse just under my skin.

Nodding numbly, I turned from her gaze.

Behind me, footsteps came in through the door and stopped a few feet away. As I turned in my spot, I locked eyes with Eric. He looked tense, his shoulders were squared and his lips in a straight line.

He turned to Emelia. "You've got a call."

A call? Seriously? Did he think I was a complete idiot? I scoffed, turning from him. Phones, computers, anything which made life bearable, in fact, died in the first two weeks.

Emelia disappeared to take her *call,* leaving me and Eric alone in the suddenly crowded kitchen.

"Thanks for dressing me and feeding me, but I'm leaving."

Our eyes met and for a moment he did nothing. His hands opened and closed at his sides and when I stood and made a move to leave, he sidestepped me and blocked off my path.

At that point, my heart kicked up.

His deep, piercing eyes bore right through me and a short breath got stuck in my throat.

Chancing a move, I stepped back and Eric stepped forward.

"What are you doing?" I demanded.

"You can't leave," Emelia said from behind Eric, startling me.

"What do you mean I can't leave?" I said firmly, keeping my eyes on her brother.

And this was it, this is how all those girls died when the serial killer got them into a secluded house with nowhere to go. Idiot. So, so stupid. I knew I should have run. *Damn it, Alex.*

I stopped my racing mind and tried to think. There had to be a way out. Emelia was tall and slender, Eric was built like a wall and towered over me, but I could run, really well. All I had to do was push past them and somehow find my way out of this maze and make a run for it. Piece of cake.

"It's not safe out there for you." Emelia came to stand beside her brother.

"Pretty sure I was safe long before you two came along." I narrowed my eyes at Eric.

"You had your parents then," he said calmly.

His words forced my mouth shut like a punch to the gut, and any response I had died on my lips. The sentence was cold and cruel and somehow it hurt even more coming from him.

Emelia folded her petit hands across her riding pants. "What he means is that your mom and dad helped to guard you—there are

69

loads of creepy people who will take advantage of a girl on her own."

"Your brother seems to know exactly what he's saying," I said calmly, keeping my eyes firmly locked on his. "Right?"

Eric didn't say a word.

That was it. I had enough to deal with out there with the Reapers and creeps and I didn't need some hot jackass treating me like a damsel. I grit my teeth and prepared myself.

Emelia moved closer to my side and as soon as I spotted an opening, I took my chance. I pushed past her, wincing at her shocked shriek and shoved a chair behind me hoping it would slow them down, and as I neared the door, I sped up throwing all my energy into knocking it open. The old, brittle wood splintered as the lock gave way. I ignored the pain as it sliced through my shoulder and continued running. She wasn't kidding, the door definitely didn't work the way it should have. Damn. I'd be lucky if I didn't jar my entire right side.

The clearing of woods around the property thinned, opening onto a main road. As I ran up and over the final embankment I sped across the pavement and back down into the woods on the other side.

They were hot on my heels, I could hear them nearing, rushing through the lower hanging branches, some of them snapping against the pressure and then, the gut-wrenching stench of death permeated the air just as the ground cover and trees started to rot away.

I chanced a look over my shoulder nearly stumbling in terror; the group of Reapers Eric had convinced to let me go were hot on my heels, and behind Eric and Emelia were Scavengers. Dozens of them. *How many of these people did the Reapers recruit?*

CHAPTER SIX
NASCAR PRO

"Run!" Emelia screamed.

I chanced another look, terrified to see them running after us. Their eyes were the brightest blue I'd ever seen. Nothing was natural about them—not their speed, not their pallor. Not that Emelia or Eric seemed normal either.

Somehow Emelia and Eric got in front of the Scavengers and I didn't need to stop and see what happened to them as their screams sounded through the woods. The Reapers had taken them out—so much for working together.

"Take a right!" Emelia screamed. "There's a clearing at the end!"

I followed her instructions and ducked under a low-hanging branch, following the path around to the right, and just like she'd said, a clearing came into view. A truck was parked just at the edge.

"Take Alex and go!" I heard Eric yell after his sister who'd gotten ahead of him.

As I turned to check on her, I heard a large explosion in the direction of the house. It was the same sound I'd heard before Eric intervened yesterday…before I became Reaper dinner.

What was happening?

My stomach lurched, where was Eric? Was he alright?

"Keep moving, Alex!" she shouted again as I pushed through the pain in my side. "Head toward the truck!"

I kept my eyes on the path ahead as I closed in on the truck.

With enough force to rip the door off the hinge, I pulled it open and threw myself in. Seconds later Emelia was by my side and the engine roared to life. We took off at dizzying speeds and swerved through the clearing. I braced myself as we sped through, coming out onto an open highway.

We didn't stay on the road long before she changed gears and drove up and over an embankment into the other side of the woods, making my entire body lurch forward as we hit rough terrain.

I kept my eyes on the road, scanning the horizon trying in vain to find the source of the loud explosion, and more importantly, Eric. Where was he? Was he okay? There were too many of them chasing him, chasing us because of me—because I ran.

My eyes began to water.

What the hell is going on? What have I done?

"Hold on," she said. Roughly kicking the truck into second gear, she drove up and over another embankment and pushed the engine harder. "Put your belt on."

"Where's Eric?" I breathed, working the seatbelt, quickly locking it into place while I kept checking behind us. I couldn't see anything.

"Eric's fine," she said quickly, flicking her eyes to the rearview mirror as we sped between the trees.

The truck took another rough dip into a shallow pit of bushes and roared over them onto the other side.

"How do you know? There were at least eight of them, how can he have taken them all on?"

72

"He's good at what he does, Alex," she said turning her head to me briefly, giving me a reassuring nod. "Trust me. My brother is fine."

"I don't understand."

"I know." She looked at me quickly before returning her attention back to the road. "But you will."

***

Emelia pulled the truck into a heavy cover of trees and killed the engine, composing herself. After a few moments of silence, she turned to me with a smile. She looked like we'd just taken a casual drive by the beach; no strand of hair was out of place and her clothes were still neat and prim. I looked like I'd completed the Mud Run and hadn't showered in a week.

"Are you okay?" she asked softly, her eyes traveling over me.

Somehow, I managed a nod though I had no idea why. I wasn't okay. I wasn't even close to *okay*.

"Who are you?" I pleaded.

For a moment she remained quiet, and when she finally turned back to me, she pursed her pink lips into a straight line.

"We're friends."

"I had friends in high school, none of them could outrun what we just did and none of them would have just driven a truck through the woods like they were Nascar pros."

She chuckled and motioned for me to follow.

"Well then, we're really skilled friends."

Somehow, I didn't buy it. What a surprise. I arched my brows at her which only earned me another smile.

Before we left the truck, she pulled the trunk open and retrieved three duffle bags. She handed me one and took the other two herself.

"What is all this?"

"Provisions." She smiled, keeping her eyes on the road ahead. "Have to plan ahead. And your bag and gun are in there too."

My eyes traveled over the bag in my hand. I didn't know what to think. I was numb. Numb and confused.

"You knew I'd come with you?"

"I hoped."

"How?"

"Call it a hunch. Okay?"

"No, not okay, Emelia. We just outran that hoard of Reapers, you're telling me Eric somehow survived, and you are like freaking Captain Marvel. What is going on?"

She drew a long breath and then released it before nodding. "Whatever I tell you is going to seem ridiculous. Which is why I can't tell you anything right now."

"Fine," I muttered walking ahead.

Eventually we both fell into step.

She gave me a sympathetic smile. "You okay?"

"I'm fine," I said quickly, not giving her an opportunity to ask again.

"We're heading this way."

As I followed her through the woods, I let my mind wander.

In the time that the rumors began to spread to the time the last communications went down, we were informed that there were certain government departments, including the CDC, who'd been set up to research and look for answers. That was at least two months ago, maybe more now. Time and everything else slipped by in a blur. Some days I was sure everything had just been a bad dream; others, I felt like the nightmare was never ending. What I knew for sure, though, was that I'd irrevocably lost everything I had known and things would never be the same.

The next communication that came through was that the Coast Guard and the United States Army had been taken out. One systematic attack that wiped out our entire defense system.

Then there was nothing.

They came hard and fast after that. They had strength and speed; some say even telekinetic abilities. My own freaky powers didn't elude me. Something big, something I didn't understand was happening.

But with each unanswered question, one persistent thought kept coming back to me, it was the same thing I'd said to Evan, the same thing which seemed so right even though it was so unbelievably impossible. They were from another time, another dimension. After seeing Eric and Emelia out here, it didn't seem so crazy anymore.

As impossible as it might have seemed then, humans knew that no one had any control over them, least of all regular citizens. The Reapers were inhuman, there was almost nothing that could take them out. They'd surprise you and take you out in an ambush...but I'd managed to sense them...

"We're almost there," Emelia announced, breaking my chain of thought.

"Where are we?"

"Just a few miles away from the farm," she said quietly, sweeping her eyes across the horizon.

My heart sunk. The farm. They couldn't go back now.

"I'm sorry...I..."

"You were scared," she finished for me. "I get it. Eric has always had the worst manners. He means well, he just doesn't know how to get it across...with you."

"With me?"

*Why would he have trouble getting anything across with me? He doesn't even know me...*but that familiar feeling in the pit of my stomach said otherwise and that same feeling made me shut my mouth.

"I mean I'm his sister, so he doesn't have to be nice or anything." She lowered her voice. "But there aren't many others left, you know? So, speaking to other people is a bit weird—we've been alone a while."

Oh.

She opened the front door of an abandoned house and pressed her finger to her lips, gesturing for me to stay by the door. As she took off upstairs to clear the space, I did the same on the lower level.

Digging out my gun, I got to work. Something about this arrangement felt oddly comforting. I'd been used to doing this alone since it all went down. Dad told me how to check and where to look.

"We're clear up here," she announced, taking the stairs back down, two at a time, landing with a graceful hop.

"Clear down here too." I tucked the gun back into my yoga pants.

"You should eat something," she added, nodding to the kitchen. "You've used up a lot of energy and you're looking a bit pale. I know I'm starving."

As soon as the thought of bacon, cheese, bread, anything full of carbs filled my mind, my stomach grumbled.

Emelia rummaged through the pantry and retrieved a couple of cans of beans and corn. "Hope you love carbs."

Catching the can she threw to me, I looked down at the chirpy mascot holding up a bunch of string beans and corn in an overly cheery yellow pair of overalls. Not the kind of carbs I was hoping for.

"Delicious." I made a face earning a laugh from Emelia.

"I appreciate you trusting us," she said quietly.

"I don't really have a choice, to be fair."

She didn't reply.

We sat around the table and popped our cans open eating in silence. Once we'd both finished, she took the cans and tossed them in the trash.

"I'm going to get cleaned up, there're some clothes for you in that bag." She nodded toward the duffle I'd carried in.

As I swept my gaze down to the bag, a sudden feeling rushed through me. Familiarity nearly bowled me over. A warm flutter of feelings spread throughout my stomach and through my heart. I felt like I knew this bag, like I knew where it had come from.

CHAPTER SEVEN
LOST LOVE

As the door upstairs closed, I rushed over to the bag and pulled it open.

It was stuffed full of clothes. Yoga pants, sweaters, sneakers, and boots. A jacket and vest were folded at the bottom. I couldn't shake the feeling that rolled through me. Why did it feel so familiar? Why did I feel like I knew where this had come from?

As quickly as the feeling came, it was gone again. No. I rummaged through it again, frustration getting the better of me.

A quiet noise just outside the front door attracted my attention. Quickly I drew back and retrieved my gun, pressing myself close to the wall beside the front door.

"Stand down," Eric called from around the corner.

Letting out a long breath, I replaced my gun.

"Are you two okay?" he asked, looking me up and down, and I was quick to notice the way his eyes lingered on my lips for far too long.

"What happened?" I managed, turning my eyes away.

"Reapers."

"Obviously."

Saying no more, he walked past me, grazing his shoulder against mine. A brief, almost undetectable rush of energy floored me. I stopped, dead in my tracks. He had to have felt that.

A glance up at him told me he didn't, or he didn't let on.

Why did it bother me so much that he was so disinterested in talking? He'd literally spoken like twelve words in total to me. Now that the world was broken, this kind of thing wasn't really a priority, but it bugged me. He sat at the table and opened a can of corn.

"Do you have a problem with me?"

His eyes flicked up to mine and we stared at each other before he looked back down at his corn.

"No," he replied, keeping his voice even. "Did you eat?"

"Yeah, I ate," I replied dryly.

"Good."

He started eating again.

He wasn't being an asshole on purpose, he was broken. I'd seen that look before, and God knew I'd felt it. Tearing my eyes from him, and the slightly scarred surface of his right hand, I retreated upstairs.

I closed the door to one of the bedrooms and leaned against it. Releasing a long breath, I reevaluated my situation and quickly came to the same conclusion. There was a longing, deep and painful and as always, my mind went into overdrive, overthinking everything.

Sadness quickly filled my eyes with tears. Mom would have loved to know that I met my *dream boyfriend.*

God. This was all too much. I ran my hands through my hair and pulled it free of the elastic.

I couldn't stay here. I didn't want this.

But another part of me, the one that was capable of logical thought, reminded me that safety came in numbers, just like I'd said to Mom. I wished that I had known why Dad wanted to leave so badly that night. I wished that he had told me, I wished so many things.

Groaning, I found the bathroom and turned on the shower.

Once I was done, I dressed in the clean denims Emelia had conveniently packed and threw on a dark sweater with a hood. I squeezed out the excess water from my hair and pinned the blonde mass in a twist.

As I pulled the door open, I stepped back in surprise. Eric was in the doorway, his eyes downcast and dark and only the smallest part of his green eyes shone through his dark lashes.

Now, in tight proximity, I stifled a small gasp when I found his eyes. His right eye was slightly clouded over, only enough that you could see it when you were this close. The scar ran deep, and I had the urge to reach up and smooth my fingers over his cheek. But as the thought formed and he blinked, I snapped myself out of it.

"We're moving," he murmured leaning up against the doorframe, almost like he was trying to get closer. "Wanted to give you a heads-up."

"Were you waiting out here the whole time?"

He shook his head, pushing away from the door. "Only when I heard the water turn off."

For a painful moment we stood silently, almost toe to toe until he dragged his eyes away from me and stepped back.

Something akin to a smile laced his lips for the briefest moment and then it was gone, and that same broken look I'd recognized in myself replaced it again.

"Can I ask you something?" I asked quickly, as he turned to leave.

"Sure."

"You're annoyed that I'm here?"

"I'm not annoyed."

"Could have fooled me."

He opened his mouth like something was on the tip of his tongue, but when nothing came out his chest rose in a deep breath before a sigh came out instead.

"Emelia gets attached, and then if we lose you, she'll be hurt again."

"Why do you think you'll lose me?"

"Because that's how it goes." He shook his head.

"Why do you think that?"

"I don't *think*, Alex. I know. I've seen so much."

And suddenly this conversation wasn't going in the direction I thought it was.

Eric was talking about something personal, and the way vulnerability crept across his eyes, turning them to a pale shade of moss, made me want to rush over to him and hold him.

"I'll get my things," I whispered.

"Okay."

***

Sometime later we'd crossed the border into Canada, and I swapped my napping for looking out over the spectacular scenery.

Nature had reclaimed a lot of the rest stops along the road and it looked eerily beautiful. Trees had grown into their unrestricted beauty, roots climbing in all directions, slipping in and weaving through the long since loosened rooftiles of the occasional house we drove by. It was magical how quickly nature flourished when man stopped interfering.

Every so often Emelia would turn to me and when I didn't say a word, she would turn away. The drive was quiet and awkward to say the least.

Eric was silent the whole time; a haunted expression was permanently etched onto his face, and every time I'd catch his eyes searching mine in the rearview mirror, he'd quickly look away and continue the silent treatment.

When I finally cracked, I shifted into the middle. "What does the rest of the world look like? Do you know?"

"As far as we know, the Reapers have invaded most, if not every continent," Eric said.

I shrunk back.

"But everyone is fighting back the best way they know how, this isn't the end of civilization," Emelia added.

"I don't see how we can survive this."

"We can and we will," she said sternly, turning her face slightly.

Her sternness caught me off guard and I moved back to my seat and turned my eyes to the tree line again. No matter what we did here, I couldn't see how we could possibly make a difference. I couldn't see how the people out there would come out on top. We were helpless against them…well, not *we* considering I had more in common with some sort of paranormal story character than humans, but the point remained—we couldn't fight the Reapers. We were outnumbered, underpowered, uneducated.

But the more time I spent with Eric and Emelia, watching their strange exchanges and cool demeanor, the more I thought that they knew more than they were letting on. Maybe they knew how to fight them, maybe that's why they were confident. Either way, I wasn't about to let my guard down even if Eric's eyes had the power to turn me into a puddle of gooey Jell-O.

Finally, we pulled around to the highway exit and Eric took us through the dilapidated turnstiles which once used to house cashiers; today it housed little more than birds and the occasional animal.

"We need to get off the main road," he said sweeping his gaze across the horizon. "If anyone's been watching us, they'll be waiting for us to stop."

"Do you think someone's been following us?" I asked, turning to look out the back window.

Emelia did the same and then turned to her brother, waiting for an answer.

"I have no doubt," he replied, keeping his voice low. "A working vehicle is invaluable."

My eyes scanned the horizon again. There were no cars, zero people, positively no one in sight. My brows knotted.

"The national park," Emelia suggested, nodding ahead. "There's a turnoff coming up."

"Sure that's a good idea?" Eric looked across at her.

"It's remote."

"That it is." Eric nodded, turning back. "But remote is also the Scavenger's favorite kind of place to hide out."

"We can handle the Scavengers." Emelia gave him a knowing look. "We take our chances. The fact that we still have Dad's truck is a miracle."

"Agreed." He nodded, following the sign to the Gatineau National Park.

"How do you still have the truck?" I asked, leaning forward between them.

"Keeping it hidden when we stop and staying off main roads when we're moving," Eric explained.

"What about fuel?"

"Grandad was always worried about doomsday, so he had a ton of fuel hidden away at the farm, and we just keep jerrycans in the trunk," Emelia added.

My heart sunk again. Now it made sense, that's why they stayed at the farm, why they always regrouped there, and I felt even worse than before. They couldn't go back which meant they'd lost all that fuel and the security that came with it.

"I'm so sorry," I whispered.

Eric gave me a quick look before turning back to the road. "Why are you sorry?"

"Your grandparents' farm, the fuel…"

Emelia turned to me with a smile. "We were running out anyway."

"We'll manage." Eric forced a smile. "We always do."

They were both lying.

"We should go to the Elders," Emelia said quietly, turning her attention to her brother.

"No. Not yet."

"If we get swarmed…"

"We won't," he insisted.

"Who are the elders?" I asked, ignoring the way his hands tightened around the wheel.

Tension suddenly filled the truck again. I glanced between the siblings, neither spoke yet so many words were right there, on the surface, unspoken. Emelia shifted in her seat and scratched the back of her neck nervously.

"I'll explain when the time is right," Eric said, finding my eyes in the rearview. "I promise."

His gaze knocked the wind from me and without a second thought, I nodded, agreeing to his less than forthcoming answer. All I knew was that his promise was iron clad, but how I knew that eluded me.

Chapter Eight
Asteraki Mou

By lunchtime the next day, I was ready to call it quits, ditch the siblings and chance my time out there on my own, however long that time may be.

Eric's mood had gradually got darker as the hours went by until eventually, even Emelia couldn't get him to crack a smile.

He was hurting, badly, and whatever was causing him the pain was getting worse. Whenever he looked at me, I couldn't help but think it was my fault. I frowned. *What did I do?*

We'd pulled over for another rest stop, somewhere along the snowy mountainside of the park, and I jumped out of the truck the second it stopped.

And my God it was beautiful. My eyes followed each jagged edge, each rock, each icy river that flowed along the naturally formed landscape around us. Ice and snow created the most stunning backdrop for the sun low on the horizon.

Emelia came out after me and jogged over, catching up.

"My brother doesn't have a problem with you," she said, easing her arm through mine, linking our elbows together.

"It's fine. You don't have to explain anything to me."

"Trust me. He's an ass on a good day, on a bad, well, you can see for yourself. But he's a good person."

"I'm not questioning that."

"I know." She smiled. "But you are questioning why he's being a douche."

"Yeah, a little bit."

"Look, I'm not all about *team Eric,* or anything like that, but give him a chance. He's been through some stuff."

Our eyes met and I found that faraway stare coming over her, the same that Eric got lost in often.

"Does it have anything to do with his burns?" I asked.

Emelia nodded.

"How…what happened?"

"There was an attack on one of our camps and there was a bad fire."

"When?"

"Before the Takeovers."

"I don't understand," I said.

She looked away for a moment before returning her gaze to me. "New Year's Eve wasn't the first assault on Earth."

My brows shot up.

"This has happened on smaller scales all over the planet."

"That's ridiculous, how could they have covered something like that up?"

"Terrorism. Natural Disasters. You think the government can't hide things from us?"

My mind immediately shot to Roswell. I believed beyond a doubt that the government been hiding something big from us.

"Anyway, the attack on our camp hurt him a lot. We lost a lot."

"Oh." I bowed my head.

Emelia shifted in her spot, looking over the snowy picture on the horizon.

"He's strong, he hides his feelings a lot, but I can see it taking a toll. I think it's getting worse and I don't know how to help him."

"I'm sorry, is there anything I can do?"

"No but thank you." She folded her hand over mine and smiled again. "He's just trying to deal. That's all."

"I get it."

She gave me a small smile. "Believe me. He really doesn't have a problem with you at all."

"Got it." I nodded, looking over at him.

He was leaning against the car, his eyes cast up to the snow-covered mountain; the sun had just crested and dipped below the light covering of clouds giving the whole valley an ethereal appearance. He seemed so content, like in this moment in time he was at peace.

"There's a ranger's station just behind that turn. We should walk ahead; Eric will hide the truck."

When I remained transfixed on Eric, she nudged me gently.

"You coming?"

"I don't even know you two," I blurted out. "I don't even know you, and I've been running around from house to house, evading those things like we're friends or something."

Emelia flinched, only just but it was impossible to miss. She folded her hands in front of her again, taking a moment. When she looked back at me her green eyes softened.

"You don't know us. But I'm asking you to trust us."

"Why? Why would I trust you? Why now? Why do you two care?" I demanded.

"Because we do. I'm asking you to have some faith."

"No." I shook my head, maintaining eye contact. "I need answers. Now."

She scratched her head and gave me a tightlipped smile.

"Answers, or I walk. And something tells me you care enough not to let me leave."

Emelia considered me for a moment before conceding. "A long time ago, a very good friend of mine told me that she had to do something that would break her. She said that even with what she was about to ask the man she loved to do, she would always remember him, and she would trust him regardless of what happened, even after everything."

My mouth gaped and my throat dried up. My head shook on its own as if in response to the impossible thing I'd just heard.

"Come inside, where it's safe, and we'll talk," Emelia said.

I followed without a word. What did this mean? What did this mean for me, and for Eric…was that real?

When we sat at the dining table in the ranger station, I found myself staring at her, trying hard to work out whether I was going completely crazy or whether she was. When Eric joined us, everything went out the window. My face heated up as memories I couldn't have possibly owned started to play through my mind.

But the man sitting in front of me wasn't the same man I had dreamed about, or maybe I imagined him, maybe I just conjured someone up because I was so lonely and he fit the bill.

Maybe they'd overheard me at the camp or maybe…I scrubbed my face and found Emelia's eyes.

"Eric and I are your friends. I know you don't believe it right now, and I know you have no reason to. But there are things we can't tell you yet. We have to keep you safe, that's all we can say right now."

I turned my eyes slightly in Eric's direction.

"The world has been brought down by a race of intergalactic demons, if you will," Eric said, "and we have the ability to fight them. We all play a part in this and right now your part is to stay alive."

"Am I meant to just accept that?" I shot to my feet.

"You're meant to do whatever your heart tells you to," he said dryly.

I looked over at his sister, hoping she'd tell me he was just being a smart ass. When she said nothing, I planted my hands on the table in front of me.

The words Emelia had spoken, the ones I'd uttered to Eric in my dream and later repeated to my mom kept running through my mind. Over and over.

Whatever this meant, whoever they were, I needed to know, and if that meant playing this game, I could do that. I *had* to do it.

Eric got to his feet and crossed the small room stopping at the door to look at me. "What is your heart telling you to do, Alex?"

Rapid breaths made my chest rise and fall sharply as my eyes searched his and the sincerity in them.

He held my gaze, his intense stare invaded every private thought cradled safely in my heart where I never knew anyone could reach.

With each passing second, I felt my resolve fading away.

I dropped my gaze and sat.

"Thank you, Alex," he said and then left.

The evening passed slowly as I found myself wandering the halls, though it was a small cabin, if you could even call it that. Emelia had made herself at home in the kitchen and Eric had taken residence in the lounge.

He had one leg draped over the arm of the sofa while his other rested on the floor. His dark shirt had risen a few inches above his jeans, revealing the taut lines of his muscular stomach which I saw was also not spared from the fire.

I swallowed the breath that caught in my lungs and as my eyes swung up to his face, I caught the grin he was wearing. His mood was evidently a lot lighter than before.

My cheeks instantly flushed and burned with embarrassment. He smirked, rising to his feet with that same expression.

Oh God.

Eric stepped forward. "You really do make it a habit to stare, don't you?"

I sucked in a mortified breath and cleared my throat. "I'm sorry."

"Don't apologize." He narrowed his eyes. They flared intensely and the green in them seemed somehow more vibrant than before, completely drawing me in. "I'm staring too."

Sometime between getting lost in those eyes and imagining how his lips would feel on mine, time seemed to slow, and then I was shocked to lucidity when I realized I was doing the thing again.

He, too, drew in a sharp breath and pulled back, my attention rapidly snapping to the small space between us. His eyes broke contact and the feeling that held me in place dissipated and I found myself blinking away the almost hypnotic daze.

What just happened?

"Am I interrupting something?" Emelia's voice made me jump.

Eric stepped back and shook his head. *Damn it, Emelia.*

"No," I muttered.

"Good, because that'd just be awkward. At least wait until I'm asleep." She winked. "I found food. It's in the kitchen…when you're ready."

Again, my cheeks reddened and if she didn't leave, I'd have combusted. I ran a hand over my hair and chanced a look at Eric. His eyes were again fixated on me.

Forcing my heart to stop doing somersaults and my breath to remain even, I kept my eyes locked on his. The intensity in his stare broke down the walls of composure I'd built.

"Do you trust me?" he asked suddenly, his hand closing around my arm where the scar stopped just above my wrist.

I cocked my head.

My mom's last words, *my* last words from my dream, hit me. *Trust him, even after everything.* This was crazy, it wasn't even the same person, it couldn't be…it was just a dream…

But my breath faltered just the same rebutting the statement.

"Alex." His voice was low as he gently swept his hand up to my elbow and stopped. "I need to know that you trust me."

My eyes followed his hand and stopped. I wanted to say that I didn't even know him, but I knew that was a lie.

"Yes. I trust you. After everything."

A hint of confusion widened his eyes.

I didn't let him say anything, I didn't know if I'd be able to handle whatever came next.

Before he could say anything, I ducked out of his way and removed myself from the living room.

Instinct told me that I knew more about him than I believed; instinct told me that I could trust them; *instinct* told me to stay.

All while Emelia worked in the kitchen, I stood completely frozen with my hand on my arm where Eric's fingers had left their mark.

There was some sort of connection there and I didn't think if I asked him that he'd be able to lie to me and keep a straight face to deny it.

There was something in that touch, there had to be. I didn't imagine the way his lips parted slightly, like it was hard to breathe. And when I looked into his eyes, I knew what I'd seen there. Fear and hope. A crazy combination which made no sense until that moment.

Forcing myself to snap out of it, I swallowed hard and made my way into the kitchen. Emelia had managed to cook up a storm with very limited ingredients and a tiny fire pit she'd made out of a discarded barbeque lid and some oven trays jammed in the sink.

My stomach grumbled as soon as the scent of food pricked my nostrils.

"Good invention." I nodded at the makeshift stove.

She chuckled, fishing out a potato.

"It's not ideal, but it's better than cans of peas." She laughed, looking down at her makeshift stove with pride. "Also, I reckon I'd give the guys on *Iron Chef* a run for their money."

"Where'd you even find this?" I looked around.

"They had a stash of supplies out the back." She nodded to the door I assumed led to the basement. "Serious preppers these guys."

Guess people really did go all out when they thought the world was going to end. I searched through the overhead cupboards and took out three plates, setting them to the side.

"Do you like potato?" She looked to me.

"Absolutely."

"Awesome." She handed me the pot of freshly baked potatoes and returned her attention to the rest of the food—plain rice.

I spooned enough potato into each plate paying careful attention to give Eric enough. He looked exhausted and I thought it might have had something to do with lack of food.

I took my plate and Emelia's to the table and sat, leaving Eric's on the counter until he finished with whatever he was doing.

He joined us not long after, silently taking the plate from the counter and sitting down opposite me.

"If you want more potatoes there's a bit left..." I said, hoping it'd draw some conversation from him.

He gave me a half smile and proceeded to eat without looking at either of us.

Emelia kept her eyes darting between me and her brother and eventually she snapped when he gave her a pointed look. She delicately dropped her fork beside her plate and glared at him.

Although a kind of unspoken agreement was made between the three of us, there was still a lot of tension, tension Eric seemed to be creating. I stayed because, well, I couldn't really face all of the Reapers alone and they helped me because it was some sort of duty they felt they had. Why? I had no idea. I also learned to stop being so insensitive but that memo didn't seem to have reached Eric.

"What?" he snapped glaring back at his sister.

"What?" Emelia rolled her eyes. "Are you serious right now?"

"I don't get why you're shitty with me."

"Because you're being rude."

"Honestly, it's fine guys," I said, sensing the absolute shit about to hit the fan.

"No, it's not fine, the least he can do is be polite and not just when it suits him." Emelia shot her brother another look.

He dropped his fork and pushed away from the table, leaving his half-eaten food behind.

"I'm sorry about that," Emelia said softly trying to hide her frown.

"Don't be. I get it."

My heart ached for him and I felt a deep pain settle. I looked down at the table where Eric's unfinished food remained.

I'd seen mourning and I'd seen pain but whatever haunted him went much deeper than that, and something told me that no matter what I tried to do, it wouldn't make it any better between us and it wasn't my place to try.

"Thanks for making all this." I nodded to the food.

She smiled and shrugged. "Helps me feel normal."

Together we emptied the scraps from the plates and I carefully placed what was left on Eric's plate into a small container and set it aside while I cleaned the dishes and returned the dried plates in their spot.

Once it was all done, Emelia gave me a quick hug and for a moment I froze, not really knowing how to react but the gesture was comforting, so I returned her hug and smiled.

"Thanks for helping." She squeezed my hand.

"No problem. Helps me feel normal."

She laughed, pressing a gentle hand to my shoulder. "We should try and get some sleep. It's pretty late."

After she took off upstairs leaving me alone, I let out a long breath and let my mind wander to Eric and the sadness in his eyes. Before I knew what I was doing, I was walking upstairs with his cold food, almost like I was being guided by some unseen force who clearly wanted me to make a fool of myself.

What am I thinking? I sucked in a deep breath and forced myself to stop being such a baby. I could have a grown-up conversation. I could do this, it wasn't like I was going to profess my love to him or anything, I was bringing him food.

No big deal. I scoffed, mentally berating myself.

No big deal, yeah right.

Why was I sweating so much then? Nerves made my hands shake and the butterflies in my stomach raged around like they were caught in a storm.

As I came to the final step clutching the container like a lifeline, I found myself barely able to walk straight.

Emelia had taken the final room at the end of the hall and she'd given me the one closest to the bathroom, leaving the one to my right the last option.

Gathering as much courage as I could, I took a deep breath and tapped gently on the door. A few minutes passed in silence and I mentally scolded myself. What did I think was going to happen?

As I was about to leave, the door opened, and Eric stuck his head out. A questioning look found me as his tired eyes traveled down to my hands and then back up to my face. Immediately my mind went to what I was wearing. I was pretty certain that the hoodie I had on was covered in dish soap and the yoga pants were probably way too tight since they were Emelia's and she was considerably slimmer than I was...

"Alex?"

Oh right, my mind snapped back to him. Seeing him in his low-hanging track pants and tight shirt winded me and I almost forgot why I came.

"I...you left, and I thought you might have still been hungry."

I was talking too much. I needed to stop, but I didn't.

"There's no power, so the microwave, well…I couldn't heat it up for you…"

"It's fine." He said, looking at the space between our hands before turning his right side away from me. I flinched. He was hiding his scars.

The tension was unbearable. I shook my head, wetting my lips. *I shouldn't have come.*

"Thank you," he said, stopping my racing mind.

I quickly shoved the container into his hand giving him no chance to respond before I turned.

"Alex. Wait," he said just as I'd reached the top of the stairs.

I stopped with my back to him and took in a slow and calculated breath before turning slightly to face him.

"I'm sorry for before. Emelia is right, I should be polite, all the time."

"You don't have to apologize. You don't have to explain anything to me."

"I do, and I will. I just need some time, is that okay?"

"Of course."

He smiled a very sad smile. "Thanks."

"Good night."

"Night, Alex."

And just before the door closed, I heard a whisper of words which shot right through me and again, like a memory just out of my grasp or a long-forgotten dream, I recognized them.

"Asteraki Mou."

"What did you just say?" I spun on the spot, desperately clinging onto the fading memory.

The subtlest hint of a smile, a real, hopeful smile, crossed his lips before he closed his eyes for a moment. "Nothing, good night, Alex."

Chapter Nine
The First Sign

He closed the door, taking with him my answers.

I rushed back to his room and was a second away from banging on it, demanding answers but as the sound of the bed shifting under his weight came through the wood, I stopped myself. He was tired. He needed sleep. I needed sleep.

Damn it. I ran my fingers through my hair, shaking my head. Why did that sound so familiar? I swear I'd heard it before. It was Greek, I knew that much. My mind wandered all over the place racking my brain trying to work out just how I'd known it.

Maybe I'd seen it on TV or read it in a book, but like always, I realized I was trying to convince myself of something I knew deep in my heart wasn't the case. No, I hadn't heard it on TV or read it in a book, I'd heard from a person, it was spoken *to* me.

It was too much. Too confusing. I made my way back to my room and gently closed the door. I found my gun, tucked it safely under my pillow and climbed under the covers. I closed my eyes and willed thoughts of those emerald eyes out of my head. I willed my heart to stop thinking about the way those words felt so right, the way his hands felt on me, but mostly, I willed my mind to quieten.

As a sigh left my lips and sleep came to claim me, I closed my eyes with images of Eric's smile and full lips, and somewhere among the last shreds of consciousness, I felt his arms around me like I'd felt them a thousand times before—I felt the way he pressed his lips to my wildly beating pulse and the way he ran his fingers gently through my hair.

"You're doing the thing again," I said.

"What thing?" he asked quietly, bringing his eyes to mine.

"The thing where you stare off, are you not interested in being here?"

His eyes snapped to me. "How could you think that? I'm always interested in being with you."

"Well," I started, lowering my eyes to his lips. "Maybe you should show me then."

A glint in his vibrant emerald eyes reached his smile and without more than a quick breath, he moved toward me, winding me with his speed.

Before I could react, he'd already spun me on the spot and fit me against his body.

His lips found my pulse and his hands snaked around my waist coming to rest over my stomach. When he held me like that, whatever resolve I had in my mind was somehow gone and all that mattered was us. We didn't care about the Council, or what they allowed or banned.

His hand stilled over mine.

"What is it?" I asked carefully.

"They're not going to allow this."

"I don't care."

"I care," he whispered, his breath tickling my ear. "You're too important."

"Then what I want should matter to them."

"It should," he agreed. "But it won't. They don't care about the emotional side."

"They will if I tell them to."

He shook his head against my cheek and let out a long breath. "Asteraki mou, they won't, not when we're at risk. Your position on the Council is all that matters, your ability to save us."

"What about what I want? Doesn't that matter?"

"Of course, it does, but this is bigger than me and you."

"What are you saying?"

"I'm saying, I don't want to hurt you but I don't want to fail you, as who I am and who I need to be for you."

"All you need to be for me, is Eric. My Eric."

"I'll always be that for you."

"Then why do I feel you're taking this conversation where I don't want it to go?"

He flinched.

"Eric. Don't do this, please."

"I don't want to. But you're going to make me."

"What—"

The caring gaze turned from warmth to ice and the blue, terrifying eyes I'd dreaded found me.

My eyes flew open. *What was that?* My fingers hovered over my neck where his lips had been, and the words he'd spoken to me, the *Council*...what the hell was all that about? I was dreaming about Eric, but it felt like so much more...I wish it had been—the Eric in my dream was so happy, so warm and it broke my heart because his burns...they were gone...and so were mine.

Once again, I forced those horrible blue eyes out of my mind and focused on Eric's. God, my head, everything felt like it was

101

scrambled. I pressed my palm to my clammy cheek and the strangest sensation of not being alone jolted me to the darkness surrounding me. I carefully moved, silently scanning the room around me. There was only a small trickle of light coming through the blinds from the moon outside, other than that it was practically pitch black. I couldn't see anything, but I *felt* it. Somewhere in the shadows, there was something with me. Two things to be precise. One was sinister the other, warm and calming. The two sensations overlapped and threw me off.

Reapers had a certain vibe they exuded; but I didn't feel that now. Whatever this was, wasn't a Reaper and that put me on edge. I ran my hand under the cover toward my pillow as silently as I could, searching for the cold steel of my gun. I held my breath, praying that whatever it was I could fight it.

A short breath caught on my lips as the calming presence moved in the room right beside me, closing in on the sinister one, and as I was about to scream, a hand closed over my mouth and I was pulled off the bed and back against a hard body.

"Stay quiet."

Eric's voice was harsh in my ear. A desperate edge laced his words as his arm around my waist tightened and he moved, repositioning his body in front of mine, shielding me.

Terror seized me; I couldn't move a muscle. Before I could let it consume me, he turned around, swiftly bringing his hand to my cheek.

"I won't let them take you," he breathed letting his touch linger. "I swear it."

Take me? Who are they?

I nodded, silently looking up into his eyes, they were wide and full of promise and in the shallow light of the moon creeping in through the blinds, I saw them come to life. There was something so desperate in them, so full of conviction in the way he held on, and it shattered me.

A quick moment later, he turned around and pressed himself in front of me again. Suddenly my mind ran to Emelia. Was she alright? Why was he in here with me instead of her?

As the other presence in the room shifted, I held my breath. It was searching, lurking around in the dark and suddenly I felt so violated. Whatever it was had been in here when I was sleeping, watching me in bed. Eric stood frozen, tense and on guard. When it moved again, I pressed myself flat against the wall. It was coming toward us.

Could it see in the dark? Maybe if I stayed still it couldn't sense us? I squeezed my eyes shut in the painful silence and slowly opened them only when I felt it move away and finally leave.

Eric dropped his guard and moved away from me.

"You okay?"

Nodding, I looked around the room. Everything felt normal again.

A breath left my lips and I slumped against the wall. I'd never felt anything like that before. It wasn't even a solid presence.

Emelia rushed into the room, the light from the hallway flooding the bedroom. She threw her arms around Eric and then around me.

"Are you two okay?"

Breathlessly nodding, I turned to her. "You?"

"Fine," she confirmed, wrapping her arms around herself.

In the short time I'd known her, I'd never seen her show anything other than composure—right now, though, she was tense.

She chewed her bottom lip, her eyes darting around from me to her brother.

"We have to move, Eric. This isn't safe."

"I know that." His response was quick.

"We have to go to the Elders. We can't risk it anymore."

"Who are you talking about?" I asked.

He turned abruptly in his spot, and his posture tensed as he switched his gaze between me and his sister.

"Eric," Emelia warned.

"Not now."

"When, Eric? When they come for her? When the Reapers finally get a hold of her?"

My eyes widened. "Wait, what? Why are they coming for me?"

Neither of them said a word, but they didn't have to. This big secret, this whole charade, was about me. I figured that part out for myself. But why? That was something I was yet to work out.

"I will not do this again," Eric conceded, shaking his head.

Again?

"Guys. I'm sorry, but that thing came for me and you're not giving me anything to go on."

Eric shot me a look which I quickly returned.

"I get you've got your own personal stuff going on," I offered, careful not to sound inconsiderate. "But it came for me, and I want to know why. I'm scared."

Emelia gave me a sympathetic look and turned her attention to Eric who looked like he was waging an internal battle.

"She won't get another chance, and neither will you. You know that."

Eric turned his face in my direction. For a moment we all stood silently in the dark of my room with the faint moonlight shining through the shutters while I watched the exchange and seriously questioned whether I should have said something.

"I can't," he all but pleaded.

Emelia threw her hands up in defeat. "The next time they come, if we're not prepared they will take her, and you won't be able to stop them."

"Get your stuff together. We have to leave, now." Eric turned to me, casting his sister a look which said there'd be a conversation coming later. "They'll be hunting us now."

"Okay." I nodded, quickly gathering my things. He didn't need to tell me twice.

They both left me to pack, and when I was done I made my way back downstairs, hauled my bag onto the table and sat.

At least ten minutes passed and eventually Emelia emerged, and Eric followed. Neither made eye contact with me as they walked by, motioning for me to follow them outside.

"Is someone going to tell me what that thing was?"

Emelia swung her eyes to me and drew in a deep breath. "They are a little specialty the Reapers have learned to produce."

"I've never heard of anything like that before."

"You wouldn't have. They don't usually go for…groups."

"What was it?"

Emelia stopped what she was doing and focused her attention on me. "It's a sort of force they can send out, it scopes out the area and sends information back."

"Like a drone?"

"Exactly, an organic matter drone."

My eyes widened. If they'd been using that thing to scope out campsites, no one was ever really safe.

"They're always out there? Looking for people?" I asked.

"No, not always. Just sometimes. Some people. It takes a lot of strength for them to produce those things, so they use them sparingly."

"How do you guys know about all this?"

"Remember when I told you Dad was a doomsday prepper? Well, he wasn't as crazy as they all thought." Emelia gave me a sideways look.

"He knew about this?"

"He was prepared. Did a lot of reading, a lot of research," Eric added.

"So, there was something out there to make him think this was coming?"

"I guess so."

"Right. You said this drone thing is hard for the Reapers to produce."

"That's right," Eric confirmed, leading us to the truck.

"So, they don't just do it offhandedly for anyone then."

The pieces started to click.

Eric's gaze landed on me for a moment and then he gave me a quick nod. "They're searching for something."

Someone, I wanted to correct. My mouth dried up and the hairs on my neck stood on end. We threw our stuff into the truck and got in. Eric took off along the road we'd driven down earlier and once again, we began our long drive.

"That's also a part of what we have to tell you. And there's a lot, but right now isn't the time," Emelia explained, handing me a bottle of water.

"Why?"

She looked across at Eric.

"It's a matter of safety. And that's the truth," Eric said, finding my eyes in the rearview. "I want to be the one to tell you, but right now we have to focus on getting us all out of here. Alive."

"Are we safe from their leader?"

"Silus," Emelia said.

"We're safe as long as we stay off the main roads. Let us do our job," Eric said and returned his attention to the silent drive.

My mouth clamped shut. Couldn't argue with staying alive. But the deflecting of questions felt a lot like the last night I was with Mom and Dad. They, too, were growing impatient with my questions, trying to dodge and evade at all costs to the point where Mom snapped at me, and Mom never snapped at anyone.

Maybe I was grateful for the chance to collect my thoughts, maybe the silence was exactly what I needed.

CHAPTER TEN
THE PENNY DROPS

As we crossed the Ottawa river, Eric pulled into the driveway of a house which looked like it could have once been an opulent mansion. I craned my neck, searching the horizon for Reapers. It looked like they hadn't yet been here. The countryside was still green, trees still flourished and small beds of flowers were still alive despite the turbulent temperatures.

Regardless, it was eerily still, not even birds sounded—although it wasn't completely unusual; most of the animals died when the humans did. I didn't know whether the Reapers *ate* them or whether it was just the putrid presence they left behind.

"We need to rest and try to gather as many supplies as possible," Emelia said, turning to me from the front seat.

"Do you really think there's anything left here?" I asked, looking up at the busted windows. There wasn't much of anything going for this place, let alone supplies for three grown adults to survive off.

She turned her attention to where my eyes were focused and then turned back to me. "Maybe."

"We can manage one night without," I supplied.

When Eric nodded, I balked. *Did he just agree with me?*

"You should get some rest, though." He directed his words at me as the three of us headed toward the house. "That's something you can't go without."

"True. What are you going to do?"

He turned back, stopping at the door. "I have to get some parts for the truck, saw a garage out there. Emelia, I might need your help."

Either he had killer eyesight, or he was lying. I didn't see a garage.

"I can help," I said suddenly.

Both Emelia and Eric looked at me and he almost looked like he was considering it. But then, he spoke. "We've got it, just get some rest."

Deflated, I opened my mouth to argue but Emelia stepped in.

"Both of us have mechanical experience from Dad. So, it'll go a lot quicker."

My mouth dried up. She was right. It was dangerous to be out there longer than necessary, and I'd slow them down. That was something I could agree on.

"Be careful."

"We will." Eric nodded, casting me a quick look before he left.

When I closed the front door, I stood for a while staring at it and eventually, I picked up my bag and went upstairs.

I carefully checked each room, though I was certain there was nothing here. I could sense it after all, and stopped when I reached the final room at the end of the hall. The rooms were bigger than my whole living room back in my old house. The old world was a constant echo wherever I went. There were too many reminders of the way things were, the way things would never be again.

There was something so definitive in the way the boards creaked under my feet. This was someone's home once, not long ago. Walls and windows had been masked like they were in the middle of a renovation, now it was barely a reminder of everything we'd lost. I trailed my fingers along the exposed drywall where the paint had been sanded off.

I pushed the door open and set my bag beside the bed. My eyes scanned the furniture and all the possessions which had been left behind. There was a modern polaroid camera, a bunch of books, and a pretty green dress draped over an armchair complete with a pair of nude heels. I inched closer to the haunting reminder of how many people simply ceased to exist and took it all in. I drew my fingers across the delicate fabric and stopped when I noticed a note folded up on the seat. I carefully opened it up. It was roughly scribbled in barely legible writing but the message was unmistakable.

"Tommy is dead, maybe Kara too. We don't have anywhere to go. Sarah and I are going to look for Dad. If you read this, come and find us. Please. I'm scared and I don't know what to do. Love Andy."

Tears quickly welled behind my eyes and my throat tightened a little more each time I read the note. I recognized those names. They were the kids at the camp. Tommy and Kara, the little redhead boy and girl I'd looked after. My hands shook as I held onto the tiny scrap of paper. They'd made it out of there after all, but not for long.

I'd seen death. I'd escaped situations no one should have walked away from. I'd lived out there alone. But this moment, reading this note, made everything real.

An uncontrollable surge of tears rushed through me.

I missed my family so much. I missed my old life. I missed school and my friends and my home and my clothes.

I dropped to my knees beside the bed which used to belong to a girl I now knew had been Andy, and I brought my knees to my chest and held my bag and my gun close to me.

Was Andy still alive? Did she and Kara find her dad? Or had she become another number, another person lost and condemned to a list that would never stop growing?

As the pain settled in my heart and the darkness came, I closed my eyes hoping to calm myself, before I could stop myself from dozing off, sleep claimed me.

Suffocating silence filled my head, the rushing of blood in my ears was deafening. There was nothing around me, everything was gone. I'd made this choice. I'd made it, yet somehow I couldn't make peace with it.

My heart raced, threatening never to slow and maybe, it wouldn't. Maybe I'd always feel this terror, even when the memories were gone.

As the hand of reasoning closed over my eyes, I steadied my breath and prayed that everything I was doing was going to work, they were all that mattered.

If the Map was protected, the Bridge would be protected.

Another heavy weight settled beside me and I knew it was him, it was time.

Diving deep into the memories, I breathed in his scent and braced myself, and as I relaxed into his touch, a loud, piercing cry forced my eyes open. He was gone and I was in an unfamiliar space. I looked around, fear replacing the initial shock.

I was alone.

"Alex!"

My name jolted me and my eyes darted around.

There was no one around.

"You're in danger! You must wake up! You must move now!"
What was going on? Where was the voice coming from?
"Alex, wake up!"

My eyes shot open. I'd fallen asleep. Shit. My guard was up in two seconds flat. I searched the floor around me for my gun. Once I had it in my grip I kept my breathing even and my eyes scanning the room.

But there was nothing. No one was in my room.

A breath caught in my lungs as I got to my knees and looked around.

Nothing.

There was nothing anywhere.

But the voice was as clear as day, I'd felt the breath on my cheek. Whoever it was had been right here, right beside me.

Chills settled over my skin, flushing me with coldness. Why didn't the dream feel like a dream? Why did it feel so damn real?

Again, I looked around, but this time I sensed something I didn't pick up on before. There was something weird about the blackness. It was too dense, blacker than black if that was even possible. *How much time had passed? How long was I out?*

Catching my breath, I looked around again keeping low and quiet.

As I crawled toward the door, a gut-wrenching feeling coiled around my heart. I wasn't alone, and something stirred inside me telling me that whatever had woken me wanted me to be able to fight back and to have a chance to survive.

That same heaviness I'd felt last night, before the drone thing had tried to attack me, filled my veins, stopping my heart in place.

Oh God. Eric wasn't here this time, no one was. Fear gripped my heart in a vice, forcing my pulse to skyrocket. Shaking some sense into myself, I grit my teeth. I could do this. I could fight on my own, I didn't need them. But a thought kept creeping up on me—maybe they'd gotten to them first, maybe they were dead, that's why they weren't here.

No. No they're not dead, they're safe, sleeping right next door. You can do this, I reminded myself and forced up a brave front.

It was in the room with me. It too was being silent, but thanks to its heavy presence, I could sense the general direction it was in, therefore I avoided moving that way.

As the breath inside my lungs grew stale and panic slowly started to consume me, I pressed myself flat against the wall.

Slowly, quietly, I let the breath out and closed my eyes, praying to God that it hadn't heard me. As my weight shifted from the breath I'd just released, the floorboard beneath me creaked and in that moment, my heart stopped. Crap.

My eyes shot down. The floor beneath me began to decay and the air surrounding me was sucked out, filling the room with stagnant air.

It knew where I was, and it was coming fast. At that point, several things happened: first, I realized I'd blown it, second, it wasn't just a drone, it was a Reaper, and third, it was coming for me.

Without a second to react, I threw my hand out in front of me, throwing a burst of wind at the Reaper. It stunned it for a second buying me enough time to get up. But the gust was nothing in comparison to the power it possessed. It hit me right back with twice as much power and knocked me down, just short of the door.

A scream was ripped from me as the Reaper hurled its weight into me, throwing me to the ground. Cold fingers clamped down around my throat and pushed my face into the floor. I choked out a sob as its hot breath neared my face.

This couldn't be it; this couldn't be how I died. Eric was just next door, separated by a thin sheet of plasterboard and a cheap door…I'd never get to see his eyes again, those eyes I *knew* I'd seen before, whether I remembered them or not.

I tried in vain to extend my arm and push it off me. Nothing I did made a difference. Its bony fingers crushed my airway and useless tears poured out of me. In the few terrifying moments it took for my vision to completely dim, I snapped out of it and found the strength I'd been searching for. I swung up into the darkness hoping that my arm would connect with something, and it did.

The Reaper let out a gargled cry as my open palm hit what I imagined to be its face. It quickly released me, and I heard the slight stumble on the floor as it came back toward me. This time I was on my feet. I couldn't let it come that close again. I threw my hands up, calling on whatever power it was that ran through me, and as a burst escaped my hands, throwing the Reaper back, Eric broke through the door, splintering the hinges. His face was marred in fresh bruises, his arms too. It could have only meant one thing. There had been another Reaper, maybe more. Shit.

Eric's wide eyes darted between me and the Reaper which was now charging at me. As its creepy, cold eyes landed on Eric, second nature kicked in and I recalled that same power. The Reaper lunged at Eric and I didn't even stop to think as I threw everything I had inside me at the creature. It went down, the impact throwing Eric back at the same time. His shock was short-lived as was my celebration.

In the second it took to suck in another breath, the Reaper's attention was on me. I was pushed back down, the immovable pressure of air holding me in place growing as the drone I now realized was accompanying the Reaper hovered over me, and from the corner of my eye, I saw Eric struggling against its hold too. It was powerful, nothing Eric did broke the hold.

Somewhere outside, I heard fighting. Emelia. There had been more Reapers. How many more I had no idea.

Adrenaline kicked in and I jerked back, fighting to get up and get to Eric, to help him, to help Emelia. But this time, as the Reaper staggered toward me, it didn't bother trying to grab me, this time it went straight for the kill. It pulled out a long, shiny blade from its pocket and lunged at me. I screamed and prepared for the impact.

"Alex!" Eric cried out from across the room. "No!"

All I could muster was a broken cry.

The blade came closer and closer to my chest like it was toying with me. The Reaper lowered it just below my collarbone and pressed.

A scream was ripped from me as it pierced through my shirt and into my skin, just beneath the surface.

"No!" Eric cried out again. "Get off her!"

To say that I was scared would have been a gross understatement. To say that I was brave would have been a lie. I'd never known that level of fear, never experienced such uncertainty. While the blade was slowly pushed deeper, Eric's terrified cries broke through the blood racing in my ears and I felt shock start to take hold. My body trembled involuntarily, breaking out in sweat that felt like ice.

This was it. This is how I died. Not old, not with a bunch of pets and a warm bed. But on a cold, damp floor seared with pain and fear. I was drifting. Everything was fading from me.

"Alex, fight!" Eric yelled, snapping me back to the present.

As if his voice had somehow given me courage, I did just that. I used the newly found strength to reach up, grab the blade and force it back.

The Reaper was stunned. Enough so that its control over Eric broke. In that moment, Eric rushed the Reaper and threw its body down. I wasted no time grabbing the blade and without even thinking, I screamed as I rushed over to where they were struggling on the floor and I plunged the blade into the Reaper, all the way to the hilt until I couldn't push it any further.

My hands shook as its sickly, yellow-tinged blood poured out onto my hands. I held onto the blade, gripped it while I kept shaking my head over and over.

Eric slowly rose, his hand gently cupping over mine.

"It's okay, let go. Alex, let go," he said.

Terror ripped through the last shreds of confusion and I let go. My eyes shot up and stopped on his face.

"Alex?"

Looking around breathlessly, I took in my surroundings. Where was Emelia, was she okay?

"Alex, say something."

"Emelia?"

"She's okay." He let out a quick breath and pressed a hand to the back of his neck shaking his head. "Are you okay?"

"I think so?"

"Your chest."

"Just a scratch," I mumbled.

Behind Eric, I heard footsteps rush in and then a gentle hand fell to my shoulder. I turned my head slightly and found myself looking at a pair of terrified eyes. Emelia looked almost as shocked as Eric.

"Are you okay?" I threw my arms around her.

"I'm fine. Are you?" She looked over my face and then my hands and then the dead Reaper.

I instinctively pulled back and wiped them on my pants. "They came for me again, didn't they?"

As soon as I tried to take a step, black dots exploded across my vision and forced me to the wall.

"Easy," Eric bit, steadying me. "And yes, they came for you."

When I winced, I saw his body stiffen and before I could tell him that I was fine, he shook his head and left the room.

"Are you ready to listen to me now?" Emelia yelled after him.

He didn't try to hide his anger as he slammed the door.

"The Reapers aren't going to stop coming," Emelia said softly, helping me forward. She gave me a rag and guided my hand to the wound in my chest. Thankfully the blade didn't get further than half an inch. If it did, well I'd be far from standing.

When I looked at her again, I got a good look at the purple bruise rapidly forming along her jaw.

"Are you—" My words were ripped from my mouth as a very distinctive pain rushed through me stopping just above my collarbone. Exactly where the blade had pierced my skin to be precise.

When I froze, Emelia narrowed her eyes and moved toward me. As she pressed her hand to my shoulder I jerked back.

"That, oh God, why did that hurt?" I stammered, moving away from her, desperately forcing back the burning which began to spread like acid all over me. "It wasn't that deep."

117

Tears sprung in my eyes, welling over before I could stop them.

My hands reached for my chest, desperately clawing at the fabric...the pain, the heat, the acid...

As she moved toward me again, I moved out of the way and pressed myself against the wall. Heat began to flush through my skin as quickly as the panic started to set in. I pressed my hand to the source of the pain and cried out when my knees gave way.

Emelia quickly ran to the door and disappeared before I could say anything. Not a minute later, Eric ran in and straight to me, Emelia on his heel.

"Get towels!" he shouted over his shoulder.

My head lolled to the side.

"Get up," he demanded, dragging me to my feet.

He pushed me backward, stopping any chance of me getting away and pressed me against the wall. His hands worked quickly, tearing the top of the already ripped fabric of my shirt.

"What are you doing?" I shouted, trying to pull back and push his hand away.

Ignoring me he pressed his hand to my shoulder. "Trust me."

That's what he asked...wasn't it? Whether I trusted him? I did, I said I did, and now...oh God, now the pain—

"Trust me."

Words were lost as another bout of fiery pain spread through me and my eyes snapped up to his. I gave him a quick nod. The only gesture I could manage.

He got to work. He moved the fabric of my shirt again and inhaled sharply as if he was shocked by what he saw.

In a far corner, tucked deeply in my mind, I knew this wasn't normal. Pain like this shouldn't have come from such a small cut. I'd been hurt before; I'd been through worse.

Eric placed his palm flat over the scratch and the gentle touch drew my eyes straight to his.

"Does it hurt?" he asked quietly, keeping his voice low.

My heart thundered in my chest. I couldn't even bring myself to speak. Of course it hurt.

When he applied more pressure, I winced, expecting the pain to fire through me again, but when it didn't, I furrowed my brows and looked down at his hand.

When I opened my mouth to speak I noticed two things: one, he was standing close, too close, and his hand was still on my chest, and the second thing, the pain that felt like acid moments ago was subsiding, and in its place there was a warmth, not burning and not fierce like before.

"Does it hurt?" His voice shook with a very subtle tremble.

"No. No, it's better."

He released me, letting my shirt fall into place.

Meeting his vibrant green eyes which seemed to almost glow in an unnatural hue, I let out a small breath.

He bowed his head, nodding. If I wasn't standing so close, I wouldn't have heard the low breath he expelled; he almost sounded like he was in pain, but he kept his eyes down and his body close to mine. When I gently pressed my hand to his forearm, his gaze slowly returned to mine.

Here in the darkness, in the silent stillness of the night, I closed my eyes and took in a deep breath before looking back up at him. He, too, was still, his focus solely on me and our proximity. Before I had a chance to speak, he stunned me into silence by bringing his hand to my cheek and brushing my hair behind my ears, and when I gently pressed my hand over his, he sucked in a sharp breath, but he didn't pull away.

There was a knock at the door and Emelia came in.

The moment was gone.

A shaky sigh left my lips and I had to lean back against the wall to hold my wobbly legs up.

"How bad was it?" I heard her ask, handing over a towel.

Why is she using the past tense?

Eric handed the towel to me and cupped his hand over mine, guiding the warm towel over my chest. "Hold it there. It helps."

I couldn't feel the pain anymore, but then again, maybe that was because I was so intoxicated with him.

Clinging onto the towel, I looked between the siblings.

"You and I both know what that blade does to us. She's lucky it wasn't worse," Emelia muttered in a hushed voice. "And now they know for sure."

Eric's eyes shot to me and then to Emelia.

Us? Know what for sure?

"We cannot risk it anymore; you know I'm right." She stepped closer to him.

"Wait, what are you talking about, what are you?" I asked.

Emelia ignored me. "We need to go and see the Elders. Now."

"Please move." Eric scratched the back of his neck.

Emelia stood her ground and my heart rate was starting to rise. What the hell was going on?

"Eric." She sidestepped him and stopped him from leaving. "If they get that close again, there won't be another chance to stop them. They'll take her. And now they know exactly where she is."

"What is going on?" I pleaded.

Again, no one answered me. Eric's body tensed, his shoulders squaring in response.

"We can't keep her safe anymore. It's over."

"Guys?" I shifted from one foot to the other.

Eric pressed his hand against the doorframe.

"You know I'm right. Look at this. Look what they were able to do to her, with you in the next room." She pointed her hand outside. "We can't do this anymore. It is over."

"Guys!" I said louder this time.

"I'm not okay with going back there," he replied to his sister, still ignoring me.

"I know you're not. I wouldn't ask if there was another way."

"Guys," I shouted again, stomping my foot which, admittedly felt a bit stupid, but it worked. This time they looked at me. "They're after me, right?"

Eric's stricken face reflected exactly what I was feeling.

"I'm not human, am I?"

Emelia's gaze dropped and with it, my stomach.

"Holy shit," I muttered and dropped onto the bed. "Well, guess that answers a lot."

Uncharacteristic silence fell between the three of us.

"Fine," Eric muttered. "We'll go."

Chapter Eleven
Welcome Home

By sunrise, none of us had moved from the small room.

Emelia had tried to pry me out, Eric did too but eventually they both left because I was shell-shocked.

I couldn't talk. I couldn't piece more than one coherent thought together and whatever I managed was fragmented, like my memories.

The only thing I did manage was to rummage through Andy's room and collect some clothes from the raided closet. There wasn't much, but the glittery pink-and-blue shirt I did find was my size.

I looked at myself in the mirror. The cheery writing on the *LA ROX* shirt was a stark contrast to the dull, lifeless expression on my face. My hair was probably the worst hit. There was blood in the dark blonde strands, probably dirt and who knew what else.

I smoothed down the shirt and then stopped, looking at my hands.

They grew clammy as I stared at them like they didn't belong to me. This power I had, these surges of energy that seemed to come to life whenever the Reapers were around made me think that I didn't really want to know what I was.

I wasn't human.

That was going to take a while to sink in.

I'm not human.

The more I repeated it, the more ludicrous it was.

But the more I recalled the little things I'd done, the more I realized that it was stupid to pretend otherwise.

What was I?

It was clear Eric and Emelia weren't Reapers, obviously I wasn't either, so what the hell were we?

"Alex?" Emelia's soft voice sounded through the door.

I opened my mouth to answer, but my tongue was too heavy.

"Can I please come in?"

A barely audible whimper was all I could muster as I balled my fists at my side.

"Alex, please."

When I was certain I wouldn't burst into tears again, I walked over to the door, letting her in.

Her eyes stopped on mine and she quickly frowned. I wiped my face with the back of my hand and walked back to the bed and continued packing.

"We're leaving," she said softly.

"I can't."

"You can."

"No." A hysterical laugh crept up on me. "I'm done."

"No, you're not. You're going to be okay."

"How am I supposed to be okay?" I shouted.

"Because you don't have another choice and you have to get yourself together."

I stepped back, clamping my mouth shut.

"We have to go, Alex. You can hate us later."

"For what?" I challenged. "For lying to me? Or keeping something this huge from me? Or maybe for treating me like an idiot?"

"You knew all along something was different about you."

"That's beside the point."

"No, it isn't," she snapped. "It's exactly the point. You're taking your anger out on us which is fine, but don't pretend that you were completely oblivious to what you are before we came along."

I flinched and she stepped closer.

"I get you're pissed. I understand you're scared, but is it really fair to be taking it out on us?"

"You lied to me," I spat.

"I never lied."

"Well you kept the truth from me!"

"Enough," Eric's voice boomed from behind us.

"And you"—I turned to Eric—"how dare you act like you're some sort of martyr, you've been lying to me too. All along you knew those things would be hunting me, why wouldn't you say anything?"

His eyes flicked away from me. "I couldn't tell you."

"Why?"

"Can we do this later?" he asked.

"No. We're doing it now." I stood firmly in place. I was so done with the lies.

Emelia crossed her arms. "Like I said, you can hate us later, but we have to move, now."

"Not until you give me something more concrete to go on."

She let out an exasperated breath but nodded.

Eric was the one who stepped closer this time. "You're one of us, and we're the good guys. Okay?"

"That's it?" I scoffed.

"For now. Yes." Eric gestured to the door. "We have to go. It's not safe."

"Fine."

I pushed past him and Emelia, rushed downstairs and planted my butt in the back seat of the truck. Both of them had officially gotten on every last nerve, not that there were many left to begin with, but God I could have killed them.

It only took them a few minutes to join me in the truck, and within the minute we were on our way to see the Elders, and the conversation that had just taken place was shoved to the back of my mind ready for another time. If he thought he'd gotten off without telling me what I wanted to know, he was sorely mistaken.

There'd be answers, there'd be clarity. There'd be a lot more than they had given me.

As the drive reached the three-hour mark and my butt grew numb, I demanded Eric pull over for a pit stop.

"I need to get out for a bit," I said.

"Make it quick," he instructed, looking around before stopping the car completely.

Emelia got out first, making sure we were clear before letting me out. At that point, I rolled my eyes. I felt like I was getting followed around by bodyguards and not the cool ones that celebrities got. Mine were hormonal teenagers, one of which was way too broody for his own good.

I glanced back at him and felt all that anger quickly fizzle out as his eyes dipped down and his shoulders hung. He drew both hands over his hat and dropped his head. I officially felt like a total jerk.

We'd all been heated. We'd all over reacted.

As though Emelia read my mind, she gave me an apologetic smile and stepped back. Besides, I'd come too far not to see this through. I was too invested now.

Emelia went back to the truck and leaned against the passenger side door, watching me while Eric stayed seated inside. They were talking between themselves and keeping their voices low.

My guard went up; they were being secretive and it didn't take a genius to work out they were talking about me. Maybe they were discussing how unhinged I'd been acting. I sighed.

Turning my face away, I scanned the horizon; cars, motorbikes, people's possessions littered the side of the once bustling highway.

I stopped at the seventh upturned car and leaned against the chassis, letting my eyes sweep the surrounding tree line while I breathed in the fresh air. After the Takeover, most things shut down, factories and manufacturing, the sky cleared up within a month, the waterways not long after. It was like the earth took a deep, shuddering breath and came to life. Ironic really. I shook my head taking it all in. It never got easier seeing the world like this.

"Alex, we have to go," Emelia called.

Reluctantly, I made my way back to the truck and got in.

"Good to go?" Eric asked, catching my eye in the mirror.

"Yep."

He took the truck back onto the main road and resumed driving in silence. It was fine by me. I wasn't in the mood to talk weather and the general state of things.

My mind was scattered, and I was still trying to get my head around everything. Finding out you're not human, well it's a game changer. It kind of makes you put your life into perspective.

"We're nearly there," Eric said, drawing my attention to him.

His knuckles blanched as he gripped the wheel.

For a quick second I contemplated questioning why he was so edgy, but in the last moment I changed my mind.

"Where is there exactly?"

126

Emelia turned back to me. "It's a compound a few miles from here. They built it a few years back when they first got word about the attacks."

"They?"

Emelia froze for a moment and then probably realized there was no point lying to me anymore. "The government, they had these kinds of buildings set up all over the world. Specifically designed to shelter those of us who were left."

"How many?"

"Seven," she said, turning back to the front. "All around the world."

"The government knew this was coming?"

She shook her head. "Not exactly *this*, but there was chatter. I guess they decided it was better to be safe than sorry. Like in those movies you see, alien invasions and whatever else. Government preps these places for the super elite."

I stared at her. "You can't be serious. That stuff isn't real."

"Well apparently neither are we."

I shut my mouth.

"Anyway, this is kind of like that," she said. "The government readied these places in the event of some sort of cataclysmic world event. They didn't think aliens would take over, but they thought Russia or China might finally snap and retaliate, so they prepared these in case."

"For the elite?"

"Not just the elite. People with...gifts, you could say."

"People like us."

She nodded.

That made sense. With the new presidential campaign heating up tempers around the world, many people thought heads would clash and eventually blow up.

"What did they use the shelters for before?"

"No one really knows for sure, they could have been unoccupied as far as we know," she explained. "But most of the soldiers here said it was government research into diseases and airborne viruses. Either way, they were fully equipped when the Takeover happened."

"Cozy." I cringed.

She shrugged. "Now they're refuges, open to whoever needs help."

"So, there are other survivors?" I asked.

"Yeah."

I craned my neck, looking ahead, hoping to see the building coming up on the horizon. I couldn't see a thing.

"Who are the Elders you keep talking about?" I asked instead.

This time she turned her attention to Eric and then returned her gaze to me, studying me for a moment.

"That's something Eric will need to tell you."

"I hoped someone would."

I turned my face but not before I saw her frown.

It was a good thing that I didn't feel obligated to be nice just for the sake of politeness. I had nothing in me. And it was the last thing I wanted to do when they'd lied to me about something so huge. It was unforgivable.

"There it is," Emelia said.

Leaning on the center console, I looked outside and up at the vast expanse of nothingness and then, it came into view. A large white building in the middle of the desert-like terrain appeared on the horizon circled by a large fence topped with barbed wire coils.

"Where exactly are we?" I asked.

"Osoyoos."

"Oh." I craned my neck.

"Well on the outskirts of the city to be specific."

I imagined this is what Area 51 looked like. Though I hadn't actually been there because, well, I mean people get shot just for crossing the barriers.

"You might want to sit back down, they're pretty serious about security here," Eric said.

Heeding his warning, I sat back and buckled up.

He pulled over in front of the entrance gate and we waited a couple of minutes, before a small rectangular door opened up in the sand. I couldn't have hidden my shock even if I tried. An elevator from nowhere appeared from underground. Two men dressed in army fatigues came up, and as soon as they were clear of the platform it descended, disappearing back into the earth.

One soldier moved to either side of the truck. Eric lowered the windows.

"We're here to see the Elders," Eric said.

"Major Raine," the first soldier said.

"Colonel Rogers."

"We didn't think we'd see you again after last time."

A cord in Eric's jaw popped but he remained stoic.

Seeing his reaction forced an ugly feeling of anger to the surface. *Are these people responsible for what happened to him?* Then, the same feeling of anger turned on him. He was still a liar, he'd still kept this monolithic secret from me.

But the way his shoulders trembled slightly made the anger fizzle out again. *Damn it, Alex, when are you going to get off the Eric Raine rollercoaster?*

When the second soldier stopped at my window, he did a double take and then his gaze shot back to Eric.

"We weren't advised that Chancellor Wynter was back."

"She isn't," Eric said dryly.

"Wait, Chancellor?" My mouth dropped open.

"That's just the start of it," Emelia said. "You're kind of a big deal here."

"Seriously?"

"You're one of the youngest ones too. So yeah."

She looked back to the front and the conversation died down. Wow.

The soldier looked at me again and then holstered his weapon nodding to the other.

"Let them through."

Rogers nodded and walked over to the gate. He pressed his thumb to a code reader and when it opened, we were waved through.

The soldier at Emelia's window looked down at her with a smile as Eric shifted the truck into drive. As we drove through, I noticed a faint blush spreading over Emelia's cheeks.

Eric seemed to be oblivious to the whole exchange, which was a good thing because his current mood made me think that seeing someone putting moves on his sister would end badly.

We drove through several long streets until we finally reached an underground parking lot. How did something this huge exist out here?

Eric took the car down and stopped by a discarded ambulance.

Emelia got out and I promptly followed.

Silently, Eric led us through the garage. Fueling stations were set up throughout and late model vehicles lined the space. We continued until we reached an elevator. Another two soldiers stood by the doors. I was starting to think that this setup wasn't just left over from before the Takeover. And knowing how easily these two lied about something so huge like being a freaking alien, well, everything else could have easily been a lie too.

We rode down two floors, and each time the doors opened I caught a glimpse of people working in what looked like some kind of lab. There were screens and computers, tablets, and other things I hadn't seen work for months.

Not only was the tech here still functional, but it was also highly advanced, more so than anything I'd seen before, setting in stone exactly what I already thought. They knew a lot more than they let on—and I was a major idiot for falling for it.

As Eric led us out and across the hall, my mind started to stray…hot shower, warm bed, microwave.

"Alex?"

"What?" My eyes snapped to his.

"We're through here."

I looked up and realized I'd stopped walking which in turn had made Emelia and Eric stop too.

"Sorry."

He nodded and continued walking ahead.

My heart ached for the creature comforts. Hopefully this place had at least some of those things, something that could ease some of the crap weighing me down.

Emelia smiled nervously beside me and nudged me toward yet another elevator. *How deep does this go underground?*

As we stepped in, one of the soldiers gave me a quick look. He kind of looked confused... *Guess that makes two of us, buddy.*

When the doors closed, Emelia let out a long sigh while Eric buzzed beside me.

"Relax, Eric," she said.

"I'll relax when we get answers."

"I'll second that," I muttered.

Eric didn't say anything, but he caught what I was throwing.

The sound of the elevator chiming drew my attention back to the doors.

"I'll let you two talk," Emelia said getting out, and before Eric could question her, she was already gone.

Probably rendezvousing with the soldier...

Unfortunately for me, my rendezvous wasn't going to be as fun. Which, admittedly, irritated me a bit. How could she just leave, go out and get busy with soldier boy while I had to deal with the shitshow that had become my life?

I let out a long breath and watched as the doors closed, sealing me and Eric in its steel embrace. The numbers lit up one by one taking us down to BG5 and then BG6.

"Are we literally six floors beneath the ground?" I asked.

"Yeah. All our living quarters are on five, six or seven."

The silence resumed.

Finally, when we got down to BG7, the elevator stopped, and Eric gently nudged me forward.

"Are you okay?" he asked softly.

"How can you even ask me that?"

"Sorry, dumb question."

"Really dumb," I muttered, walking ahead.

"Take a left at the end." His voice behind me sent tremors down my spine.

Taking a left at the end I saw that it opened up to yet another set of dizzying hallways. I kept walking and waited for his next instructions. When he caught up, he steered me toward a door to the left.

"This is your room."

I stopped at the door and repositioned my bag across my shoulder. "My room? I don't understand?"

"I'll explain everything later, I gave you my word. But I think you should get some rest first. You'll need it," he said, and as an afterthought, added, "I know I do."

"I don't want rest, I want answers."

"And there will be answers, but I need to get my head together, I need to get this right."

I was about to argue but when he looked down frowning, I dropped it.

"Alright," I said.

"There's a shower and some new clothes for you inside."

Eric pushed the door open and my eyes followed his.

A retort died on my lips when my eyes fell on the contents of the room.

His gaze followed mine as I stood in shock, rooted to the floor. All the things I'd loved, all my belongings, my hobbies my books.

"Welcome home, Alex," he whispered before disappearing from the doorway.

CHAPTER TWELVE
THE TRUTH, FINALLY

My eyes swept the room. There was no possible way that this was real. The bookshelves at the far end were stacked with the books I'd read over and over; the small writing desk was lined with notepads and colored markers; the bed was made up with blue-and-purple covers; and the coat slung over the chair was the one I'd worn on New Year's Day when we went out for lunch. I'd changed later that night—it was the last time I ever saw my house.

But this was it, my room, from the house I lived in with my parents, the house I never saw again.

Yet here it all was. The stuff didn't fit as neatly here as it did back home, but it worked. It was crammed in, the books overflowing a bit, some had to be placed on the floor, but it worked, nonetheless.

How did all of this stuff get here?

I finally moved, stepping toward the small desk to the far right. I trailed my fingers along the soft sheets lining the bed and breathed in the familiar scent.

Closing my eyes tightly, I took in a deep breath and moved to the neatly stacked shelf that stood towering above the small desk. There were more books, an old iPod, notepads and sketchbooks, and on the middle shelf, surrounded by two small candles, there was a framed photo. I blinked back the mist in my eyes as my hand instinctively reached for it. This wasn't in my house, not the one I'd left behind.

My fingers grazed the smooth, white edges of the provincial frame and when I gathered enough strength, I picked it up and let my mind accept what I was seeing.

It was a photo taken of me, probably years ago. I knew because I had short hair then, cropped at my shoulders, the wispy ends framing my face, highlighted with soft accents of darker blonde, and my blue eyes were bright and alive. Right beside me, Eric and Emelia. Not the strangers I knew them as, but friends. Like she'd said.

They were different now though, so was I. My eyes weren't as bright now, my hair sat well below my shoulders and there were no highlights anymore.

My muscle tone was well defined now compared to then and I attributed a lot of that to being on the run, constantly hiking and eating barely anything that wasn't protein.

All of that was a lifetime ago, but this photo, this was before all of that happened. My smiling face looked up at me. I was laughing, caught in a completely candid shot. It looked like Emelia had thrown something at her brother and he was trying to get her back.

In this picture, Eric's tanned skin was clear, there were no scars, no burns, no haunted expression in his eyes. I looked at my face and my arms, carefully studying the curves and lines. There were no scars there either, no sign of the burns I'd sustained.

A breath caught on my lips. How did I have no memory of this? Nothing. There was no inkling of anything at all. And that girl in the photo was me without a doubt and she was happy, truly happy beside Eric, and he was smiling.

We're friends...that's what Emelia said, and I hadn't believed her. But staring at this now, how could she have lied about that?

Placing the photo back down with trembling hands, I trailed my eyes along the rest of the things in here. There was a small bag beside the shelf. I toed it open and yet another pang of familiarity shot through me. There were sweaters and yoga pants, similar to the ones Emelia had given me, but these were in my size, because these were my things.

Beside all of that was a Yankees cap. I smiled. I knew this, I hadn't seen it in weeks, and I swore I'd lost it at the camp. Suddenly, my mind went back to all the small things Eric and Emelia had said which now made sense.

How did I remember snippets, but not the siblings? How did my mind wander to the familiarity yet had no recollection? I shook my head in frustration. I pulled the cap free and held it up, hoping that touching it would bring back some sort of memory, and when that didn't work, I tossed it on the bed and groaned.

I looked around the room, which I now realized was a makeshift civilian quarter. I'd seen rooms like this when Mom and I had visited Dad at the barracks. There were exposed pipes and steel all running over the walls and across the ceiling.

And from what I remembered, there was always a small bathroom and toilet in places like this. And I sincerely hoped that the shower Eric mentioned had hot water. I crossed my fingers with hopeful anticipation and opened the door.

Just like that, my prayers were answered. Like a tiny slice of heaven in a hell we'd learned to adapt to, the shower stared me in the face in all its glory. Quickly checking that there was hot water, I grinned when steam started to fog the mirror.

Doubling back to the room, I rummaged through the small wardrobe and chose a pair of jeans and a sweater and tossed it over the towel rack.

Grinning again, I pulled the shower door open and without even pausing, I stepped into the stream and laughed.

As the hot water cascaded over my tired and achy body, I groaned into the vacant air and pressed my forehead to the tiles.

God, it had been so long, I'd forgotten what this felt like. Things we'd taken for granted seemed like such blessings now. The chance to heat up a TV dinner and watch movies when you were bored, the heater, a warm shower…popcorn. I could have killed a man for some popcorn.

As the water rushed over me, I settled into the comfort of the moment. It wasn't about a shower or a bed. It was about peace and safety.

I never thought I'd feel any of those things again, let alone all of them. Granted, I was still cautious, I wasn't about to let my guard down completely. I needed answers. The photograph, the books, and the personal possessions were one thing, but the memories that failed me, they were another. And then, to top it off, my entire existence. I mean I just found out I wasn't human, not a big deal, just a tiny detail.

Yeah right.

I pressed my palms above my head, and shamelessly started sobbing. To hell with it. Who would judge me? And if anyone did, I'd like to see what their laundry list of issues looked like. I was allowed to cry, I was allowed to grieve and be angry, at least for now. When I was done moping, I'd face Eric like the strong woman that I was, and I would get the answers I deserved.

When I collected myself, I waited for a few minutes, making sure that the tears were done before turning the water off. I wiped myself down and took my time squeezing the water out of my hair.

My reflection caught my attention as I threw the towel over the rack. I stopped and looked at myself in the mirror. I'd almost forgotten what that felt like. I wiped the steam off and leaned heavily against the counter letting my eyes wander over my body.

There'd been too many things that changed, not only mentally but physically. My body was a lot more toned, less shapely but it was okay. My face was gaunt and tiny freckles dotted my nose and dispersed around my full lips. I trailed my fingers through the ropes of wet hair around my face and traced the small scratches along my arms and chest.

Letting my eyes wander down, I lowered my head and turned away. I swallowed the lump in my throat. None of this sat well with me. This whole arrangement, the siblings, and that photo. I drew in a shallow breath and talked myself into following this through even though all I wanted to do was run and never look back.

I'd been doing that a lot lately.

Giving my hair a final squeeze, I left it out and dressed in the jeans and sweater, arranged the damp strands around my shoulders, and took a deep breath. I could do this. I had to.

I sat on the bed, absorbing everything. I didn't know how many hours passed, probably hours I should have been sleeping, or resting, but neither of those seemed to be an option. My mind was busy racing through a bucket load of scenarios.

Maybe I was from Mars, or Venus, that's where women came from wasn't it? Or maybe I was from a different dimension or made of space dust, or maybe I was an idiot.

Tired of waiting around, I got up and crossed the room, rummaging around the small bathroom in hopes of finding a hair dryer. Once I was satisfied that my blow out looked decent enough, I put everything away and made a beeline for the front door. I needed to see Eric.

As I reached for the handle, a quiet tap drew my attention and my hand instinctively jerked back. I contemplated whether I wanted to see who was on the other side of the thin sheet of wood. Deciding that I needed as many answers as possible and as little mystery as possible, I pulled it open.

My eyes widened. It was a total brain overload. Eric stood at my door, with his hands tucked neatly in his dark jeans while a tight, grey T-shirt covered his insanely muscular body and I made no attempt to hide the fact that I was, in fact, staring this time.

Then, I promptly reminded myself that I was mad at him.

I crossed my arms.

Welcome back to the Eric Raine rollercoaster.

His deep, emerald eyes swept across me, swinging from my face down across my body and back up to my eyes. Whatever was on his mind seemed to be on par with mine and I had to remind myself to breathe. Also, that I was mad.

"May I come in?"

A deep breath rolled though me. *No, no you cannot,* I wanted to say. Instead, I nodded and stepped aside.

"Did you rest?"

"Sure," I muttered when he walked around the tiny quarters, finally stopping at my desk.

"It suits you."

"What does?" I looked away, suddenly feeling overly exposed. Did I leave my bra on the bed? No, definitely not. I put that away.

139

Sinking into myself, I snapped my attention back to him.

He looked around, examining my room.

When he turned back to me, he produced a smile that didn't reach his eyes. "The clothes…the perfume."

"I'm not, there's no perfume…"

Two inky brows shot into his hairline.

"I think it's the shampoo," I clarified, shifting my weight onto my other leg.

"It's nice."

The tension inside the room doubled.

"You said you'd tell me what all of this is about…" I tried.

He was practically rooted to the floor, standing with his feet firmly planted to the ground like he was afraid to move.

"You know me," I said, "and you know a lot more than you've said."

"Yes. I promised you answers. Come with me."

He didn't need to tell me twice. I nodded and pushed past him reaching for the keys which he'd already snatched up from the small side table by the door.

"I can lock my own door," I muttered, taking the keys from him. He didn't argue.

As soon as the door was locked, I walked beside him without making any eye contact.

"I'm taking you up to BG1," he explained as we reached the elevator. "It's the closest to the business sector."

I nodded like I understood what he was telling me.

He stopped and turned to face me.

"I know you're angry, you have every right to be. I just hope that when you hear what I have to tell you, you'll understand why I did what I did."

"You mean lie to me."

"Yes."

"We'll see," I said, turning my eyes ahead.

My stupid heart was refusing to get on the same page as my head, and that page was lined with several reasons outlining why I shouldn't trust him or forgive him.

Yet, somehow, my heart seemed to know exactly how to cross out all those reasons and supply justification for his actions.

But now as the truth stood in front of me, ready to be seen and heard, I found myself freaking out. I had no idea what he was going to tell me. I'd already worked out that we shared a history and whatever that history was, it cut him up, a lot.

Fidgeting with the cuff of my sleeve, I looked at the elevator doors and then at him. He pushed BG1 and we started going up.

"I want to tell you everything. I can't promise you that it's what you want to hear, but it's the truth."

One of the things I'd promised myself when all of this began was to be strong. No matter how much fear or pain came, I had to stand tall and survive because that's all I had. So, I nodded. Whatever he was about to tell me, I had to hear it.

"I'm ready."

CHAPTER THIRTEEN
THE CEORAN

The elevator opened above several hundred people in white medical suits working around monitors down below in the workspace. In the center, arranged in two neat rows there were at least a hundred beds with people in them.

Meticulously dressed doctors were tending to those people, some had clipboards and were taking notes, others with stethoscopes were checking their heart rates.

The more I strained my eyes to see who these patients were, the more I realized I didn't like the answer that had miraculously formed in my mind—they were regular humans.

I swallowed hard and ignored the cotton ball sensation closing my throat. A part of me believed they were simply helping the patients. Another part of me, however, felt a sinister feeling wash over me. Maybe they were experimenting on them.

"What is all this?" I asked.

Eric's eyes landed on me. "A hospital."

"Were they sick?"

"Unfortunately. Yes. Come on," he said gently.

Casting another look over the *hospital*, I shuddered. There were kids, elderly, men and women of all ages. Some mobile, some not so much. Some looked like they were in pain while others were chatting lightheartedly with their doctor.

Peeling my gaze away, I followed him, jogging to catch up.

He led me across the grates and over the doctors working below. My eyes darted around the facility, stopping on nothing and everything. My mind was in overload and I couldn't figure out what I was feeling, I couldn't understand what I was seeing.

As we moved further in, I spotted a large set of black doors that was sealed off from the medical floor.

"What's in there?" I nodded to the door.

"There are some dark things about this world, things I wish I could lie to you about, but I won't. Not anymore. But that is for another time, once I explain everything else."

"Okay."

When Eric continued walking, I pulled my gaze away from the doors and followed him. There were soldiers dressed in fatigues and dress blues. And then there were others that looked like Wallstreet suits ready to land a hot deal.

Eric gave curt nods to each of the soldiers dressed in uniform as we walked, though each of them almost bowed when I walked past.

My head snapped back, watching in awe as they refrained from making eye contact with me, but the Wallstreet suits showed no problem with the contemptuous look they gave Eric. *What the actual…?*

"Why are they looking at us like that?"

Panic began to rush through my veins and that soul-consuming fear began to replace it. Before it took hold, Eric stopped and turned his face toward me. He crossed the distance between us and gently pulled me away from the walkway and moved us against the wall. He stopped in front of me and searched my face. The intense gaze bore right through me. I looked away. Over his shoulder I noticed that we were being watched, but his tense, almost soldier-like stance brought my attention back to him.

His hands were folded neatly behind his back and a conservative foot separated us.

"Class division here is a real issue and we have to—" he said.

"What did you just say?"

"Class division," he reiterated, shaking his head. "These people live and die by their rules."

Everything he just said went over my head but those two words...those two words tasted like acid in my mouth.

Class division.

Class division is what the Eric in my dream was talking about, that he and I...we couldn't...because of it...

"Alex?" He cleared his throat. "Did you hear me?"

"Yes."

"Come on." He nodded, leading me down a set of steps and into a meeting room.

Two soldiers dressed like the two earlier stepped out, both gave Eric a curt nod and me a half bow. Interesting.

Eric gestured at the door, letting me in first before he followed and closed it behind us.

I took in the room—it was decked out in tech I'd never seen before, just like the rest of the facility. Time seemed to have progressed and advanced rapidly here while the rest of the world sat hidden in darkness. A sharp contrast to the hell out there. Sleek white and black lines flowed through the entire facility, and from what I'd picked up it didn't stop in this room.

The large rectangle table was white while sleek black chairs surrounded it contrasting brilliantly against the stark white floors.

There was super minimalist monochromatic artwork on the walls which honestly looked more like something a kid drew than something I would call art. Then again, I liked color, and lots of it.

He nodded to the chairs and when I sat down at the end, he took a seat on the corner closest to me. He swiveled his chair so that we were face to face.

"What I'm going to tell you is going to change everything for you, Alex. I wish to God there was another way, but the truth is, everything we've done so far has failed and we can't take any more risks. *I* can't take any more risks."

He tipped his face forward searching my eyes. I collected myself and nodded, letting him continue.

"You saw the photo in your room?"

"Yeah."

"It was taken a year ago. That's when the first Reapers descended."

No. "Reaper's descended on New Year's Day, not a year ago."

"There was a reported plane crash, all five hundred people on board died. It was the first demonstration of their power," he explained.

"I don't understand. We would have known about something like this. It would have been in the news."

"It was. But not in the way you would have expected. All the public were told was that it was a freak, electrical storm that took the plane out."

"They kill electricity…" I found myself whispering. I'd seen power shut down around them, all through the New Year's Eve celebrations when we were on the run.

Eric nodded and looked away momentarily.

145

"I remember that." A deep sorrow filled my heart. "So many people were searching for their loves ones. There was so much chaos, I didn't know if it was a terrorist attack."

"So many were lost." He paused for a moment and returned his gaze to me, "The plane fell and hit the resort in Hampton. You were there with your family, holidaying while your dad was back from tour. It was a compound we'd set up, one of seven."

My mind went back to that trip, that's when Mom's friends died, there was fire, commotion everywhere.

"This is where your memory stops and mine begins."

My hand moved on its own, running over the burn marks on my arm.

"Okay," I murmured skeptically.

As he spoke, pieces that seemed out of reach before were slowly fitting into place.

"The resort you were in was leveled by the plane. Your family was killed and despite the rescue efforts, many couldn't be saved. But you were."

My eyes narrowed, and my head instinctively shook in response to the words he was telling me.

"My parents didn't die, my parents were with me until a few months ago." I jerked back when he tried to come closer, shooting up from the chair.

There is no way, he's wrong, he's lying.

"Don't." I held my hand out, watching it tremble in response to the oncoming tears. I didn't imagine being with my mom and dad, being with the sisters and Evan.

"I'm sorry," he said quietly, his hands balled into fists on the table in front of him.

146

But he remained seated, his eyes studying me under a scrupulous gaze.

My attention fell to the scarred hand and I dropped back into the chair.

His eyes were solely focused on mine, watching me intently, watching the way my reactions changed, the way I refused to hear what he was telling me.

Shaking my head, I managed to form some sort of coherent sentence. "I was with my mom when she told me to run. I washed pots with her."

Eric frowned and looked down at his feet.

"You're telling me I imagined people, that I imagined being in a group and I was actually alone?" My voice rose.

"No," he said, "you were with people, two people who cared about you, and lived with you among others in those camps, but Alex, they weren't your parents."

"You're crazy."

"They were soldiers, highly trained and incredibly good at their jobs. They were entrusted by the Council; they were tasked with protecting you. The memories you have, they're not real."

My jaw locked, and I couldn't speak. No matter what I tried to say, no matter what thoughts I tried to hold onto, the memories, they slipped from my grasp.

"Think, Alex. What do you remember before the camps? Before New Year's Day?"

"I remember everything," I shot.

He rubbed his eyes, pausing for a moment. "Really?"

Before I answered, an insidious voice deep inside me told me I already knew the answer.

My mouth closed.

The realization brought fresh tears to my eyes. It was strange, it was like on the surface I remembered my childhood and school and going out to the movies. I remembered the resort and the crash. But when I dug deeper, there was nothing. I didn't remember getting my scars, I didn't remember anything before New Year's Day.

"You don't remember anything because those memories aren't real," he said sadly. "You didn't go to school at Mission Lodge, you didn't bake cakes for the Fourth of July. You lived here at the compound until the Hampton compound was destroyed. The people who died at your camp were picked because they resembled your real family, they were picked because they resembled you. Your hair, your eyes."

"No," I whispered. "That...that's crazy. I remember their faces."

"You remember what we needed you to. The photo you carry with you, they're your parents, look back at it now. They're not the people you lost at the camp."

Every muscle inside me locked up, an instantaneous mechanism I'd employed to help myself hold everything together. But it did very little to stop the avalanche coming right at me.

Thought after thought crashed into my fragile wall, drowning me in one false memory after the other. There was no way, I couldn't believe what he was saying, it was too much...

"The Reapers descended that day; they broke through the portal which divides this world and ours. Unfortunately, the plane was their first contact. When that tear in space happened, the rest of us came up too, to stop them."

"We?" I whispered.

"The rest of us, the ones who weren't living here."

"I don't understand." My voice was barely above a whisper.

148

He looked away, a cord popping in his neck. "I've been here a while."

"Oh," I said, completely numb.

"There are races, people like us who exist—we are the Ceoran and they are the Reapers. We have a council, a whole political setup, everything a powerful race requires to live, including bureaucracy."

"Ceoran?"

He nodded and when I remained transfixed in my chair, he looked down at the space between our hands and then back up at me.

"You heard the solider out there call you Chancellor?"

"Yes."

"You sit on our council; you have advisors in our Elders. For all intents and purposes, you're royalty here."

My throat constricted.

"You're one of the youngest with a seat and had your family lived they might have waited a few more years to appoint you, but there needed to be a Wynter to step up."

"I don't…" I cleared my throat again. "This is a lot."

"There's more," he said gently. "The Ceoran come from our gods, The Karatoi—they rule over us. Some live on earth, like us, while others live in our time on our world. The Karatoi and their essence gives us the abilities we have."

"Abilities?"

"We pull the power from a source just outside this universe, called the Cradle of Esper. It's a pool just beneath the Bridge that links our world to this one."

My head continued shaking and he continued talking.

"Some of us can see ahead of time, not by a lot but usually it's enough; we can manipulate elements like fire, water, and air; some of us even have telekinetic abilities, though that's rare…"

"And you can heal?" I breathed, before I could stop myself.

His brows rose.

"At the house. Whatever that Reaper did, you healed me." I wet my lips, struggling to swallow through the dryness in my throat.

Eric didn't say anything for the longest time, and finally, he nodded.

"And I can do things with my mind," I said.

"Didn't you ever question it?"

"I did, but I, well I never told anyone."

"That's wise." He smiled gently.

"God, this is big, Eric, this is too big."

"I told you it wouldn't be easy."

Well he wasn't wrong. I shifted in my seat and looked down at my hands. "What are they? The Reapers?"

He looked pointedly at me, one brow arched. "You know what they are."

"They're the other side of the coin."

"Everything works off the same principles. If there is good, by definition, there must be evil."

I blew out a long breath. So much for my theory about the government creating them. Though I'd accept that easier than what he was telling me. Portals and dimensions, tears in space. I swallowed the bile and looked up at him.

"The Reapers have always waged war against us," he explained.

"Why?"

"Because we're the only ones strong enough to protect the universe and the humans on this planet."

"But why are they here? I don't understand." I rubbed my eyes furiously.

"They're here because they've exhausted all their resources and they need access to other accessible planets."

"They've killed everyone on their world?"

"And many other worlds out there."

This was a bad dream, a really bad and twisted dream that I'd wake up from any moment.

"What do they do, eat us, absorb us?"

"More or less."

"Wow."

He paused and I took a moment to compose myself. When I was sure I wouldn't vomit all over him, I looked up at him.

"We don't, well, we don't eat people, do we?"

He chuckled and shook his head making a knot of tension fizzle away. Thank god. I didn't think I could deal with the fact that I'd have to *eat* people.

"They exist to claim the lives of those whose time has run out, but recently they've stopped abiding by the laws of the universe, and they've started killing everyone they come into contact with."

"Why?"

"It gives them extra endurance to travel across the galaxy."

"This is insane."

"I know." He nodded. "Usually they go for the native species on the planet they've invaded because they're an easier target, but in some cases, when they're desperate, they come after us. But that's rare."

"Rare?"

"Very. We can kill them, we're the only ones who can. So if they're coming for us, it's purely out of desperation."

151

"And they do this across the whole universe?"

"Not just this one."

Letting that thought settle, my eyes shot up, my brain finally coming to the party. "What attacked me in my sleep?"

Eric made a face. "That's a much more sinister version of the Reapers. They're extremely dangerous and even we can't always stop them—we're strong but they're stronger."

"Humans don't know about this?" It felt weird talking about humans like I wasn't one of them.

"If anyone sees, they're compelled to forget."

Oh, hell. This was a whole world of stuff I couldn't get my head around.

"You can make people forget things?"

"Not completely, there's a separate procedure we use for that." His eyes dropped from mine and as he trailed off and silence descended, everything clicked into place.

The memories I couldn't reach, the fleeting moments of comfort around him, the understanding…the dreams. I finally understood.

"Oh my God, Eric. Why?" I pleaded, preparing myself for the barrage of answers I knew I was afraid of.

Why was all I could ask, *why* was what I needed to know. Why would someone make me forget everything? Why was this happening to me?

A breath shuddered through my body on the heel of the most painful realization yet. *He'd* taken my memories. And as the shock of that information settled deep in my veins, I ignored the burn of tears building in the back of my eyes and forced my eyes up to his.

"When that building fell on you, and I went into the fire, I knew that it was the final straw. The Council finally knew you weren't

152

safe anywhere." He took my hand in his and turned my arm over, touching the scars.

This couldn't be real.

"I did what I did to save you but I failed and you're in danger because of it."

He poured us each a glass of water and set one in front of me.

I looked at the glass, my mind racing in every direction except the one I wanted to focus on.

Maybe I'd finally lost it after all the hits I'd taken to the head.

He cleared his throat and took a sip of water. Once he'd set it back down, a heavy silence fell between us until he spoke.

"Do you want me to continue?"

"Why did you make me forget?"

"Because you are a Ceoran Chancellor and you are on the Reaper's most wanted list. If you were out there with knowledge of that, it would have painted a beacon on you."

"I'm not following, Eric. Why am I on any list? I don't understand. Who am I? Why...why is this happening to me?"

He leaned forward in the chair, resting his elbows on his knees and pressing the tips of his fingers together.

For a painful moment he didn't say a word, only sharp, shallow breaths and the raging of blood in my head sounded in the sterile room.

Eric was right, it wasn't easy, and it wasn't what I wanted to hear. Not by a long shot. I wasn't ready to accept what he was telling me, I wasn't ready to accept that this wasn't a freak accident and someone, *something* out there planned this, to take down the world, to come after me and that I wasn't who I thought I was. My whole life, everything I could remember was false.

My eyes burned.

153

"After your memories were taken, it was agreed that you were going to live among the humans. Two guardians from the Council would stay with you and you would be safe. For a year you were safe with them, a year exactly since the Hampton Compound was taken out and they descended again this New Year's Day. We watched from afar, Emelia and I."

"Did you...did *you* plant the false memories?"

When he didn't reply, I had my answer.

"Wow. Okay." I shot up to my feet and paced the small room reminding myself to take a few deep breaths.

The sadness of the situation was quickly replaced by a heat in my cheeks and a burning anger building in the pit of my stomach. I clenched my fists at my side and looked across at him.

"It was the only way," he added. "If they thought you were lost, they'd leave you alone, and for a while it worked, but now..." He shook his head, letting out a long breath. "Now they're coming for you anyway."

"Why?"

"Because they got to you, and now they know who you are, your anonymity is blown. You're remembering."

"I don't remember anything!"

"Is that really true?"

His eyes burned through me. I immediately felt a hot flush rush through my veins. I looked away. No, no it wasn't true. I was remembering things; I was remembering *him*.

"All of this was for nothing? Wiping my memories...making me forget, it was all for nothing?"

"I was trying to protect you."

"If you didn't get involved, none of that would have mattered." I realized my voice was getting louder as the heat in my cheeks grew.

His eyes flared as he pushed away from the table and pressed his hand over his heart. "You think I don't know that? Damn it, Alex. I knew, I always knew I had to stay away from you."

"Why?" I begged. "Why did you have to stay away?"

At this point, I didn't care. I just wanted to know why I felt like I was missing him in my life, why it hurt so much whenever his eyes turned cold looking at me even though I saw the pleading in them. And why, why was I dreaming about a man I couldn't remember but loved so deeply beyond any doubt.

"You owe me an answer!" I stalked over to him. His back was to me but the shaking in his shoulders was evident.

"Because you're one of them and I am not!"

"One of the Wallstreet suits?" I flinched.

He turned and blinked like he was surprised by my astuteness in this situation. I was surprised too. But it didn't take a damn genius to work out what he was talking about. He'd mentioned the class division more than once.

"You're royalty, Alex. I can't compete with that."

"Yet you had a choice, and I didn't. I lost everything and you're still you."

"I had no choice, Alex, and I *still* have no choice!"

"But you have the audacity to treat me like I'm a burden! Like you regret intervening!"

He stepped toward me so quickly it nearly winded me. His eyes were an unforgiving shade and heat radiated from his body.

"You're not a burden." His voice was dangerously low, and he was achingly close. "And I don't regret anything I've done."

"And that includes wiping my memories too, right?"

"Yes," he bit.

"Good, at least I know."

Shock and anger set in. Without giving him another opportunity to speak, I turned toward the exit and as I reached for the door, he caught my wrist and turned me around, gently pressing me against the cool metal. And that's when my breath caught in my lungs as his fierce expression floored me. That was when those dreams seemed realer than real.

When he froze, completely unmoving, my brain took a back seat and I let every other part of me take control. I stepped closer, my confidence radiating through the warnings in my head. I didn't care about the lines I was about to cross, or the proverbial barrier between us or whatever the hell the *class division* meant to us.

I reached up and gently drew my hand across the line marring his beautiful, tanned skin letting my fingers dance across the pinkish burns, tracing them down over his jaw. It was so innocent yet so deeply intimate.

For an eternal moment, neither of us moved, neither breathed, silence wrapped us up and consumed us and then, like time slowed, he closed his eyes and lowered his forehead against mine. I didn't know whether to hold my breath or say something. So, I stayed perfectly still and I let down my walls. This moment, this tiny piece of something I'd been missing, was back.

He cupped his hand over mine and drew it away from the scar, turning his face from me.

"You shouldn't worry about this, especially not with me," I said.

Eric frowned.

"I have them too," I whispered.

"Because of me."

"I'm alive because of you." All that anger from minutes ago seemed so small, so irrelevant in the grand scheme of what my life now seemed to be.

When he pulled back, my heart cracked, threatening to burst at any given moment and as his hand reached up and cupped my cheek, a shallow breath came free from the both of us.

Instinctively, I leaned into his touch. I knew this, I *remembered* this even if I didn't remember anything else.

He swept his fingers across my skin, letting his touch linger. His hands were soft and rough all at the same time, calloused from working on his truck, from fighting the monsters out there, but they were soft too, gentle, like someone who knew how to nurture and love.

"You're too important, Alex. I have to keep you safe; we have to keep you alive."

His voice tore me apart. There was a tremble in his words that reflected the furrow in his brow.

We stood painfully close, breathing in the same air, letting the static burn and light up the air around us. He tightened his hold on me and the way his breath kept coming in short bursts told me that this was as hard for him as it was for me.

Forcing myself to snap out of it, I slowly opened my eyes and searched his face. His expression was unreadable, damn he had a good poker face. I removed myself from his personal space and took a moment to recover from that earth-shattering proximity.

"Can you bring my memories back?" I asked, shifting the conversation into much safer territory.

"I can't. I don't have that sort of power."

"So, I'll never remember any of this?"

"That was the whole point, Alex." His face twisted.

"You said you don't have that kind of power. Does anyone?"

"There are rumors, but nothing concrete."

"How is that possible?"

157

"This kind of thing has never had to be undone before."

"You're still lying to me," I said.

"Alex, I'm—"

"What I don't understand is why you're lying about what we had, because I've been having these dreams and I—"

"We were friends, Alex, that's all. Everything else was forbidden."

"And we wanted more?"

He didn't reply.

I shut my mouth as two red circles heated my cheeks.

"Okay," I heard myself say. I had my answer.

My feet carried me back to the table and all I could manage was to sit down, and then he was gone.

Chapter Fourteen
Clean Slate

He lied to my face. A complete and utter lie that was laced with more lies.

A bittersweet taste coated me and set in motion my determination to find out exactly what they were keeping from me.

How was I meant to digest everything he'd just told me?

How was I meant to look him in the eyes again and know that he'd just shut me down without even trying to entertain the idea that my dreams meant something.

Maybe they actually didn't. Maybe I was right before, maybe I was just making them up because I was lonely. It wasn't a long shot, was it? I mean loads of girls found guys with dark hair and green eyes attractive, right?

But I shot that idea down as soon as it formed.

I didn't make up words like *class division* that held so much meaning for both of us it hurt. And the thing I'd told him in my dream before he obviously wiped my memories? That wasn't just a coincidence.

And what was that thing my favorite podcaster said...oh yeah, it was too much of a coincidence to be a coincidence. You were onto something, Jim. I sighed and looked down at my hands like, somehow, I'd see the signs of this supposed being I was meant to be. And just like I thought there was nothing. My hands were normal, just like I was, at least before they dropped the *you're not human* bombshell.

But there had been signs. I wasn't in complete denial. My *weird gift*, my powers. That wasn't your average girl next door secret. That was an alien level secret. A secret that supposedly lay in the universe somewhere, pooled under a bridge.

My thoughts were chased away when the door behind me slid open and a man dressed in military uniform stepped in. I got up.

The soldier gave me a curt nod. "Please, sit."

I did.

"I was hoping you'd still be here, Chancellor Wynter," he said. His voice didn't seem to match the hard exterior.

And I was still getting used to whole *Chancellor* thing.

"When Mr. Raine told us you were back, I had to ensure I had the opportunity to speak with you myself."

I let out an even breath and nodded, not really knowing how else to respond.

"I'm General Corteza, it's a pleasure having you back with us."

When I failed to reply, he gave me a smile which I didn't really think was genuine, and pulled up the chair opposite.

"I understand a lot of this is out of your grasp, and if there was any other way, we would have done it. I assure you, your protection is our priority."

"I'm not sure why I'm even here," I said, cutting to the chase.

He shifted in his seat and nodded. "I understand Eric has explained what was done?"

"Yes." I looked down. "He told me he wiped my memories."

"It was an unfortunate yet necessary occurrence. But you have to understand, Chancellor Wynter, we'd never intended this conversation to take place."

Those words hit me harder than I wanted to admit. A coil of anger tightened around my heart. Was I meant to be okay with that? Just take it lying down, accept that my brain was poked and prodded only to have them say it wasn't ever meant to be brought up again, and what? They were sorry. That it was an inconvenience now? That trying to bring me up to speed was going to be a challenge?

"Believe me, Chancellor, the decision wasn't made lightly. Many people were involved with the Clean Slate."

Clean Slate. It all sounded so clinical.

"What exactly is the Clean Slate?"

"An injection composed of highly potent drugs we've synthesized to work with our genetics."

"An injection," I stated, like it made sense.

Did they just have lab rats lying around? Maybe that's what was locked behind those black doors.

"Indeed. It was developed centuries ago when we started sending our soldiers out on missions. If they were compromised, they swallowed a pill; it wiped their memories and the Ceoran were safe."

"Just like that."

"Soldiers know what is expected of them."

"They're expected to sacrifice for everyone else." Disgust forced anger to the surface. "I've worked that part out for myself, General. So, did I know?"

His shoulders squared.

"Did I know what was expected, did I know what had to be sacrificed?" I repeated.

"You knew what needed to be done, yes. Mr. Raine didn't agree with your reasoning, but he did as you asked. We all did."

"I'm sorry, I'm not following."

"You gave the order, Chancellor Wynter. It was your call, and as such, due to your position on the Council, we were obligated to obey."

The wind was knocked from me. That's not at all what Eric was saying. Had he lied to me or was the general lying?

I'd made this choice, I'd made it. Yet, somehow, I couldn't make peace with it.

My eyes snapped up to his.

"My position?" I whispered.

"You commanded a group of Ceoran here. That is why you're so important and why the Reapers are after you. Evidently you have some information that is relevant and invaluable."

"What information?"

"That was something you never discussed with those of us without clearance. It was between you and your guardians. But seeing how you're remembering parts of your life even after the Clean Slate, which is unprecedented in itself, we had to bring you in."

To say that I was shocked at this point would have been grossly understated. Each time I opened my mouth, I promptly shut it, then I shook my head like somehow that would shake loose the rest of the memories, and when nothing else came out he cleared his throat. I couldn't believe it. No. I refused. Not possible.

"When it came time to discuss what needed to be done, you made the executive decision," he said. "Now, while I understand you must be feeling out of sorts, we need to get you up to speed. If you're ready, we'd like to bring you back to the Elders. They have questions and I'm sure they're quite relieved to have you back."

The Elders...the Clean Slate...I couldn't, my mind wasn't keeping up.

"Please, Chancellor. If you will."

I nodded because what else did I have right now?

***

The Elders were a bunch of old men and women in suits. They sat at a ridiculous high table which looked like it had been dragged through history and plopped right down here in the twenty-first century, with the bones and armor from the knights of the round table barely dusted off it before use.

I stood before the four of them, several feet away, my eyes coasting from one wrinkly face to the next. There was still one empty spot. Maybe they'd kicked the bucket.

Behind me, Eric and General Corteza stood by the door. As stupid as it was, I felt safer knowing they were there, at the very least, Eric. Corteza seemed to have some sort of issue with me.

As the final old guy arrived and sat, I straightened in my spot.

Not one of them cracked a smile, or even said a word.

All I got were scrutinizing gazes like I was some sort of juvenile delinquent facing court and waiting to hear the outcome of my future.

Maybe they'd send me to Ceoran juvie, or maybe they'd give me community service. What would that even entail? Cleaning the soldier's boots, making their beds?

"Chancellor Wynter."

"Yes," I said, unsure of what their titles were and still unsure how I held mine.

"We're pleased that you have returned."

I squinted and made out the small golden plaque in front of the woman, Sharia.

163

"Thank you, ma'am."

"Please, that's not necessary. Sharia is fine." She smiled. Actually smiled.

I relaxed slightly.

"We're not here to question what has happened but merely to advise you of what will come."

"Advise?"

"Yes, Chancellor Wynter, that is our purpose to you. We're your advisors, though, granted, we do still have the final say in important matters."

Right. Okay. So, I was a big deal here. Eric and Emelia weren't blowing that out of proportion.

I didn't know if I was meant to reply, so I stayed silent.

The man beside her, Jonathan, spoke next. "We're truly sorry for the pain this has caused you. It is unheard of for someone to break through the Clean Slate."

"So I've been told."

"We know the Reapers have been trying to get close to you for some time and Major Eric Raine and Lance Corporal Emelia Raine have done an excellent job in keeping you safe after your guardians were killed."

"My parents."

"Yes, your assigned *parents.*"

I felt Eric shift behind me and once again I felt that unexplainable pull drawing me to him. It took everything inside me not to turn.

"What happens now?" I asked, keeping my eyes ahead.

"Now, you resume your duties here, relearn everything," Sharia said. "You were working on some important things before you were pulled away, we would like you to continue that work."

"I'm sorry, what work would that be?"

"You were working on uniting our galactic forces."

Umm. Did someone say *Star Wars*? My brain backpedaled. This was real. Like really real. Holy cannoli. I shifted my weight onto my other foot and folded my hands in front of me, consciously reminded myself not to fiddle.

These were big and serious people with serious roles. I was supposed to be one of them.

With each second that passed where they kept telling me about the contacts I'd made with other Ceoran around the galaxy, I found myself getting more and more breathless. I'd made serious connections, well-respected relationships, and I couldn't remember any of it.

Eric appeared beside me and a gentle hand fell to the small of my back. "Elder Sharia, Elder Jonathan, might we resume this later? Chancellor Wynter has been through a great deal and would probably like to rest."

"Of course, dear boy," Jonathan said, and then looked at me. "Take some time for yourself, Chancellor Wynter. But not too much time, this work is important now more than ever as I'm sure you're aware. We need whatever help we can get to defeat the Reapers, and it's starting to look like most of our allies will have to be from the contacts you've made."

"Yes, sir. Thank you."

Everything he just said went over my head. Contacts. My contacts on the other side of the galaxy were meant to help. What in God's name was I doing here?

I stood, mouth dry and throat achingly raw. I couldn't do this, oh God, I couldn't...

"Relax," Eric whispered beside me. "Just breathe."

The second the Elders left the room I slumped my shoulders and doubled over pressing my hands on my knees.

"You okay?" he asked, keeping his voice low.

I was hyperaware of Corteza's eyes on us. Maybe he knew about this relationship that supposedly never happened.

"Yeah, fine," I muttered, straightening up.

"Chancellor, if you will?" Corteza gestured to the door. "We have to present you to rest of the military."

"She needs rest," Eric said.

"And she can rest after this."

"It's fine," I said, not wanting to be responsible for anyone else having reason to be pissed with me.

I followed Corteza into another room. This one was filled with people. Great.

Eric stopped by the door while Corteza led me to the front, up onto a podium. Every eye landed on me and my nerves went up tenfold.

I searched the room for familiar faces and came up empty, but at the far end, my eyes locked onto Eric's and I released a slow breath.

As Corteza took the stage, the chatter in the room died down.

Most, if not all, of the eyes in the room darted between Eric and me. Confusion seemed the be the word of the day as each of them gave me quick looks of awe while some looked on in pity.

"Please sit," Corteza began, stepping in front of the lectern. "I know most of you have been hearing chatter about the return of Chancellor Wynter. While she is present, the situation remains arduous."

I avoided looking up. Everyone was staring.

As soon as Corteza started talking again, their attention shifted.

But Eric's gaze remained on me. I tipped my head up slightly and kept a neutral expression.

Something about the way he was looking at me said there was so much more under the surface he wanted to say. Yet if he said we were just friends, what else could I go by?

My cheeks flushed when I thought back to the first dream I had about him and the way his body felt so right against mine…

General Corteza turned toward me, bringing my thoughts back to him and I realized I'd missed everything else he'd said.

"In conclusion, Chancellor Wynter has spoken with the Elders and she will be resuming her relations with the galactic Senators."

I looked back out over the soldiers. Some looked at me with cynicism, others with hope. And Eric, well he looked like he was proud. A flutter of a breath rolled through me. Class Division, that's what set him on edge, that's what the Eric in my dream was afraid of and that was enough to know that I was here for a reason. Whatever the reason was, whatever stars aligned to bring me here to this moment, I knew in my heart that I could make a difference, and it was my duty then and now, to do so.

"I'm holding another briefing later this afternoon for those who weren't in this group. It's imperative we get everyone up to speed on Chancellor Wynter's arrival. If we go by the information given to us by the Elders, we have to believe there is a possibility of an attack and we have to be prepared," Corteza said.

Outraged chatter broke out and one soldier, dressed differently to the rest, stood. He had a plain polo top and jeans on that looked like they cost more than half the equipment in this room.

"Why are we letting her back in when we know what happened last time?" he asked with a smug grin. "I mean, don't get me wrong, it's great that we get to see her shining face again, but isn't it a risk?"

My eyes shot to him and then to Eric. A scowl appeared on his face and his eyes went straight to the guy.

He was tall and defined, and judging by the way he stood beside the others I didn't think he belonged to this crowd; the smug grin widened accentuating deep dimples and dark brown eyes.

The general gave that man a curt nod before answering his question. "Aside from that comment treading dangerously close to disrespecting the Council and Chancellor Wynter, when have we turned our back on our own, Ashfield?"

Ashfield seemed to have missed the memo on being polite and respectful to generals, because his response was a scoff.

Corteza gave him a half smile and turned up the level of hardass leader. "We all know your question comes from a personal place, Ashfield, and being that this is not of a personal nature, I'd suggest you keep whatever else you've got rattling around in that head of yours to yourself."

I balked, as did half the platoon. Ashfield, however, looked like he'd just swallowed a lemon.

When Corteza continued, my eyes traveled across the crowd to Eric. A half smile on his face shocked me as our eyes met. He seemed to know what Corteza was talking about.

"Now," Corteza said, "any more questions that pertain to this matter?"

Unanimous "no sirs" met him and when he nodded in return, he got up and everyone else followed.

Ashfield shot out of the doors first.

"Good. Now I expect business as usual with Chancellor Wynter while she's on site. Dismissed."

The room cleared out in a few minutes and Emelia, who'd been missing the whole time, came running up to me with a wide smile on her face. Guess she missed the whole part of me still being mad at her. I pulled back and readjusted my hoodie. She didn't seem to notice. Instead, she gestured for me to follow her.

As much as I wanted to go back to my own room, sulk and be alone, I had no idea how to get there, so, I followed.

"Why didn't you tell me any of this?" I questioned her as we walked.

"I haven't told you because it's not my place."

"What does that even mean?"

"It means that a lot of it is between you and Eric."

"Right. Because friends have such intimate secrets."

She stilled.

"He lied to my face," I said. "I've been having these dreams, Em."

"What kind of dreams?"

I looked away before bringing my eyes back to hers. I was suddenly unsure about whether I should say anything. I mean, she was his sister.

"Dreams about me and Eric, and after hearing and seeing some stuff here, I'm starting to think they're a lot more than…" How was I meant to say *fantasies* to his sister?

"More than what?"

"More than just something I'm imagining."

She folded her arms and exhaled. "It's probably because your mind is piecing memories together."

"Right. So, I'm not losing it. He lied, about everything."

"If he did, then he has his reasons."

"You're defending him again."

Her mouth straightened into a line.

"He lied about me, about what he and I had and everything in between. And so did you."

"It's not that simple."

"I think it is, and I think you're both treating me like an idiot, and honestly, I expected more than that from you."

She ran her hand over her throat and stepped back, shifting her weight.

At that moment I felt like a total bitch.

"I'm sorry." I took the higher ground.

"You don't have anything to be sorry about." She gave me a tight smile.

When she didn't say anything else, I shook my head and continued down the same path we were on. I had no idea where we were going or what I was doing. All I knew was I couldn't just stand there, arguing back and forth about something I knew in my heart I was right about.

Emelia caught up.

This place was a maze, doors upon doors and hallways I wouldn't remember if I had to.

When we reached another set of doors, she stopped and looked at me for a moment before she let out a long sigh.

"I can't tell you about what was there between you and Eric, and believe me, as his sister, I really don't want to get into that."

I could understand that.

"But when it comes to other stuff here, well, some Ceoran are unhappy that the Reapers came for you in the safety of our own facilities and they believe that if you'd been hidden from the start, none of this would have happened to us."

People thought *I* was responsible for the end of the world. Well that was an epic kick in the gut, one for the record books.

"But most of us believe if you were hidden to begin with, all of this"—she waved around us—"would have been way worse."

"I don't get it." Irritation started to get the better of me and I felt bad for being short with her. "What do they want with me?"

"Apparently you were close to uncovering something."

"What?"

"I don't know."

I rolled my eyes and began to walk when she caught my hand.

"Alex, wait," she said. "I really don't. I don't have the clearance for that."

"Clearance?" I turned in my spot. "Seriously?"

She nodded and a frown crossed her lips. "I'm on the low end of the food chain here, I'm a soldier like Eric. But at least he's a Major, I'm just Lance Corporal. We don't get to know anything other than what's on a need-to-know basis. That's the truth."

It pained her to say it. The class division struck again. I could understand it now, it was awful, and it made me angry for her.

"Don't be mad at him," she said. "He only did what he had to. We, well no one thought we'd have to reverse a Clean Slate."

A *Clean Slate*. A simple term, a simple name designed to explain away possibly decades of someone's memory, someone's existence.

"I'm not mad. But I'm not going to sit around and continue getting lied to." Before she could argue with me, I pulled my arm free and left. "I'll see you later."

I didn't miss the look of hurt that crossed her eyes, but I had to be alone.

Chapter Fifteen
Class Division

Eric and Emelia had officially gotten on every last nerve. Emelia was sweet but her undying defense of her brother's actions made me want to slap her, and Eric, God, he was another story. I alternated between wanting to punch him in the face and kiss him and as soon as that thought formed, I wanted to punch myself.

Pushing through the last of the corridors I found myself walking over a large grate which overlooked the medical floor. The doctors working down below were tending to their patients and monitoring equipment just like I'd seen earlier. This time, though, there were a few extra people, some soldiers and Council members, I assumed, watching them work. I continued over the grate, taking everything in. I stopped when I spotted the large ominous black doors off to my right. For a moment I watched, waiting to see whether anyone went in or came out. Eric said some dark stuff happened behind there and nothing he'd told me about this place and their way of life made me think he was lying. A shudder rolled through me and when a soldier walked past, I jumped, startled by his presence. All I got in return was a curt nod, with no eye contact of course. I ignored him and brought my eyes back to the doors.

There was a keypad beside them and what looked like a fingerprint scanner, the same one we had to pass through when we were let in. And by the look of it, only certain staff had access to what lay beyond.

Two doctors approached, followed by someone I assumed was a member of the Council. She had a long black coat on, thick rimmed glasses and long red hair. She was striking and whatever she muttered to the doctors beside her earned a series of curt nods. They stepped aside, and she pressed her thumb to the scanner.

As the doors opened, I straightened on the grate and craned my neck. Just inside I could see more plain doors, with small square windows, along a corridor, a bunch of framed signs, and some thick red arrows on the floor on either side of a thick black line dividing the walkway. One of the doors had a giant sign printed in block letters: *Observation Room 1*.

The doctors walked in after the redhead and the doors closed.

What were they cooking up in there?

Peeling my eyes away, I resumed my way along the grate and stepped through the double doors dividing the business quarters and the elevator bay. I rode the lift down to BG7 and made my way back toward what I hoped was my hallway. When I spotted the familiar signs, I let out a breath of relief. This place was worse than a maze.

I stopped when I spotted Ashfield leaning lazily against my door. I glanced around. *Is he waiting for me?*

An uneasy feeling spread through me, putting me on guard. Slowly, I moved closer to my door but stopped just short, folding my arms over my chest.

"Can I help you?"

He smirked but said nothing.

Seeing him this close, I now saw that his dark eyes were an almost unnatural hue—the color was somewhere between cognac and whiskey, neither brown nor golden.

His short, styled hair was dark brown and matched the three o'clock shadow on his jaw.

"Ashfield, right?"

He nodded, pushing away from the door and edging closer to me. "Indeed, Chancellor."

As he neared, I moved back. I didn't need to remember anything to feel that this guy was bad news. He was basically undressing me with his eyes.

"You don't remember me?"

"I don't remember anyone," I countered.

"Interesting."

His eyes sparkled with a glint that I didn't like, and my senses put me on edge setting every hair on end.

"I'm Lucas, you and I grew up in the regal quarters."

"Regal quarters?"

He chuckled. "Yes, where the royals, of sorts, live."

"Royals? Seriously?"

"Yep." He nodded. "Natural leaders of things, so to speak."

"Right."

I tried to sidestep him.

"You look worried," he said, cocking his head.

"Should I be?"

He laughed. "Where's Raine?"

"Why would I know?"

"I thought you two would have hit it off."

"I don't even know him," I snapped back, and it hurt.

174

Lying about Eric like that made my chest tighten. Not that I had to explain or justify anything to this asshat.

"That's not what it looked like when he was saying goodbye."

"Guess it's lucky for me I don't remember a thing. So, was there something I could help you with?"

His eyes narrowed and then he was moving toward me again.

A breath caught in my lungs as I assessed my next move.

There were doors upon doors and dizzying corridors surrounding me. Wherever I went, I'd probably get lost. How I'd made it back to my room was a miracle in itself.

I could try the medical floor, there were thousands of people there but there were kids, people that were sick. No, I couldn't do that to them.

Taking that out of the equation, I was left with one choice. I could hit him, push him back if he tried anything and then run into my room.

"Well then," he started. "If you don't remember, then I guess there's nothing to hold on to. Right?"

"What are you talking about?"

He stepped closer and I stepped back until I was flush against the wall making a shudder roll through me.

"I'm sure by now you've figured that you're a big deal around here."

My eyes darted around, I didn't want to look at him. God, he was getting closer.

"And that means that you're back on top of the food chain, which means…" He stopped talking long enough to step closer and effectively force me into the corner I'd backed into. "Chancellors and soldier-boys don't mix."

"What are you talking about?" I repeated.

175

"Don't waste your time with the lower spectrum of the Ceoran, Chancellor Wynter. You're better than that, you're better than him, and I…well let's just say that I've got the right colored blood to stand by your side."

Oh hell no, this guy was a complete nut job.

I sucked in a deep breath as he neared and made a quick attempt to move, but I was too slow. He threw out his hand above my head and when I turned the other way, he repeated the gesture, caging me in. His eyes dipped to the low collar of my sweater making another shudder roll through my body.

"Why are you running away from me, gorgeous?"

"Don't call me that," I hissed, pressing my palms to his chest to push him away.

Only he didn't budge. "Maybe you prefer babe?"

I turned my face.

"Or princess?"

"Move, or I'll make you move." I found my voice.

This was about to get bad. I felt the coil of heat inside me rising, signaling either a potential meltdown or a shot of power. Neither were appealing. I didn't know if I would get into trouble, I didn't know whether they knew what I could do here and I wasn't about to paint a flashing sign above my head.

I tried to push him again. He smirked.

"You didn't seem to want me to move the last time we were here."

My eyes shot back to his and the glint in his whiskey orbs stunned me into silence. *Did we have some sort of thing going? No. There is no way I'd have ever gone for a guy like this.*

"I must have had a head injury then," I muttered.

His breath rasped in a way that made my blood boil. "Making snide remarks doesn't make it less true."

Hands shaking, I bit down on my molars and stood my ground. "Move, asshole."

"Don't use that kind of language, it's unbecoming of someone as refined as you."

"You won't think I'm so refined when I slam my fist into your face."

A low grumble left his lips and he simply grinned and pressed his body closer, making me flinch and turn my face away.

Wherever I turned, his face followed, his hot breath invading my space. And then his hand was on my hip and the panic went up tenfold.

"People like you and me, people of our class don't belong in these hallways with them." He looked around like he was disgusted. "I can get you back to the top, where you should be."

"I don't need you getting me anywhere." I pressed my palms against the statue of a man and pushed but to no avail. He was solid and immovable and the thoughts assaulting my mind sent my heart skyrocketing.

As his other hand slipped to my lower back, I lost it.

Why wasn't that crazy power working for me now? It was right there. I prayed that whatever made it rise, that the *Cradle of Esper,* that's what they called it right, that it would let me draw from it and as he inched his face closer to mine, I realized that it was a no show.

Damn it! What do I need to do to make this work?

"Get away from me!"

He laughed in my ear and when I pressed my hands against him again and pushed, he was flung away. The impact threw us both down, and when I landed heavily on my butt, I looked up at the space where he'd just been.

That wasn't me, I didn't feel the power surge.

I looked across to where he sat in shock and my eyes landed on Eric.

His body was rigid, wired up with so much tension I thought if he moved, he'd snap.

A deep and low breath left his mouth as he looked down at Ashfield. His eyes flared in the deepest green I'd ever seen; it was completely unnatural.

"I strongly suggest that you get out of my sight, now."

Ashfield's eyes darted between me and Eric and when he finally got up, he shot me a threatening look earning him a warning glare from Eric.

"Assaulting an officer of the Council is a publishable offense, Raine."

Eric's lip twitched into a smirk. "And the attempted sexual assault of a Chancellor isn't?"

Ashfield's eyes widened in shock. Whatever retort he had fell flat and all he could muster up was a glare at Eric.

"Something you want to say to me?" Eric added.

"Watch your back, *Scarface.*"

I flinched, even though Eric didn't move a muscle.

Unphased, he stepped closer and I had to hand it to Ashfield, the crazy idiot looked like he was about to argue but at the last moment, he shot me a look. "It's so like you to always have your watchdog on hand."

"Shut the hell up, Ashfield," I snapped.

Without another word he backed up, storming away, leaving me shaking by the wall and Eric wired like a coil.

Eric let out a long breath and dropped his shoulders.

"Are you okay?" he asked without turning to me.

"I'm fine." I breathed, pushing up to my feet. "Are you?"

"Did he hurt you?" He ignored my question and turned his face toward me slightly.

I shook my head.

"What were you doing out here?" he asked.

"I was walking back to my room."

"I thought you were with Emelia; you shouldn't be out here alone."

"I'm inside a compound, I'm pretty sure Reapers aren't going to get me in here."

He didn't look amused. "It's not the Reapers I'm worried about."

"Are you worried about Ashfield?"

No reply.

"I mean sure, he's a jerk, but Eric, I don't think he'd actually do anything. He was just trying to rile me up." I looked down at my jeans noticing the dust clinging to the fabric.

"It isn't just Ashfield."

Twisting around to wipe it off, I looked back at him.

He let out another long breath and pressed both hands to the back of his neck.

"Is there something I should know about this place?"

Eric shook his head; he was still for about five seconds before he held out his hand and I gave him my keys.

"You don't trust them, do you?" I asked.

He reached for the door and stopped.

"Eric," I began, my lungs expanding with each nervous breath. Being in such proximity to him was dangerous. "Why don't you trust them?"

"Because everyone has an agenda," he said, finally letting his hand settle on the door when the key failed to open it.

"What does that mean?"

"You're smart, Alex, I'm sure you'll figure it out."

My eyes widened and then fell to the space between us. His hands shook at the door.

"Let me," I said taking the key from him.

He stepped back and I kept my eyes glued to the door and worked the key. When it unlocked, I pushed it open and turned back to face him.

His lips slowly parted like he was about to say something and then he closed them and pushed past me into my room.

I followed him in, shutting the door behind me.

"What's Ashfield's deal?" I asked, twisting to face him.

"He's a jerk."

"Yeah I got that part. But why?"

"There's a lot of history there."

History? I looked away, surely not between me and him.

"What kind of history?"

"He's jealous," he added, keeping his voice low.

"Of what?"

"Of me."

A chill settled over me and I folded my arms across my chest.

"Like I said, there's a lot of history there."

He tried to move past me again toward my small desk and signal the end of the conversation but there was no way he was getting away with that, not again.

"Eric. Stop."

He didn't. He kept busying himself with rearranging the items on the shelf and he only stopped when I cupped my hand over his. He drew in a sharp breath and pulled back, startling me.

"I…I'm sorry," I said.

"Don't apologize."

"But I—"

"It's fine."

A heavy silence fell between us and he sat.

"Are you going to tell me about the jealousy, or do I have to go pry it from someone else?"

"There isn't much to tell, politics and all that."

He scowled at the word making me flinch.

"I don't understand."

"It's your world, Alex, your people, not mine. I can't help you understand."

"What is that supposed to mean?" There was attitude and then there was this, this personal dig at me. "They're not *my* people. They're materialistic jerks, I'm nothing like that."

"You're right, that was a shitty thing to say, I'm sorry."

"It's fine," I muttered.

"But you need to stay away from him."

"Fine, I'll stay away from him."

Eric didn't say a word, he didn't react. He just remained silent and still, hands pressed flat to my desk like a lifeline.

He'd told me about this world and who I was, though I still had a hard time grasping it all.

"What is he jealous of? Really?" I asked again.

Finally, after what seemed like the longest time, he dropped into the chair at my desk and let out a long breath, his eyes never once leaving mine.

"He was jealous of my relationship with you."

The air disappeared from my lungs.

Words kind of failed me. Where I would have really benefited from my inability to stop talking, I was silent. A few moments passed before I cleared my throat and spoke.

"Why would he be jealous?" I asked gently.

Eric's eyes found mine and without having to say a word, I saw the apprehension coursing through him.

"We were just friends, right? Why would he be jealous?" I asked, keeping my voice light.

Because we weren't just friends. That's why, genius.

"It was rare for my class to be friends with yours."

There was that word again.

My gaze fell to his hand on my table. His scarred fist balled into a tight circle and he showed no sign of relaxing. It made sense to me now: Eric was a soldier, and Ashfield and I, we were on the Council, or *royal,* whatever the hell he said we were.

And if that dream I had meant anything, it meant that this Eric was afraid to get close not because he didn't feel anything for me, but because it was forbidden.

Stalling, looking for the right words, I moved closer to him and ignored the way he tensed. So maybe that was it then, I'd just conjured up fantasies where Eric and I ignored the rulebook and ran off together.

"Did I care about that?" I rested my hip on the desk, right beside him.

His eyes shot up to mine.

I arched my brows, waiting for an answer.

Eric shook his head.

"So, I don't understand."

He tilted his head.

"You said the Council are serious about the Class Division, but if I didn't care…why…?"

"Because I did."

Our eyes locked.

I don't want to hurt you. I don't want to fail you. That's what the Eric in my dream had said. He'd meant it, he was convinced that I wouldn't be safe.

Pain replaced the curiosity in my heart. Everything that was done here, was for the protection of me, and no one had been able to tell me why.

But now I understood, now I felt it.

Looking down at the space between our hands again, I reached over and gently cupped my hand over his.

He flinched, but he stayed this time. His body was still tense. He was protective, he hated me looking at his scars, he hated me touching them. I understood. I felt the same about my own.

His eyes traveled up to mine. His expression was haunted, and he looked wounded, like he was grieving and mourning all at once, but his lips curled up into a half smile, the kind of smile that said he was going to be okay. If only I believed it.

For a moment, he stared at me and I thought he was going to say something and when he opened his mouth, my heart raced but then he closed it, pushing to his feet, taking his hand away from me.

"Don't wander the halls," he said and then quickly crossed the distance between me and the door in a couple of strides.

"Thanks for before," I mumbled.

He nodded and then he was gone.

Chapter Sixteen
The Set-up

My eyes opened long after my body had woken up. I let myself lie in silence, embracing the rare opportunity to relax. It'd been a while since I'd had the luxury of sleeping without worrying whether someone was going to steal my things or try to attack me.

And then, without even realizing what was happening, a chain of broken memories started to flash through my mind.

Like a flicker of a memory I felt Eric's lingering touch on my cheek as I slept, his gentle whispers when I cried, his soft caress when we danced.

I shot up in the bed and looked around.

Eric looked up at me from the picture in the frame.

I *remembered* when this picture was taken. Emelia had thrown something at Eric, she had thrown a book at him, a book me and her had cried over, swooned over, and Eric was teasing us. Someone else had taken the picture just as the book hit the back of his head, someone I'd been good friends with.

Tears started to form as I desperately tried to drag air in. I laughed out loud when I remembered that Emelia crashed the picnic at this gorgeous retreat. Eric had been planning it for days, making sure that she wouldn't annoy us, but there she was.

It had been my seventeenth birthday.

The threads of memory started to solidify.

Maybe being here was helping, maybe being in the compound was somehow triggering it. All I knew was that the desperation to hold onto the threads was stronger than anything I'd ever felt.

I stumbled getting out of the bed and got dressed. I shook my head as I stuffed my feet into a pair of sneakers and rushed into the bathroom. Another image jolted me: me and Eric, in here. He was standing behind me, fastening a necklace and his eyes never once left mine.

Tears stung the back of my eyes. *Why would he lie to me?*

It didn't matter. I had to talk to him. I pulled myself away from my reflection and ran to the door. I had to see him. I had to tell him.

As I pulled the door open, I nearly ran into two people I wasn't expecting to see.

General Corteza and Emelia. Her eyes were glazed with tears.

"It's Eric," she blurted out. "He's gone."

"What? Gone where?"

"I don't know. He was talking about a lead." Emelia was a mess, tears streaming down her face.

I pushed past them both and stormed down the corridor toward the lifts. I didn't know exactly where I was going but my gut told me I'd know when I got there.

"I think I know where he's going."

"What?" Emelia's high-pitched voice shook me. "Did he say something?"

"No but I think he's trying to find the Ceoran who can undo what he did."

I pushed the button for BG1 and tapped my foot impatiently as we went up. The moment the doors opened, I made my way down the hallway, Emelia and Corteza followed.

"They're just rumors," she choked, shaking her head. "No one can do that."

"I know that, you know that. But he's holding onto hope that they're not."

"Alex, I don't understand, how do you know this?"

Without slowing, I turned my face toward them both. "I don't know how, but I'm starting to remember."

Corteza shot me a look.

"I know it's not possible," I said, "but it's happening. Only a few things, but they're there."

Reaching the same double doors I'd walked through yesterday, I pushed them open and walked past some stunned soldiers who threw me curious expressions, yet none of them failed to nod their acknowledgement as we walked by. It was surreal, like I was being guided by an unseen force.

"Who told him about the Ceoran?" I asked.

"What do you mean?" Emelia jogged to catch up.

"He said he heard rumors, but he didn't have a lead."

Emelia ploughed into me when I stopped abruptly.

"Who told him?" I demanded.

She shook her head but nothing came out of her mouth.

Crap.

"Someone's setting him up," I ground out.

When I reached the end of a large workspace surrounded by monitors, soldiers, and techs, I knew I'd reached the right area. It was part of a bigger workspace but sectioned off with a small partition giving minimal privacy. This was the head of operations. Off to my left there were two small boardrooms separated by glass walls and frosted glass. Off to my right, two more board rooms with sheer curtains for more privacy.

I stopped beside a young lieutenant until he looked up at me and then he jerked up out of his seat.

"Sorry, ma'am."

"It's fine," I said, taking a seat.

Emelia remained quiet beside me as I pulled the keyboard closer to me and brought up a screen which felt like second nature.

I had no idea how I knew where to go and what to do; my hands were doing everything on their own, my mind was barely keeping up and the only thought coherent in my mind was Eric and getting through to him. *The memories are coming back, he doesn't need to do this.*

Those same nagging pieces of broken thoughts kept rushing through my head and with each minute they started to seem clearer, but they still didn't make complete sense; I saw Ashfield and Eric arguing in a hall, Ashfield had pulled a prank on him. I didn't know what it was, I couldn't remember that far, but Eric was being blamed for a fire breaking out in the recreation room and being a soldier, he was the only one taking the blame.

My jaw set into a hard line. Ashfield was an asshole, he'd always riled Eric up and I wouldn't be surprised if he'd done something now. If he'd been the one sending Eric out there with false information to get him out of the compound and out of the way. We could be in for a long night.

As if right on cue, Ashfield strutted into the room and stood by the door, one foot lazily resting on the wall behind him.

As the screen in front of me locked onto a grid of the surrounding desert, I took a deep breath and pulled up another feed. It was a few miles from here, a small town with no power and no signs of life. By my very limited knowledge of the geography of this area, I figured it must have been the city of Osoyoos. Everything was still and blank as the satellite kept tracing the location and feeding the information back to me. There were no heat signatures detected.

I executed instructions for the satellite to do another run of the area. And just as the satellite came back, I saw a tiny dot of orange fill the screen with a simple message: heat signature detected. Bingo.

Next, I pulled an earpiece off a charging dock and put it on. "Please work."

"What are you doing?" Corteza asked.

"Eric always carries an earpiece." I remembered the *call* back at the farm, and I remembered Corteza sternly telling him to do so as another hazy memory solidified in my head.

In this memory, Corteza was chastising Eric for running off unprepared. He'd been on his designated break but Corteza still gave him a hard time. Little did he know Eric and I had snuck out beyond the walls to go sightseeing. We'd done it often, sometimes alone, sometimes with Emelia and her then girlfriend, Lana.

I ground my teeth and pulled myself back to the present. The Corteza here gave me a curt nod and stepped back letting me work.

I tried the first frequency that seemed to pop into my mind. Nothing.

Not even a blip.

Emelia shifted beside me, stilling for a moment.

I tried another.

Static.

It was excruciating.

189

When another frequency popped into my mind, I gave it a shot. When that failed too, I composed myself before I tried another one. This time it worked.

Thank the Karatoi and whatever other gods are looking out for us.

A breath on the other end cracked through the static. Damn these lines were so sketchy.

"Eric?" I tried.

No one said a word and I closed my eyes, pressing my palm flat to the surface of the table.

Corteza and Emelia were silently waiting. I still had no idea how I managed to do this, just looking at the trail of what I'd typed in to bring up this link blew my mind. I was never good at anything like this, I barely managed to use Twitter—this was a whole other world for me.

"Eric, say something," I said.

"Alex?"

"Yes, it's me." I let out a huge breath.

"I'm so sorry."

"It's okay, just come back."

"I can't. I have to find him."

"No one can do what you're asking," I said, pleading with him to understand what I was saying.

Movement off to my right caught my eye, Ashfield was talking to someone, someone who wasn't there. He tapped his ear and nodded.

"He can," Eric said, dragging my eyes back to the screen.

"No, he can't. Someone is setting you up."

Silence.

"My memories are coming back, Eric. You don't have to do this."

"I have to try," he said quietly, though the angst in his voice was loud and clear, "for you."

There was no nice way to say it. "Someone set you up. There's no magical Ceoran who can undo a Clean Slate, you know this, you said so yourself, you looked into the leads."

"This is a new lead."

"Eric, it's probably a prank."

"No."

I heard the apprehension on the other end of the line.

"The lead is false. You know it is," I said gently. And then something else made me think. "Eric, what if someone sent you out there to get you away from me?" Someone whom I knew almost without a doubt had been Ashfield.

"Stay with Corteza," Eric said suddenly. "Stay there and don't move."

"Okay."

He disconnected the call and my eyes scanned the room. Ashfield was gone.

I turned to Corteza. "Where is he?"

He turned, searching the room, and then stopped when his shoulders squared.

Crap. I stood. "We need to find him now."

"What's going on?" Emelia asked.

"Not sure, but Ashfield is up to something."

"How do you know?"

"I don't know how to explain it, but it's a feeling, a very bad feeling. I saw him talking to someone through an earpiece just as I made contact with Eric," I explained to them both.

Corteza seemed to be entertaining my accusations but the look of skepticism made my stomach tumble.

There was something under the surface that was making a very prominent appearance. He didn't like me; he didn't trust me; and he sure as hell didn't want me anywhere near Eric…but, he had to listen to me.

As his stern features softened, he turned from me and called over a pair of soldiers.

"Sir?"

"I need you two to locate Ashfield, is that understood?"

"Yes, sir."

Once they were gone, his attention returned to me. I glanced up at Emelia and then back at the screen where the orange dot had been. Eric was moving, he was no longer on the radar of the satellite and that put me on edge.

"Stay put, Chancellor," Corteza said.

"Alex," I insisted.

He nodded and then turned toward me, speaking in a low voice. "You think Ashfield has been working with someone out there?"

"They had a history of pranks, right? Dumb stuff?"

"Yes."

"What if he made this lead up, to get Eric out of here. Everyone knows he's my guardian, right?"

His jaw squared. He must have thought the same.

"I need you to stay here," he said to me then turned to Emilia. "Do not leave her side."

"Where are you going?" I asked.

"To look into something."

He excused himself and disappeared.

Emelia sat herself down beside me and kept the small talk to a minimum. It was oddly soothing while being nerve-wracking all at once. I would have actually enjoyed a distraction right now, but I

192

realized that her source of anxiety was the same as mine. We were both painfully worried for Eric.

It didn't take a Ceoran high council chancellor to understand the limitations of what these people would do for a soldier. The whole thing left a sour taste in my mouth.

Corteza obviously cared about Eric, he respected him and that begged the biggest question of all: why wasn't he out there searching for him? What exactly was he looking into that was more important than helping one of his finest soldiers?

I huffed and sat back in my chair. If I was so important like they said, why hadn't I done anything about that, why hadn't I made them change their laws to treat everyone equally?

One way or another, I would find out.

Hours had passed since I'd spoken to Eric, and I was starting to feel each second weighing down on me. Ashfield still hadn't been brought back which could have meant a million things.

I'd been out there long enough to know how volatile the world was when night fell and the last thing you needed was someone hunting for you.

After repositioning herself for the hundredth time, Emelia stiffened beside me drawing my attention to the approaching figure— Ashfield strode up to us with a smug grin, the two soldiers Corteza sent in tow.

"What did you do?" Emelia spat, placing herself between us.

I stood beside her.

There was absolutely something irritating about him, but it was a lot more than that. I folded my arms across my chest and watched silently as he came a few steps closer.

"What did you do?" I repeated Emelia's earlier question.

"I'm insulted that you think I would have anything to do with this," he said like he was bored.

"I'm insulted that you're even questioning me. What did you do?"

"I simply gave him information."

"What information?" I stepped forward, my face inches from him.

"Whoa, easy Chancellor, someone might get the wrong idea." He grinned.

Yuck. My body recoiled at the suggestion and I stepped back.

"What did you say to him?" Corteza appeared behind Ashfield and his whole body stiffened.

Huh. Guess the smug asshat wasn't as tough as he made out.

He turned and tipped his head back.

"I won't ask again," Corteza warned.

"I told him about the mage."

"The mage doesn't exist," Emelia spat, narrowing her eyes.

And when neither Corteza nor Ashfield said a word, Emelia sunk back, her eyes wide.

"What is it, what's going on?" I asked. "What is the mage?"

"Someone whose powers are unheard of; they're said to possess the power of the Reaper through magic." Emelia sighed, like the fact that we were having this conversation was a huge waste of time.

"What does that mean?" I demanded.

"It means Ashfield sent Eric out there knowing that he was chasing a ghost." Corteza added, "Is that right, Ashfield?"

Ashfield laughed. "It was just a joke."

"What kind of joke is that!" I shouted. Angry tears welled in the back of my eyes when I thought about what kind of sick person would do that. Set someone up with false hope just to get a laugh.

"Relax, Wynter, he's going to be fine, he'll be back before night-fall."

"You're a jerk," I snapped back.

"Come on, it was funny—"

"I think that's quite enough, Ashfield," Corteza muttered when I opened my mouth to argue. "Your childish prank could have ended badly."

"He's a tough boy, he's fine." He shrugged, and he knew no one here could do a damn thing to punish him. He was practically royalty and he would get away with it. Even if something bad happened to Eric.

I wanted to scream and probably punch him in the throat. But I reined it in and backed down. One way or another, I would use whatever power I supposedly held here to make equality a priority.

"He's on his way back," I said.

"Let's hope that he makes it back safely." Ashfield smirked.

Oh, that asshat.

Before I made my move toward him, Emelia pressed her hand on my shoulder and gently squeezed.

That earned a smug grin from Ashfield. Someday, someone was going to beat that expression off his face and I sincerely hoped it would be me.

"Get out of here," Corteza muttered to Ashfield.

Thankfully, he was done testing his position and he left. I exhaled through my nose and sat back down.

"Stay at this station, I'm going to make sure Ashfield returns to his quarters," Corteza said.

"Good." She ground out and then turned to me. "What a dick."

After all the bravado she put on outside of these walls, I realized now it was all a front to keep herself from breaking and it was obvious that Eric was her life, her only family, and if he were gone, she would be lost. I could relate.

I glanced at the time in the corner of the screen and really tried to pretend that the tightening in my chest wasn't worry for Eric.

"It's been more than five hours." I turned to her.

She hadn't left my side the entire time and she was quickly growing impatient.

As General Corteza approached, I stood. "Can we send a search party?"

"Not unless he's been missing for at least twelve hours."

Emelia shifted beside me. I ignored her and shook my head.

"There have to be extenuating circumstances."

"There aren't any, not for soldiers I'm afraid."

"Because they're not the same class as the Council?"

"Unfortunately, those are the rules," he said.

"Those rules are ridiculous," I shot back, attracting the attention of a few officers by the entrance.

"Careful, Chancellor Wynter."

"You know they're a joke," I said sternly.

Emelia glared at me, her eyes the size of saucers.

I stood my ground and looked Corteza right in the eyes.

It was time to make something happen, time to use the power I supposedly had here at the compound.

Emelia pressed her hand to my arm, but I wasn't done.

"I need you to launch a search party for him."

"Chancellor Wynter—"

"I know that you have to listen to orders from Council members, General. And as far as I'm aware, although I haven't yet been reinstated as a Chancellor, I am in fact still legally allowed to exercise those rights, am I not?"

Hoping that what I said held some sort of merit, I stood tall and waited, and by the look on his face, I knew that I was right.

Before Corteza answered, a voice interjected, drawing my attention behind me.

"She is right, sir. Section fifteen of the guidebook confirms that despite the absence of a council member, their rights remain intact unless they revoke their position or are confirmed deceased. And, since Chancellor Wynter is very much alive, unless she's revoked her position, her request is warranted."

My jaw dropped.

A tall—much taller than Eric—guy stood with his hands tucked neatly into beige chinos wearing a simple white polo and a leather satchel slung over his shoulder. His eyes were the brightest blue I'd ever seen, and his face was dusted with tiny freckles matching his fiery hair.

A broad smile accentuated his perfect white teeth and cocky, yet respectful, attitude. My brows shot into my hairline.

"While that is true, Mr. Kelly, Chancellor Wynter has been absent for more than six months. Section eighteen stipulates that there is a statute of limitation."

"Please, Kieran is fine." He flashed a pearly smile. "And that rule only applies to involuntary expulsion from the compound. Chancellor Wynter left of her own accord."

My eyes shot back to him and his broad smile widened, revealing dimples.

"By the way, it's great to see you, kid," he said.

I looked around, certain that he wasn't talking to me and when he chuckled, I felt stupid. Of course he was talking to me. How did I have no recollection of him, not even a teeny tiny image?

"If Raine isn't back within the hour, we'll task a search party," Corteza said.

"Thank you, General," I said as politely as I could.

His response was a small nod and then his attention was back on the men who'd entered the room. He moved over to them and gave orders I couldn't hear. My attention, however, went back to Kieran.

As I opened my mouth to thank him, Emelia rushed him and threw her arms around his neck, pulling him into a bear hug. The force nearly bowled him over.

"You're the best!" She jumped him again, this time he held her at arm's length with a laugh.

"And you said reading the guidebook was for losers."

"I said no such thing." She slapped his shoulder.

I watched the exchange with fascination and felt a smile tug at my lips.

"Thank you for stepping in there," I said.

He waved it off and smiled. "No need. I was actually coming to see you."

"Me, why?"

"Yup." He nodded. "I have some things to give you."

He set down his satchel, unzipped it, and nodded to its contents—a large, full manila folder was tucked between a bundle of newspapers and a book. Emelia gave him a knowing look and then quietly excused herself.

"You're safe with Kieran, I'm going to wait for Eric."

Kieran gave her a pearly smile and then pulled the book out, set it on the table before following up with the folder the bunch of newspapers and a few smaller bundles.

"What is all this?" I asked.

"This is the guidebook, for one. You should read it. It's most definitely not for losers." He handed me the heavy, dusty old book and grinned. "The rest are your files, things you kept here and were working on. You asked me to keep them safe."

How could I not remember him? I'd obviously trusted him with...whatever these were.

Flicking through the files, I sighed when nothing made sense.

"It will come back."

"You're the only one who seems to think so." I groaned.

"Let's just say I've seen more than most."

"I'm really hoping you're going to tell me what that means."

He chuckled. "It means that you and I have worked closely on a lot of clandestine stuff, so you and I have seen some things that would push the boundaries of what's possible and what's not."

"More than intergalactic empires?"

He laughed. "Well, when you say it like that."

"To be completely honest with you, I'm still digesting the fact that I'm one of..." I couldn't bring myself to say it. "You."

"I wouldn't worry too much, you're a quick study. Have a read of your files and see if anything sticks. In the meantime, I think we should go."

"What?" My eyes snapped up in the direction he was looking, and he quickly made his way toward the commotion.

Eric, two other soldiers, and Emelia came rushing down the small walkway seemingly unfazed by anyone trying to stop them or ask questions. He stormed his way through a set of doors, and into

199

one of the glassed off boardrooms. Kieran didn't slow down and I found myself jogging behind the forming crowd.

Oh no, Ashfield. He was going for Ashfield. As the glass unfrosted, I saw that he and two others were seated in the small boardroom.

My heart kicked up, I dropped the files on the first table I ran past and rushed toward him.

His face was hard, every muscle was set tightly, and I wasn't blind to the fact that he wasn't even looking at me, not even a quick glance, nothing. I focused on the shitstorm that was about to be unleashed.

Commotion broke out as Eric burst through the boardroom door and surprised the trio who were seated around the table. Emelia shrieked for Eric to stop while the other two soldiers pulled her back, trying to get into the room after Eric.

Neither of them were quick enough.

Eric shoved Ashfield so hard he fell off his chair, landing on his back on the floor. The other two with him tried to stop Eric, but with little more than a side kick and a punch, Eric took them both down and turned his attention to Ashfield.

"You think you're funny?" he spat.

Ashfield was back on his feet. "You're a fucking psycho!" he snapped, dusting off his pants. "Just like your girlfriend!"

Oh hell no.

Eric rushed forward and shoved Ashfield again, who this time reacted with a forceful thrust back.

Corteza appeared behind Emelia and pushed through the two soldiers who'd done a stellar job of keeping everyone else out but not much else.

As I reached the boardroom Emelia pulled me back, keeping me from getting closer.

"How does it feel knowing you lobotomized her?" Ashfield challenged.

"Stand down, Raine!" Corteza yelled.

Eric ignored the general's warning and charged Ashfield again. This time, though, he raised his hand and launched a fist right into his face. Ashfield flew back with a lot more force than a normal punch should have given, landing against the wall, cracking the plaster behind him.

I stifled a scream with my free hand and watched on in horror as Ashfield recovered and moved faster than I'd ever seen anyone move. He got his hand around Eric's throat and slammed him back into the glass wall, breaking it into a million pieces, sending fragments of it shattering all around.

As it came falling, I darted out of the way and collided with a strong body behind me. Kieran pulled me back and turned me away as the glass rained down over us, his body taking the brunt of it.

My eyes quickly shot up looking for Emelia. I breathed out in relief when I saw that Corteza had done the same, shielding her.

Kieran released me and moved past everyone who'd gathered and stormed right into the fight.

Eric was back on his feet, blood dripping from a cut along the right side of his face, his fists balled at his sides. I'd seen Eric fight; I'd seen him move. There was no reason he shouldn't have had Ashfield whimpering like a baby in one clean shot. Maybe he was holding back, maybe he knew that hurting Ashfield any more was going to be detrimental to him.

As Ashfield chanced another move, Kieran stepped in and shoved him back. "Enough!"

"Move," Ashfield spat.

"You're both being moronic. Stop," Kieran yelled again towering over them both.

How Ashfield had the guts to stand up to him was beyond me. Eric did back off; he gave Kieran a quick look which I imagined was laced with pure annoyance and then he wiped the blood with his sleeve and turned from the room walking away.

"Raine!" Corteza shouted.

"If he isn't punished for this I will go to the Elders!" Ashfield yelled, nursing a violent-looking bruise on his face.

"Shut it, and back the hell off," Kieran muttered.

Ashfield's eyes widened so much I thought he'd give himself an aneurism.

"Now," Kieran barked. "Or do you want me to start listing all the times you've defied those on the Council higher than you?"

Ashfield scowled and for a moment I thought he'd fight him on it. But even he must have sensed that enough was enough. With little more than a look, he left.

As I let out the breath I'd been holding, I looked down the hall about to follow Eric, but then promptly stopped when I saw him walk toward a tall and pretty brunette who quickly appeared at his side and wrapped her arms around his waist, pulling him away.

Hands shaking, I moved toward the blown-out room and looked at all the carnage. The glass was at least an inch thick, some sort of reinforced, double-glazed glass by the look of it. I'd been told they—we—were strong, but this was crazy. Impact like that should have killed him, but he got up and walked away. They both did.

Emelia linked her arm through mine and drew my attention to her. She was crying, and her brilliant green eyes were surrounded by red rings.

"You're hurt," she gasped, looking down at my arm.

My eyes followed hers. I hadn't even felt the cut but there was blood steadily flowing to prove it.

Instinctively, I pressed my free hand over the wound and winced when the pain finally registered. I breathed as the burn settled and let Emelia lead me away.

I chanced a look over my shoulder. Corteza was yelling some creative remarks at Ashfield and while Eric was gone, I knew there'd be repercussions. Why did he have to do that?

He'd drawn first blood in an otherwise tame battle of egos. Not only that, he'd instigated a fight against not one, but three Council members at once.

"Alex!" Kieran yelled after us. "Wait!"

Emelia slowed just enough to let him catch up but didn't turn to look at him. She was still in shock and I didn't think she'd manage a coherent sentence even if she tried.

"You're hurt." Kieran's jaw clamped shut.

"I'm okay, I'll just wrap it up."

He stopped us, and gently pried my hand away sucking in a sharp breath as his eyes flicked up to mine.

"Come with me."

"I was taking her to the med bay," Emelia managed.

Kieran looked at her and then back at me. "I've got this. Okay?"

Her usually perky responses were absent. Instead she just shot him a warning look.

"I'll be fine. It's just between us," he urged.

"Fine," she snapped and left.

"What was that?" I asked.

"I'll explain, come with me. Keep this over the wound." He pulled out a handkerchief and handed it to me.

My lips tugged into a smile.

He chuckled. "What?"

"I haven't seen anyone carry a handkerchief, like, ever."

"Well I'm old fashioned, what can I say? Press tightly, got it?"

Silently nodding, I followed him through the maze of corridors.

"How you doing?" he asked.

"I told you before. I'm fine."

"You're probably still running off adrenalin, when that wears off, you'll feel it. It looks deep."

I could feel the tingling now, it was still bearable though, but I didn't want to wait around and see how much this bad boy would start to burn.

"Just through here." He nodded at a door with an obscure entrance.

It looked like a walkway into a service stairwell, not something I'd expect would lead to a med bay. When he pushed the door open, I held back my surprise. It wasn't the med bay; it wasn't even a service stairwell. It was a bedroom, *his* bedroom.

"What are we doing here?" I looked around. "I thought all rooms were down in the lower levels."

He smiled and shook his head. "Nothing too exciting, I assure you. And you're right, almost all the rooms are, mine was a special request."

Right. I turned away. I'd obviously turned bright red.

"Sit." He motioned to a large leather chair beside a writing desk which matched a smaller version by the window.

My eyes traveled around the room. He *was* old fashioned.

The armchair I sat in matched a mahogany writing desk; the shelves beside it were stacked to the brim with early editions of Dickens and Poe. The rug beneath a large, wooden framed bed was adorned in red-and-gold detailing and a large golden framed mirror was fixed to the wall.

He smiled at me sheepishly.

"Is this your grandad's stuff?"

"Ouch, Wynter." He grinned.

"I'm joking. It's nice," I said, nodding at the décor.

"I feel like a massive dork. But I like books and writing, this seems fitting."

"It is." I swallowed hard and looked down at my arm.

"Why couldn't we do this at the med bay? Whatever *this* is."

"Because *this* isn't really allowed here."

Before I had a chance to ask him to elaborate, he disappeared behind a door and quickly came back with a couple of towels. He dropped them on the bedside table and dragged his relic of an armchair over, sitting right in front of me. He took my arm, pulling the handkerchief free.

At first, he didn't do anything, just kind of looked at the gross, gushing cut and then he cupped his hand over it.

Flinching slightly, I winced when he applied more pressure. As he did, I watched him, and his expression changed, hardening, like he was in pain.

His bright blue eyes steadily turned to a piercing shade of grey and then, I felt it. A warm, almost tingly sensation spread from the spot he was touching on my arm into my entire body and then it was over, and I felt like I'd run a marathon.

"Lean back for a bit," he instructed, reaching under the desk and retrieving a small bottle of milk from the minibar. "Drink this."

"Milk?" I looked skeptically at his choice of medicine.

"It's the tryptophan. It helps."

"With what?"

"Rest and mindfulness, especially after what you just went through."

Taking his word for it, I drank the milk and as I did, I felt slightly better.

My eyes widened when I dropped my gaze back to my arm and took it in. The wound which had been at least an inch wide, and probably the same deep, was healing before my eyes. Kieran looked at me, slowly leaning back in the chair.

He pulled over the small towels and handed me one while he cleaned his hands with the other.

When his gaze found mine again, he quickly looked away and down at his hands. They shook violently and while he tried to hide it underneath the towel, I didn't miss it. His lips quirked into a half smile, but every movement seemed to be filled with pain.

"Are you okay?" I asked.

"I'm fine."

"You look really hurt, Kieran."

"Perks of the power," he stammered.

"Does this affect you?"

"Only a bit."

"Are you lying to me?"

He smirked and closed his eyes leaning his head back.

Taken aback, I frowned. "Why are you smirking at me?"

"I'm not smirking at you."

I narrowed my eyes at him, perfectly aware that he couldn't see me.

"And now you're doing the eye thing," he murmured.

"Now you're being creepy."

He chuckled softly and brought his eyes back to me.

A smile crept across my face before I could stop it. *Yeah, we'd definitely known each other well.*

"Will you be alright?" I asked.

He nodded and sat up, bringing both knees to his chest, his fiery hair falling over his eyes as he scrubbed the back of his neck.

"Kind of the reason they don't like us doing this sort of thing."

"Why?"

"They don't like us exerting too much power, especially not on the lower class."

"So we can't even help each other?"

"No. They hate us wasting power. They have dedicated doctors that can do it, people that are willing."

"Willing to sacrifice." I scowled.

"Exactly."

I shook my head. "So they're the *lower* class too then?"

"Yes, Alex. Soldiers, cooks, workers, nurses. They're all the same. If they're not like us, they're not worth anything to them."

"This is bullshit."

"I know. I don't believe in the division," he clarified. "But they do, so, it's not allowed, and I have to be careful."

"The power affects us long term?"

"Yeah," he mused. "The more we use it, the more it weakens us. So, they don't like the High Council using it at risk of wasting away. But we do, obviously, when we need to."

"Eric can do it too," I blurted out and then quickly shut my mouth. I had no idea what compelled me to say that.

Kieran nodded.

"I'm sorry." I looked away. "I don't know why I said that."

207

"You don't have to say sorry."

"I do. I just came across as the biggest jerk."

He chuckled again, diffusing the tension.

"Eric is a lot better at it than I am."

Thinking back to the farmhouse, the pain I felt was severe, like soul consuming, heart lurching severe, and when Eric did what he did, it was gone almost instantly and I felt lightheaded, but he walked away like nothing happened.

"Is it something you can practice?"

Kieran shook his head. "It's something you're born with, you kind of get the gift and you're meant to nurture it. Those who don't, don't get good at it."

"Eric said we can do other things."

"Yeah, but it's really rare, but some can home in on a certain gift or power and amplify it."

"Could I do any of those things?"

"You are a whole other story, Chancellor Wynter."

"How so?"

"Well, for starters, you can sense the Reapers. No one has ever been able to do that before."

My mind raced. I had always sensed something, even when I had no idea what it was, but I thought back to the Chrysler building and how I made the Reapers leave.

"And I can make things happen with my mind."

He nodded. "You're a mystery, which is why you are so important."

As I opened my mouth to ask him what they wanted with me, I felt my eyes start to close. Why was I so sleepy?

A warm haze spread through me and before I knew it, I was leaning against Kieran's hard chest as he carried me through the dark halls.

"Sleep, Alex. You'll get all your answers soon."

CHAPTER SEVENTEEN
THE FRIEND

The light coming on in the room woke me when it started to blare through my closed eyelids. I swatted away the cover and groaned into the pillow turning onto my stomach.

I pulled my arm out from under the pillow and looked at the spot where the cut was. It was now a faint, pinkish line barely visible unless you really looked for it, which made my eyes skeptically travel up to my left arm. Like with all the other memories, tiny pieces started to come back to me.

The fire, the heat, the burning of flesh and the screams echoing through the shifting rubble. I traced a line over the pink scarring, letting my fingers linger. The coloring of those burns was the same as Eric's. It didn't take much more detective work to figure it out.

Releasing a shallow breath, I dropped my sleeve and looked around realizing I was still in the same clothes as yesterday but now comfortably tucked in my own bed. I had to find Eric and I needed to make sure Emelia was alright.

I quickly showered, throwing on some fresh clothes and made my way out.

Once I'd reached the right floor, I wasted no time making my way past the operations room, I hurried past the yellow strips of tape sectioning off the boardroom that had become an impromptu gladiator arena yesterday.

A few men in fatigues stopped me to ask about Eric and what happened, to which I had no answer. Once I worked out that Eric wasn't up here, I headed back to the lift and hit BG7 and navigated my way in the direction I thought Emelia's room was in.

Just as I thought I'd taken a wrong turn; I saw her up ahead. She was talking with someone in a really hushed tone, her posture was tense, and her hair was in the same messy braid it had been in yesterday.

My stomach twisted into tight coils and as I neared, the feeling got worse, like maybe I shouldn't be here, and as the last few feet came, I saw the person she was arguing with was Eric. An ugly mess of emotions rattled through me.

He stood at her door leaning heavily against the frame. His hair was messy, probably from when he tried to clean his cut and he was in the same clothes as yesterday too.

Getting closer I could make out a little of what they were saying, so I stepped off to the side and slipped into a doorway staying out of view.

"You're going to get yourself killed acting like that," Emelia hissed; her usual warmth was replaced by a venom I never knew was possible from her.

"Ashfield played me."

"Obviously," she muttered in response. "And you couldn't have taken the high road?"

"I don't get why you're so pissed."

"You don't get why I'm pissed?" Emelia said.

"No. I don't get why you're getting so worked up. Ashfield is a piece of shit."

211

"Yeah, he is, but he's still a Council member, and so were his two friends."

"I did what I had to."

"No, your ego did what it had to."

"Ashfield's an asshole."

"Yeah, I got that part." She ran her hand over her ponytail. "But you shouldn't have done that. You're about to get thrown out for assaulting a Council member. Again! And you've brought too much attention to us."

"This isn't about us."

"No, it isn't. It's about Alex and it's about you, and now she's got a target on her back."

"That's not what this is about."

"Oh yeah?" Emelia snapped back. "So, seeing her with Ashfield had nothing to do with it then?"

"Seeing her with Ashfield reminded me of the last time I saw them together."

What? I recoiled. *The last time we were together?*

"Exactly." She stood tall. "And you're throwing your life here at the compound away for what? Jealousy?"

"He's still here and I'm still being jerked around. It's going to be the same, all over again."

"Yeah, maybe, but now you've just shown that Ashfield's ranting was right. And you know what that means?"

Eric remained uncharacteristically quiet.

"It means that now the Council will have more than enough ammunition to throw you out—they have proof of mixing classes. They have proof that you overstepped your bounds as her guardian and they won't punish her, but they will not hesitate to lock you up or kick you out. And with you gone, there's no cover, no pro-tection."

"I'm doing what I have to," he repeated. "She'll be safer this way."

"I get that you're trying to throw them off your relationship, but you're doing the exact opposite."

He'd taken a tentative step back and cast his eyes down.

"I'm doing this for her."

"You're doing this to make yourself feel better."

A long, silent pause passed between them.

"You're right," Eric said suddenly. "I'm doing all of this because all of this is on me."

"Eric, that's not, I didn't mean that."

"It's fine, it's the truth, right? So, there it is. I feel guilty. That is why I'm doing this, because I hate feeling guilty. I want to set things straight." His voice broke. "So she can go and sit up on her throne among all those assholes, beside the biggest dick of all and forget me like she should have the first time around."

A pang of hurt shot through me.

When Emelia retreated and dropped her gaze, Eric stepped back into the frame and laughed.

"I am doing this, *all* of this because I feel bad. It's all I've felt, from the beginning, from the day I met her, to the day it happened and even more when we saw her again. And I'm done. I don't want that anymore. I don't want to feel this, I don't want to *feel* anything, let alone for her!"

"Eric…I'm sorry."

"And the fire, the building, this shit"—he gestured to the scars on his arm—"all of this is another reminder of how I fucked up. She could have died because my feelings got in the way."

213

My chest tightened.

"But she didn't."

"No, thank God, but I will not make that mistake again. She can never know. Understand?"

She nodded and my heart sank. Tears welled in my eyes before I could register them falling. I'd heard enough. God, I couldn't do this.

I shot out of the hallway and rushed down into the common room. I walked as fast as I could, evading their rapidly nearing footsteps.

I made my way up to the ground floor and took a sharp left and pulled open a door to what I was sure was a service stairwell this time and not the way to Kieran's room, and quickly shut it behind me. Swatting away the tears I rushed down the stairs and took another door out.

Following that corridor down, I found myself just outside the artificial garden I'd seen from afar. Off to the left I spotted Kieran sitting on a park bench with a book. As I stopped by the glass doors, he looked up at me with a smile and then that smile quickly dropped when he saw my face.

He got to his feet and walked over, opening the door.

"Everything alright?"

"Sure," I muttered, following him in. "Peachy."

"How's your arm?" he said, changing the subject, obviously tactful enough not to press the matter.

"It's perfect, thank you."

He nodded and led me down to the park bench he'd been sitting at.

"Eric?"

"He's fine too." I tried to keep my voice even.

"Considering what happened, he's lucky to have Corteza exonerating him."

"No shit."

We fell into a comfortable silence and I kept reminding myself to stop thinking about Eric and what I'd heard.

After about half an hour of sitting beside Kieran while he read his book, I'd had enough. I shifted and he caught that as his cue to start on the small talk. I reciprocated, only until he launched into a very detailed explanation about how the artificial garden's irrigation system worked.

"Look, I'm sorry, I'm not the best company right now, I think I just want to head back to my room. I shouldn't have bothered you. I'm sorry."

"Sure, got it. I'll walk you back. And you didn't bother me. This book is painful. No idea how I'll ever finish it."

"Thanks." I tried to force a tight smile.

With minimal talking, he led me outside and back into the hallways, down the familiar lifts and into the familiarity of my own area. Kieran led me to my door.

"This is you." He nodded to my door. "Just remember to stay away from the south side and everything else will lead you back to the common room."

My brows knotted. "Why?"

"It hasn't been used in years, it's old, unsafe in places, most of the security cameras and perimeter lighting are busted so they have patrols going out there to make sure everything's Kosher."

"Oh."

"But you don't have to worry about that, the doors are usually locked. They keep the corridors and the small walkways around the perimeter open for maintenance but even they're fenced off. That's about it."

"Good to know." I nodded with a smile. "Thanks for walking me and I'm sorry for being shitty company."

He chuckled. "No problem. And I understand. I'll catch you later."

Watching him disappear down the hall, I let myself in and let another long breath out.

Great. I was alone with my thoughts. Again and again, they escaped from my grasp and wandered back to those green eyes.

I sighed toeing my shoes off and slumping into the bed.

I turned my attention to the bookshelf, stretched my arm out for a random book, and started reading.

Chapter Eighteen
The Breach

I knew without a doubt that my aim was to help the Ceoran, those who were soldiers and those born to the council with royal blood flowing through their veins. I still didn't know how I knew that or how I was meant to achieve it, but baby steps seemed to be the way to go.

Whether my memories ever came back or not, I knew in my heart that this was why I was here, it was what I was born to do, and I would do whatever I could to get it done. Maybe I was over being a nobody, maybe I was done with being on the run. Whatever the reason, I was just glad to have a purpose even if it was in this weird, supernatural world I'd been thrust into. I was still scared, and the thought of taking all of this on made my whole body break out into a cold sweat. But I had to be brave. That's what Dad taught me, at least I thought he did.

Once I managed to shake the last shreds of sleep away, I showered, changed into something a little less boring than I was reduced to, and stopped in front of the mirror admiring the well-fitted green sweater and black jeans. That same feeling of overwhelming yearning shot through me when my mind decided to throw up more memories of me and Eric standing in front of the mirror here.

He'd done a lot and he'd been through even more. The angst that was constantly written on his face wasn't just easily forgotten, not even with my memories being wiped.

I sighed. I knew that with Eric's actions, the sacrifices he and I both made, that we could make the Council see what we were worth, whether he was with me the way we were before, or not. I just had to work out how.

I peeled my gaze from the mirror and found myself sitting at my desk staring at the large folder Kieran had given me. *Better get started.*

As I skimmed through the first few pages and made my way to the heavily highlighted sections, I started to get an understanding of what Kieran and I were working on. There was one passage beside which I'd made a buttload of notes.

The Class Division rule was enacted by the Elders in past generations. It was created in order to maintain a level of compartmentalization should the Ceoran become compromised. If there was a mixed couple in a romantic relationship and an attack on the Ceoran compound took place, it is feared that the Ceoran soldier would be compromised in the effectiveness of their role. They might choose to protect their partner rather than complete their duty to protect the High Council.

A flurry of emotions raced through me. I squeezed my hands around the bulky folder and ground my teeth, reminding myself to stay on track. This was outrageous. Duty was ingrained into everyone here, hell, even I remembered it when I wasn't meant to remember a damn thing.

I closed my giant folder with a huff and read through mine and Kieran's notes. Despite the rage I was left feeling confident. I knew what I was doing now, and Kieran had been actively pushing the *fairness for all* angle from his side while I was gone. Along with his parents who had been on the Council for years, we'd made some leeway. Apparently, I'd also managed to convince someone in power, out near the Canis Major constellation, that we were all equal and all lives were worth being saved. It seems my position here on Earth meant something to them.

That made me force back my own feelings about what was going on because, as cliché as it all was, the universe depended on it. It was still ridiculous, I could still barely get my mind around it, but it was starting to sink in.

So, today, all the Council, Ceoran, and life-changing stuff that had occupied my mind for the better part of three months would be put aside. I was going to find Eric, talk to him and see what came next, because as far as I could tell, everything stemmed from the supposedly relationship we 'never' had. But first, I had to get ready, I had to do something important, something that couldn't wait.

***

"You're being a baby."

"Maybe." I shrugged, toying with the nail polish on Emelia's side table.

All that big talk about seeing Eric and seeing what came next fizzled out in a puff of smoke when I saw Emelia and her vibrant eyes that reminded me too much of his.

My bravado was gone, and I was wussing out.

Luckily, she was too busy pouting in the mirror attempting to get the perfect line around her lips to notice.

As she kept talking about the miracle of makeup and how lost she'd be had it all been wiped out along with Saks, I rolled my eyes.

I sat on her bed in yoga pants and a sad excuse of a T-shirt that didn't even fit properly while she looked like a model in her form-fitting jumpsuit and heels. Where was there even to go around here dressed like that?

I should have kept the green sweater and jeans on. Damn it.

"I really think you should talk to him," she said, turning from the mirror, presenting her face. "Does this look okay?"

"It looks great, so did the last four colors." I opened a perfume bottle beside the bed and sniffed it, snorting as the liquid puffed in my face. "I don't have anything to say to him."

She dropped the red lipstick she'd settled on into her small purse and gave me a look.

"Sure you do. Tell him you love him and that you want to be with him."

My eyes widened, and I was sure they were about to pop out of my head.

"What?" She laughed, taking the perfume from me and spritzing herself. "You think I don't see the way you ogle him? You might not remember your time together, but you sure seem to be feeling it."

"I don't ogle," I snapped back, quickly feeling my cheeks heating up. "And I'm not having this conversation with you."

"Good, because it's weird and gross." She grinned.

Sighing, I leaned back against the hundred cushions adorning her bed and frowned. "How long have you and the soldier been together?"

The smile from her face disappeared and she sat. "A few months, I don't really know if it's serious or not yet."

"You don't feel that strongly about him?"

She toyed with the cuff of her green sweater before meeting my eyes again.

"Before James, I was dating this wonderfully beautiful girl called Zoe. She was my everything. I knew before she even asked me out that we would be together forever." Her eyes coasted across the room and landed on a small, framed photo of her and a blonde girl. They were hugging, a brilliant laugh adorned both their faces.

"I'm so sorry."

"Zoe was lost in the first wave a year ago. She was running the ground operation and I was second response. Her team stood no chance."

"You look really happy there."

She nodded, casting a faraway look at the photo. "Anyway, that was a long time ago, I don't like to dwell on past memories."

"Funny about that," I mused. "It's the one thing I wish I had."

She ignored the offhanded comment and resumed getting ready.

"You should talk to him. That's why you came here right? Looking for my brother?"

"Maybe. But he's made it clear that he's got no interest in me."

"Did he say that?"

"No."

"Well then?"

"He's got someone else." I shrugged. "As if he wouldn't have moved on in that time."

"You're not talking about Mariana, are you?"

When I didn't reply, she straightened up in her spot and grimaced.

"Please tell me you're not."

The name hurt my ears, it sounded like nails on a chalk board. Pretty, sparkly, and perfect nails. I didn't remember her but inside,

221

somewhere deep down where the hidden memories lay, I knew who she was.

How does she always know where he'll be? It's like she has a homing device on him. Creep. She probably does.

"My brother can be a total idiot at times, but he's not stupid."

"Why would he be stupid? She's tall, she's pretty...her hair is nice."

Emelia's brows shot up. "You're pretty, you're not the tallest girl around, but your hair is nice."

"Stop talking."

"You're being a baby."

I rolled my eyes.

"Besides, she's not his type."

"How do you know?" I shot her a look. "Maybe this whole mind wiping deal has changed him; he seems pretty broken up about it. People change."

"They do. But this hasn't changed. Trust me, I'm his sister. I know these things even though I really don't want to."

And when I remained quiet and skeptical, her penetrating stare made me think she was about to throw her purse at me.

"Trust me and go and talk to him. Please?"

Once I was sure she wasn't going to attack me with her makeup, I shook my head and folded my arms across my chest.

"Are you seriously doing that right now?"

"What?"

She mimicked my action. "You look like a child whose mom just told her she can't have any more candy. Now get up."

I did.

"Will you please go and talk to him?"

"Yeah. Fine," I conceded. "You just want me gone so you can see James."

I ducked and narrowly escaped the wrath of her shoe. A smirk quickly found her lips when I stuck my tongue out at her and escaped her room.

"He's in Boardroom 2, on the ground floor, don't forget!" she shouted just as I slammed the door.

As I left, James arrived. He tipped his chin and then disappeared into her room.

***

I'd spent a good fifteen minutes looking at myself in the mirror. Somehow, I'd managed to smooth my hair into a pretty side braid and even found a soft blue sweater to pair up with black skinny jeans, and I'd traded my sneakers for a pair of cute, low-heeled boots. These were Emelia's and that in itself made me nervous. I had literally thousands of dollars of clothing on me.

There was no way Mom would have ever let me spend that much on anything that wasn't a laptop or phone.

Tugging on the sleeve, I admired the outfit; it was a huge change from the usual yoga pants and hoodie combo I'd been accustomed to and the finishing touch was the makeup she'd let me borrow. Yep. I was proud of the work I'd done.

After a few more moments of silent deliberation, I nervously left my room conscious that it was getting late. *What am I doing?*

Once I'd made my way down to ground, I forced a tight smile every time the council members I'd come to know waved as I walked past them.

It had been about two weeks since Emelia and Eric brought me here and, in that time, I'd met some nice people, and some not so nice ones, and even got to know Emelia better.

The betrayal was still there in the back of my mind which kept reminding me not to get too close, but overall, the things they'd both done for me, and explained to me, started to chip away that anguish. I didn't agree with it, but I could kind of understand it.

Had it been me, I wondered what I would have done.

I couldn't take the moral high ground on this one, because each time I asked myself that question, I seemed to come up with the same answer. I would have done the same thing he had.

Some things came back to me, things like who always ate all the communal bread and earned a chastising from the supplies lady. I also remembered the compound's training facilities and how they favored actual hand-to-hand training versus the dummy and punching bag method.

"Hi Alex!" A young girl I'd seen around the compound jogged by with a group of fourteen- or fifteen-year-olds, training up as new recruits. I waved as they ran past, jumping out of the way. They were heading outside; it was still light out, but the night was rapidly approaching. The large, panoramic glass windows which looked to be made of solid, bulletproof glass circled the room leading out into the courtyard which was surrounded by the polished, concrete walls that kept us safe.

Dodging two more groups, I sidestepped through a small doorway and entered a large hall with a set of glassed-in offices.

"Okay, *Boardroom 2,* where are you?" I said to myself as I walked past room after room.

Boardroom 4 came up to my left which meant it would be a couple of rooms down.

224

As I neared, a heavy feeling in the pit of my stomach drew my attention. It was strange, and I could have sworn I'd felt it before, I just couldn't figure out when.

It was like that feeling you get when you really don't want to sit through an exam because you tried to cram the night before and you knew you'd fail miserably.

Then it slowly came to me, it was the same feeling I had when I walked up on Eric and Emelia arguing. Something I shouldn't have heard, something that would hurt me if I didn't stop and turn back now.

It was as though the feeling, whatever it was, was warning me of something.

Ignoring it, I walked past another empty meeting room and then stopped abruptly when I spotted Eric inside the glassed walls of *Boardroom 2*.

He was just where Emelia said he'd be, but he wasn't alone. Oh no. He was cozy in the company of one very handy brunette. His face was all over hers and his hands—I didn't stay long enough to see that.

Briskly turning I stormed back the same way I came only this time I rushed past wordlessly whenever anyone tried to speak to me, and at some point, I even ran into Kieran and told him to leave me alone. I felt a pang of hurt as soon as I did, but that hurt was nothing in comparison to the pain I felt seeing Eric with *her*.

Stupid, stupid Alex. What did you think? You were going to be his girlfriend?

I immediately felt childish—we weren't together, he didn't owe me anything, but damn it, I felt my ego crumbling into an unrecognizable mess.

When I shoved the next door which failed to open, I practically ploughed into it and shrieked. I stepped back and rubbed the sore spot forming on my shoulder. The realization quickly hit me when I saw that I was on the south side garden of the compound, the side I most definitely shouldn't have been on.

My eyes darted from one direction and then the other, every hair stood on end and my heart rate tripled.

I continued down and tried one more door. This one worked.

The door led outside and as I stepped through, the wind blew right through my light sweater, chilling me in an instant. I wrapped my arms around my chest, squinting my eyes against the piercing cold.

The rest of the compound grounds were serene and even the twenty-foot wall was polished and easy on the eyes. This wall was rusted where the concrete met the sleepers, and there weren't any guards in these lookout towers like there was everywhere else. Kieran wasn't kidding when he said it was old. This looked ancient.

An uneasy feeling started to build and spread through me as the same heart-stopping feeling reared its head. Deep in the pit of my stomach I felt dread building, creeping into every vein and infecting it. A breath got stuck in my throat as a subtle shift in the darkness drew my attention and then my blood turned cold.

The few working lights fixed to the wall began to flicker and as I slowly turned my head, my eyes followed each of the dying globes. One by one they dimmed then blew, plunging everything into darkness.

The steel began to rust, creeping along the wall as the sleepers began to rot and then, as the tendrils of death crept closer and closer, my stomach twisted into tight knots and the temperature started to drop.

They were coming.

I didn't stick around to see if I was right.

I ran.

Adrenaline pushed me, keeping me on my feet, keeping me moving. I chanced a look back as I ran through the unfamiliar territory. I didn't see them, but I felt them. I didn't know how, but Reapers were inside the compound.

Chapter Nineteen
Breaking Protocol

My heart was in my throat as I ran, not daring to chance another look back. This was bad news; a breach like this could be detrimental for the whole compound and everyone inside its walls. If they did some serious damage here, it could take years to rebuild, if they could at all.

The fear in the pit of my stomach doubled. I ran along the perimeter fence until I reached the fenced-off area that separated the dodgy south end of the compound and the new end. It took little effort to scale the fence and jump to safety. It wouldn't stop the Reapers though. I paced myself and took several deep breaths as I continued running. When I neared the familiar walls I spotted the young girl from earlier with two friends, sitting in the outdoor area.

"Run!" I screamed, ignoring the confused looks they cast at me. "Get help!"

As their eyes shot up to me and over my shoulders, I watched as they unanimously understood what was about to happen and fled inside to safety.

We were under attack.

Beyond the safety of the glass doors I saw the young girl alerting the men inside; they were safe and if I could hold them off long enough, I could make it too.

Swallowing the tightness in my throat I stopped and spun on my heel, ready for whatever was coming.

One way or another, they weren't getting past me.

Whatever fear I had before was now replaced by courage. I had something to protect other than my life. There were young kids inside, vulnerable and exposed in the compound grounds, not to mention all the sick people in there.

I stepped back a few feet, forcing myself to think back to all the lessons my *parents* taught me. Be brave and be strong. That was their motto. We could fight whatever came if we were brave and strong.

My muscles tightened as I faced down the blue-eyed demons. No matter what I'd told myself, I didn't feel so brave or strong. Unsteady breaths came hard and fast as I looked from one Reaper to the other.

My stand-in parents succumbed to them, regardless of their skill, so what hope did I have? I was so far from the person I should have been that I stood little chance against the Reapers.

I wanted the other Ceoran here with me, I didn't want to face this alone, I didn't want to face this at all. I didn't want to die.

Three of them stood tall, inching toward me, their pale blue eyes glistening from the fluorescent spotlights above. This wasn't how I pictured my death. I thought I'd overdose on Twinkies or die of old age surrounded by a hundred dogs and the man of my dreams, not outside in the cold, alone and terrified—despite my mantra.

One of the Reapers with particularly pale skin stepped forward, its face contorted into a sickening grin. My stomach churned as the other two began to laugh beside it, the shrill and unnatural sound filling my ears.

"Why are you so afraid, child?"

229

"I'm not a child," I spat back. *Great. What a good remark.*

Its lips quirked into a mock smile.

"We won't hurt you, all we need is the Map."

"What are you talking about?"

As it stepped toward me, I stepped back. And with each movement, my brave face was slowly slipping. Was no one coming to help? Was I really going to die out here? Then, like a slap to the face, the reality of what they were doing dawned on me.

They were protecting everyone inside because what was one Ceoran lost in the grand scheme of things? I was a Chancellor, but that's all. Surely there were other important royals to protect. What was one dead?

The gates engaged and large bars dropped directly along the glass windows I'd been admiring earlier, sealing the compound from the outside walls with a loud thud that echoed entirely too loudly.

My eyes snapped back to the Reapers when I realized that I was on the wrong side of the bars.

"Don't you know how these things work, princess?"

Refusing to give in to their taunts, I tightened my fists and stepped back, looking around for any form of escape.

Much to my dismay, there was nowhere to go. Of course there was no escape. These walls were built to keep people in and Reapers out, yet here we were.

"They won't risk a dozen soldiers for one little Ceoran."

But I wasn't just an ordinary Ceoran, was I? That's what they'd all said. Confusion tore through me. Was it all a lie?

Or maybe it was a tactic the Ceoran employed, maybe they were trying to keep my anonymity. To the Reapers, I was a nobody—guess that was the silver lining, right?

But one of the Reapers didn't look convinced. Its twisted face turned in my direction, almost questioning what the other Reaper had just said. Maybe it knew more? That thought chilled me. If that was true, I had nothing protecting me.

Inside, behind the glass, behind the steel, I heard muffled screams and shouting. I didn't want to look, I knew one of the voices belonged to Emelia, maybe even the young girl I'd seen around a couple of times, and somewhere deep down, in my irrational heart I also hoped that Eric would be there. Worrying, trying to get to me, but that part of me was naïve, just like the part of me which thought I'd somehow get out of this alive.

I had to do something. I wasn't about to hand them a fresh meal on a silver platter. I didn't want to become that girl on the park bench in Times Square. I didn't want them remembering my face like that. I grit my teeth, getting ready to make a run for it. If I managed to get past them, at least a few yards, I'd have a shot and at least I'd make them work for it.

Readying myself, I moved back about to sprint off and as I did, bright spotlights came on blinding me momentarily, drawing my attention to the roof behind the Reapers. Eric's eyes quickly found mine and the determination in them gave me back whatever courage I'd lost.

Two more soldiers appeared on the ground behind the Reapers and their pale orbs locked onto them, confusion coloring their pasty skin.

"Alex, run. Now!"

As the Reapers darted toward the two soldiers, I pulled my eyes away from Eric and weighed up my options—stay and probably die or run. I did as he said.

The cold air whipped at my face with each step making my eyes water, but I kept my attention on the bars up ahead. As I got closer, Corteza and Kieran raised them up.

My eyes narrowed in confusion as Kieran started to wave his arms frantically, but whatever he was trying to tell me was lost as a heavy, bone crushing weight smashed into me, sending us both to the ground, the impact shattering my wrist. I screamed as the pain ripped through my arm and into my stomach. I was certain I was about to throw up.

The weight on me shifted and flipped me over onto my back and then there was darkness. An immovable mass pressed down on me, its hand clamped tightly over my mouth and its pale, haunting eyes burning through me. If I thought the pain in my hand was bad, it was nothing compared to what came next.

I screamed, the sound was muffled and cut off as the Reaper pressed down harder.

Endless waves of energy were being pulled from me.

My body jolted up into the air a few inches with each convulsion and then landed lifelessly against the concrete beneath.

Somewhere off in the distance I heard Eric call my name, but the salvation never came. The frantic tone cut through me, but he wouldn't get to me on time.

The waves of energy continued to leave me.

The kind of pain that came was the sort that made your breath stop in your lungs and dry up your throat. Small, painful attempts of breathing were the only thing I could focus on, that and the way my body burned, lighting up at every nerve ending.

Biting down through each convulsion I begged it to stop but it wouldn't. It kept coming harder and with more force. Wave after wave made me scream, only I knew the screams were in my head. I felt the rest of my body, but nothing worked, I couldn't move my arms or legs, I couldn't fight back—the Reaper was winning.

It was pulling my essence from me, sucking everything it could and as each wave continued to crash into me, I felt the blood struggling through my veins, I felt my heart slowing like everything inside me was being ripped apart. And then it dawned on me, this is how every single person that had succumbed to them by whatever means, left this world.

Not in a peaceful sleep, not in a comfortable bed, but in pain, afraid, forever etching their agony into the world they left behind, in a burst of lasting energy that would forever be imprinted into the very soil they died in. Mom was taken out by a blade but what came next, I imagined would have been the real hell, the same one I was in now.

Drowning in an ocean of pain I forced my eyes open coming face to face with the Reaper's blue ones. Almost as though it was surprised, it stopped what it was doing and looked down at me with childish awe; the paleness in its contorted face made me sick. I didn't waste any more time analyzing its expression, instead I forced my fingers to move. Every tiny bit of movement was agonizing, every inch I managed tore through me.

With more effort than I'd ever given anything in my life I bit down on my molars and forced everything into the motion, knowing I needed to regain control of my body to survive.

After an epic battle with my mind I felt the sensation ripple through my fingertips and then white pain exploded across my vision as I moved the broken hand.

Choking back a gargled scream I stopped and attempted to move my other hand. When it finally shifted it took everything inside me to lift it up and wrap it around the Reaper's wrist.

Its arm snapped back, breaking contact with me, the same look of confusion contorting its face. Not giving it a moment's reprieve, I watched on in shock as Kieran tackled the Reaper off my body.

My arm dropped limply to my side, and that was it. That was all the energy I had left. I couldn't move my head, but my eyes darted in the direction of the fight.

Where were the other two?

Kieran wouldn't be able to fight all three of them. Before I could attempt another agonizing move, my whole body exploded with pain; the adrenalin must have worn off because I was feeling everything full force.

Swallowing the bile in the back of my throat I forced my eyes open. Eric appeared above me, his gorgeous face twisted into agony, smears of blood smudged across his cheeks. *Is he hurt?*

I wanted nothing more than to touch his face, to feel his skin underneath my fingertips. Funny how everything was forgotten when death was calling you into its murky depths.

"Don't try to move," he said quickly, pressing his hand down on my shoulders. "Take care of the bodies," he shouted to someone outside my line of vision and then his eyes were back on me.

"Alex?"

My mouth dried up. I swallowed the roughness in my throat, and it felt like I'd eaten a bag of cotton wool.

"Can you hear me?"

All that came out was a low moan and then my body was lifted off the ground and we were moving.

Eric's eyes found mine every few seconds and then we were inside, the bright lights above blinding me.

"You're going to be fine, Alex. Just stay awake."

I wanted to answer him. I just wanted to tell him how afraid I was.

"I need you to keep your eyes on me. Don't fall asleep."

As much as I wanted to keep staring into those emerald pools, I couldn't.

"Get everyone out. Now," he barked as he pushed a door open with his foot. As it swung shut it closed off the sounds from outside, and among the sea of voices Emelia yelled at someone to let her in, but no one did.

"You need to stay awake, Alex. It's so important that you don't fall asleep. Do you understand me?"

He left my side for a moment and the light in this room dimmed to a comfortable level and then he was back beside me. My body was tingling like I'd just had a bad case of pins and needles, and I barely felt his touch, but I couldn't mistake the gentle squeeze of his hand around mine.

But what really worried me was the fact that I was starting to grow weaker as the minutes passed, and with each of those minutes, his touch was becoming fainter.

For hours we stayed silent. A doctor came and went several times, I recognized him as one of the doctors I'd seen talking to a little boy in the huge hospital area.

When I zoned out, Eric got up and gently shook my shoulders. I hadn't managed to move or get up, but coherency was quickly returning.

Tears rapidly filled my eyes and spilled out of the corners. Is this what death was? Is this all that was left?

After what felt like another hour going past painfully slow, the doctor came back. Tests were run, questions were asked—blink once for yes and twice for no—Eric and the doctor argued and then he was gone.

My core…my core is left, and they've taken everything else.

This wasn't how my life was meant to go. I squeezed my eyes shut and let the tears fall.

As the door closed leaving me and Eric alone, I heard him let out a long breath and sit down, the chair beside the bed groaning under the pressure.

"God, Alex. Why didn't you get out of there?"

Why? Because those Reapers would have killed the kids.

I didn't open my eyes, but I felt his gaze on me.

"What were you doing out there alone?"

Where do I even begin? Even if I could answer him, how did I tell him that it was my stupid jealousy that got the better of me.

"I'm so sorry," he said quietly. His voice was so raw it startled me.

Slowly, I opened my eyes and looked across at him. His head was buried in his hands. As he let out a disbelieving laugh, he shook his head like he wasn't sure how we got here. When his eyes found mine again, I quickly looked away when I saw the red rings around them.

Fresh tears spilled onto my cheeks.

How was I meant to be brave when he was pulling me down, drowning me in my own fear? I couldn't do this, oh God, I couldn't…

"Do you want me to leave?"

No. I wanted him to stay. I wanted him by my side, I wanted to have him here with me. I wanted to tell him this wasn't his fault.

But instead of all those things, I looked up at him and blinked once.

CHAPTER TWENTY
EXCUSES

Eric

Balling my fists at my side did nothing to settle the anger inside me. In fact, it made the rage stronger. Ignoring the whispers and stares I got as I walked past, I moved through the halls with my eyes dead ahead.

There was no way the Reapers got in on their own. This whole place was just short of being a fortress even at the weaker parts of the compound perimeter. I slipped outside past the stationed guards, knowing exactly where their blind spots were, and stepped into the shadows keeping close to the walls.

They were still treating the courtyard like a crime scene and everything was cordoned off. I ducked under a strip of yellow tape and kept moving. This wasn't of interest to me, this isn't where they came in, there had to be something else. I grit my teeth as images of Alex rushed through my mind, haunting me. The way she ran and then stopped to face up to them, to protect the younger kids. Anger forced my jaw to clench. She was so brave, probably stronger than she believed.

But I should have been quicker, Kelly should have been quicker. She'd been in so much pain and I couldn't do a damn thing about it. They were monitoring her room and if they saw me heal her, they'd lock me up and I couldn't afford to let that happen.

Swallowing the bitter taste, I kept moving, keeping my eyes ahead, scanning every inch of the wall, searching for something out of the ordinary. I looked across the grounds and off to my right I spotted the dark alley leading to the south garden. Corteza said the girls had seen Alex running from that direction. I followed the dimly lit path and kept scanning the wall.

One salvaged light post stood at either end. The bare minimum they could get back up and running for the cleanup.

"What were you doing out here, Alex?" I whispered to myself as the path got darker and darker.

I grazed my fingers along the rough and unpolished surface of the heavyset gate at the very end of the alley. Just as I was about to leave, my fingers scraped along something which shouldn't have been there. I reached into my pocket and switched on the flashlight. Again, I drew my fingers over the marks, there were several scratches along the edge of the gate where the hinges were. I narrowed my eyes looking up and down the length of the structure. They were on every hinge and I'd bet it looked the same on the outside. If someone wasn't specifically looking for this, no one would have ever noticed it.

Curiosity piqued, and I reached into my pocket, happy that I'd brought the earpiece. Hitting the button to redial the last station, I waited for Corteza to answer.

"Corteza."

"It's me. Meet me at the south garden," I said.

"What's going on?"

"I'll explain when you get here, sir."

Corteza disconnected the call and I turned off the flashlight slipping back into the shadows cast by the moon above.

In the few minutes it took him to leave the operations room and cross the compound grounds, I waited patiently against the wall, keeping my eyes open for any signs of movement.

Off to my right, footsteps drew my attention.

"Raine?"

"Here, sir."

"What's going on?"

"Take a look." I motioned to the gate.

Corteza pulled out his own flashlight and shone it on the spot I pointed to. He inspected the marks closely, studying the pattern around the hinges. A few moments later, he straightened and holstered his flashlight.

"What's your take on this?"

I looked back at the scratches. "Someone was trying to weaken the hinges."

"To let the Reapers in?"

"It makes sense."

"Coincidental that Chancellor Wynter was out here tonight?"

"I doubt it."

He knotted his brows considering what I'd told him. Her safety and her protection were of utmost importance to all of us.

Only a handful of us knew who she really was. Alex's parents, me and Emelia, and of course, Corteza. None of us would risk her like this.

"Someone else must know." I looked back at the general.

"Ideas?"

"You know what I think."

"Aside from your personal history with Ashfield, has he given you any other reason to believe he could do something like this?"

"I don't know, sir."

He sighed. "They've failed this time, but that doesn't mean they won't try again."

"Agreed."

"Keep your eyes on her."

"I will, sir."

"And Raine?"

"Sir?"

"I don't want to see any more theatrics with you and Ashfield. Am I clear?"

"Yes, sir." I nodded, averting my gaze.

"Good, because there are only so many excuses I can use to cover your ass. The Council are getting shitty as it is."

"Got it, sir. No more theatrics."

Corteza gave me a quick nod and left.

I turned back to the dark path and looked around.

Where was she hours ago?

Hoping the path would shed some light, I reached the door she would have taken and stopped, looking at the map on the wall.

Deciding that going straight through was the best idea, I followed the corridors until they led me to a service stairwell. I stopped again and looked at the map—I could go up, or down to the living quarters. That didn't seem right, so I headed up the stairs wracking my brain about where she'd been.

None of this made sense to me, she knew about the south side, she was warned not to come out here alone.

Stopping briefly at each floor I swept the level and then something crossed my mind. She could have been with Emelia and then left when James came around. That had been much earlier, I was sure of it.

And I was—. I stopped midway up the staircase. I was with Mariana.

No. My stomach jumped into my throat. I took the rest of the stairs two at a time and rushed toward the lifts. It felt like it took forever for the slow beeping of each floor to finally alert me to BG7. As soon as the doors released me, I sprinted the rest of the way to her room.

Banging my fist against the door, I ignored the soldier from the next room who told me to go to hell because he couldn't hear his TV.

A few loud knocks later she pulled the door open and the look of surprise was quickly replaced with anger. She slapped her hand against my chest shoving me back.

"What is your problem?" she shouted. "I came by the hospital three times and you wouldn't let me see her."

"Was Alex with you earlier?"

"You're a real ass sometimes, you know that?" She shook her head scoffing as she leaned against the frame.

"Just answer the question, Emelia."

"Yes," she answered firmly. "She was with me until James came."

Damn it. I pushed past her into the room and ignored the way she snorted at me. She shut the door and followed me in. I glanced at the clock beside her unmade bed.

"Where did she go after she left?"

Emelia sat on the edge of her bed tightening her robe—it was cold in here. It always baffled me as to why she slept with the fan on and the heater blaring. It made no sense.

241

"I told her to stop sulking and go and find you."

Fuck. "You told her where I was?"

"Yeah, not like she would have found you without me telling her."

"Damn it."

Emelia's face hardened, and she was back on her feet in an instant.

"Oh. My. God. Eric. Tell me you weren't with Mariana." Her voice shot up two octaves.

"I shouldn't have been," I managed.

"Damn straight you shouldn't have."

"No, you don't understand. There was no way she would have known I was there. I was working, looking into Alex's past, looking up leads."

"Okay, so how did she find you?"

"I don't know, that's the problem. You didn't tell anyone else about that room?"

"Of course not, Eric."

Shoving her clothes aside, I dropped into the chair beside her desk.

"What were you thinking letting her stay?"

"She just turned up and I—"

I was an idiot. Plain and simple.

She sat down in the other chair. "God, Eric. For once in your life you should have listened to your heart and not your—"

"You think I wanted her there?"

"Did you tell her to leave?"

Letting out a long breath, I closed my eyes, massaging my temples. She was right. I didn't tell her to leave. Christ.

"You chose to push Alex away; *you* chose to keep her in the dark so don't go around acting all righteous like you've done nothing wrong."

My sister really knew how to say what she was thinking, and she didn't care how it came across. Sometimes I needed it, other times—

"Alex cares about you," she said with a firm persistence.

"I'm not good for her."

"That's not just for you to decide."

"She's in this mess because of me."

"Because you kept her in the dark."

"I wiped her mind!"

"She asked you to!"

Neither of us would back down. I couldn't win this argument with her and when she turned away, I cursed under my breath.

Emelia groaned, returning her attention to me. "Look, I know this is hard, but you have to be honest with her, and yourself."

"I don't know how to do that."

"Start by getting your head out of your ass. Did you even see that Alex got hurt when you and Ashfield took down the meeting room?"

My eyes widened. How had I missed that? I felt the blood drain from my face.

Emelia shook her head and wrapped her arms tighter around her robe. "Doesn't matter. Kieran took care of it; he's not as strong as you but he managed."

Damn it.

"You have to make things right. Because if Alex doesn't recover from this…"

"She will."

243

"If she doesn't, I don't care that you're my brother. We're done and you're on your own and see how far that gets you when you need your ass bailed out for punching one of them."

The graceful simplicity of that statement stunned me into silence.

"I need to get some sleep. You do too. You look like shit, Eric."

She was right, about everything. I got up and left her to sleep. I had to make things right. But first I had to see Kieran and set some plans into motion.

Chapter Twenty-One
Trust No One

Alex

I was getting sick of crying. I could say that I was on the verge of hysterically losing it. My mind went from anger to denial right through to sadness and back to anger again, and so the cycle went. I couldn't feel anything. I couldn't move anything. I couldn't speak. All I could do was cry.

Over and over. I'd alternate between hyperventilating and needing to be sedated. I hated that I'd become such a coward.

Emelia came to see me, the doctor showed up a few times and even Kieran stopped by. Eric was a no-show. I hadn't seen him since I'd told him to leave. That coupled with this crappy situation I was in was just the icing on the cake.

It had been three days, and still, nothing worked.

The little sensations I kind of had after the first few hours were completely gone now.

Phantom pains the doctor had said.

There was no improvement, not even a tingle.

The doctor kept telling me things could change, Emelia kept insisting they would, and I lay in silence, staring up at the five thousand small dots on the ceiling I'd counted at least seven times.

"You're going to pull through this," Emelia whispered, sitting beside me. I didn't feel her pull my hand into hers, but I saw it.

She repositioned herself and sat on the edge of my bed and held up a brush.

Before she got started, a tap at the door drew her attention then the loud hiss of the hydraulic door opening made her curse.

"What are you doing here?" she hissed.

I couldn't turn my head to see who she was talking to but the feeling I got from whomever it was made my stomach tumble into knots and I knew instantly that it was Eric.

"I can help her," Eric said.

"You need to get out."

"I've heard that Silus can—"

"Don't you say that name. That monster destroys everything it comes by. You think trying to reason with a Reaper like that will end well?"

"I have to try."

"You have to get the hell out."

A moment of silence passed between the siblings.

"I'm sorry. You're right," Eric said quietly.

Before Emelia could say anything else, the door hissed open and then whirred shut again.

What is he talking about? What could Silus do? The name made me shudder. It was pure evil and made terror fill my veins. I couldn't imagine what Eric was thinking about doing.

Emelia was back at my side. "I thought I'd braid your hair, I could even do your makeup, you kind of suck doing the smoky eye." She held up a palette that had far too much glitter to belong to a grown up. "I can put this gold on you, it would really suit your eyes."

If I could tell her to leave me alone, I would. But unfortunately for me, I was doomed to this pity party with no way to get bailed out. Her fingers gently tugged my hair free from underneath me. She ran her fingers through the long blonde strands and smiled.

"My mom used to braid my hair like this, it used to help me sleep."

Like I needed help sleeping. It's all I did. What I did want was to know why Silus came up.

She gently ran the brush through the ends and paused for a moment, looking down at me.

"You're going to get better. You'll see."

I looked away.

"Alex."

Keeping my eyes glued to the ceiling, I squeezed them shut when another tear trickled down my cheek.

"Eric knows you saw him with Mariana."

That drew my attention back to her, though she kept her eyes down and busy with my hair.

"It was a mistake, he knows that. She really means nothing to him; they had a one-night stand ages ago and she became attached. God, I'd told him a hundred times he had to stop seeing her. She's bad news. She runs around with the Ashfield boys—there're like three brothers in a clan—she's probably sleeping with them all. But he insists she wasn't even meant to be there, she kind of just turned up. I don't know if I believe him. But he has no reason to lie."

My heart began to race.

"What if she just sprung him, you know? I mean he's a guy and well, she's hot."

I focused on keeping myself calm, freaking out now wouldn't do me any favors.

247

"He swore to me that she came on her own, but my question is, how did she know where he'd be?" He only told me about that office, no one else used it after hours and I told you right before you went, there's no way someone else would know."

No. They didn't. Someone set him up. The same someone who knew I'd see them and run, probably the same someone who sent Eric on a wild goose chase because it was *fun.* Ashfield.

It was all too convenient, too coincidental. I took the corridors down myself, though, but thinking back to it, most of the doors were locked. I didn't think much of it then, but it made sense now. Someone set us both up.

Emelia looked at me and then stopped and I really hoped that she figured it out since I couldn't tell her.

"What is it?" she asked.

If only I could work out some way to tell her.

She looked around and then got up and rushed over to the table. She grabbed a pen and pad and scribbled something down.

"Blink toward the word."

"Yes" I blinked to the *yes,* she'd written down.

"Did you see the Reapers come in?"

No.

"Did you see anyone else?"

No.

She sat back down and paused for a moment.

"So, someone let them in before, someone who knew you'd be down there."

Yes, exactly, someone who ensured all the doors would be locked and I'd have no choice but to go down the corridor and out into the yard.

"Eric doesn't trust people here; he didn't want us to bring you back. We need to be careful, Alex. I don't know who we can trust."

I looked at the pad, she'd only written yes and no on it. I needed to tell her more. I kept flicking my eyes to the pad and eventually she got it.

She wrote the alphabet on it and turned the pad slightly and started going down the list with her pen.

When she reached "K" I blinked.

"Okay. K," she said and started with the alphabet again.

This time when she reached the "I", I blinked again, and she moved back to the start quicker this time and this time when I stopped her at "E", she got it.

"Kieran. Tell Kieran?"

Yes. Yes, we have to tell Kieran.

"I will be back, okay?"

I blinked to confirm that I was okay with that plan. As she left, my heart sort of settled down into a comfortable rhythm and I felt some sort of semblance that things might be alright.

Chapter Twenty-Two
The Escape

Eric

Kieran agreed to meet at the head of operations. Luckily for me, our conversation three days ago went well, more or less. He didn't completely shut me down but there would be a bit more convincing needed.

It took me less than a minute to locate Kelly. He was in a heated conversation with Corteza which immediately set me on guard.

When I came closer, they both stopped talking and turned their attention to me.

"What's going on?" I asked.

"Kelly was expressing his disdain at the handling of the rescue mission," Corteza said.

"You mean the mission where we almost lost the most valuable Ceoran in existence?" I tested.

"We had to wait until we were certain we could get her back," Corteza said.

Biting my tongue I nodded, earning a look from Kieran. I quickly shook my head hoping he'd get the idea that this was a conversation for later.

He did.

I turned my attention to the general and stood tall. "Lance Cor-poral Rain is keeping Chancellor Wynter company and has asked for some privacy from all medical staff this evening."

He looked at me skeptically.

"Is there any particular reason?" Corteza asked.

"Lance Corporal Raine has advised me that she would like to help Chancellor Wynter with some…feminine stuff."

Both Kelly and Corteza shifted slightly and cleared their throats.

"Very well. I will advise the medical staff."

"Thank you, sir," I said. "If it's alright with you, sir, could I have a word with Kelly?"

Corteza nodded and left us alone.

"Feminine stuff?" he said.

"Don't even ask. It's the only thing I could think of."

"Well, it worked. The old man turned green."

I shielded a grin. "Knew it would."

"How is she?" he asked.

"That's why I'm here."

"I figured. Let's speak in my room."

On our way toward his quarters we were eyed suspiciously by no less than a dozen Ceoran, some of which were my people. I shook my head. I'd never understand how easily people just con-formed even when they knew it was wrong.

"Do you want water or anything?" Kelly asked when we were secure inside his room with the door shut and locked.

"No thanks."

Kelly took a bottle from his minibar which I saw was only stocked with milk and water now. Damn we'd had some good times before everything went to shit.

He must have thought the same.

"Remember the time old man Locke chased us down the hall?"
He chuckled, taking a seat at his desk, leaving me the other arm-chair.

"Guess he didn't approve of underage drinking."

"Like it matters. Look at the state of the world."

"It wasn't this bad then."

"No, but it wasn't like home either." He frowned.

"No. It wasn't."

"So, have you had a chance to think about the idiotic plan you came to me with?" he asked.

"I still want to take her away from here."

"No."

"I didn't even explain everything."

"There's nothing else to explain, Raine. That's a bloody stupid idea and you're smart enough to know that. I told you then and I'm telling you now."

"As a Council member?"

"As a friend."

I scoffed earning a scowl.

"Mature."

"She's not safe here," I said, ignoring him.

"And in the state she's in, she's not safe out there."

"I can keep her safe."

"Not alone you can't. This goes against everything we've fought for, Eric. Everything we've tried so hard to change. You do this now, we undo all of that."

"Then help me."

"I can't do that"—he frowned—"you know I can't."

"Can't or won't."

For a moment we looked at each other in silence. That was answer enough for me.

"Fine, glad to know where we stand." I shot to my feet and reached the door before he followed me.

"Eric, wait."

"Just keep everyone off my scent until I'm gone. Could you at least do that?"

He knotted his brows but nodded. "I'll make some calls and get you backup."

"Fine." I slammed the door shut behind me and headed back to my room.

Damn the rules to hell. Kelly didn't want to come with us but at least I knew he would help here. I was going to get Alex out and he was going to help make that happen.

When I reached my room, I wasted no time getting my things together. I grabbed my coat and satchel and threw them on, rushing out of the door, quickly shutting it behind me.

Speeding up my pace, I took a few extra turns and ensured no one had followed me. It was quite late for anyone to be wandering the halls, but it didn't mean someone wouldn't be.

I rounded the corner to Alex's room, picked the lock and quickly packed a few things she might need. Before I left, I stopped and scanned the bookshelf. My lips quirked into a smile as I reached for *Vampire Academy* and shoved it into the bag, and then I was out.

As I moved toward the hospital wing, I stopped abruptly around a corner and waited for the two figures at the end to move. I couldn't make out who they were, but they looked like nurses. They weren't coming from Alex's room since Corteza had ordered all staff to stay out this evening but they were in my way nonetheless. I had to wait it out.

Just as I was preparing to make my move, a firm hand grabbed my wrist and pulled me back.

"What are you doing here?" I hissed at Emelia.

Her eyes were wide, but she kept hidden. "I was looking for you and when you left your room in a rush, I followed you down to Alex's room and then here."

"Stay quiet and come with me. You might as well make yourself useful."

She gave me a pointed look but nodded and followed me.

When the two nurses moved on from the end of the corridor, we moved. When we reached Alex's room I stopped, turning to my sister. "Stay here and keep watch."

"What are you doing?"

"I'm getting Alex. We have to get out of here."

"We're leaving?"

"Not you, Em. Me and Alex."

"I don't understand," she said.

"I don't have time to explain."

"Make time."

"It's the only way I can do my job. They're going to keep coming for her. I have to keep her safe."

"What about me?"

I smiled. "You're more than capable of looking after yourself, and besides, you've got James to back you up if you need."

"You hate James."

"No." I shook my head, pressing a kiss to her forehead. "I just hated the idea of my baby sister getting close to another soldier. I don't want you to go through that pain again."

"Oh, Eric."

"He's a good man, Em. I trust him. Which is why I want you to stay here. He knows what's going down and he's going to keep you safe."

"You told him about Alex?"

"Not the important stuff, just enough to explain why we need to get her out."

"What about Kieran?"

"He's helping too."

When a painful silence filled the usually light air between us, I gently squeezed her shoulder. "It was a mistake coming back here. We never should have returned."

She opened her mouth and promptly closed it, looking over my shoulder to the door separating us from Alex.

"Someone's been setting us up from the minute we got here," I said.

"I came to tell you the same thing. Alex wanted Kieran to know, maybe they suspected someone before, maybe it was in her notes. I don't know."

"I'll find out."

"You're going to heal her?"

I nodded.

"Eric, that's a huge task."

"I know. I can do it," I said. There wasn't much time, it was now or never. I looked at Emelia, hoping that she'd understand and deep down, in that pure heart of hers I knew she did. She stepped aside, taking guard by the door letting me slip inside.

Alex was asleep, but her eyes moved rapidly. My stomach twisted into tight coils knowing what she was going through, knowing that it was my fault.

Pain was something I was familiar with, on an intimate level, so I never wished for anyone to experience the soul consuming horror where you didn't know where the pain began and where it ended.

Carefully moving around her, I unhooked the monitors ensuring they were switched off and wouldn't alert anyone that she was "flatlining."

I took a moment to read through her chart. The last update stated that some feeling was starting to come back. When I moved back to her, I gently sat down beside her and swept my fingers across her cheek until her eyes fluttered open.

"We don't have much time, but I need you to trust me, Alex."

Her eyes focused on me.

"I'm getting you out of here."

She blinked once, and I smiled.

"I have to take these syringes out, it might hurt, okay?"

Again, she blinked.

Carefully I grabbed some cotton wool from the supplies closet, pressed it over the needle, and slowly pulled it free from her arm. A single bead of blood pooled at the site, and I stuck a Band-Aid over it.

"Okay, one more." I moved over to her other arm, the one which was set in a cast up to her elbow, and slowly I pulled that syringe free, then placed another Band-Aid over it. "We're going to go down into the parking level, and then go out the same way the Reapers came in."

She squeezed her eyes shut and then looked up at me.

"I swear to you, Alex. I will fix this."

Turning back to the supplies, I threw a few things into a bag and shoved it into my satchel. Along with that, I loaded Alex's small bag of possessions and zipped it all up.

I looped my arm under hers and gently pulled her up into a seated position then, sweeping my other arm under her knees I pulled her up and against me ensuring her head was comfortable against my chest.

I tapped twice at the door and waited for Emelia to give me the all clear.

When she pulled the door open, she quickly looked up at me and then Alex. Her eyes were full of tears, but she smiled giving Alex a quick hug.

"Take this. She'll be cold." She pulled her coat off and draped it over her.

My throat tightened. This was the right thing to do, I knew it as soon as I looked down at Alex.

Taking the stairs down to the parking, I kept as silent as I could and kept her as steady as possible. The last thing I wanted to do was hurt her even more. I cringed when I saw her squeeze her eyes shut.

"We're nearly there."

She kept her eyes closed.

The door to the basement came into view and my heart raced.

As Emelia opened it and let us pass, I smiled at the small bag of supplies tucked behind a laundry basket, just where James said it would be.

"Good luck, Eric. Be careful and please, please look after yourself too." She pressed a kiss to my cheek and one to Alex's, then she shut the door, locking it from the other side.

I moved to the far corner and eased us both down. I leaned back against the wall and pulled Alex to me, holding her up against my chest.

"We have to wait a few minutes then we're out of here."

I sucked in a deep breath and carefully put my hands down beside us.

"I know you're wondering how all of this even happened. I'm sure you figured most of it out for yourself. I have no doubt Ashfield's involved, if not directly responsible. But why?"

I took another deep breath and continued.

"Mariana and I, it's nothing." I didn't even know why I'd said anything. "She isn't important to me. I wanted you to know."

Knowing I'd say something else I probably shouldn't, I kept my mouth shut and remained silent.

The rest of the wait was filled with quiet breaths and the occasional scurry of a rat somewhere among the forgotten supplies. When a series of taps at the far end of the basement sounded, I eased Alex back into my arms and got up.

"Time to go."

When I reached the door, I gave it a quick tap with my foot and stepped back. James came inside and helped me with the bags.

"Come on, man, we gotta hurry."

I nodded and followed him out and into the garage.

His eyes darted around the dark, keeping tabs on everything. He was a highly strung individual but that's what made him deadly.

He had the highest number of kills aside from Corteza; the man was a machine. Having him on our side was a blessing and I really owed Emelia for it.

In the beginning, I'd given him a hard time, but he was there when Lana, Emilia's ex-girlfriend, passed away and he always took care of Emelia and always came through when she asked him for help. I meant it when I said it, he was a good man and I trusted him.

"Thank you." I shook his hand as soon as I'd seated Alex inside the truck he'd sourced for us.

"Just be safe, brother," he said.

"Will do."

He closed the door and tapped the top of the roof sending us off. I navigated the truck through the garage and took it up the winding ramps which felt infinitely longer than ever before and finally led out to the barren desert.

The night was cold and flurries quickly covered the windshield before the wipers took over.

As the exit came into view, I floored the truck and sped down the road. This was it. Now or never. The gates swung open just as planned and I passed through without a second thought.

I looked across at Alex and swore to myself that I would make this right.

I had to.

I couldn't fail.

Chapter Twenty-Three
The Map

Alex

My hand burned, inside and out like I was on fire. The bones were creaking and settling, and I was hyperaware of every nerve in my hand firing at once with each bump and turn of the car. I squeezed my eyes shut. That's all I could do. Eric turned his attention to me every so often and grimaced when he did.

After what seemed like the longest drive of my life, he pulled over and from my limited field of vision I figured we were at some sort of cottage.

"I'll be right back," he said and then disappeared.

When he returned his face hardened when he looked at me.

A line in his jaw spasmed before he slammed the door shut and walked round to my side. He pulled the door open and very carefully moved my arm over his shoulder, and as gently as before, he slipped his arms under my knees and pulled me up to his chest.

I was numb and I felt everything all at once. I didn't know if I was falling apart from the pain or if I'd completely lost it. I wanted all of him and I wanted none of him. Every part of this situation was chipping away at my composure. I never thought I'd feel like this about anyone.

Eric wasn't just anyone though. As much as he tried to deny it, I saw the same look in his eyes.

He pushed the door open with his foot and walked us both in. From what I could see, it looked to be in good condition, nothing was broken or damaged, and then when the windows and doors sealed shut with high-tech metal bars it all made sense. This was a facility created by the Ceoran, this wasn't just a house.

Silently, he walked over to the bed and kneeled, laying me down against the soft mattress. If I could have groaned in comfort, I would have. This was the best bed I'd been on in years. The pillows were like clouds and my head sunk right into them.

Eric disappeared for a moment and then he was back. He took off his coat and rolled up the sleeves of the long black sweater he had on.

"Do I still have your trust, Alex?"

I blinked once without even thinking. *Yes, Eric, I trust you and I wish you'd trust me enough to tell me the truth. And tell me why you would risk speaking to Silus.*

"If this doesn't work, I need you to know that I'm sorry for what happened, I'm so sorry for what you've gone through, for what I've done."

If what doesn't work? What are you about to do?

He moved toward me and sat on the bed, the mattress dipping beneath his weight. He gently cupped one hand around my broken wrist and the other on my cheek and then he closed his eyes. Before another thought could form, I felt a rush of pain and then white noise filled my ears to a point of agonizing static.

And then, there was nothing.

***

There were moments in my life where I thought that things were bad, that things had been sucky. One of those moments was in tenth grade when Aaron Somers broke up with me. I thought my heart would stop beating that day—he said he'd found Carissa Lockhart more appealing. I knew it was only because she was rich and had a pool at home. Whatever.

But now, after experiencing the pain of my parents' death and watching the world turn to ash, learning that my pit of made-up memories were all fake, and I wasn't even human, I didn't think there'd be anything worse…and then I was proven wrong.

My insides screamed for my body to move but nothing did. My hand pulsed with pain I'd never felt before, and worse than that I couldn't seem to shake the persistent thought that something else was wrong. I almost laughed at that point, what else could possibly be more wrong than what was happening to me?

Despite that, I still felt it. Something kept creeping up on me, telling me to get up and move, telling me that I had to get up, had to act.

Something was wrong, something bad…

So, as far as my sucky situations in life went, this was high on my list.

My body didn't want to respond, my arm tingled when I tried to move it but it barely budged. That was still better than what it was like yesterday before Eric brought me here, before he asked me to trust him. And then it hit me—it was Eric.

Eric wasn't with me; I didn't feel his presence beside me, not like I had before I passed out.

I forced my eyes open through the confusion and looked around. Again I tried my body and this time it worked. My arms kind of spasmed beside me and I managed to somehow roll over onto my side and pull my legs up to my chest even though they felt like they weighed a ton.

"Eric?" I croaked. My voice sounded like I'd been screaming at a concert all night. "Where are you?"

No answer. My stomach twisted into a tight coil.

Flipping over onto my stomach, I crawled up to my knees letting out a long breath. If someone told me last week I'd be doing a mini celebration about being able to crawl, I would have probably laughed. Now I was counting my blessings.

Two days earlier the doctor had pretty much told me there was nothing he could do for me; today, I was recovering, learning how to use my limbs again.

The nagging feeling intensified. Pushing it aside, I crawled to the edge of the bed and looked around, my eyes falling on a figure laying on his stomach on the floor. My heart leaped into my throat.

"Eric?"

I hauled myself over the edge and landed with a thump. Pulling my legs across the floor I dragged myself as quickly as I could.

The lower half of my body seemed to still be waking up but as long as my arms worked, I was grateful.

"Eric?"

There was no response.

His face was turned from me, but his arms were beside him in a way which suggested that he'd tried to take hold of the bedside table but fallen. The lamp lay shattered beside him along with a note pad and pen.

I reached his side and gently pressed my hand to his arm and shook it. Nothing.

"Eric, wake up."

Maybe he'd just fallen asleep. I'd seen Kieran get exhausted after he healed me, maybe Eric was just tired since it was a bigger job, but the logical reasoning inside me said no—Eric wouldn't have taken a nap on the floor.

As carefully as I could, I took hold of his shoulders and turned him on his back. His head lolled to the side and remained motionless.

Oh God. Oh God. Oh God. He was completely still and positively unresponsive. I had no idea what to do. *Should I try CPR?* Would that have even worked? He didn't drown, he was drained of energy saving me, what kind of CPR would that even entail?

Instead of letting the fear control me, I moved closer to him as best as my body would allow and pressed my fingers to his neck.

Feeling a pulse, I let out a breath and calmed myself. At least he was still breathing, and his heart was still beating.

I closed my eyes and pressed my hands to his chest, aware of the hard lines of his muscles underneath the thin fabric of his sweater. I pushed that thought to the back of my head and focused on what I was doing.

Swallowing the doubt and taking a deep breath, I looked down at his still face and decided that I had to try. He'd risked everything for me, on multiple occasions, even if I couldn't remember them. My eyes landed on the scars across his arm and the ones across mine. I owed him my life.

I pressed my hands over his chest again and closed my eyes and began wondering if I had to chant or anything. I immediately felt stupid and shook my head. I didn't hear him chant, I didn't hear him whisper or say a word, all he did was press his hands to me. Surely there had to be a trick to it, but I didn't know what.

Damn it.

All I wanted was for Eric to be okay. I wanted to know that he didn't hurt himself to save me. The thought that he traded places with me made my heart sink, no one deserved to feel what I felt. I couldn't bear to have him go through it.

Tears formed rapidly and constricted my throat. I couldn't lose him, not when I'd just found someone, not when I'd lost my family, my whole life, he needed to be okay, *I* needed him to be okay.

As I clutched the fabric of his sweater, pleading with whatever god would listen, a subtle pulse of energy began to heat up under my fingers. My eyes shot open and looked down.

Nothing was visibly happening, but the feeling was growing— heat began to spread through my hands and just as I was about to break contact, a bolt of energy rushed out of my hand and shot into Eric.

His body jolted under my touch and then his eyes snapped open, scaring me half to death.

He gasped and spluttered, his hand shooting up to his chest and then he sucked in a violent breath and jolted upright.

Whatever just happened didn't feel like my energy, this was new. More powerful and far more intense.

I stammered backward and landed on my butt.

"Whoa. What just happened?" I breathed, holding my hands out, watching Eric stare at me like he'd just witnessed the birth of a unicorn. "Holy shit."

His eyes were wide.

"What did you do, Alex?" he croaked.

"I—I was like a human defibrillator...I Emperor Palpatined you!"

"How?" He shook his head, drawing my attention to his eyes. "How did you do that?"

265

"I don't know," I answered truthfully. "I just, I put my hands on you and that happened."

He clutched at his chest and shook his head breathlessly.

"You've never been able to do that before."

"What?"

He looked across at me. "In the past. We all have an ability to heal, even on a basic level, but your healing powers never evolved. That was some serious shit, Alex. Powerful, almost as powerful as me."

Kieran had said that Eric was one of the strongest healers and he'd also said that if you didn't have the gift it didn't suddenly appear.

"Maybe I just didn't know how…"

Shaking his head, he got to his knees and slowly moved toward me, holding his hand out.

"No. We tried, we did all sorts of tests, you couldn't do it."

"Am I…is something wrong with me?"

He didn't answer. Instead, he helped me to my feet holding me steady since I was still walking on jelly legs.

"Sit down," he said quietly, moving me toward the edge of the bed.

When I sat, he kneeled in front of me and ran a hand across his jaw.

"Are you okay?" he asked finally. "Do you feel okay?"

"You saved me."

A weak smile formed on his full lips, but it didn't reach his eyes. "Are you feeling lightheaded?"

"No," I kept my eyes on his. "I'm fine."

And I really was…that in itself begged the question, how? How was I completely unaffected when I just did that but Kieran and Eric both took on the pain when they healed?

He retrieved a small bottle of milk from the minibar just the same and handed it to me, before getting one for himself.

I looked at the bottle in my hand before looking up at Eric.

"I need to ask you something," I said.

His brows rose into his hairline. "Okay."

"I overheard you saying something to Emelia about Silus."

"It was stupid."

"What was it exactly?"

Eric drank his milk, quietly looking over at me. When he set the empty bottle down, he sighed. "I wanted to ask him for help. I wasn't sure I could bring you back."

"Silus would do that?"

"For you and for a price."

I drank my milk down in a couple of gulps and then found his eyes again, processing what he just said.

"What do you mean for me?"

"Because you're a Chancellor."

"No." I shook my head. "That's not it. Just like no one should have risked their life for me at the compound. No one gets risked for another, no one is that important. Not even a Chancellor. So, I'll ask again. Why did you risk your life for me?"

He looked at me like I'd just punched him in the gut.

Eric drew in a long breath and stood. For a moment, I thought he was going to bail. Instead, he sat down beside me on the bed and lowered his head, raking his hand through his hair.

"You came across the Map when you were reading up on your notes?"

Slightly recalling that I'd skimmed over that subject, I nodded hoping that this pop quiz wouldn't show how little I knew. "It's some kind of Map that leads to a sparkly bridge and the Cradle of Esper—the source of my, *our*, power."

"What else do you know about it?"

"Not much." I shrugged.

"In short, yes, the Map leads to the Bridge. The Bridge is how the Karatoi travel from world to world. It's where they plant our DNA."

"Okay?"

"So you already know that everything in the universe is made up of a series of complex formations, we're no different. Atoms and molecules come together and make a molecular chain. Every so often, a molecular chain that is more exceptional than every other, is created. This special Ceoran is linked to the Map, well, more accurately, imprinted with it."

"I think I'm following."

"There was a rumor, centuries ago, that the Reapers learned how to harness the blood of Ceoran who were implanted with human DNA, eventually making a sketchy version of Ceoran in order to blend in and infiltrate us. Obviously, they don't look as human as we do but they're still just as powerful as they are in their true forms."

"Wait, true forms?"

"There's this extra part…"

"Of course, there is." I pinched the bridge of my nose.

"Ceoran and Reapers don't always look *human*. We, and they, can create a form of light, in our case, or dark matter in theirs. That's when we're strongest. If we need to fight, that's how we're best equipped."

"So, we're like balls of bright light?"

"Something like that. It's like a dissolution of our cells, less complex than the human bodies we have to don."

"This is crazy."

"The power we have in our true form is completely raw and unfiltered, the Reapers want to get to the Bridge so they can cross over the realms we're protecting and the only way they can do that is in our form."

"And I'm guessing they can't do that."

"No, not without Esper and some complex DNA splicing."

"Where does the Map come in?"

"The Map would show them how to get there and how to accurately splice their DNA. They would also need the power that Esper holds—without that they wouldn't make it very far."

"And, I'm starting to think this Map isn't a map."

He pinched the bridge of his nose and looked at me. "It's a person."

I let out a long breath.

He turned away from me and lowered his head. "Every few thousand years, when we're at risk, a Ceoran is born and they're the Chosen…"

"The exceptional molecular chain…"

My mind doubled back to the last night at the camp: the Reapers were searching for a Map, they were desperate, they killed everyone they came into contact with for it, didn't even bother feeding. That said a lot and it made me shiver.

"This Ceoran is chosen to be the Map. Their mind is imprinted with the coordinates of the Bridge at birth. No one else knows the location of this Bridge, only the chosen Ceoran and the Karatoi."

269

My mouth went dry. "Why would they do that? Plant their Map in someone?"

Eric kind of cocked his head and then looked back at me.

"If the Karatoi become compromised, someone needs to know how to protect the Bridge."

"Like an insurance policy."

"Exactly."

I pressed my fingers to my lips, trying to digest all the information. "Does the chosen Ceoran, the *Map,* get an insurance policy? Like someone who looks after them. Do they even know?"

Eric's body tensed; I'd seen that sign before. He was getting uncomfortable.

"Eric?"

"Normally, yes. The Ceoran knows, and yes they have someone who's assigned to protect them at all costs."

"So, they're pretty important then."

"They're the most important Ceoran, Alex. Their protection, their life, is the only thing that matters. Above any rules, above any laws."

And like a kick to the gut, the wind was knocked out of me. A choked breath caught in my lungs as Eric's gaze held mine.

It all made sense.

For you and for a price.

Eric and Emelia following me in the woods, keeping me safe, being my *guardians,* having advisors in the Elders.

That's why they risked soldiers for me. That's why they risked everything for me. He'd told those Reapers in the woods all those months ago when we first met that he would speak to him when he was ready. *Is this what he meant?*

A dizzying rise of panic swept through me, making me double over. I was about a second away from throwing up.

I pressed my hand over my heart, about to hyperventilate, and when Eric moved toward me, I shoved him back. I shook my head over and over, ignoring everything he was saying. Whatever he tried to tell me, I didn't want to hear it. I stumbled to my feet and rushed away from him.

It didn't matter where I went, I just had to get away, I had to breathe. I couldn't catch my breath. I tripped over my feet as I ran through the cabin and into the bathroom where I slammed the door shut behind me. My knees failed me. I crashed to the floor and threw up all over the tiles.

I gave myself a few moments to suck in some air until I finally pulled myself to my knees and expelled a long, painful breath.

"Alex?" A loud succession of knocks on the door reverberated through the bathroom. "Please open the door."

Words got stuck in my throat like the breath that wouldn't budge.

"Alex."

"Go away."

"No," he said firmly. "Your mind is adjusting to the memories, and the information. You're in shock."

"I need you to leave me alone."

"Not going to happen."

"Get away from me, Eric!"

"I will not leave you alone. You need to breathe through this."

"Go!"

I raked my fingers through my hair and replayed every moment that somehow now made sense. My memories, my family, my life in the woods, alone. It was because of who I was, who I had always been.

But I didn't feel like a leader. I felt weak and afraid. I couldn't be what he was telling me. I wasn't even old enough to buy a drink. I didn't even know how to cook properly!

"Alex…" His voice was laced with a painful edge and it cut me deep. "Please come out."

How did I go out and face him now?

"Please," he said again.

Sadness crept through me and before I knew it, another bout of annoying tears was streaming down my face, and even worse than that, my body was moving on its own, opening the door, yearning to be near Eric and shoving all the logical thoughts I had aside. I cringed when he pushed it open and stopped, his eyes taking in everything.

Without another word, he crossed the space between us, and I let him tug me toward him. He wrapped his arms around my shoulders and swept his hand through my hair.

That was all it took to break down the last shreds of my crumbly wall. I cried shamelessly into his sweater and let him hold me. What else was I going to do?

Chapter Twenty-Four
Her Guardian

Eric had brought some food, a change of clothes, and a pouch full of things from my room.

Gently prying my bag open, I smiled when I saw the tattered book in the bottom beneath my Yankees cap and a few snacks. When I didn't feel so sick, I would definitely devour them. Until then, I would settle for reading. I pulled out the *Vampire Academy* and smiled. He really did know me.

As I mindlessly flicked through the pages, a small picture fell out.

I frowned when it disappeared under the oven. I kneeled, stuck my hand under it and felt around. Once my fingers touched the edge of the photo, I dragged it out and froze. It was a picture of me and Eric, a very personal one.

His hand was cupping my cheek while the other had obviously taken the picture of the very intimate moment. We were lost in a kiss, the kind that makes the earth feel like it stops spinning. I couldn't *remember* feeling that way but my entire being felt it through to my bones.

I turned the picture over in my hand and instantly felt the reactive tears forming. In elegant, black handwriting there was a simple, definitive phrase written: *Asteraki Mou, forever yours, whatever it takes.*

As all the air was stolen from my lungs, I leaned heavily against the counter and placed the photo back in the book. Then I stumbled into the living room and sat down.

"Alex?"

"In here."

"You okay?"

"Fine."

He walked around the table where I was sat and stopped, his eyes narrowing and a dark expression forming.

"Can I ask you something, Eric?"

He glanced down at me and nodded.

"And please, don't lie to me anymore."

"Okay."

Breathing in deeply, I looked up at him. "You told me we were just friends, right?"

"Yes." He folded his arms across his chest.

"You were pretty convincing," I whispered. "I mean I started to believe it despite the way you look at me sometimes and the stupid dreams I've been having, but then I found this." I pulled the photo out of the book.

As his eyes landed on the picture, his face paled several shades.

"Where did you get that?"

"I found it in here. Obviously, you knew I loved this book because you knew me really well, that's why you brought it here, isn't it?" I said. "Do you know what's written on the back?"

He swallowed hard and ran a hand through his hair.

"Because I'm pretty sure this is your handwriting." I flipped the photo in my hand and read it out loud. "*Asteraki Mou, forever yours, whatever it takes.*"

He blew out a long breath but remained quiet.

"It's what you called me, back at the farmhouse. You remember?" I tossed it on the table.

His gaze followed as it slid across the slick surface and stopped just in front of his hands.

"It's Greek, right? Means, *my star*?" I said quietly. "I racked my brain for days trying to work out how I knew it and where I'd heard it. I know now, I'd heard it from you."

He remained abnormally unresponsive. Not even the rise and fall of his chest made a muscle on his body move. Eventually, he reached out for the photo, his hand trembling as his gaze found mine.

"So, what was it then?"

"Alex—"

"Don't." I stopped him midway. "Don't you dare shut me down."

He looked down.

"Was all of this because it was convenient, because it was your job and getting close to me was what, fun, easy? Spend a lot of time together, late nights?"

"No." He shifted, standing firmly in his spot. "God no."

"Then what?"

"I was your guardian; we became friends and then…"

"Then what?"

"Then I…"

"What, Eric?"

"Then I fell in love with you."

I closed my mouth and everything else on the tip of my tongue just vanished.

Finally, his lips parted, and he looked down at the photo.

"I fell in love with you and I fucked everything up from that moment onwards. Because the Council came after me, I jeopardized my position to watch over you, I jeopardized your position on the Council, I fucked everything, Alex."

There weren't enough words to describe what my heart was doing in that moment. It was somewhere between wanting to explode and tighten into a tiny ball and implode. Eric looked across at me, those full lips tightened into a straight line.

"But I won't make that mistake again because what I want doesn't mean shit if they get to you," he said. "What I *want* is irrelevant. You matter and that is all."

And that was the nail in the coffin. He'd admitted it all but then he just threw in the selfless spiel. How could I push him on that? I couldn't. Everything was riding on the Reapers coming for me because they wanted the Map, and as long as they did, they'd keep coming for us.

I couldn't do that. Anger started to simmer inside me.

How long could I keep running, hiding in the shadows, and letting others risk themselves for me?

I ground my teeth as Eric retreated into the kitchen.

When I heard the sound of the tap being turned on, I quickly packed my things. I found my sneakers and stuffed my feet into them before snatching up the bag of supplies he'd taken from the compound basement and slung it over my shoulder.

I snatched a gun from the black duffle and moved.

Being alone wasn't an issue for me and I knew how to look after myself. I didn't need him risking any more for me, guardian or not.

In the kitchen, I heard him open and close a few cupboards and start plating the food.

I shoved the door open and snuck out.

I didn't wait to hear whether he was coming after me, nor did I take any chances. I sped through the coming darkness faster than I'd ever run in my life, leaped over upturned trees and dove under low-hanging branches, all while my eyes darted around the unfamiliar surroundings trying to work out where I was.

Figuring I must have still been in the same state, I kept moving in the same direction. I'd been out here long enough alone to know where to go and where to avoid at all costs. So as a clearing came into view, I diverted my direction and ducked into the cover of trees.

The moon was peeking over the horizon playing hide and seek with the canopy of clouds sweeping the sky. The little light it shed over the vast blackness quickly descending was enough to guide me toward a dark path which seemed to have been reclaimed by nature.

Markers which once guided tourists down its shady walkways now lay hidden under a cover of moss and insects which had made it their home.

I tightened my hold on the bag over my shoulder and wrapped my arms around my chest keeping as warm as possible. It was so hard getting used to the odd weather changes.

The creatures of the night were also oddly quiet sending chills all over my body. Finding a small rock formation in the side of a hill, I dropped the bag at my feet and looked around. There weren't any footprints that I could make out, nor were there any telltale signs that anyone had been here in the recent weeks.

The branches were still holding onto small green leaves, evidence that the Reapers' destruction hadn't made itself known in these woods...yet.

It would do for tonight. Tomorrow, I'd work out where to look for Silus and how to end this. Eric wanted to barter with him to save me, I wanted to barter with him to stop this war.

Granted, it wasn't my best thought-out plan, but it was still mine. Still something *I'd* chosen to do and not some crap I'd been born for.

As I settled down against the cold rocks in the tiny cave, Eric's eyes haunted me and a restless night quickly found me.

Chapter Twenty-Five
Silus

Eric

My hands shook and balled into fists at my side. How could I have been so stupid? How did I think that she wouldn't work it out, that she wouldn't have had contingencies in place when I had?

I threw my belongings into the bag she left behind and slung it over my shoulder.

My breath caught when I noticed one of the guns was missing. Damn it, Alex.

I shut the door and stepped outside. It was getting dark quickly these days and it made me incredibly anxious to know that she'd be out there alone, with the Reapers hunting her. Anger settled in my bones; I should have just told her the truth from the start. I shouldn't have danced around and played along with the damn charade. I should have just told her how I felt and this wouldn't have happened.

Grinding my teeth, I pushed through the branches in my way and stopped when a fork in the path stared me in the face.

I breathed through gritted teeth and looked left and then right.

"Where are you, Alex?" I whispered to the cold night.

When nothing but the cloud of my breath spoke back, I forced my eyes shut and stilled. I concentrated on her, on the smell of her skin, the touch of her soft hands, the waves of her hair.

Slowly, fragments of her started to piece together in my mind— like a beacon, her energy pulsed and called to me.

Ceoran were gifted in many ways; some more skilled Ceoran could do things like this. Reach out to others, follow their essence or aura, read into their feelings and emotions, and I could do all those things.

Alex's mom told me it was because I was chosen to protect her and because I was the Chosen's guardian and keeper. In some cases, it helped, in others, I just wanted to shut myself off from the world. It was too much.

Three years ago when she told me, I was seventeen, I was just a kid myself. I was nervous as hell and terrified out of my mind but when I met Alex, all those worries disappeared. She was a fiery fif-teen-year-old who ran rings around the older Ceoran, we became friends immediately and a few years on, whether I wanted to admit it or not, I'd fallen for her, hard. I couldn't lie about that and I hated myself for lying now.

I thought if she'd forgotten about me and this world, she'd be safe, and then it went to hell. The Reapers found a slip in time and started their war.

Alex never stood a chance.

None of us did.

Hurrying through the woods, I stopped at each clearing and checked for footprints. Each one came up empty until one didn't.

My heart leaped into my throat. I crouched and looked around. A scuffle of some sort looked like it had taken place, three or four sets of large footprints scattered among the dirt and then, a smaller set, probably belonging to a female, rushing away.

I followed the smaller set and stopped abruptly. A slow, shallow breath escaped my lips before I could process what I was seeing and what it meant.

With trembling hands, I reached for the torn jacket, stained with blood. I recognized it immediately, it was Emelia's, the one she'd given Alex. The sleeve was ripped clean off. My heart rapidly kicked into overdrive meeting the fast pace at which my mind was throwing up scenarios of everything that went down.

I'd failed. I'd been too stuck in my own head to do my damn job. By trying to keep her safe by lying to her, I'd no doubt been solely responsible for whatever happened here.

Heat filled my veins making the anger rise to the surface quicker than I could contain it.

I clamped my jaw shut and got to my feet. I inspected the fabric for clues. When I turned it over and saw the small, precise hole in the back, a new sensation ripped through me.

Pure, unfiltered rage coursed through my body.

I closed my eyes and focused. Slowly, fragments of Alex's form started to come to me. I felt her fear, her desperation to fight and survive, I felt which way she went and along with her essence, a dozen Reapers, including Silus.

I dropped the jacket and homed in on the direction I needed to travel.

***

Alex

281

"You're afraid."

"Of course I'm afraid," I whispered, letting him draw me closer.

His hot breath tickled my cheek when he exhaled.

"Don't be, I'm here with you. You know I won't let anything happen to you."

"I'm not afraid for me, I'm afraid for you, Eric."

He raised himself up on his elbow and gently turned my face toward him. "Why are you afraid for me?"

"Because I don't want to lose you."

"Why do you think you're going to lose me?"

"Because you would die for me, right?"

He stiffened beside me and looked away.

"I know you, it's in your bones, Eric. You'd do whatever it takes, you would die for me without a second thought. I don't want you to ever have to make that decision."

"And it won't come to that."

"It will, one day, I can sense it."

Eric ran his hand over my cheek, pressing a soft, yet definitive kiss to my lips. There he let them linger and I wasn't about to complain.

I tasted everything between us; every touch, every breath was intoxicating to a point where I thought I'd stop breathing without him.

"Lexi, I'm not going anywhere. Stop worrying."

"I wish I could."

Eric slipped out of my grasp and the image shifted. His gentle gaze full of warmth and depth faded out and the same, awful vision replaced him. Those blue, shallow pools frosted over, and I jerked.

Shock woke me. I yanked my arms and the first thing that stole my breath was confusion and finally the pain. I groaned and quickly realized that I wasn't where I'd fallen asleep.

God, my head was pounding. Why couldn't I move?

Trying to get into a more comfortable position was a bad idea. I cried out, my back was on fire, a burning sensation was localized to the upper right part of my shoulder and it hurt something fierce.

My eyes darted from corner to corner and nothing but blackness stared back at me.

There wasn't another soul around, nothing moved, nothing sounded. I was alone with my ragged breaths and terrified whimpers. It was the unknown that worried me.

Fear coated my insides and squeezed my heart.

Where was I? Who brought me here? Why was I still alive?

All questions which burned inside me. Why couldn't I remember anything?

And then, as the newest realization formed, the real shit hit the fan.

My arms were tied above me. Thick, cold, iron shackles stopped any movement I tried to make, and to top it off, they seemed to be attached to some sort of cage. As far as I could tell, I was locked inside it like an animal.

An ugly mess of emotions quickly filled my heart.

"And she's awake." A rough voice sounded, somewhere, I couldn't tell where.

I glanced around in the dark.

"I hope you're feeling okay. You took quite a hit yesterday."

Yesterday? What happened yesterday? My head was fuzzy. I was in the cave, I'd fallen asleep despite my best efforts not to, then there were sounds…noises…someone else was there—

"I ensured my men didn't hurt you too much. After all, you're no good to us dead."

Who was speaking?

"You might be a little disoriented. That's normal, you should be familiar with the Clean Slate procedure."

My brain spiraled.

"We only altered a few small details; the rest is as you were."

"Who…who are you?" I stammered.

"In time," the voice said. "First I have questions for you."

"No," I said as firmly as I could. I was terrified out of my mind, but I wasn't ready to cower.

"No?" The voice laughed. "You don't even know what I'm asking."

"I don't care." God, the pain was slicing through me.

"Painful, isn't it?"

"What did you do to me?"

The voice bellowed again, a low, inhuman sound carrying through the dark and then, several high-powered reflectors came on, throwing the whole space into blinding light.

"Just a little bullet, nothing to cry about."

I squeezed my eyes shut, but the heat of the lamp burned through my lids simultaneously making my head feel like a fire prodder was being shoved into my brain.

Booted feet pounded against the floor.

Orders were barked out.

And my heart rammed into my ribcage.

As I shook against my restraints, tension inside me began building. What had I gotten myself into? *What is about to happen?* Where was I?

A jingle of keys drew my attention to my left. Oh no. I held my breath and stilled, not daring to move.

As the latch gave way and the door was pulled open, I felt another presence beside me. Instinctively, I jerked back. It took every ounce of self-control I had not to thrash out.

A rough hand squeezed my cheeks and pulled me up to my feet, my shoulders jarring in the constraints and I couldn't help the shout that came from my lips.

"Open your eyes." A different voice spoke. One that sounded less relaxed and chatty, one that sounded like it was annoyed that it was assigned to this job.

I tried to shake my head. I didn't want to see it. I didn't want to see the monster who was about to do God only knew what to me.

And before I could force another thought to the surface, a hard fist connected with my stomach, sending me crashing into the ground and another scream ripped from my throat.

"Open your eyes."

Cracking them open through the haze of tears coating my eyes, I looked up and my heart fell. A pair of crystal blue eyes surrounded by deathly pale skin looked back at me. The first voice belonged to this terrifying face.

A wicked grin formed on its paper-thin lips.

"What's the matter, Chancellor? Are you surprised to see me?"

Words literally failed me. I couldn't open my mouth.

Nothing came out. Those eyes haunted my dreams. Those eyes I'd seen a dozen times waking me in the middle of the night. Those eyes I could never forget regardless of the Clean Slate.

"You're Silus…" I breathed, barely above a whisper.

I'd come looking for him, I'd set out on a mission and now that he was staring me in the face, I seriously questioned what was wrong with me? *Why on Earth did I think this was a good idea?*

"I'm so flattered you haven't forgotten me," he said. "Sorry. That was a poor choice of words."

My heart cracked into a million pieces.

"When I heard what you did, asking them to wipe your mind. I have to say, I was shocked." He leaned against the cage, his hip resting lazily against the bar. "It was very brave, very noble of you. A true hero, one might say," he added.

I couldn't say a word.

Two figures moved behind him, drawing my attention over his shoulder. "And then, I was even more shocked when your reappearance at the compound caused some chatter."

"You have people on the inside." The realization floored me.

"Of course, my dear. How else do you think we were going to find you?"

"You were waiting for me."

"Yes. And it was only a matter of time until the siblings broke and brought you back to where I was guaranteed my answer."

"You knew who I was?"

"Not exactly. But I had my ideas."

"What do you want?" I looked up at him, ignoring the way my voice shook.

"You gave yourself away, you know?"

My eyes shot up.

"When you fought back at the camp with your guard dogs."

For a moment I couldn't breathe. I couldn't think.

"You gave away your anonymity. My soldiers were told that you were important in there, and maybe you knew someone who can help me. So, I sent them in for you, but then, lo and behold, they break protocol because you know who the Map is, don't you?"

He grinned and moved his body closer to my side of the cage, and I watched on as his hand moved to the side and up, gripping the chain that was connected to the restraints around my wrists.

"So, my dear Alexia, tell me who the Map is."

When I mustered a very weak, and very scared "no" he yanked the chain and forced my body up. Another shocked cry left my lips and he laughed.

"Location of the Map. Now."

I forced my head up slowly as fresh tears rolled down my face. *They don't know.* All I could think was thank God, they didn't know.

"Map, Chancellor Wynter, if you don't mind."

"I don't know."

"I don't believe you."

Silus remained silent for the longest time before he brought his face closer and yanked the chain again making me scream.

He smirked and released it. I slid to the floor, my knees barely catching me.

"I'm going to ask you one more time, nicely, before things get ugly for you—where is the Map?"

"I. Don't. Know."

"That's your final answer?"

I didn't bother with a reply.

"That's fine with me."

Too panicked to pay attention to what was happening, I failed to see that one of the Reapers was quickly coming toward me.

Before I could take my next breath, its hand tightened around my throat and in an instant, my world was transformed into pure darkness lit only by the blinding pain that surged through me.

The encompassing fear blocked everything else out and as each bout passed through my veins, a scream stopped short as my breath was stolen from me and I felt my heart slow, and then nothing…

Chapter Twenty-Six
The Fallen Angel

Eric

Something wasn't right. I felt a shift inside me, almost like something was breaking. I sped up my pace and focused on the feeling while struggling not to trip over my own feet.

I'd never felt anything like it. I walked, though each step felt like it was getting more and more difficult. About a minute or so in I started to feel sweat beading on my forehead even though it was close to forty degrees. I wasn't exerting enough energy to be breaking a sweat, and then my heart started pounding.

Careful not to trip on a rock, I stopped at the next tree and steadied myself. I clutched my chest taking a deep breath and let it out slowly.

This wasn't normal.

Something bad was going on.

My mind kept wandering back to Alex and those footprints. It could have been my worry for her, that would make sense...but it felt stronger than that.

My vision faltered and black dots kept interfering with my line of sight. I shook my head trying to clear my mind and began moving again, quicker this time. Maybe I was weakened from healing Alex, maybe it'd finally taken its toll on me like the Elders kept saying it would. But as another twinge of fear shot through me, I realized that it wasn't my healing abilities going haywire, it wasn't me at all—something was happening to Alex.

I swallowed the dryness in my throat and ignored the myriad of scenarios I refused to entertain.

She had to be alright because I still felt her presence, even though an insidious voice said that just because she was alive it didn't mean she wasn't hurt.

When I reached another clearing, I stopped and checked the surrounding earth—just like last time, there were more footsteps, further apart this time and the smaller ones disappeared. My stomach lurched. Maybe she'd gotten away and hidden, or maybe they got to her.

Yes, Eric. They got to her and this is your fault.

I bit down hard and followed the footprints through the wooded area until the trees grew sparse and the dirt covered more land. It was hard to make out in the dark, but there was some sort of structure up ahead. I knelt and took cover behind a smaller shrub. A large mound of earth resembling an embankment surrounded the entire perimeter with the building nestled inside.

Craning my neck to get a better look, I gave up when I noticed that the perimeter was also encircled by a large fence. I needed to get closer; whatever was hidden in there was going to lead me to Alex.

A movement off to the right caught my attention and I ducked, staying low and in the cover of shadows. Reapers. At least five or six, roaming around the building, and they conjured up a drone. Piece of cake.

Ducking lower, I dropped my bag beside me and rummaged through it. I fished out the tracker James forced me to take. He was always thinking one step ahead which was just as well. I didn't have time to wait for backup, I had to move now. I pushed the button and dropped the tracker in the shrubs, and then moved down the embankment taking my time, careful not to slip down the sheer drop. The whole damn place was built like a fort.

Nothing but getting her out was driving me at this point. Not only was it my job, my destiny as her mom had put it, but she meant a lot more to me than that. Admitting it made it hurt, it made it real and I couldn't entertain that right now. Right now I had to do what I was sent here for. I had to see her as my objective and not someone I wanted a relationship with. It wasn't possible then and it wasn't possible now. Not with the class division, not when she was so perfect, and I was just a soldier. My *destiny* landed me the job, my skillset allowed me to do it well.

So, focusing on the task at hand, I surveyed the building. It looked like an old jail from afar, one that hadn't been used for decades and only a more concentrated look at the perimeter security told me that was just a front. The building might not have been used as a prison anymore but it certainly wasn't abandoned.

The aging brick walls towered into turrets with small, rectangular windows dotting the walls every few feet or so. They were closed off by thick iron bars and by the look of the damage around them, I imagined they had been through some battles.

A quick glance around the surrounding landscape confirmed my theory that this had in fact been utilized recently as a shelter.

The trees directly against the brickwork were broken off at unnatural angles like something had pulled them apart with force, the earth was scorched, and the bricks smudged with something brown. I didn't need to get closer to know that it was most likely dried blood.

Pushing the possibility of how many humans died to make that much of an imprint on the wall out of my head, I assessed my next move.

Lifting my head, I looked across at the fence. There were several panels that had been patched which meant they were compromised. Ensuring it was clear, I made a run for it and skidded to a halt on my knees stopping just on the cusp. I found a section which had been rewelded and applied enough pressure to make it fracture. When the panel gave way, I slipped through and looked around for my next move. There was a rusted container with half of its walls rotted through. I leaped onto it, using the height to boost me onto the building. It took me little effort to scale the wall and reach the first barred window; I was thankful for my years of training, for the strength and stamina to do things most couldn't.

I took a moment to look through the bars and when I was sure I hadn't attracted any unwanted attention, I continued to the first turret and swung up, landing safely inside the open top.

My soft landing didn't draw their attention but the emergency lights that came on with my proximity did.

Shit.

Sirens started wailing all around causing the previously silent building to come to life.

I ran across the rooftop to a small arched door and threw myself in. As I started rushing down the round staircase, several Reapers started running up.

Not good, not good.

I gripped the railing and swung my legs over the balustrade and kicked the first Reaper, forcing it back into the one behind. Together they dropped, tumbling over the railing and falling down below.

I quickly scanned the area. Pipes from the ancient plumbing were exposed in the ceilings and the walls. I could use that.

The Reaper's pale eyes darted up to me. I ran down, hoping to make it to the next landing and prepared myself for everything they could throw at me. I jumped over the railing onto the second landing and swung from one pipe onto another as the Reapers down below followed me up. Damn it. When did they get so good? I released my hold on the pipe and prayed that I'd gained enough momentum to reach the other side. I landed with a heavy crash, but I'd made it. I continued along the platform reaching another pipe which led to the next landing all while fighting new Reapers at every turn. They kept coming and I kept fighting. The burn in my muscles intensified with each kick and each punch.

Commotion erupted below, and I was sure the Reapers had alerted whoever was in charge. It didn't matter now. I had to get to Alex. Enough games. I spun on the spot and as each Reaper neared me, I took them out. It wasn't easy work, but it wasn't as challenging as they once were to me. The years out there, learning to rely on no one but myself and my sister taught me a lot. It taught me how to maximize my own strength and how to fight on my terms.

I grabbed the next Reaper by the scruff of its neck and pulled it forward, slamming my knee into its midsection and then its face when it doubled over.

As each Reaper took me on, I employed the same tactic. Brute force and speed.

Once they were all down, I expelled a long breath and slowed my heart.

Damn it. So much for my stealthy approach.

I dusted myself off and ran down the remainder of the staircase, leaping over the railing.

Taking the next landing a little harder than I wanted, I hissed when my knee cracked against the hard concrete. I ignored the pain and pressed myself flat against the wall and looked down. So far so good. It appeared that I'd taken out the first response of Reapers and that hopefully bought me some time before the next wave came at me.

I crept along the grate walking by the empty cells paying attention to the shouting coming from the far right. They were coming. When I reached the end, I spotted several Reapers keeping watch down below and there, behind them was Alex.

She was in a cage, bound by her wrists which were attached to chains held firmly above her head. She wasn't moving.

"Kill the alarms!" I heard a voice yell.

Moments later the sirens were out.

I peered around the remainder of the floor I was on. The doors to the cells were wide open, each once-occupied room was filled to the brim with discarded barrels of oil and chemicals. Some were stacked to the ceiling with car parts and other mechanical stuff. If I needed to, I could definitely use them to fight.

Sweeping my gaze around the lower level of the jail, I made a mental note of the closest cell door and used the railing along the side of the wall to climb down. I paused for a moment to look back at Alex and sped up my pace—her head and shoulders were slumped forward, her long blonde hair was matted and wet and hung in messy strings across her face.

It dawned on me then, they were using Alex to draw me out and I had no choice.

Forcing myself to stop and think, I kneeled behind a pillar and looked around. I only hoped that Corteza was checking on the signal and would be coming soon.

294

I reached behind me and found two larger rocks and crushed them between my fingers. I concentrated on the rubble and with little effort the pile of crushed rock levitated out of my hand. I closed my eyes, focused on the material, and with a single thought I cast it outward. With full force the pieces flew outward, landing in several locations all around the prison, causing the Reapers who were keeping watch to rush away from Alex in search of the sound.

I made my move. Getting her out was all that mattered. If they made her talk it was game over for everyone.

Once I got close enough to really see her, my throat constricted— a fine sheen of sweat coated her whole body. She trembled faintly, and where her hair had stuck to her face, I noticed that it had done so with dried blood.

I moved quickly, picking the lock on the cage and proceeded to the shackles on her wrists. Once she was free, I caught her against my chest.

"It's okay," I whispered. "Can you hear me?"

She remained still.

I felt air shift behind me and at that point, I realized that I'd made my first mistake. I'd turned my back and that distraction earned me a sharp jab to my ribs. Crying out I held onto her as tightly as I could. When another jab threw me off balance, I lowered her to the ground gently. Before another hit could throw me down, I sprung to my feet and spun on the spot stopping the incoming right hook.

Dodging another fist coming at me from another Reaper, I slipped underneath its legs and sprung up behind it, surprising it with a forward kick.

The Reaper was stunned for a moment before it regained its composure. It came at me with a scissor kick and I moved out of the way, narrowly stopping it with my shin.

Hissing through the pain I darted off to the left, and using the momentum of my jump, I bounced off one rail and up onto the next, catching the overhead pipe and used it to swing over onto the grate of the floor above. The prison was laid out in such a way that the rectangle structure had walkways running around all four sides with cells every few feet. The same layout was repeated across all five floors. The middle was open so I could see all the way through which made my job assessing where my attacks were coming from, easier.

The kicker was, there had been construction equipment set out throughout the prison which meant there were platforms, cranes and a bunch of other stuff impeding my escape.

It didn't matter. I'd worked with worse. As if on cue, the Reaper came hard and fast and swiped at me with a large blade. Damn. I darted out of the way just in time. I had to concentrate.

I jumped up again using the pipe above me to swing away from it, landing on the next platform over. There were paint buckets and rollers left behind on this one. I picked up an extension pole and ducked as the Reaper leaped, taking the whole distance in a single jump.

Soon, I was joined by another three. Crap.

Undeterred, I swung the pole and effectively knocked the first one down and then the next. When the pole broke on the third, I tossed it and jumped, grabbing hold of the railing on the level above. I moved fast, using whatever I could to my advantage, Reapers hot on my tail wherever I went. I pushed myself and when I reached the top level, I spun on the spot kicking out, and dropped low to avoid their retaliation.

The one closest to me made a guttural sound, its face contorted in confusion, and I smirked.

Taking the momentary break in the assault, I reached for my gun and aimed. The Reaper stopped.

Shooting them in the head was the only way, as far as we knew, to kill them, and it knew that I knew.

I fired, but somehow, it dodged the bullet and as it lost its footing and began falling, tumbling over the edge that had been missing its railing, it grabbed my foot and pulled. A breathless shout erupted from me as I dropped the gun and went down with it.

My breath stalled. This was not good. The fall wouldn't kill me but I sure as hell wouldn't be walking away.

Survival instinct kicked in and I desperately reached out, catching hold of the edge.

Hoisting myself up, I rolled myself onto the safety of the grate I'd just been on and let out a panting breath and got to my knees. Down below, the Reaper landed with a loud thud which made my stomach turn. It wouldn't be dead, but it would be out for a while.

I looked across at Alex and panic quickly set in—another Reaper was stalking toward her.

"Hey!" I shouted without thinking.

It turned toward me, its blue eyes flaring with anger.

"Need to kill a wounded girl? Don't have the guts to come after someone who'll fight back?"

Its mouth broke into a creepy grin, setting me on edge. As soon as I felt the presence behind me, I knew that I'd messed up.

It didn't take long to work out what it was smirking at. I was screwed, because I'd made yet another mistake, probably my biggest, possibly my last. I turned slowly.

Not only was this Reaper bigger than the others and faster, it was *The* Reaper.

"Silus," I breathed.

"I thoroughly enjoyed the show, even if you did take out half my soldiers," he said and I followed his eyes as he looked around at the carnage of Reaper bodies. He seemed inconvenienced more than anything else.

Silus was the kind of leader who didn't mind getting his hands dirty, like the night he personally led the attack on New York. Our gods never came here, the Karatoi never helped, but right now would have been the perfect time for them to start.

My chest constricted as he let out a short and mirthless laugh.

He stepped toward me folding his arms behind his back, like he was just casually taking a stroll. I swallowed hard and retreated, the edge of the platform getting close.

I chanced a look down. Damn it. The gun was on the grate below. I looked to the other side and froze when I saw Alex. The other Reaper had his hand around her throat, holding her up on her knees. She was awake, and her wide eyes were focused on me. She was deathly still and sickeningly pale, a tiny trickle of blood streaming from her lips.

If I fought him, if I at least got the chance to get to lower ground I could get us both out of here, but the realization of how bad my shoulder was hurt was like a punch to the gut. I clenched my fist at my side, testing the strength of it and when I winced at the pain, Silus gave me an amused, half smirk.

"Yet again, the Ceoran break protocol." He looked down at Alex and then back at me. "For a girl who supposedly knows nothing."

He took another leisurely step toward me.

"Or is this personal?"

Ignoring every word coming out of his mouth, I kept my eyes on Alex.

"Ah, it is personal, of course it is." He looked away. "Thought you'd have learned your lesson when you lost half your face."

Alex's eyes snapped up to us.

"Chivalry at its finest," Silus said, nodding to Alex.

Alex began to cry, and my heart fractured.

Silus turned his attention back to her. No one dared to move or even breathe.

"It's a good thing you healed her, mostly. Would have been a shame to see such a pretty face scarred up."

Alex's crying turned into angry shouting.

"Too bad you didn't have enough in you to fix yourself."

"Leave him alone!" Alex shouted.

"Enough," Silus barked at her. "I'll ask you again, Alexia—where is the location of the Map?"

Meeting her horrified gaze, I shook my head.

"Go to hell!" she screamed.

"I'm growing impatient now," Silus said taking another step toward me.

This time, though, he moved quicker than I'd anticipated and in the second it took me to realize what was happening, his large hand was wrapped around my throat. "Are you really testing me, Raine?"

"She can't tell you what she doesn't know," I ground out.

Silus kept his attention on Alex and I didn't need to see her to know that her beautiful blue eyes were wide with fear. I felt the tension dip the whole building into a sort of dark cocoon.

The feeling was so strong, so overpowering I could barely think around it and then my mind went back to the woods. The odd feeling that spread through me like I was in pain. But it was her I'd been feeling. Alex. My eyes wet with tears, what had they done to her?

"Now I know the two of you have some secret attraction, which means you both care greatly about what happens to the other," Silus said.

Alex remained silent, and I prayed that she wouldn't give the Map up, not for me.

"I know you both hide it from the Council," he taunted. "I know you both quiver with passion every time you're in the same room."

Silus moved us both backward toward the ledge and my stomach soured. *Why did they think removing the safety railing on a platform this high was a good idea?*

"Now, I'm going to ask one last time, Alexia—where is the Map?"

She thrashed against the Reaper holding her.

"She doesn't know!" I managed.

Silus didn't believe me.

"Do you really want to see how gravity treats a falling angel?" Silus muttered, yet again keeping his eyes on her. "Because I can't imagine your fragile, human-like bones handling a fall like this very well." He looked at me and then over the ledge as though he was sizing up the distance.

"Leave him alone!" Alex's voice carried through the jail.

Silus inched us closer to the edge and I squeezed my eyes shut as Alex cried out below.

"She doesn't know," I said again. This time Silus turned his attention back to me.

Those pale, lifeless eyes turned a brighter blue, almost glowing from within.

"I don't believe you."

"She doesn't know because I wiped her memories," I spat back. "But you already know that."

He looked back at Alex with genuine surprise.

"Your man here has some brass ones."

"Please, stop!" Alex cried out again.

I knew better though. I knew where this was going, and I only hoped that he wouldn't make her watch.

I cast a quick look down at Alex, her eyes filled with tears, crying and pleading. I smiled through the terror, the kind of smile which said I was sorry for failing, and I was sorry I lied, but most of all I was so sorry that her tears were because of me.

"No!" Her voice seared me.

Another mirthless laugh filled the silent warehouse and then Silus pressed his lips against my ear. "Do you really think she'll let you suffer for this secret?"

The reality of the situation must have dawned on her just like it had on me. If she spoke to help me, our people and probably the rest of the world, whatever was left of it, would be wiped out.

But we knew the outcome, we both did.

One person or the whole world.

She wouldn't break, and I'd never expect her to.

"She will because she doesn't know anything," I hissed back, pulling my face away. "Do it, you coward. Or do you get off on playing?"

It was obviously not the outcome he was hoping for because the next thing I heard was a low, animalistic growl of fury rumbling deep from within his throat. I braced myself for what came next because what came next, was not good.

"Don't!" Alex screamed out.

And in a moment of terror, he tightened his hold around my throat and rushed us backward toward the ledge, and in a split second which lasted an eternity, he let go and I fell.

Nothing but Alex's screams sounded through the eternally silent jail. As the ground came hard and fast, I felt nothing but the split second of pain cracking through me and then the endless dark.

Chapter Twenty-Seven
Courage

Alex

"No!" I thrashed against the hold around my throat. "Eric!"

The Reaper's hand tightened but I couldn't care less. I didn't pay attention to the way its nails dug into my skin or the way it pulled my arms back, jarring my shoulders. All I cared about was the way Eric lay motionless, unmoving, deathly still.

"Eric!" I screamed again. "Dear God, no, Eric!"

I couldn't take my eyes off him; I couldn't stop calling for him through the endless mess of tears streaming down my face. For the first time in my life, as far as I could remember, I felt what true fear was.

Red-hot rage turned my insides into liquid fire. Anger exploded inside me and I didn't think when I acted next. I thrashed against the Reaper and fought against every bone crushing sob ripping through my body.

One of the Reapers rushed behind me and grabbed my arms while another tried to stop my flailing legs.

Without a second thought I threw my head back and connected with its face. It released me giving me a quick second to regain my bearings. As the Reaper in front of me lunged, I threw my leg out and hit it square in the jaw.

I ran. I didn't stop to see where the Reapers were. All I could think about was Eric, all I wanted to do was help him.

Silus jumped off the ledge he'd thrown Eric from and landed beside his body, his knee coming an inch from Eric's head causing me to stop abruptly. The Reapers behind me quickly took the opportunity to take hold of my arms. As Silus stood, he nudged Eric with his foot and pushed his body turning him onto his back.

I yelled, pulling my arms to no avail.

"Release her," Silus muttered.

The Reaper holding me hesitated for a moment before it obeyed his order.

I scrambled over to Eric and threw my hands around his shoulders. His head lolled to the side revealing a pool of blood. I couldn't tell where it came from or if it was still flowing.

"Eric," I whispered, gently turning his face. "Please wake up."

But he didn't. He was still. His eyes closed and unmoving.

"Eric, please, please open your eyes."

With trembling hands, I pressed my fingers to his pulse and choked back a sob while Silus stalked around us and knelt on the other side of Eric's body.

He was alive but only just.

"Talk. Now," Silus said, his voice lacking any amusement. "I think you know we're serious, Chancellor Wynter. Don't waste my time."

I shook my head, the shock still holding me down.

"Believe me. There are many creative ways we can get you to talk."

"Do whatever you want to me, I don't have what you're asking," I spat, surprised at the venom in my voice.

He laughed and then he wrapped his hand around my throat and pulled me up to my knees. I refused to let go of Eric. I gripped his shirt in my hand and my mind zoned out. Silus's mouth moved, but the words didn't even register. I couldn't even hear the threats or feel the fear. All I registered was the pain inside me, Eric's pain, *my* pain. The horror of what he'd done to Eric and of what they'd done to me.

"I'm done talking. Tell us the location. Now."

"No," I spat back. "You can go to hell."

The other Reaper looked across at me with a bemused expression while Silus tightened his grip around my throat.

As Silus reached down for me with his other hand, a loud and bright explosion reverberated through the jail and plunged it into darkness.

The force of the explosion threw us apart and Silus landed with a thud a few feet from me. I didn't even think as I scrambled back to Eric and threw my body over his as flames caught hold of the cluttered mess around the building and licked the walls and caught the wooden slats.

Another explosion sent debris showering down around us.

"They're coming for you!" I screamed.

Silus looked back between me and the ceiling which was about to cave. I wasn't leaving and if he stayed, he'd be caught. I smirked through the tears and tightened my hold on Eric.

As the dust grew denser and more beams from above came crashing down, Silus took off, disappearing through the flames leaving me and Eric alone. I lowered my body over his face and coughed as the smoke started to wear me down.

A beam crashed through the upper levels and landed in a fiery heap beside us. I looked through watery eyes as I thought I saw two figures approaching. It was either help, or I was losing it.

"Raine!" I recognized Kieran's voice shouting above the roar of fire. "Alex!"

"Here," I choked. "We're here. Please...help."

Gripping Eric's shirt, I shielded him as another beam came crashing down, sending embers into the air. I ignored the pinches of pain as they burned and settled on my exposed skin.

"He's...he's hurt, please, please help him."

Kieran quickly appeared beside us, dropping to his knees, pulling me away from Eric.

"Let go, Alex, we have to move. They've got him."

My eyes shot up to see Corteza and another soldier I'd never met running toward us to help Eric.

"Move out," Corteza shouted over the noise, never once looking at me. "Get her out of here."

Kieran nodded and helped me up, setting me on my feet.

"Can you walk?"

"Yes," I yelled back.

Together we navigated the burning building and got out through the blown-out hole in the side. I dropped to my knees in the cool grass, gasping in gulps of fresh air, the wet blades beneath my fingers soothing the heat on my skin.

As I looked back, taking in the sight, I broke.

Chapter Twenty-Eight
Rock Bottom

The night was a blur and the last sixteen hours felt like a bad dream. But no matter how much I wished for the impossible it didn't happen. I watched on through endless tears as they took Eric away and I was led in the other direction, away from him. We were both in the same building, but the distance felt unnaturally infinite.

He'd woken up when they put him on the stretcher and the screams that came from him completely undid me. It was the worst kind of torture.

I'd thrown up a couple of times and then the guilt set in.

Kieran came and checked on me a few times in the early morning and once more an hour ago. This time he left only to refill his coffee and when he came back, he stayed for good. I didn't have it in me to chat or even tell him to get out, but he seemed to be fine with that.

He'd made himself at home in my small room and kept himself busy looking through the files Eric had brought along, scribbling furiously on a pad he produced out of nowhere. When he finally finished that, he did a few laps of the small room and sat back down with a long exhale.

I couldn't believe we were back at the Compound. The walls had been repaired and it seemed like business as usual around the grounds. How could they just go on when Eric was in there suffering?

Each time my mind went back to the jail and the look on Eric's face as he fell, a furious torrent of tears began.

If only I'd stayed, if only I hadn't been such an emotional brat…Eric would be okay.

Not only did I risk my life and everyone who had to come for us, I'd nearly cost him his. I'd been so careless and for what? To ask Silus to spare us? I was an idiot. If Eric hadn't come, would Silus have made me talk? Would I have been the downfall of all the Ceoran in the universe and all mankind here? God. That was a heavy thought. Another relentless tear fell and splattered in my lap.

I pulled my knees to my chest and buried my face in the crook.

My mind kept going back to the fire, to the way they came in and got us out. Not much was said, Corteza looked pissed and he didn't even look at me. They knew where to come; Eric must have contacted them somehow. He could've waited, but he didn't, he risked his life, for me, again.

I sobbed even harder when I remembered how Eric's face broke as Silus taunted him. He'd mocked his scars, the injuries he'd sustained.

Kieran stirred, breaking my chain of thought. Slowly he stood and walked over toward me pulling up a chair.

He spun it the wrong way around and sat with his legs on either side.

For a moment, I looked up at him and tried to read into the blue eyes peering at me. When I saw sadness and disappointment, I turned away like a coward and looked outside the barred windows and absentmindedly wiped the flowing tears from my face.

The skin there was starting to feel raw from scrubbing it so much but the pain in my shoulder was long since gone. Kieran had done his healing trick and somehow fixed me, though I didn't deserve it. The bullet should have stayed lodged in there just to remind me how much of an idiot I'd been.

When I stayed silent, he ran a hand through his long hair and shook his head. His knuckles were grazed and raw where the training gloves didn't cover, and looking further up his arms, I saw the cuts and scrapes no doubt received while running through the ruins of the jail. Wordlessly, he unstrapped the tactical vest and tossed it aside. My eyes followed it as it landed on the small armchair beside the window.

None of us had taken the time to change or shower, or even wash off the blood. It had all happened so quickly that everything following was a slow-motion reaction to the shock.

He folded his arms across the backrest of the chair and leaned in. My eyes caught the same logo on his T-shirt like I'd seen on Eric's all those months ago in the woods. He wasn't a soldier—I'd learned that weeks ago—yet here he was, on the front lines stepping in when he didn't need to. This wasn't his calling or his duty. He made his choice to work in the field and help because he told me he thought he could do more here. I wondered now whether it was all worth it?

All these Ceoran, soldiers and council members, who'd stepped up to the plate to protect the Map. Little did they know the Map was a selfish person who barely deserved the friendship of these people, let alone such a huge responsibility.

"I know you're not up to talking. But I need to know what happened. We need to know where we stand," he said.

"I didn't give up the Map, if that's what you're asking."

"Okay, that's good. Can you tell me what happened?"

What was I supposed to say? That I was planning on starting a crusade all on my own, against an entire army of them? Yeah, not going to go down well.

"Alex?" he said softly, tilting my chin up with his fingers. "What happened?"

Tears welled before I could stop them and spilled over onto my cheeks. He quickly reached for a box of tissues and handed them to me. I ripped out a whole bunch and squeezed them like a lifeline.

"I ran. I…I got caught, I couldn't fight them and Eric, he came after me."

"He tracked you to the jail."

Nodding, I wiped the fresh tears with my ball of tissues.

"Why did you run?"

"I wanted to give him his life back. He was stuck watching after me, it isn't fair."

Kieran sighed. "That is his job."

"It shouldn't be. I'm a mess, I'm bad for him."

He didn't say anything else.

"How bad is it?" I looked up at him through wet lashes.

"It's bad."

"How bad?"

He massaged the back of his neck and looked down at me. "The fall was pretty bad, Alex, he broke some bones and, the impact broke his back…"

My brain refused to hear what he was saying, flat out denied what he was telling me. I shot to my feet and rushed over to the window quickly winding it open. I gulped in as much cool air as I could and pretended that it wasn't because I was too much of a coward to hear what Kieran was telling me.

An ugly mess of emotions invaded me and sat there, sour and heavy in my gut and I deserved nothing less. As much as I wanted to run, as easy as it would have been, I stayed. I listened to the things Kieran was telling me. I listened to the things I was responsible for. I pressed my forehead to the cool wall.

After a while Kieran cleared his throat.

"This isn't on you," he said.

"Don't"—I shook my head, and turned to meet his gaze—"this is on me. Every last thing he is going to go through. Not only now, but in the future when he realizes that he has to live with the mistakes I've made."

Kieran dropped his gaze.

It is my fault. Pure and simple and no amount of sugarcoating would make it less true.

Kieran stood and walked over to where I was standing. As he reached for my arm, I moved out of his way, jerking back. I crossed my arms and turned from him.

The Reapers wanted the Map and I wanted what they could give me. It was time for me to stop running and start bargaining. And this time, there would be no mistakes.

Chapter Twenty-Nine
Failing the Chosen

Eric

My eyes snapped open and darted around. The dimly lit room was unfamiliar. There was a small, plain bulb suspended from the ceiling and it cast a moody, yellowish light around me. And as my eyes trailed down over the walls, I made note of the bars inside the window, the linoleum floor tiles and beige paint: Ceoran made, and the gaudy décor littering the side table gave it away.

There was also a book, the title of which I couldn't make out, and a candle on top of a mahogany side table. I cringed; it was almost like a bedside vigil was being held.

Where am I?

When I tried to sit up and couldn't, my heart rate skyrocketed. A choked sob got stuck in my throat as I looked down at my legs and nothing moved.

The events of yesterday came crashing back, flooding my mind quicker that I could keep up.

The last thing I remembered seeing was Alex's face, the last thing I heard were her screams and then I was falling.

It felt like an eternity, yet it was over before I could take a breath. I vaguely remembered explosions and heat…had I been dreaming?

I tried my legs again.

Nothing.

I pressed my hands to my face and that's when I lost it. The breath I'd tried to release came out in a sort of broken cry which I barely recognized as my own voice.

The door opened but I was so far beyond comprehension that I didn't even recognize the man speaking to me.

"Eric."

"Dad," I choked out.

"Where am I?"

"One of the old infirmary rooms at the Compound. I'm afraid the newer facility is still under repair after the attack."

My heart was thundering so loudly I couldn't silence the blood rushing through my head. Bile rapidly formed and before I could stop it, the back of my throat started constricting and the contents of my stomach came up.

A bowl was quickly placed in my hands which I eagerly gripped and utilized. Ignoring the new coating of acid tears, I swatted them away and heaved until nothing was left.

A firm hand gently took the bowl away.

Corteza pressed a gentle hand to my shoulder and squeezed it.

"Son. Look at me."

I could barely muster the courage to look up, but when he asked again I listened. How could I even look him in the eyes when I'd failed so miserably?

"Everything is going to be alright, my boy," he said quietly, squeezing my hand.

"How is this going to be alright?"

"We will get through this together, you, me and your sister."

Oh God. I couldn't imagine dealing with this *and* Emelia's reaction. She would cry and make a huge deal and I didn't have the energy for that.

As scenario after scenario rolled through my head, my mind instantly snapped back to Alex.

"Is Alex okay? Did she get out?" I asked quickly.

His shoulders squared but he nodded. "Kelly got her out. She's fine."

"She was hurt, they…they shot her."

"Kelly took care of it. Here." He placed a glass of water in my hands. "Drink."

When I was done, I handed the glass back, and found his eyes. "Don't let her in here. Please."

"If that's what you wish."

"It is."

A few moments later, he repositioned himself and sat down in the chair beside the bed. He rubbed the side of his jaw which seemed to have greyed overnight.

He had the same sharp jawline as me and the same green eyes Emelia and I both shared, but his complexion was fairer and his hair lighter.

How Emelia and I got our features eluded me. We'd never known our birth mother because she died when we were very young, but the woman who raised us, our Mom, was a beautiful redhead, a strong soldier. Emelia was just like her and she reminded me of Mom every day. I missed her so much. I missed her cooking, her singing in the mornings, her sweet perfume and the way she danced with Dad when she thought we weren't looking.

"I'm sorry, Dad," I said, keeping my eyes on the ceiling.

"Eric, you don't have anything to apologize for."

314

"I do. I'm sorry for failing, for not being the guardian Alex needs. For falling short in my duties. You trained me better."

He didn't say anything and for a while I thought he wouldn't, then he spoke. "Son, these laws, these prophecies and things they expect of us…they're complicated. We're always expected to risk our lives for them—"

Stopping him mid-sentence, I shook my head. I knew where he was going with this and even though I knew he'd never dare breathe a word of it outside of these walls, I still didn't want to hear it. "I would always risk my life for her. Not because it's my job."

"Why? Because you *love* her?"

I winced at the tone he used.

"Because you said goodbye to her, you made peace with that and now that she's back, she's reckless and risking not only your life but everyone else here."

My mouth snapped shut. "Can we do this later?"

"Eric."

"I just want to be alone, Dad," I said quietly and turned away from him.

"Alright, son. Get some rest." He stopped at the door and a few moments later, he obliged, closing it behind him.

As he left, I reminded myself that I was strong; I'd seen difficult situations, I'd fought battles, escaped certain death. I could do this.

Only as I lay in the bed, barely able to hold my shit together I laughed at the absurdity of that statement.

I wasn't strong and I didn't know how I could do this. I was scared and I didn't know what to do.

***

Alex

I was beyond angry, beyond rational thought.

Silus hurt Eric because of me, he tore him down with taunts and threats and he knew that Eric would do everything in his power to protect me.

I didn't deserve his sacrifice; I didn't deserve what he did. Not then, not now.

I could try and heal him. But I didn't know what I was doing or how it worked, but I owed it to him to do whatever I could to make this better.

For the first few hours I debated what to do, I contemplated trying to somehow make this work. So, when I mustered up some courage, I stormed my way to where I knew the makeshift infirmary was in the old part of the compound and stopped abruptly when I saw the heavily armed soldier by the door.

"Chancellor."

"I'm here to see Corporal Raine," I said.

"I'm sorry, ma'am, he's not taking visitors."

"Not even…not even me?"

Clearly sensing my confusion, the soldier stepped closer. "I'm sorry, ma'am, he said no visitors."

"I see."

"I'm sorry."

"No, that's fine. Thank you."

I couldn't pretend that it didn't hurt, but I respected his wishes. I wouldn't have wanted to see anyone either, let alone the person responsible. Without wasting any more time, I opted for another plan, one that Kieran would hate.

He'd even try to stop me, but I dared anyone to breathe a word of destiny and prophecy because I was so well and truly done.

When I reached my room I was surprised to see a very wound up, flustered Kieran.

"I've been looking everywhere for you."

"Am I under room arrest?" I challenged.

"No, of course not."

"You're acting like I've been missing for days."

"I'm just worried, given everything that's happened."

"You mean you're worried that I'm out of your sight and I might do something stupid."

His eyes flicked away, and I pushed past him and proceeded to pack my bag. It didn't take a genius to work out that I was planning something, but Kieran was pretty switched on.

"Where are you going?"

"Get out of my way," I said.

"Not until you tell me what you're planning."

"I'm not telling you anything. Move."

Kieran stood his ground, tall and immovable. His eyes scanned my attire, black pants, black hoodie, compound cap. Then his eyes widened, and he stepped forward.

"You have to stay here. Where it's safe."

"I've already risked everyone's lives too much," I said.

"And you'll risk them even more if you leave now."

Musing over that, I still came to the same conclusion, and stood my ground. Maybe, maybe not. All I knew was that if I stayed, Eric would never get better which was absolutely not an option.

"Not if no one comes after me."

"You know that's not going to happen. There's no way." He stepped in front of me.

Ignoring him, I tried my shot at the door handle, but he moved his hip into my way making me jerk my hand back.

"Alex. Seriously. What are you planning on doing?"

"I'm going to see Silus."

"I'm going to pretend I didn't hear you say that."

"Whatever helps you sleep."

"Jesus, Alex. Tell me you're not being serious?"

"He can help. I have to fix this."

"You have to think straight."

"He's in there because of me. He's never going to walk again."

Kieran flinched. "If you do this, and you get yourself killed. How do you think he'll feel?"

"It doesn't matter."

"It doesn't matter? Oh Alex." He stepped back and ran his hands through his hair. "He did that for you."

"He shouldn't have done anything!"

"Yet he did. And he would do it again, like we all would." His voice rose to match mine.

I didn't think I would ever hear anything but laughter and jokes from him. He was so sweet and gentle, but the man standing in front of me looked like he'd been through hell and came back barely breathing.

"You don't even know what we've done and would do for you, Alex. You have no idea."

"What?" I whispered.

"You might not remember us and everything that went down before the Reapers came, but we remember you." His voice was quiet.

"Kieran…" I stepped toward him and pressed a hand to his arm. "I have to."

318

He moved out of my grasp. "What you're talking about is just short of suicide."

"I have to help…"

"You have to wake up and open your eyes."

His tone cut right through me.

"We care about you and not because it's his job or because you're my friend."

"How can I just stand back?" My voice faltered with each word. But Kieran stood his ground.

"He knew the risks, Alex. But walking to your death isn't what you should be doing."

"I appreciate everything you've both done, even if I don't remember it, but I *have* to do this. I know in my heart it's the right thing to do and I know in my heart that it's going to work."

"You're about to throw all of that away."

"I know you don't understand—"

He laughed, a low and humorless laugh. "Don't even try that with me, Alex. I understand. You feel bad, I get it, but this isn't okay. If you go out there and they get you to talk. We're all done. Do you understand?"

"Yes," I said.

For the first time since this whole thing began, it was the first time I felt sure about anything, the first time I understood what was happening. The first time I *knew* what I was doing without a doubt and I knew Silus would help me.

"You're making a mistake."

"I'm sorry," I whispered.

"No," he muttered back, stepping closer to me until we were toe to toe. "You're not."

Anger and something else started to rise inside me; the anger I understood, the something else…worried me.

Kieran was talking, I could see his mouth moving but I couldn't hear a thing…everything descended into silence, heavy and thick. Only my blood sounded, rushing inside my head, weaving and tearing its way through my veins.

I didn't know what made me do it, or what I was thinking, but the only coherent thought inside my head was Eric. Eric was hurt. Eric needed my help. I could do it and Kieran was in my way and he needed to be stopped.

When he reached for me I closed my hand around his wrist and he quickly tried to back away. But I held on and pressed my palm to his chest, feeling the buildup of power from the Cradle of Esper, and when the sensation reached its peak, I locked eyes with his wide gaze and pushed with little more than a flick, and he went down.

He didn't speak anymore. He didn't do anything.

I stepped over his body and calmly walked out the door.

Silus would give me the power I needed, and I would do whatever I had to, I would get it and I would help Eric.

That thought alone fueled me, everything else wasn't important.

Chapter Thirty
The Mage

Eric

My dad kept his distance after that argument and somehow, God only knew how, he'd managed to keep his mouth shut and not tell Emelia. She was worse than Mom when she worried, and I couldn't deal with that now.

My heart kept racing whenever I thought about the accident. I passed out from working myself up and then like a bad dream I hoped that when I woke, it'd be over.

But hour after hour, nothing changed. The only thing that kept playing on my mind was Alex. I'd told them not to let her see me. But I wanted to see her so badly. I wanted to know how she was. I wanted to hear her voice and see her face, but I couldn't shake the image of her chained up and hurt and I couldn't shake the hoarseness in her voice when she was pleading.

That's what kept me shying away like a coward, that's what kept me hidden in here afraid to face her.

Whatever happened to me was shit, no doubt, but I wouldn't change it. Alex was important, she mattered, and she was okay.

Despite the denial in my heart, I did care about her. More than I wanted to admit to myself. When I said goodbye, I closed that part of my life and filled that part of my heart with cement. Now that she was back, the hardness there couldn't be undone that easily.

Every time she looked at me and smiled, every time she grazed her hand across my skin, it slowly chipped the stone away. But it hurt, seeing her, remembering what we'd had, knowing she'd never remember me that way. It killed me. I could admit it. It hurt. Badly.

The scars were a reminder too—I hated that she had to see them, I hated that she had to touch them, feel them under her perfect fingertips. I hated that this is the world we had to meet back in.

But most of all, I hated that I couldn't heal her. She was always perfect to me, even with the small speckling of scars on her arm, and the dark shadows that were cast over her heart.

A series of loud knocks at the door snapped my attention back to the room and before I could tell whoever it was to get lost, Kelly pushed the door open and stepped through, the soldier on guard in tow.

"I'm sorry, Corporal, he just pushed through," he said.

"It's fine."

Kieran's eyes were wide and a shocked expression was etched onto his face.

When he shut the door he looked at me for a moment before striding over to my bed.

"What is it?" I asked.

Kelly and I hadn't really spoken much since everything went down, but we'd always been civil. Seeing him like this reminded me of a day I'd never forget, something which was etched into my memory and would be for the rest of my life. I'd nearly lost Alex then and the horror of how that felt refused to leave my memory.

My guard immediately went up and I pulled myself up into a seated position.

"What's going on?" I repeated.

"Alex."

"Alex what?" I challenged.

"She left."

This was one of those times where I looked at him dumbstruck and really hoped he was just being stupid and trying to get a rise out of me. But the way he stood, uncharacteristically serious, said otherwise.

"What did she do? Where's she going?"

He remained frozen and speechless.

"Damn it, Kelly. There's no time for this shit. Where is she?"

He shook his head. "She, she stopped me. I don't know what happened."

"What do you mean? What happened?"

"We were arguing, she was trying to leave—I tried to stop her and when I tried to take her hand, she pressed her palm to my chest and when she pushed me, Eric, I, I just dropped."

"You dropped?"

"Like a stone."

"What do you mean?"

My brows shot up as he carefully pulled the collar of his shirt down, my eyes following his. A red imprint of her hand was burned into his chest.

"No one can know," I whispered.

"What the hell did she do to me?"

"You can never tell a soul. Do you understand?"

"What did she do?" he asked again.

323

I drew in a sharp breath and quickly motioned for him to come closer. He sat and I began.

"Reaper's power."

"What?"

"When her mother first told me about who Alex was, she told me that there were things she couldn't tell me at first, not until she knew I could be trusted."

"Holy shit, Eric, that's one hell of a secret."

"When Alex was born, she was sick, the human doctors and the Ceoran said there was nothing they could do for her. They had no idea what was wrong and everything they tried had failed."

Kieran paled.

"But there was a woman who could, she and her husband were cast out by the Council decades ago, for dabbling in some dark shit."

"The mage."

"Yes, but when the war came to Earth, they disappeared. I haven't been able to track them down and when I heard there was a lead, I took it."

"Christ." Kelly rubbed his jaw and sat on the edge of my bed. "But Ashfield was full of shit, feeding you false leads."

"Yeah, I thought so too, but maybe there was some truth to it, probably more than even he knew."

"So how does Alex come into this?"

"The mage found Alex's mother and told her that there was a chance. It involved fusing Alex's blood with a Reaper's."

"And of course, she'd do anything to save her daughter."

Rubbing the back of my neck, I looked across at him. "She agreed, and Alex lived. Nothing happened, she grew up completely normal and healthy, the only thing she couldn't do—"

"Was heal."

"Yeah." I nodded. "And now, something must have switched inside her—she brought me back after I revived her. I've never seen anyone that strong. She's stronger than me, Kelly."

"There's something else," he said quietly.

"What?"

"She left to find the Reapers."

"What? Why would she do that?"

"To help you."

Holy shit. They'd lock her up an use her until they got everything they wanted.

"You have to find her. She doesn't know how powerful she is."

Kelly gave me a curt nod and got up.

"Kelly."

He stopped at the door and looked at me.

"They cannot find out who she is. Promise me you'll find her first."

"I will. I swear to you." As soon as the door was shut, I threw my head back and ran my hands over my face in frustration, letting out a long breath.

Not even fifteen minutes later, my dad came rushing through the door, his face set in a furious line.

"If that girl doesn't get someone killed, it'll be a damn miracle."

I shot him a warning look that he completely ignored.

"She's taken off from the facility. Kelly has disappeared too, want to bet they ran off together?"

My already nonexistent patience was wearing thin.

"She's reckless and dangerous and just because she's a chancellor it does not mean she's exempt from repercussions—"

"Stop," I said. "She's not reckless and she's not careless. She's afraid!"

"You're going to be in wheelchair for the rest of your life."

"Enough!" I shouted, ignoring the wave of emotion running through me. "You don't know what you're talking about."

"Eric. Listen to me, you're blinded by her."

"No, Dad. I'm not. I'd do it all again if it meant that she would get to walk away and live. Every. Single. Time."

"I understand what it is to be in love."

"Dad, no. That's not all this is about."

"Then what?"

"She is important to us, you know that, you know she is the key to everything."

"And does she appreciate what you've done? What we've all done for her? The Council and the race, and what about you, your face, your burns!"

My jaw clenched and he continued.

"She's the same as all the other Council Ceoran, spoiled and entitled."

"She is not. She is nothing like the rest of them."

"I'm not going to let her harm anyone else."

He turned to walk away and as he did, the last words he said registered and immediately set me on edge. "Wait, Dad, stop, what are you going to do?"

"I'm going to make sure she and Kelly are brought in. Then we'll deal with the rest."

"No. You can't. Dad, please."

"I can, and I will. You need to remember your place."

"You need to back the hell down!"

His brows shot up, disappearing into his silver hairline.

"Alex is in danger," I blurted out. "She didn't run off with Kelly, I asked him to go after her."

Corteza stepped closer to my bed and straightened up.

"You need to start talking now. Explain."

"I can't."

"Eric." He sighed, running his hand through his hair.

My father had a lot of patience, he had to in the commanding role he was in, but that patience was quickly wearing out.

"She's in real danger, Kelly can find her, he can bring her back. I trust him."

He looked at me hesitantly.

"Please, Dad. I'm begging you to trust me."

His eyes pulled away from me, but when they found mine again, they softened.

"You have always been my best soldier, son, I mean it. Always. But you're asking me to trust you without giving me anything."

"I know that, but it's all I can give you right now. I swear it."

"Seventy-two hours. That's it."

"Thank you," I murmured.

He didn't say anything further as he left my room and shut the door with a loud thud.

Praying to whoever was listening, I closed my eyes and squeezed my palms over my face. Kelly had to find her; he couldn't fail.

Chapter Thirty-One
Pirate Pa and the Scavengers

Alex

Figuring out the time based on the position of the rising moon on the horizon was a skill I'd learned very quickly. Had it not been for my *dad's* knowledge from all his years of training, we'd have been so lost and screwed for a long time.

As I walked through the dark woods, I found myself oddly at ease. I wondered what my real parents were like, and I wondered whether they were proud of me. Mostly, I wondered whether I would ever remember them again. Though I didn't want them to see the last few months of my life. I'd acted like a child, a spoiled and undeserving child. I was ashamed of myself. But what I was doing now was making amends, the only way I knew how. I had to be brave.

A rustling in the low-hanging branches set my nerves on edge. I gripped my bag tighter and looked around, keeping a close eye on anything and everything that could have possibly made the sound.

Obviously, it could have been an animal, though unlikely. Which meant it could have been Scavengers, which meant I had to change my approach. I could take care of myself, but I didn't want to get into anything tonight, not when I had more important things to focus on and save my energy for.

Keeping alert, I began moving again, keeping low to the ground and close to the cover of trees. It was nearing nightfall and if they were looking for me, they'd be coming out now, and I was counting on it.

The moon started to crest the horizon and a thousand stars quickly followed. I increased my pace and moved into the thicker canopy of trees, using the darkness to shield me.

Continuing down toward the sound of a rushing river, I kept an eye out on the uneven terrain I was crossing and carefully stepped over the larger boulders which were scattered all over this area.

As I raised my leg to step over another rock, I stopped abruptly when a glistening object about ten yards ahead of me caught my attention. I placed my foot back down and swept the horizon.

There was nothing else out of place. Taking another cautious step, I froze, my heart jumping into my throat as a crunch beneath my feet made my throat fill with bile. I had no time to react before I registered what was happening and then it was too late.

The trap beneath my feet triggered the glistening object in the distance, a large, human sized net. It sped toward me and no matter how fast I thought I ran, I was too slow. It caught me with a body crushing thud, scooped me up, and catapulted me into the air. I suppressed a scream as the net tightened around me and pulled me high into the tree line.

I scanned the area around me. Nothing. There was no one. Maybe that was good. Maybe it was an abandoned trap, maybe they'd moved on and, oh crap. I looked down when the net started to move. They hadn't left. Oh no. A group of six stood beneath me, cooing and jeering and jerking their guns up and down in the air.

I'd come across the worst kind of Scavengers. Hillbillies with semis. Perfect.

As the net moved lower and lower to the ground, I could make out two teenage boys about my age and four older men. My stomach recoiled at the sight. Some of them were missing teeth and looking up at me with sadistic grins, while one of them in denim overalls and a literal pitchfork was missing an eye. Pirate Hillbilly was going to stone me to death.

"What you think this one here has, Pa?" one of the younger boys asked.

The man nearest to him readjusted his belt and smirked up at me, nudging the boy in the ribs. "I'm sure we're about to find out, son."

No, no, no. I looked around, there had to be some way of getting out of there. My mind raced back to the things I'd packed: had I brought a knife? My gun? Anything useful? No. Damn it.

"Look, Pa, she's scared," the other young boy said to his father. "Think she's a crier?"

"They're more fun when they're scared," he replied with a smirk. "And even better when they cry."

My eyes darted from one to the other, growing more and more scared as the net got lower.

"Who gets to go first, Pa?"

"Easy, son, we have to check what she's got on her first."

I ground my teeth. I was not going to go down without a fight. Not to this bunch of idiots not when I'd been surviving *Reapers* for God's sake.

Holding my hand out at my side, I wriggled my fingers, hoping to God that the power would course when I needed it.

"Look at that feisty face. She's kind of pretty, isn't she?" One of the younger ones said.

"I've seen better," another replied.

My stomach twisted into angry coils.

The net stopped, jarring in the air, about three feet off the ground.

"Get back," Pirate Hillbilly said forcing his way to me. "Cut her down."

What was he going to do, take me out back and go deer hunting? When he reached for the net and his dirty fingers grazed mine, I stifled a surprised cry and moved back quickly.

Jerking back from him made the net spin, which made them laugh and the fear inside me rise.

He gripped the net fisting a handful of my hair with it. He yanked the blade through the rope and stepped back as it fell with me in it, crashing to the ground.

Gaining my bearings, I sucked in a deep breath and scrambled out of the net, stammering away as quickly as I could.

Ignoring the jeers and laughter from behind me, I kept running, and just as I was about to jump over a boulder, a painful thud buckled my knees and as I went down I caught a look at my legs: a long silver chain with balls at either end coiled around my shins. Great. I'd been taken down by a bola. Never in my life had I thought I'd say those words in the same sentence.

I reached down and frantically pulled at the chain. There was no give. If anything, it seemed to get tighter. I grit my teeth and groaned. The more I struggled, the more the chain seemed to tighten around me. I chanced a look back and my breath caught.

They were walking toward me, stalking, taking their time, like a predator taunting its prey. I looked back down at the chain and desperately pulled again, and this time, by some miracle, it loosened enough for me to pull one foot out and then the other. I didn't waste any time scrambling to my feet. I ran again, taking off in the other direction and, like I'd messed up their plans, I heard them cursing and calling orders to come after me.

As I glanced back over my shoulder, running through ragged breaths, I only saw two. They'd split up. Oh God. I ran faster, pushing my body as hard as I could.

This would have been the best time for the power to show, but again, it did not. I sucked in greedy breaths and kept pushing. What made it come to the surface? Did I literally need to be at death's door for it to shine?

"Take her from the embankment!" I heard one of them shout through the dark woods and I immediately changed my course away from the river and up into the less wooded areas.

It was a risky move, but if I had a clearing and a chance to run, I knew I could outrun them. They knew these woods, so it was an advantage to them, but I wasn't an ordinary girl and that was a definite advantage for me.

As the trees grew sparse up ahead, a clearing came into view and I pushed myself toward it, jumping over an upturned root. I missed one of them running toward me and a moment later, a hard body crashed into me, throwing us both to the ground.

Dried leaves and dirt and God knew what else flew up all around us as the impact disturbed the earth.

"No!" I screamed in his ear, which seemed to piss him off because without a second thought he slapped me so hard that stars exploded across my vision.

It was one of the younger boys. Pirate Hillbilly's son.

His eyes were filled with rage—what happened to these people to make them turn so savage? Tears pricked the back of my eyes, not only from the stinging in my cheek, but with anger. Why couldn't I use whatever power I had when I really needed it?

I thrashed against him, but his body was hard on top of mine. He grabbed my wrists and pinned them above me, holding me down.

"Get off me!" I screamed again, and again his eyes flared with rage. Before he could slap me again, a hand caught his.

"Enough," Pirate Pa said sternly. "Get her up."

With little more effort than picking up a small child, he dragged me by my hair and pulled me up to my feet.

I stood back, retreating as they circled me.

"Now," Pirate Pa, obviously the alpha of the group, said, "throw your bag down."

Wriggling my fingers at my side again, I cursed when nothing but panic coursed through me. *Come on!*

"Now."

Deciding that rebelling right now was a bad idea, I pulled the bag off my shoulders and tossed it to the ground.

He jerked his head toward the bag.

"Bring it to me," he muttered to his son. He did.

He eyed me off, as though he was waiting for me to make a move. I didn't. I remained rooted to the dry earth and watched with focused eyes.

As he spilled the contents onto the ground my eyes followed. He rummaged through my packs of food and water, the notes I'd made and the photo of my parents; he made me mad enough to reconsider rebelling.

"Now take off your clothes."

My eyes widened, and I shook my head, reactively wrapping my arms around my body.

"I'm not going to ask you again."

Surely he wasn't serious? I looked from one set of eyes to the next, each one more sickening than the one before. No.

My eyes snapped back to *Pa*. He slammed the heel of his pitchfork into the ground causing me to flinch.

"If you don't do it yourself, one of these boys would be more than willing. Now you don't want that, do you, missy?"

I cringed as they grinned at me.

This was officially the lowest and scariest point of my life. I slowly unzipped the jacket and shivered as the cold met my skin.

Throwing it over, the younger boy picked it up and sniffed it. Pig. Ignoring my disgusted expression, he handed it over to Pa.

"Darlene would love this."

"She sure would, Billy," he said without much emotion.

"Now the rest."

"Please," I begged. "Don't make me do this."

"Well like I said, doll, it's up to you. Either you can do it, or Billy does it for you."

It wasn't just the literal chill making me shake anymore. With trembling hands, I pulled off my tank top, thankful now that I'd worn a sports bra and not a lacy one.

"Hurry up, bitch!" the other young boy shouted making me flinch.

"That's no way to talk to a lady, now is it, Joe?"

Joe smirked.

"Now, the rest," Pa ordered.

I moved my trembling hands to my jeans; oh God I didn't want to do this. This couldn't be happening. He gave me a pointed look, urging me to hurry up.

As I undid the first button, a terrified breath left my lips and as I undid the second, the boys grinned, and as the third and final one came undone, a loud and deafening shot echoed through the woods quickly drawing my attention in that general direction.

The men dropped to the floor and I didn't wait to run. I sped through the woods, somehow managing to do my buttons back up, and ignoring the second and third shots echoing through the night. I caught a glimpse of the two younger boys running after me. Billy and Joe.

Taking no chances this time, I zigzagged through the terrain in case they had any more surprises up their sleeves.

Off in the distance, more shots were fired, and it sounded like an all-out war had broken out. My breath came out in ragged gasps as my mind went blank, and then, wave after wave of forgotten memories crashed into me.

With each flash and echo of bullets, memories started to flash between the noise—my parents, my real parents, holding me when the building started to fall, cries and screams as the fire took hold, Eric over me, holding me down as fire licked both of us.

Never once, not even through the flesh burning pain did his eyes leave mine. Never once did he let go, not until I passed out and woke with barely any visible marks.

Shock of each fresh imagine flashing through my mind made me stumble and trip over my own feet.

Scrubbing my face, I cleared my eyes and pushed the thoughts back. It didn't work though. As I raced through the night, images of Ashfield taunting Eric back in our Compound Institute high-school days raged through me, and as each gunshot cracked through the night, memories of me and Kieran standing up for Eric amplified my anger.

I sobbed openly as branches cut and scraped me at every turn, burning less than the relentless memories of my forgotten life.

The final memory that crashed into me was of Eric holding me the moment before he performed the Clean Slate. *I could never forget you, not completely, even after everything.* I'd spoken those words. I remembered them. I remembered the pain and the fear.

I screamed into the night and just as I reached the edge of a cliff, I skidded to a halt as the path ahead of me disappeared into a ravine.

Throwing my hands out to balance myself I stammered backward, stopping when I was sure the cliff wouldn't crumble beneath my feet. Fear spiked as I heard their footsteps rushing toward me.

Focusing on the present I struggled to keep my eyes clear of tears. My impromptu trip down memory lane left me shaking and breathless.

"Nowhere to run now." Joe laughed breathlessly as he stopped a few feet away.

Turning around, I clutched at my chest trying to catch my breath and remain in the present.

"Now that you've made us go through all that work, we're going to do this our way, ain't that right, Joe," Billy said and laughed.

Oh, hell no.

Billy stepped forward, obviously taking the lead.

Before either could come any closer, I held my hands out, hoping to God that my bluff would work and that if I thought really hard, the Cradle of Esper would let me tap into her power.

"Stay back!" I warned.

"Or what?"

"You don't want me to hurt you."

Billy's brows shot up. "She being serious?"

"I am being serious," I answered for him and again, pushed all my thoughts inside me on the power, hoping it would make an appearance.

"What are you going to do?" Joe asked.

"You've seen what some people can do in these woods, what *they* can do."

Billy's eyes narrowed. I'd got them thinking.

"You're not one of them." Joe laughed again, resuming his prowl toward me.

"Aren't I?"

As much as they weren't taking me seriously, a small part must have because I was still holding their attention and they were still standing back.

When I raised my hands again, Joe flinched, and when I narrowed my eyes, hoping the spark would ignite, Billy moved back, but when nothing happened, they both laughed.

They began to advance and all the anger inside me somehow simmered to the surface, but not the power.

Damn it. I didn't need it. As Joe made his move and reached out for me, I slapped his hand away and pushed him back. Taking a quick second to recover he grinned as he came at me again.

This time they came with everything they had: Joe rushed me, grabbing for my arms while Billy reached for my shirt.

Like a surprise to all of us, when I threw my hand up to stop Billy, a small burst of wind slammed into him, momentarily stunning him. Instead of scaring them, it seemed to excite them even more. Billy lunched for me again but this time when no power came to my rescue, I launched my knee into his stomach before kneeing him in the face.

When Joe released me, I stomped my foot on his and sprung forward, only to be pulled back and forced to the ground by Billy.

He flipped me over onto my back and pressed his knee down on my leg locking me in place.

He grinned, breathing heavily into my ear.

My body reacted to the cold earth and jerked. He reached for my left arm and pulled it up. Kieran had done the best he could healing me but the scarring was still visible.

"Been in an accident, love?"

"Let go." I tried to pull my arm free. He gripped it tighter.

"This looks like it must have hurt."

"Don't," I pleaded, aware of the faltering in my voice.

"Don't what?" he hissed, bringing his other hand to my hip.

His hot breath was foul, making tears burn my eyes.

"It's been lonely out here, doll," Joe said. "Real lonely."

Holy mother of God. This could not be happening.

Again, I tried to move my arms but to no avail, and when I tried to move my legs his knee somehow ended up between mine and then the real panic set in.

"Get off her," a loud voice shouted over the pounding of blood in my ears.

Looking up behind me, I cried out in relief. Kieran stepped forward holding up a gun in each hand.

I shoved Joe off me as he slowly moved his knee from between my legs. Shivering, I quickly got up, brushing off the leaves and dirt from my body and readjusted the strap of my bra.

"Get back," Kieran said to me while keeping his eyes on the two boys. He waved his guns motioning for them to move.

"Where's her stuff?" he asked firmly.

Neither of them responded.

"I killed the other four you were with, so you should know I'm not hesitant about killing out here. Not anymore. Where's her stuff?"

"He took it, one of the guys you killed," Joe hissed. "They were our family."

"And she's mine." Kieran's voice remained eerily even. "Now I'll ask again. What did you do with her things?"

"If you don't kill us. We'll come and find you and your bitch."

Kieran's jaw tightened and a cord in his neck pulsed.

"I'd seriously suggest you stop talking and tell me what I'm asking you."

"I'll kill her myself, but not before I get to have my fun." Joe made his last mistake.

Kieran didn't even blink when he fired. Joe went down, lifeless and positively dead. I stammered backward, my eyes wide and glued to the spot where he'd just been standing.

Kieran turned his attention and guns to Billy who looked like he was either about to start crying or crap himself. I wouldn't have blamed him for either.

No matter how scummy someone was—and given the things they were talking about doing I didn't feel too badly for them—my heart still ached when another life was taken. It's what separated us from them.

"Where are her things?" Kieran asked again.

Billy raised a trembling hand and pointed in the direction I'd run from.

"Good. Show me," Kieran said evenly, holstering one gun while keeping the other trained on him.

My eyes traveled back to Joe, his wide-open eyes gazed up at the stars, forever to remain here until his body became a part of the earth again.

"Come on," Kieran said quietly to me.

Silently, we followed Joe as he tripped and stumbled on everything we walked over. After tonight, he'd probably be dead. No one to protect him, no one to do his dirty work—people like him only hung out in likeminded groups. And since they were very private, I didn't see him finding one that'd take him in.

"They left it all there." He pointed to the pile of clothes I'd taken off.

"Get it," Kieran ordered.

I looked up at the iciness in his eyes. He wasn't to be messed with, obviously. I swallowed hard and watched as the boy walked around his dead family and collected my bag and stuffed all the things he'd tossed out before.

"Get her clothes," Kieran ordered next.

Once he retrieved my jacket and my tank top he walked over to us and held it out with shaking hands. Kieran snatched it from him and motioned for him to turn around. I wasted no time getting dressed. Thank God. It was freezing out.

"Walk," Kieran barked.

That's when the begging went up tenfold. The kid began to cry, and whimper and I seriously considered whether Kieran was going to kill him too.

But he didn't. Instead he gave him a kick to the butt and forced him to start jogging.

"The next time I see you in these woods, I will not hesitate to shoot you."

That was that.

I released the breath I'd been holding and doubled over, I pressed both hands to my knees and I laughed.

Kieran stood silently beside me and pressed a gentle hand to my back as I let the hysterics consume me. He let me laugh until I couldn't anymore and then he waited silently when the tears came, and when I couldn't breathe through the sobs anymore, he helped me to the ground and held me.

When the tears finally stopped, and I could breathe he helped me up and handed me my backpack.

"We should get out of here," he said. "The sun is starting to come up."

CHAPTER THIRTY-TWO
THE REVEAL

The sun came up over the horizon and a flock of birds flew through the sky, silhouetting against the bright orange backdrop. My eyes widened in awe. It'd been months since I'd seen anything alive out here.

Times like this made the world seem like it had never changed. I looked back down into the dark shades of green and brown surrounding us, there was something oddly comforting about being in the shade of these mammoth trees. It was almost like nature was welcoming us back into her arms when we'd so cruelly taken her legs from under her.

"You okay?" Kieran asked softly.

"What?"

"You're slowing down."

"Oh." I murmured and then caught up. "I'm fine, just thinking."

"About what?"

"The world," I said simply.

"Lot to think about there," he answered before we fell into another comfortable silence.

We walked for what I figured to be about four hours based on the way the sun rose and moved across the sky. Kieran was leading us toward a small hut he'd marked out on a map he kept checking every few miles or so.

"How much farther?"

"About two hours."

Nodding, I wiped my forehead and kept walking.

"We should rest up for a while." He stopped, looking over the map.

"I'm fine. We can keep moving."

He looked at me skeptically.

"Honestly. I'm okay, we should keep moving."

Taking my word, he agreed, folded the map back up and we continued.

Just like he said, a few hours later a small hut came into view. The white stone walls and cobblestone path glimmered between the branches of the low brush.

"Ceoran?"

"Yup." He swept his gaze before moving ahead. "We've got a few out here in these woods."

He led the way up the cobblestone path.

We did the usual check around back and through the windows and, satisfied that we were the only occupants, Kieran led the way in through the front. He dropped his bag beside the door and unholstered his two guns, placing them neatly on the kitchen counter.

"The bathroom is through there; do you want to take it first?"

As I took a quick look at my dirt-covered clothes, I decided that it was most definitely a good idea. Taking the jacket off, I tossed it aside and made a beeline for the bathroom.

The water was cold, but it was a welcome relief. It was a wonder how they managed to keep the facilities stocked at all, and after the night I just had I needed to cool down.

Keeping my hair out of the stream of water, I washed up and got out, drying and dressing quickly to avoid the cold air settling on my skin.

Kieran looked up when I walked out and sat down in the small living room, embracing the comfort of the sofa.

"Better?"

"Oh yeah." I nodded.

"I'll wash up quickly, stay put."

"Scout's honor." I held up my fingers.

He smirked and disappeared into the bathroom.

Letting myself relax, I leaned back and stretched out the muscles in my neck and shoulders and groaned when the bones cracked.

God, I didn't remember a time when I wasn't sore or nursing some sort of injury. Ironically all the cold showers and icy baths were probably what kept most of us in working order. Who'd have thought?

The shower shut off and a few minutes later Kieran came back in and sat down beside me.

"Thank you," I said.

"For?"

"Saving my butt back there."

"Part of the job, ma'am." He chuckled.

"It's not part of your job."

Catching the shift in my tone, he pressed a hand to my arm and gently squeezed.

"I'm kidding, Alex. You don't need to thank me; anyone would have done the same. Those guys were animals, it makes me sick knowing what freaks like that do to people."

Yeah, they really were, I didn't even want to let my mind wander to all the things they'd have done had Kieran not shown up when

344

he did. I probably could have taken them on had my power shown up, but considering the little squirts that came forth, I wasn't so sure.

"In all seriousness though, are you alright?"

"Yes." I pulled my hair free from the ponytail letting it fall around my shoulders.

"They didn't hurt you?"

"No." I shook my head.

"Are you lying to me?"

I shielded a smile when he asked me the same thing I'd asked him when he healed me. "No, I'm not lying."

"Okay." He let out a long breath and nodded. "Good. And we need to talk."

"Yep."

"That was some serious shit you did to me, Alex. I don't even know what to think."

"I don't know what to tell you..." I stretched out the tired muscles in my neck. "All I know is that power doesn't always come to me and I have no idea why. Back there would have been great for it to show up."

"No doubt, I would have loved to see you take them out. But what you did to me"—he pressed his hand over his chest and a pang of guilt shot through me—"I've never seen anything like that. You were you and then, you did that."

"Maybe it was just adrenaline?"

He shook his head and I sunk in my seat.

"Eric told me something which makes you very valuable to the Reapers, and if they ever found out...well let's just say that they'd have hit the jackpot."

"Aside from being the Map?"

"Probably even more important." He looked at me pointedly.

I knew he knew. It would have been stupid to assume otherwise. Of course Eric would have told him about his position as my guardian and me being the Map. Considering how closely they'd worked together in the past, it only made sense.

"For decades there's been this rumor that a Ceoran who is half us, half them will come along."

"The Halfling," I said and he nodded.

A cold chill settled over me. That's what the Reapers were searching for in New York, it's why they killed all those people, why they ambushed my camp, and it's what my *parents,* those soldiers, died for.

"This Ceoran is special because they can travel back and forth between realms; they can survive the shift between time dividing our dimension and others."

"We can't all do that?"

"No," he said quietly. "The Cradle of Esper gives us the tools we need to get here and live here. It's where our power comes from and it's a one-way ticket kind of deal. There have been stories passed down from generations that if a Halfling Map were to harness their power, we could find our way back to the Bridge and back home. There's never been a Halfling who's survived to adulthood. So, no one has ever traveled back home."

A few seconds of silence fell between us.

"Like ever?"

He shook his head.

"How do you, *we,* do that…just go somewhere knowing we could never go home again?"

"Well, we don't know any different, we're created up there somewhere, and when the Karatoi decide who's going where, the DNA of that host planet is planted, and we're sent here."

"Oh, right."

"Anyway, the Reapers aren't just searching for the Map; they're searching for a way to travel across the universe indefinitely," he added. "Basically it's like a free ride, piggyback off the Halfling and avoid being obliterated by the whole realm traveling thing."

"And they think it's here."

His eyes searched mine before he continued.

"There was this woman, she practiced some dark stuff, Alex, she played around with magic and all sorts of things we don't dare touch. When the Council found out, they cast her out. For decades she hid out with her husband and then, she emerged, when you were born."

My mind was starting to piece it all together and with each piece, my chest tightened. I knew where this was going, but I didn't want to hear it.

"You were sick, and you were going to die. Your mother had no choice. The mage bonded your blood with the blood of a Reaper."

My head dropped.

"She never thought anything of it, she was grateful for her help, and you grew up completely normal. But now, the Reapers know that someone like that exists, they know they're on Earth and they will stop at nothing to find them."

"I'm the Halfling they were looking for," I whispered.

"Yes." He sighed.

"So, with me, they'll have unlimited power to travel all over the universe…"

"Yes," he replied. "Alex. You see now why it is far too dangerous if they found out about you."

"Then I'll make sure they don't."

"You can't be that naïve," he said sternly. "You've seen what they can do, what they're capable of. And believe me, I wish you could walk in there and take them all out. Hell, I'd be backing you, but you can't and that's the truth. At least not right now, you don't know how to call on the power, it doesn't always show. You're walking in there unarmed."

I frowned as helpless anger filled me.

"We have to work out how to help Eric some other way. I can't let you go out there and face them."

Digesting everything he'd just told me, I shook my head. "There is no other way."

"There's always another way," he countered. "And we're going to find it. So, settle in and let's start thinking."

"You're going to help me?"

"Of course I am."

I smiled. Whatever happened between them must have been big, but Kieran still cared about Eric, he still came out here to find me and to help him and that gave me courage.

"What happened between you two?"

He raised his head and looked across at me.

"Why do you think something happened?"

"Because I wasn't born yesterday, I can see the strain a mile away."

"A lot happened."

"We have a lot of time to pass."

"Don't you want to sleep?"

"Not when there's important conversation to be had."

He smirked.

"So?" I encouraged.

"You happened."

My mouth dropped but I quickly closed it before he could see. "I don't understand, I didn't think you and I…"

"Nothing like that." He chuckled.

"Eric and I were always like brothers, he kind of stuck by me when I didn't have any friends of my own and when I started to hang with him, the other Council members stopped letting their kids socialize with me…Eric never cared about the classes and all that, you know? I always stuck up for him and he always had my back when they bullied me, and then when you were transferred over to this Compound and started at our school, I couldn't be happier for him, you two hit it off. I'd never seen anything like it, and then the Reapers descended a few years later." Kieran paused.

A heavy breath settled between us as I watched him fiddle with the cuff of his sleeve. He was a tough guy, smart and witty, always something smart and fiery to say, always a smile on his face. But this, this was hard on him. I saw the subtle frown tug at his lips as he bowed his head, recalling the memories that caused him such pain.

"He warned me about chatter he'd heard, that they were planning on coming for the Map, that's when he confided in me about you. He told me to get everyone out of the facility in Hampton and when I tried to tell them, no one wanted to listen because he was the one who gave us the information, a soldier, beneath them—they attacked, and they killed your family and dozens and dozens of other Ceoran. No one, not a single Council member fought, I watched as they died in front of you."

"The plane crash was planned," I said, suddenly understanding it all.

"They knew what they were doing and who they were killing. The poor souls in the plane were just collateral." He stopped to clear his throat and I, I was frozen with tears brimming in my eyes.

"We couldn't get to them on time, but Eric saw you fighting for your life, you were suffocating, the flames were getting higher and the smoke was killing you. He didn't even think. I heard him, heard the yelling, but he never stopped. He was in hospital for a month after that."

My throat seized up.

"No one helped him…"

"No one is allowed, you heard the rules. I tried, but I, well you saw how good I am."

He shook his head, he blamed himself. God. I reached across and squeezed his arm and I swatted the tears that slipped out onto my cheeks.

"He never forgave himself for not getting there sooner and I never forgave myself for failing to convince the Council. After that, when the compound reinforced their laws, you swore that no one else would die for you and you made him initiate the Clean Slate."

A pregnant pause filled the silent room and Kieran looked down at his hands.

"I never forgave him for doing that to you. No matter how much you demanded it, no one should have had to go through that. There was always another way, we could have gone on the run, taken you away from there. He knew that. He knew that I would have left to help. Between the two of us, we would have been more than efficient to guard you." He stopped and looked away. "But he never should have done that, never."

350

"Why did he lie to me?"

Kieran looked away and for a moment I thought he wouldn't say anything but then he turned back to me.

"Because it was too painful for him. He loved you more than anything and then you were gone. How do you think it would have gone down, Alex? He'd just meet you in the woods, a complete stranger telling you he was your long-lost boyfriend?"

His words cut through me. My mind swam, I was in complete shock. I didn't know what to say.

"The whole thing was a disaster. A huge mess," he muttered. "But one thing remains, there is always another way."

There was nothing left to say. I saw the angst in his eyes, and it was definitive, he would never forgive him. But something told me that no matter what Eric had tried to do to persuade me against the Clean Slate, I would have made him do it anyway, but Kieran didn't know that.

"Try to get some rest. We have to move soon."

Taking his advice, I reluctantly snuggled into the cushion and closed my eyes.

Chapter Thirty-Three
The Halfling

A firm hand clasped over my mouth and the suffocating feeling of fear jolted me from my broken sleep. My eyes snapped open and met Kieran's wide gaze. He released his hold on me and pressed his finger to his lips and motioned for me to stay quiet.

When I rolled off the sofa and ducked down beside him, he pressed his body in front of me and gestured for me to follow.

I couldn't hear a thing, but I felt that instant gut-churning sensation which I'd learned meant Reapers.

Judging by the intensity of the nausea forcing my stomach to do somersaults, I figured that there was at least a dozen. That were way more than any of us in our small groups had ever come across.

The stench permeated the air and just above the window frames, the plaster started to turn black and slowly rot away.

My eyes snapped back to Kieran. We were hopelessly outnumbered.

Regardless of how badass he was and how powerful I could be, when the power worked, we were still screwed. I grit my teeth, swallowing the dryness in my throat and kept low to the ground. Suddenly, he stopped, holding his hand out behind him.

"Chancellor Wynter." Silus's voice boomed through the small hut.

I cringed, ducking low.

"I heard you've been searching for me."

Kieran turned his face toward mine and shook his head silently. Warning me.

"We can do things the easy way this time, because I doubt you want to see another friend end up in a wheelchair."

The anger inside me coursed.

Kieran shook his head again, with much more force this time.

"I know you came looking for me to barter."

I held my breath.

"I'm here, if you're serious."

Kieran wrapped his hand around my wrist and mouthed a "no" to me, but this is what I came for. Despite the warning. I'd heard what he said, I *understood*, but I had to do this. Eric needed me, I *needed* to do this for him.

"Tick tock," he chided. "I don't have all day, Chancellor Wynter, and I'm sure Mr. Raine would love to get out there and hit the gym sometime this century."

Before Kieran could hold me back, I pressed my hand to his chest. "I'm sorry."

Ignoring his pleas for me to stay down, I got up and held out my hands. They'd have eyes on us by now, I had no doubt.

"Good choice," he said. "Stand down, men. She won't give us any trouble tonight."

As I opened the cabin door and stepped outside, my eyes went from Reaper to Reaper, noticing how each one was in varying states of evolving; some were pale and almost translucent, others were darker, closer to the pallor of humans. That spelled trouble, the younger ones were more volatile, less likely to obey Silus.

When he stepped closer, I cringed, hoping that he didn't see my reaction. I fisted my hands at my side.

"Now, now, Chancellor Wynter, don't even think about calling on your power."

I relaxed my hands.

"You want your friend's life back?"

"Yes."

"What are you willing to give me for it?"

"The Map."

His eyes widened. "You said you didn't know where it was."

"I lied."

"You lied," he said with a hearty laugh looking around at his men. "Oh, I do like this one."

I swallowed hard and stood my ground, refusing to let them see how terrified I was. I couldn't believe I was doing this.

"Where is the Map?" he asked.

"Can you help him?"

"Of course, I can."

"Will you?"

"If your information proves valuable, yes."

"You'll let my friend leave, unharmed?"

Silus narrowed his eyes. "Has the angel's fall changed you?"

It was oddly fitting, the name he'd given to Eric. Not only was he my guardian angel, we'd come from the dust in the stars, hadn't we?

"It's made me prioritize," I said truthfully. "Let Kieran walk free and you get the Map."

Silus waved at the Reapers keeping guard over the hut. They moved aside, and Kieran came out, stopping a few feet away.

"Alex. Don't do this."

"Tell Eric I'm sorry, tell him I made you leave."

"I'm not leaving." He stood his ground, giving the Reapers pointed looks before bringing his eyes back to mine. "I'm not going anywhere."

"Kieran. Listen to me."

When my eyes locked onto his, something happened, something I had no control over.

It started inside me, much like the power of Esper that spread through my veins when I healed Eric, only this time it was in my mind. The focus made everything around us slow, like only Kieran and I were standing in the woods.

The wind stilled and became silent, the trees too until they were motionless. I finally felt the control pour into me. He must have felt it too because his eyes widened, and a sudden understanding washed over him. He began to plead but it was too late.

I grit my teeth, taking in the rapidly forming rush of memories: Eric's green eyes, fear and pain in them, he was pleading with me too, begging me not to make him do the Clean Slate, begging me to stop, begging me not to compel him to do it.

Kieran needed to know what I did. He needed to know that Eric wasn't to blame, Eric had no choice. I made him do the Clean Slate just like I was making Kieran leave me now.

Tears filled his eyes as the transfer of my memories spilled into him and I gained full control over him. I locked on and gently pushed into his mind.

"Leave. Tell Eric I'm sorry. And please, forgive him, he had no choice, neither of you did."

Kieran turned and left. It was done.

The further he walked, the less I could feel the hold over him. Eventually it faded until all I could feel was the memory of his mind. The wind came back and the trees rustled violently. A storm was coming.

"Now that your friend is safe, give me the Map."

"Heal Eric," I said.

He smiled and stepped toward me.

Without a second to react, Silus wrapped his hand around my throat and pressed the other to my forehead, and before I could think about what he was doing, a violent rush of power ran through me forcing me backward. I was vaguely aware of his hold on me as the world rushed around me, spinning at dizzying speeds and then, it stopped, and I was looking at Eric. He was asleep in bed in a hospital room.

Holy shit. Was this real? Did I get transported through some sort of portal?

Machines beeped around him, Emelia was asleep with her head resting on his arm, and then there was a brightness that exploded around them both. I looked around like I was right in the room with them, but wherever I looked, I couldn't see its source. I couldn't feel the heat, but I was starting to get hot like a part of me, not a part that was physically connected to me, was sensing it.

And then I realized that the source of the light was me, the heat was coming from me. I was moving toward Eric, and I quickly glanced down as Emelia opened her eyes. Her stunned expression bore right through me. She quickly grabbed Eric's hand and shook him awake.

Neither of them moved but Eric didn't look afraid, he looked content, peaceful, like he'd seen this before. I realized that somehow, Silus had caused time to bend and surge until a window was opened. I was seeing Eric, miles and miles away like I was simply seeing him through a looking glass.

356

I reached my hand out toward him, which was just a giant blob of light, but he reached up for me. As our hands connected, I felt the pull of power from inside me, spill into him.

It wasn't just my power though, it was Silus's too. He was right there with us in a weird and freaky sort of three-way connection.

Emelia's eyes darted from me and back to Eric. And in one, blinding explosion of light, I felt a fire within me send a forcefield of power outward. Eric was thrown into the air and froze, tensing midair.

A violent sonic shield began to pulsate around him growing in power and in speed until the erratic flashing became one, long, blinding flash of light.

Pressure built in my head and burned the air around us and as a scream broke free from my lips I watched on as Eric's head was thrown back and a scream broke free from him.

He dropped into the bed and I dropped into the cold earth before Silus.

Eric's eyes darted around, searching for the light while I desperately tried to hold on to the fading window in time.

Emelia stiffened beside her brother and just as the window closed, I saw Eric crawl up to his knees and get up. A relieved laugh filled the void until I couldn't see him anymore.

I dragged in a ragged breath and fell to my hands.

The trees around us raged in fury as the sky opened and let out the mother of all rainstorms. I was drenched in an instant and as I looked up at Silus through strands of wet hair and breathless gasps, I knew I'd blown it.

I'd tried to keep myself hidden but Silus had ripped through all the barriers I'd built up and it was too late.

He stepped back, his eyes wide with shock, but the grin that spread across his lips told me all I needed to know.

I was screwed. We all were.

"You, my child, you've given me far more than just the Map. You're the Halfling. You're what I've been searching for."

Violeta M. Bagia is a fantasy writer from Melbourne, Australia. She is an advocate for sexual assault survivors and is passionate about writing strong female leads who learn and grow throughout the worlds they're thrown into. She is currently completing her Master of Arts and hopes to someday teach young writers and help them empower their words.

When she's taking a break from writing, Violeta can be found exploring the wilderness in her home state of Victoria with her husband and dogs, a Maltese cross called Molly and a German Shepherd called Rayne.

While she's working tirelessly to bring you new and fantastical worlds, you can follow her updates on all the links below, drop a line or just say hello.

w: vmbagia.com
t: @vmb_author
i: violeta.m.bagia_writer
f: Violeta M. Bagia

www.ingramcontent.com/pod-product-compliance
Lightning Source LLC
Chambersburg PA
CBHW021525250626
47154CB00006BA/1976